MW00976727

The
Everlasting
Spring

—BEYOND OLYMPUS—

Volume One
Benjamin and Boudica
Second Edition

FRANCIS AUDRAIN

PAGE PUBLISHING, INC.
Conneaut Lake, PA

First originally published by Page Publishing 2020

ISBN 978-1-64462-455-5 (pbk)
ISBN 978-1-64544-754-2 (hc)
ISBN 978-1-64462-456-2 (digital)

Printed in the United States of America

This second edition and it's sequels are dedicated to Dana Marie McDougall Audrain, my wife—the love of my life—who has led *the way* in everything truly meaningful in our fifty-year sacramental marriage. Over the course of that wondrous journey, her daily examples of self-sacrificing, true love have enabled a lone rider to discover the reason, the purpose, and the meaning of our lives here and beyond.

The old man thinks there's a great truth.
It dwells in a no-man's land,
Between the laws of God's nature,
And the laws of God's people,
Between Heaven and Earth.

Animals are called to live,
Fight for survival,
And die in accordance with the former.
People are called to discover the difference,
To live in accordance with the latter,
To fight for love and freedom,
And die Holy.

Blessed in life and death are the animals,
Who seem not to know.
And blessed are those who find *true love*,
In The Everlasting Spring.

—Francis Audrain

Praise for *The Everlasting Spring: Beyond Olympus*

This Second Edition of *The Everlasting Spring: Beyond Olympus—Volume I, Benjamin and Boudica* strikes me as a winner with wide appeal and a Five Star rating. It's a completely engaging story both emotionally and intellectually and certainly a rousing one in terms of level of action. The principal characters are vivid and compelling creations that will stick in a reader's mind for a long time; the supporting cast is also first-rate. The prose is consistently lively and evocative and often quite eloquent. The story's theme—the triumph of truth and reality in mankind's drift toward tangible treasure—is powerfully articulated and presented. The plot is amazingly inventive and powerfully imagined. It is also solidly thought out and put together; the story arc is excellent, bringing the rising conflicts of the whole extraordinary adventure to a thunderous climax and resolution—and a very satisfying conclusion.

Tom Hyman is a professional novelist of twenty-five years standing with six novels in print in over a dozen languages. Tom is also a former magazine and book editor. In his years of editorial experience at *LIFE Magazine* and the publishing houses of Atheneum, Doubleday, and G. P. Putnam's, he has worked with the widest of talents, including a substantial number of best-selling authors, academics, historians, and novelists.

Acknowledgment

The author is indebted to the god of our ancestors and the heroes and heroines whose dreams, sacrifices, and honorable lives were spent sourcing and securing the blessings of Judeo-Christian tradition and Greco-Roman civilization that created the rise of Western Culture and the ideas that inspired the birth of the United States of America.

The two most important days in your life are the day you are born...and the day you find out why.

—Mark Twain

Prologue

What follows is an epic tale told by an Old Man. It has three parts. Each part is a saga about brave couples who meet under unusual circumstances. The Old Man knows the characters. Some are his ancestors, and many others are known by authentic historians. The eras of their lifetimes span three millennia in the gestation period of Western culture from the first century to the postmodern era. Their connective sagas involve six souls—three men and three women, genuinely heroic people—*not* rock stars, movie stars, supermodels, actors, or other media celebrities.

Like the couples whose stories follow theirs, Ben and Boudica are anatomically modern human beings with common characteristics—both good and bad—who discerned during moments of trial and error what *mattered most*, and by doing so realized the purpose, the meaning and reason for their lives on a planet roughly divided between East and West, and where a religion called "polytheism" once reigned supreme.

The results of their being are apparent, graphically exposed in provocative conclusions as they stand up, set out, and confront face-to-face the horrific circumstances of life as it *actually was* during their terribly turbulent and violent times. Thus reminding those of us who follow, that regardless of birthplace, environment, status, or historical content of our times, *our choices truly matter*, especially when anxiety arises with the threat of imminent death and the present is diminished in the fading light, giving way to the notion that life on Earth *might not be all there is*. Possibilities beyond the "normal" are considered then looming large in the chaos of ignorance and uncertainty that reins.

But the results of a struggle to confront the unknown often adds value in new wisdom, with ideas *not* considered or dismissed in the past for some reason. Yet they seem worthy of examination in the light of a new reality dawning, as we inevitably follow the deceased mystically, fast-blazing our own trails through life on this side of the cosmic divide that our minds attempt to penetrate as we gaze into a night sky sprinkled with myriad points of light winking in the distance, perhaps suggestively: to alert us about possibilities beyond our daily existence, like the presence of dimensions in time and space, and distant domains, impossible to conceive clearly given the limitations of science and religion, even in times when both are in harmony. Yet many earthly authorities continue to believe that *Homo sapiens* will solve those timeless mysteries, *if given more time*.

Over many eras, including the present, human beings have gazed into the surrounding vastness of our universe to wonder what dwells beyond the black wall sprinkled with impossible numbers of twinkling stars and the steady glow of planets nearest to ours. Then beholding the spectacular display of miraculous mystery experience a primordial sensing, inferring there might be, or *must be*, a Supreme Being who has prepared every one of us at the time of our birth, to grow in wonder about *the cause* that continues to orchestrate *the result*. Perhaps *not* an exquisite accident—

something more profound, perhaps involving a preexisting power with a mind of such enormity and genius that we might never comprehend the unmitigated magnitude of its power, its location and *form*. Yet undeniably, the thought awakens an embedded instinct to wonder what state of being our bodies might assume in order to pass "beyond the pale" and travel far enough to discover the end point: *the source* of certain knowledge about the locus of the beginning and the destination at the end of mortal life's journey from here to the "other side" beyond the limitations of our material entrapment.

No doubt there have many millions of us, in every generation, who have gone through that intense "soulful" speculation, left their mortal remains behind, and never returned to provide the solution to the greatest of all mysteries. And if they did, might they suggest to us another dimension beyond space and time: *a heaven?* Even those closest to us— our mothers, fathers, husbands, wives, and children—have *not* done for us the favor of sharing what they've found in their personal voyage through a life-changing transition and *ultimate discovery.*

So here we are with some of us anxious to get out there, to find an answer, to solve the mystery like the great explorers did in their time: Chinese, Polynesians, Vikings, Magellan, Vasco Da Gama, Columbus, Lewis and Clark, and the astronauts in manned fights with powerful telescopes and numerous other probes and "space explorations" to land on our moon, a mere 283,000 miles away, discovering vast tracts of land, sea, and sky now charted around this Earth and confirming its unique composition and special placement in our celestial safe haven surrounded by billions of hostile galaxies like our Milky Way containing stars that make our sun, just 93,000,000 miles away, seem small by comparison.

And on this mighty globe, now clearly visible in photographs from near and far, most of us remain in varying degrees of emotional and spiritual fear, confusion, uncertainty, and even indifference to what our predecessors have passed on to us in regard to philosophy, theology, geology, biology, chemistry, physics, astronomy, anatomy, quantum theory, and a mind-numbing host of religions such as Judaism, Christianity, Islam, Zoroastrianism, Hinduism, Buddhism, Taoism, Zen, mysticism, polytheism, naturalism, and atheism, not to mention "Darwinism" and a host of other "world views" of the natural and supernatural aspects of human life, since the first Adam and the first Eve and their descendants could conceive and commune with a first force, commonly referred to as the "Great Spirit," the "Creator," or "Godhead," and such, who caused (rather *Created*) a first source of white-hot fire and brimstone in a precisely ordered explosion of mass energy from the first atom that resulted in the ever-expanding complexity of a life we know, yet struggle to understand.

From the genesis of the big bang to the first fully formed civilization of the Sumerians in the middle land of Mesopotamia, there have been enormous amounts of speculation about what has survived beyond the death of Neanderthal and given us a written record like *The Bible* of the ancient Hebrews and early Christians who sprang from Semitic roots and created the foundation of the Judeo-Christian ethos, to rise and survive through hundreds of centuries *beyond* numerous civilizations that had fallen from greatness: like the Egyptians with their picture writing and pyramids; the Phoenicians with their alphabet; Syrians, Babylonians, and Persians who conquered the Semitic and Egyptian worlds; and the Macedonians who established the Greek World Empire, bringing classical mythologies that informed human reality, and great philosophers with *powerful ideas*, lofty ideals of government organization and classical art, inspiring architecture and plays that produced some of the highest forms of public entertainment and inspired men like Pythagoras who impressed the Israelites with his theological insights and beliefs.

Then came the Romans. So enthralled by the Greeks, they adopted Greek gods, translated their names into Latin, and went on to win numerous battles for ascension in the Mediterranean Basin against the Carthaginians and others, at the onset of the Roman Republic that spread Greco-Roman civilization, persecuted early followers of Jesus Christ then subsequently adopted Christianity in the Roman Catholic (universal) Church in the West and the Greek (Eastern) Orthodox churches encompassing the Roman and Byzantine empires in faraway lands overrun by hordes of Celts, Gauls, Goths, Ostrogoths, Visigoths, Vandals, Lombards, Huns, Mongols, Franks, Anglos, Saxons, Jutes, Vikings, Normans, and Arab Jihadists in search of a worldwide caliphate with religion and law spread by the sword. Yet the Catholic Church and classical culture miraculously survived centuries of horrific chaos, incredible devastation, and unconscionable slaughter of millions to become the crucible of Western civilization with the formation of the Holy Roman Empire at times including Germany, France, Spain, Netherlands, Scandinavia, and

England—with people, cultures, and languages mixed in a melting pot of ancient tribal and classical societies that held the continent of Europe in fluctuating boundaries while continuing to fight among themselves, during the Protestant and Catholic Reformations, and beyond, while two English-speaking colonies brought the seeds of a unique philosophy of government and a love-based monotheistic religion farther West across the deep waters of the vast Atlantic, to the shores of a fertile New World in the Americas.

For those who lived that history, this epic trilogy, the Old Man's tale, is a memorial. What they did was incredibly difficult. It required great sacrifices. There was suffering, disappointment, great love, redemption, and happiness along the way for those with noble dreams like Benjamin and Boudica, then Colton and Blue Star, and Aaron and Alana who followed in time with countless others—some known, most not remembered—who lived their lives during those chaotic eras. All were touched by monumental events, compelled to endure, and were often caught in the middle, as they tried to find their Creator's plan in the chaos of secular and religious mayhem that swirled around them as they struggled to find a sense of faith, law, and order in a safe place they could call "*home.*" Those and many others like them will hereby be recalled and appreciated in the narrative that follows. They helped along the way by turning their dreams into reality, in spite of contrary forces of menlike beasts with inexplicable insanities that were arrayed against the good, with behavior that degraded, weakened, and corrupted everything in ways that denied sanity, science, reason, and truth.

They did the best they could to create a special place where great ideas could flourish in freedom, dreams could be realized, and citizens with *good sense* would count their blessings, give thanks for the *givers*, and preserve rather than change the timeless markers their forefathers painstakingly created, while blazing a trail to a better way of life in a historically unique culture, saved from darkness by the heroes and heroines who carried Liberty's Light.

Thus, we turn back respectfully, through the media of unvarnished history, to join with the good for a glimpse of how it truly happened and experience history as they lived it—to feel what they felt—to learn from *their* outcomes, and truly appreciate the heritage their vision and their victories created with faith, hope, and love (charity) in the formation of values, traditions, and laws drawn from an ethos miraculously preserved since the first century in the written testimony of a few humble men whose work was subsequently reflected in the founding documents of a sovereign nation offering opportunities for life, liberty, and the pursuit of happiness in an immigrant's empire millions longed for, as they opened their bibles to repeat liturgies of hard work and noble sacrifices made and remembered by virtuous men and women throughout the ages.

Benjamin
and
Boudica

Chapter 1

Benjamin, the son of Samuel, was blessed well beyond the norm by birth and native culture. He had excellent health, female admirers, and the best education his father's money could buy. He was gifted in social status and enjoyed the highest comforts. Even under Roman rule, accepted as a practical matter by his parents, his family had flourished. His father was a shrewd businessman who cleverly orchestrated trade with silk and spice route caravans from the eastern world of the Orient. He wisely adhered to the whims of Roman civilization and its laws and was valued for his cooperation and lavish hospitality. Ben's mother was also regarded as an asset to be appreciated. Her graceful manner, exquisite beauty, and stimulating charm were reflected with great interest in the eyes of a number of powerful Roman officers and administrators to an extent that troubled Ben and his father. His parents were also favored by the Jewish inner circle. Both were skilled in the Hebrew elite's social graces, could converse in Hebrew, Aramaic, Greek, Latin, and Gaelic dialects, and were well grounded in the liberal arts. As a student of Gamaliel the Elder, Ben enjoyed regular interaction with rabbinic scholars and leaders of the Jewish religious community. He had learned to observe faithfully and participate regularly in all the rites and rituals of Hebrew traditions. He believed that Mosaic Law was delivered directly by an angry God, who held his "chosen people" closely and had served them well in the past—especially when they were confronted by Pagan attempts to lead them astray.

Ben's wife, Rachael, also came from a wealthy family. She was introduced to him after a Yom Kippur ritual in their temple. It was a perfect match, two thoroughbreds, a contemporary Rachael in name and manner, coupled with a son of David. They would replicate perfection with many children in the line of the Hebrew patriarchs. At their wedding, the couple reflected two thousand years of biblical history personified and presented in exemplary lives, a model of what belief could provide as its blessing for the world to come, during the fulfillment of the final provision of God's Covenant with Abraham, the father of their faith.

But Ben was beginning to struggle with the notion of so much hope for the future of the Israelites and a sustainable, unified state.

As he continued to make his way toward Jerusalem for the annual Passover Feast, avoiding the constant threat of deadly contact with Romans, Ben was also confronting his increasing doubts about the rigorous exercise of his faith. What had it actually produced in regard to the fundamental meaning and purpose of his life? he pondered. For him, it was beginning to be an inescapable paradox. During the years he passed through the traditional gates to maturity, he was inundated with the rites, passages, and practices of Judaism. His faith provided material wealth for the religious as well as the secular elites who benefited from an ongoing legacy of domination, abuse, and hypocrisy rather than equality for the majority of Israelites.

Ben's experience had culminated the recurring spectacles of mass crucifixions and leaders who found vocations in self-service with the benefit of alms and taxation. They took advantage of their own people and their property and cooperated with the Romans and others who would be useful to them and their extravagant lifestyles. It appeared that the fierce, demanding God of the Hebrew Scriptures, the inspirer of the Torah, the Talmud, and the Shema, the Almighty Godhead who had allowed, if not ordered, the slaughter of thousands of Gentiles and Jews as well, to prevent material corruption and spiritual enslavement of his ancestors, seemed to be condoning corruption by the current elites against the majority of Israelites, and thereby abandoning throngs of the faithful, including Ben himself, in *his* hour of need, and divine intervention.

*****

When he awoke to tremors rising from the desert floor beneath his chest, Ben was in darkness; yet still alive. He could hear a tinkling sound, and hoped it would guide him to a source of water.

As he crawled toward the sound, the tremors contin-ued, one, then another, and another, rolling through his earthbound body, he began to remember the mirage. It promised an oasis and gave him hope—the desperate kind of hope that this time he would find what he desperately needed to restore his strength, renew his will to *survive*, and reach the end of his heartbreaking journey from Damascus.

Ben's hope was restored when the sound grew louder and his outstretched hand felt water flowing over a rock face, not far from where he fell.

As he drank the cool water, a warm breeze caused a series of rasping collisions in the palm fronds high above him and swept downward over strands of curly black hair, his beard, and across the sand-flecked skin around his eyes. A flickering ray of light finally reached him. He began to blink. Perhaps it was an attempt to respond to the exhilarating presence of new energy, or a welcome release from his blindness. There was light. Perhaps his imagination. Perhaps a morning star strong enough to penetrate the overcast, or perhaps it was the revelation of lost hope returning through divine intervention or simply a reflexive effort to remove some troublesome grains of endless desert sand.

He began to pray. "Praise to you, *Yahweh*. Your will be done. A star to guide me or a sign of early dawn could be a blessing."

And as he waited, the eldest son of Samuel remembered the Passover, five days of walking in the burning sun and choking dust, and the Roman soldiers who overpowered him and hanged his wife from an olive tree.

New tears touched his cheeks and were carried away by a sudden blast of howling wind blowing across the torn fabric of his bloodstained woolen cloak. Another sudden sandstorm had tormented tranquility.

Ben slowly raised his head. "Goddamn them to hell!" he screamed. His words were carried by the howling winds to join a heartrending chorus careening through the barren hills nearby, etching his epithet on rocks like the tablets given to Moses and the stone that killed Cain—everlasting in their content, but never knowing why.

Chapter 2

A full moon's journey north from Benjamin's oasis in Palestine—across the Mediterranean Sea, through Gaul to the island home of the Briton Celts—a woman was also fighting to free herself from the darkness surrounding *her* plight.

The blood that flowed from deep gashes on her back had coagulated, hardening between her nakedness and the soil beneath her shoulders. She was struggling to free herself from the earth. Her pain was excruciating. After twice trying and failing in agony, she was finally resting on her side and realizing the nightmare she was beginning to recall. The image of Roman Procurator Decianus Catus, on an elegantly tacked white stallion, was coming into focus. He was smiling, speaking in *Gaelic*.

"Oh, my dear Boudica. How can I *not find* humor and great irony as well? The Warrior Queen of the Iceni Celts, the woman who rode into my camp shouting her displeasure. You were making demands for return of your women. And now, just look at you, wallowing helplessly, mired in a disgusting pool of filth."

Boudica turned her head to listen, staring directly up at Catus. Behind him was the pole. She could see its cross-member and the horsehide straps that suspended her, still dangling from the place where they were cut to expedite her free fall into oblivion.

"And you," Catus continued, "the wife of the great Prasutagus who became our client king. He willed half his assets to Caesar without having the courtesy to tell you I would exercise the Roman right of inventory upon his death and take it all, including the slaves you refer to as *your people*."

Boudica remained silent as his menacing charger circled her position. She continued to make slight adjustments as needed to face Catus directly as he continued his rant.

"Look at you. Long red hair, the body of a goddess, and the infantile brain of a Druid whore. Let's forego the additional reminder of your expendability for the time being. Just get up when you're able and go to the *leather tent* behind you. There you can gather what's left of your clothing and your daughters. Then never cross my path again, or I will finish my business with you while your daughters are dispatched by the most painful methods my torturers can conceive."

When he was about to turn away, Catus stopped. "Oh, by the way, Boudica, you'll soon notice your heathen gods have no power to protect your offspring, much less the pathetic wretches you left to guard them," he added then dug his heels into his horse's flanks and rode off to join a column of armor-clad cavalry.

When Catus disappeared over a ridgeline laden with fog, Boudica struggled to rise. Her mind was focusing on a glorious day when she would gallop through the chill mist to build a fire in her massive firepit. And when the fire began to roar, she would drink of her finest spirits, then reach down to pick up by its bloody hair the head of Decianus Catus, and place it firmly on top of the trophy pole next to her throne.

Chapter 3

The winds stopped suddenly. The sandstorm had passed. Ben's rage was spent. The distant light he saw earlier was burning brighter, coming nearer, leading a series of images trailing in a single file. Soon there were more lights, wavering and stretching back to the far horizon: no natural phenomenon of any kind. Ben crawled closer and closer until he could see a span of torches carried by a cohort of Roman legionnaires.

"Oh my god," he whispered as he watched the spectacle unfolding to reveal a parade of wagons, oxen, horses, and hundreds of men spreading from horizon to horizon across the field of his vision.

The ground was shaking. The blare of trumpets and the thunder of drums reached his ears. Ben cupped them with both hands and struggled to focus his eyes. Torchbearers were visible. He could see them. All were fully outfitted in Roman battle dress with armor, brass helmets, javelins, shields, short swords, and daggers appeared over short tunics and bare legs from knees down to their hobnailed leather sandals. As the dawn settled in and new light revealed more, Ben's awareness of his increasing vulnerability caused him to crawl back from the road until he found a sand dune and settled behind its cover, without losing sight of the procession.

"What in God's name were they doing?" he uttered as his mind began to evaluate the possibilities and determine his potential to react effectively given the most lethal outcome he might face. When he saw some Romans with red horsehair crests running lengthwise across the tops of their helmets, Ben remembered the Centurions his parents had hosted many in their home in Damascus. He counted up to ten and figured each would be commanding from sixty to a hundred soldiers. He marveled at the irony between the civility he experienced with Centurions in his home and the barbaric multipliers of horrifying violence they now represented. *No matter at this point*, he thought. They had shared their knowledge in past conversations. *They taught him much in their boasting*, he mused. "I'll use what I know to thwart them, if I ever get the chance."

Then he noticed the eagle-mounted standards supporting the legionary designations of the Roman units and the wagons that came near enough to see the cages they carried. There were men inside, naked and bound together in chains. When his eyes met the dreaded standard of a Roman crucifixion unit, Ben felt an involuntary rush of air from his lungs. "It couldn't be...*not again*."

As the caravan came to a halt, the annoying tremors ceased and trumpets blared the gut-wrenching knell of a low, slow, funereal dirge. Ben's eyes widened as the unloading began. Twenty men from each wagon shuffled eerily, heads bowed as if dancing to the tune of the dirge, moving slowly to the beat of the thundering drums. Down the ramps from the wagons they came. Wretched they were, pitiful, with crippled postures covered in filth and blood.

When the cages were emptied, the prisoners stood in groups of twenty along the edge of the road for as far as Ben could see in either direction. All had clearly been brutally whipped and beaten. Blood still streaked down their torsos from deep wounds and hanging chunks of flesh, caused by scourging with Roman flaying whips, like those Ben had seen in Damascus.

While the prisoners waited, some fainting from loss of blood, shock, and paralyzing anxiety, the Romans dug deep holes twenty paces apart and parallel to the far side of the road. At the same time, soldiers from the crucifixion unit were unloading lumber from the wagons, assembling crude crosses, and placing them next to the holes as each was completed. By the time the sun was directly overhead, Ben counted a hundred crosses, and the same number of holes. He closed his eyes and began to pray.

When he heard the screams of the first prisoner being led to a cross, Ben reluctantly raised his head. The man was still in chains, arms and legs held by Romans who were placing his body back down against the long beam of the cross. When his arms were spread outward along the short beam, Romans carrying wooden mallets and sharp spikes knelt by each hand, pounding spikes through the man's wrists, just below the heels of his hands. His heartrending screeches of agony and pleas for mercy were intense. Ben strained to cover his ears. He could see the victim's mouth moving. His eyes were bulging out of their sockets, fixated on the blue sky as his feet were nailed to each side of the long beam with spikes driven in just above his heels, slightly forward of the main vertical tendon, and hammered deep in the timber until the heads of the spikes were resting on the skin over his ankles. When a legionnaire drove a javelin into the man's heart to silence his unbearable shrieking, Ben lowered his hands and continued to peer at the crowd that had gathered.

Trumpets sounded attention as a mounted Roman dignitary in the company of three escorts turned off the road and stopped. After ordering the hoisting of the now-silent victim, the Roman dismounted to assume a commanding position on a nearby platform. From there, he watched with a satisfied smile. A group of soldiers lifted the cross and placed the base in a nearby hole while others gathered to push against long beam from the rear as it was hoisted from the front by members of the crucifixion unit tugging on ropes draped over the short beam. As the cross slammed into a fully upright position, the victim's dead body began to shudder with violent spasms as if he had come back to life and was suffering through a second death. When the cross was secured in place, the crowd cheered, trumpets blared again, and Ben strained to listen as the dignitary addressed the gathering.

"My message is this. Listen carefully. Sedition against the Roman Empire *will not* be tolerated! We will continue these executions, one after another until these four hundred...these Jewish rebels...have been successfully crucified and hanging, ready to relay my message of caution to pilgrims passing on this road to their Passover Feast in Jerusalem."

As the crowd shouted approval and another victim began to scream, Ben felt for his dagger. He wanted to run, with it at the ready until he buried it up to the hilt in the heart of the first Roman he could reach. Then it would be over. His nightmare would end, or would it be the start of another? He hesitated then remembered. His dagger was stolen by the Romans who murdered his wife.

Chapter 4

Boudica continued to focus on the revenge she would reap in her next encounter with Catus. She felt the surge of energy created by her imaginings. Her blood began to boil. She got to her knees then onto her feet, standing in a forward-leaning posture. The heat of her outrage was like lightning shooting through her veins, burning her wounds into centers of strength and hardening the fibers of her flesh into resolute steel. She lunged toward her whipping post, grabbed it with both hands, pulled herself up to full height, ripped the post out of the ground and continued forward, carrying the deadly weapon over her right shoulder, holding it in place with powerful hands, like the talons of an eagle.

How ironic it was, she thought through the haze of her clouded mind. Could she actually be where she was, drawing strength from the same object that held her captive during the most painful, depressing, and humiliating defeat of her lifetime? She would remember the moment. She was inspired by the thought. Boudica realized her new weapon, something so evil, could be turned into good by sheer determination and relentless persistence. She was incapable of identifying the source of what might be her ultimate salvation. She was carrying the object that held her in torture and humiliation yet was exhilarated by something *not from* her gods. It was more powerful, a unique feeling she had experienced in those joyous moments after the birth of her daughters. But this time it was more apparent, more sustained, a feeling she could not describe but deeply desired to sustain. Her muscular legs stopped shaking. Her head stopped spinning. She was able to concentrate on her will to survive for revenge and the safekeeping of her offspring.

Even the sight of her escorts' corpses, burned alive, hanging from posts could not deter Boudica from her mission. She thrust one leg forward with a step, five hands in length, then another, and another until she looked up to see the leather tent and its Roman guard, looking directly at her with an expression of shock and disbelief. When she quickened her pace running in leaps and bounds, the Roman reached for the hilt of his short sword. His mouth opened to shout the alarm, but too late. Boudica was on him. With a mighty downward heave of her club, she smashed his helmet, splitting his skull and driving his lifeless body down to the ground. He was just a lad. Boudica heard a faint groan. Then came another. But the sounds were not his. They were coming from inside the tent. She tightened her grip on the Roman's sword, found the opening, slashed through the closed leather flap, and burst through the gap with sword held high in both hands, expecting deadly resistance. But there was none. Instead she saw her daughters, unguarded, alone, lying side-by-side apparently whole and still breathing. She dropped her sword, breathed a loud sigh, and fell to her knees between the pallets where they were tightly strapped down. Ignoring the obvious, she hastened to remove the balls of cloth stuffed in their mouths.

Both began to open their eyes in recognition of her presence.

With a series sighs mixed with anger, relief, and remorse, Boudica embraced her daughters in turn. Her lips trembled. "Oh, my brave girls. My brave, brave girls. How could those bastards have done this to *you?*"

Tears streamed down her cheeks. Her chest heaved with anxiety as she used her abundant hair to wipe away the bloody messes defiling her daughter's faces then waited patiently, hoping they would respond.

Her eldest daughter was the first to speak. "Oh, Mother, it was *horrible!* There were *so many* of them. Isolda was crying. I begged for mercy. My eyes were on Catus. He was smiling."

Boudica was speechless. She bent to kiss Fiona tenderly.

"I fear for her life," Fiona whispered. "Isolda's hurt bad. She's been quiet *so long*."

Boudica turned toward Isolda. "Please tell me," she pleaded. "Are you going to stay with us…precious baby… my sweet little girl?"

Chapter 5

Ben found no joy in his decision to retreat from the Roman butchery. Those he had abandoned still prayed and begged for mercy along the road behind him. His wife was still dead, yet he had crawled back to the shade of his garden oasis, refreshed by clear water, conserving his energy and planning to flee again for the sake of his own salvation. As he considered his options, a feeling of regret began to haunt him. When it settled on his memories of the good fortune he enjoyed in his parents' home, the reason for his discontent was obvious. The suffering of others he previously scorned was becoming a matter of conscience, elevated by all he had seen. In light of the privileged life he had taken for granted, the plight of the "unclean" he and the hierarchy of his faith avoided had become a troublesome matter of conscience, looming large with mounting regrets about his former arrogance and thoughtless lack of charity for others less fortunate.

When deep darkness fell again, Ben resumed his journey. His blind spells had ended. He thought they must have been the result of the beating he received from the Romans. The thought of that and the mass crucifixions sent cold spasms to tense nerves, rushing through his body as he plodded along.

Then a stunning blow drove him to the ground. Before he could recover, another blow convulsed his abdomen and crushed his lungs. He was gasping for air, when he heard a voice commanding in Latin, "Take all that's worth a damn and bash in his head."

It was the last thing he heard. A final blow ended his agony.

When he regained full awareness, Ben rolled over, looked up at the stars, and was reassured that the god who dwelled far away, beyond the twinkling lights, had given him another chance. As he slowly rose to resume movement more cautiously, he felt the wound from the blow to his head. The bleeding had stopped. His mind was unscathed. He recalled it must be the fifth and final night's journey from Damascus to Jerusalem. His shoulder was painfully bruised. He surmised the blow intended to kill him must have glanced off his skull. He was thankful. He thought there might be good fortune, somewhere in that assessment, yet his mind hastened back to the recollection of so many ineffective years of prayers, study, sacrifices, and formal supplications. In spite of all that dedication, his physical security and spiritual salvation seemed threatened. For the first time in his life, Ben felt a gnawing ache of dread in the depths of his being, more disturbing, much more troubling than the blow to his head and the pain in his shoulder. He and his loved ones might be expendable, unworthy in the eyes of their god, unclean like those *he* had ignored so long.

"What must I do?" he asked. "Yahweh, my Godhead and my Creator, what must I do to restore your favor and your help, to receive your blessings and your eternal mercy?"

Suddenly, thoughts of the man some called Yeshua, perhaps a prophet or a promised messiah, had entered his fragile mind. Ben had heard about him. There might be hope in the ideas and ideals he shared, "the seeds" he was spreading across the land. Yet he was rejected by many, Jews and Romans alike. It was confusing. Why would they brutally torture, scourge to near death, humiliate, and murder someone who spoke about the love of God and fellow man above all else? Particularly at a time when such a way of life should be embraced by the vast majority, especially in light of all they had painfully and *personally* experienced themselves? What harm could be done by someone who focused much of his attention on the humble and the meek, the lepers and lunatics?

What little Ben knew about the man seemed to be at once a perplexing mystery and a profound source of inspiration, causing his strides to increase in length and his steps to quicken, as he prayed, "Dear God of our Fathers, it seems that I've been called to learn more about your messenger. Please heal my wounds and help me find the way to *his words.*"

Chapter 6

Boudica had regained her composure, surged back, and was confronting the reality of a horrifying conundrum. Her daughters had been ravaged, her escorts burned to death, and she was the victim of unspeakable brutality. She was seething with anger, humiliated well beyond degradation by fiends with no respect. They had caused great harm to those she most cared about, and she would do whatever was necessary to spread fear of her power, strike terror in the hearts of her Roman enemies, and be assured their atrocities would never be repeated. But her most urgent and immediate challenge was to get her daughters on their feet and safely back to the protection of their home. She turned to that task with every measure of strength and ingenuity she could muster as she released Isolda from the bloody straps binding her arms and legs.

"My dear Isolda, you *are* brave. I'm so proud of you."

Her daughter finally stirred and responded. "I can see you."

Boudica breathed a sigh of relief. "From this moment on, you must trust me more than ever before, Isolda. You'll get through this. Fiona and I are with you. In time, you'll be restored. Our revenge will be sweet. Now you must turn your mind, your thoughts, and your prayers to our Iceni goddess of war, *Andraste*. Ask for the strength you need to rise from this pallet and release your sister while I hide the body of the Roman guard, and bring you his dagger. You and Fiona must hasten to use it. Cut material from the tent and wrap it around you. It will stop your bleeding and keep you warm while we return to the safety of our homeland."

Boudica knew Isolda needed a challenge to take her mind off her own plight. Helping Fiona and doing the tasks required to leave the tent behind would concentrate her efforts and rekindle her flagging will to survive.

As Boudica was turning to address Fiona, she was relieved to hear Isolda say, "I will do as you say, Mother, but you're naked too…your back is bleeding. What will you cover *yourself* with?"

A flood of tears blurred Boudica's vision, her throat constricted. Both of her children were still bleeding from the rough pallets rubbing against their backs. "Don't worry, my dear…I'll find something," she whispered, then turned away to hide her muffled sobs.

When the sound of Isolda's movement toward Fiona reached her, Boudica walked back to the entryway, removed the guard's tunic, dressed herself with it, took his dagger to Isolda, then returned to drag his body to a nearby copse of shrubs and hemlocks. When the body was adequately concealed with twigs and leaves, Boudica sighed, wiped away her tears, glanced back at the lad's resting place, and walked to the edge of an open area where she could survey the Roman encampment and its surroundings. To her amazement, she found the quadrant of the camp nearest her unprotected, without barriers or sentries. Was it another sign of Roman arrogance, an oversight, or mere stupidity? She took note, then returned to her daughters.

"It will soon be dark," she said while inspecting their readiness to escape. "We must depart immediately and enter the deep forest by the shortest route. The Romans have left a fatal flaw in their defenses. Catus and his cavalry are out there somewhere. We'll avoid all roads and trails and travel only at night, staying in the deepest and darkest parts of the forest. We must *not be* separated in the darkness. I will lead. Isolda will follow me, and Fiona, you will bring up the rear. I will carry the Roman's short sword. Isolda will carry his dagger. The light javelin will be yours, Fiona. Turn and look to the rear from time to time as we travel. Isolda will watch to our sides. I will observe to our front. Both of you stay close enough to see me at all times, especially when we're in thick brush or dark of moon. We'll signal with whispers and touching, stop to rest as needed, and tend to our wounds. Good water is abundant. We can look for food whenever it's safe around our resting places. I can see that you are ready," she concluded. "We must go now. Follow me and do as I do."

The girls acknowledged her instructions with nods then fell in behind Boudica as she turned to depart.

At sunset, they were deep in the dark forest without incident. Boudica detected the tinkling of a small stream and led her daughters to it. They drank deeply from the clear, flowing water then cleansed each other's wounds. Boudica watched, impressed by their covering in tent flaps held with rope around their waists and high boots made of leather wrapped around their feet and legs and secured with rope above their knees. The cool water had revived their spirits, and they were soon on their way, three shadows gliding silently through towering trees while a full moon rose without clouds, causing shadows in eerie shapes, accompanied by strange sounds echoing through the depths of the primeval forest that concealed them.

"Wouldn't it be wonderful to live in a place like this? It feels so good," Isolda whispered. Fiona and Boudica nodded to signal they agreed.

Boudica recalled the Druid grove at Anglesey. She marveled at how this forest reflected the serene nature of peace and tranquility rather than the horror of human sacrifices surrounding her in a circle of fire when she took up her dual roles as warrior queen and Druid priestess. On this night, the shapes of ancient tree trunks with gnarled and twisted branches reminded her of the tormenting sacrifices. They haunted her memory. She found it strange that her thoughts dwelled so long among those sacrificial sufferers. She began to wonder. Why had it *not* appeased her gods? Why were those bloody offerings insufficient? Why not enough to inspire the gods to overcome or prevent the recent ordeals with the Romans and more suffering? Could the Roman gods be superior to hers?

As they stopped to rest for a second time, she noticed her girls seemed to be gaining. They were moving more forcefully and whispering among themselves as they bathed one another's wounds. The rigors of their lives had prepared them for many hardships. While she tended to her own wounds, Boudica realized that this hardship and the coming storm of rebellion would try them to their limits. Like the young guard whose handsome face was smashed in her rage, Fiona and Isolda were innocents cast into a cruel world, paying a heavy price at a tender age to survive and carve out a few moments of genuine happiness before they too perished in the madness they were destined to blindly accept, as a consequence of a life *she* had caused them to begin, on the eve of their conceptions.

The Roman legionnaire had soft little hairs on his body. As Boudica stripped him, she had been moved, realizing he was just a babe, a victim with a proud mother, a son who might have been *her own,* in another time, in another place. Was this the plan the gods had set in motion for Roman and Celt innocents? If so, the purpose was well beyond her understanding. Her eyes narrowed. Her lips pursed. Her jaw protruded, then set as she brushed back her hair with both hands and tilted her chin upward to gaze at the night sky. If it was their plan, she thought, her only recourse was to press on, to do the best she could to ease her daughters' pain and pray they lived long enough to bring their own children into a life of destruction, disappointment, and ultimate death, perhaps with renewed hope that there *might be* a second chance to do better and receive mercy as a just reward.

Then a light flickered ahead, filtered by thick vegetation, in the direction of their travel. Her daughters confirmed the sighting. Boudica flattened her body on the forest floor to watch and listen, and they did the same. When she flinched at the sound of voices, the girls moved closer. Their bodies touched, four eyes were focused on their mother, awaiting her response. When Boudica detected a Gaelic dialect, she knew. Heat surged through her chest. Her heartbeats accelerated rapidly. She was about to face her hated enemies, the bloodthirsty *Trinovantes!*

The warrior queen of the Iceni began to smile as her fingers passed lightly along the razor-sharp blade of her liberated Roman sword.

Chapter 7

Benjamin could see the shadows retreating. He too was retreating, but quickly dismissed the painful reminder. A new day's dawn was breaking, its light revealed the familiar hills of the Holy City.

As he approached the outskirts of Jerusalem, the light awakened his spirit. Rays from the rising sun warmed his back. His body responded with renewed energy. He stopped briefly at a public well, filled his goatskin water bag, drank deeply, then replenished the contents.

Refreshed and ready to press on, Ben quickened his pace as he entered the narrow street network that penetrated and connected the tightly packed mass of small dwellings that were the humble homes of the poor. Although those families did not enjoy the comforts of religious, government, and business functionaries, he envied the simplicity of their lives inside the stick roofs and brick and mud walls. The little boxes of beige and white were crowned with flat wooden roofs of crisscrossed poles supporting covers of palm fronds woven tightly between them. The smoke of breakfast fires drifted upward, passing through them like morning prayers visibly rising from the minds and mouths of the souls inside whose curious eyes peered out through black rectangles formed by windows without covers.

Beyond the windows where eyes watched, smoke caressed the hillsides, touching the grand architectural features surrounding the Temple Mount's massive walls and the business districts, markets, stables, lodging places, and exquisite homes of the aristocracy who socially, culturally, and religiously looked down upon the poor, the starving, the infirm, and the sick they collectively referred to as untouchables.

Passover chaos swept through it all. In every lane he chose to follow, Ben was engulfed in a flowing, pulsating mass of humanity. The noise was overwhelming. Dust covered everything including a wide variety of waste matter travelers discarded anywhere a modicum of privacy could be found. Putrid air irritated his eyes, adding to the nausea born of other offensive odors lingering in the thick dust and debilitating heat.

Over the course of the frenetic day, Ben found no place to stay. He cursed the delays that caused him to come late to a city already inundated with throngs of pilgrims. By nightfall, he managed to secure a small loaf of unleavened bread, and with that, he dived out of the chaos and entered a lovely garden on a gently sloping hillside shaded by olive trees.

"Thank God!" he exclaimed. The crowded avenues were behind him. Beyond his peaceful garden, the tension was ominous. The heart of the city was overflowing with anxiety. It hung over everything like a shroud, heavy, lingering with a sense of dread looming, without a definable cause.

After sunset, the earth beneath him gave up the heat of the day. There was a sudden chill. Ben built a small fire. He wrapped up in his cloak, removed his sandals, then placed his bare feet near the flames, and prayed.

"Almighty God, I beg you to take care of my wife's spirit. Please give it strength enough to power her soul and enable her entry into your loving embrace in the fullness of time, according to your will."

Before long, he was dozing and dreaming, oblivious to all but his haunting memories. From time to time, he awoke to strange sounds, then consoled himself with prayer until he drifted back to sleep.

Then came the nightmare. Men were approaching.

Still in the fog of sleep, Ben bolted upright, sprang to his feet, and began flailing with his arms and fists. He struck flesh. A bloody face flashed before his eyes. Then another and another. He was overwhelmed, hurled to the ground. Searing pain stunned him as his head hit a rock, enraging him. With mindless ferocity in reaction, Ben's arms and legs lashed out, striking and kicking, over and over at the hair, cloth, and flesh that tormented him.

Out of desperation he screamed, "In the name of Yahweh, be done with me, demons!"

More shouting arose in response. Words came to him in short breaths, shouting in Aramaic from distinctly different voices.

"He too is a *Jew!* One of us. Hold fast, brothers."

Then another voice: "Why do you strike us, friend?"

And another: "We don't want to harm you!"

Ben relented. He breathed deeply, staggered back, and slowly relaxed his guard.

"You surprised me. I was asleep," Ben panted. "You scared me out of my wits!"

"Whom were you expecting?"

"I thought you were Romans, here to arrest me. Or thieves who'd followed me after I left the crowds."

"Brother, we are neither. Stand assured," said the man nearest to him.

Ben's pain was receding. He could see clearly. Three men. All Jews draped in humble cloth. One appeared young; the others, much older.

"Who are you?" Ben asked, wiping blood off his face while noticing the others were doing the same.

"I'm John Mark," said the youngest, still out of breath. "Most people simply call me Mark. Next to me is my cousin Barnabas. The other is John, the Evangelist."

"Why are you here in this place, at this time, in the dark?" Ben inquired.

The man named John responded, "We must know more about you before we can answer."

His countenance appeared more serious and apprehensive than those of his companions.

Ben was neither surprised nor offended by John's concern. "Of course," he said. "My apologies. My name is Benjamin. I've come from my home in Damascus for Passover."

"How long have you been here, in this garden?" asked John.

"I arrived late because of a misfortune along the way. I have no shelter; thus, my presence here since sundown."

"And your people?"

"My family follows the lineage of King David in custom, religion, and law. My parents moved to Damascus for the trading business. We're citizens of the Roman Empire."

"So, Benjamin, from Damascus, how do you view your Roman citizenship?" John asked.

"It's what my father wanted. To facilitate his success in the merchant business," Ben replied.

"Of course," said John. "And what was it that delayed your arrival here, Benjamin?"

"Since I have not yet notified my family in Damascus about my arrival and the events of my journey, I beg you to hold in confidence any matters we might discuss while answering your questions. Suffice to say, there should be no cause for your concern. I've *not* violated any laws."

"My apologies, Benjamin," said John. "However, for good reasons of no concern to *you*, we must know more before we can speak openly and honestly. If that is not possible, we shall bid you good night and leave you to return to your slumber."

"There was a chance encounter with a small group of Romans," Ben offered. "The damage has been done. No amount of discussion can provide consolation."

"But what was the cause of the damage?" asked the man known as Barnabas.

"They rode into our camp while my wife was preparing our supper," replied Ben with obvious reluctance.

"Your wife?" Mark interjected.

"Yes. My wife," said Ben as he looked away from the three to gaze at the flames in his slow-burning fire.

"And what did you do?"

"My wife and I greeted them. They sat by our fire and drank wine. She offered them food. They accepted."

"How long did they remain with you?" asked Barnabas.

"They're still with me...a*nd will be forever!*" Ben shouted. "*It's so horrible!*"

The three drew back, shocked by Ben's outburst.

"Ben, Ben, please be calm," John softly requested.

"Yes, Ben," added Barnabas. "Please calm down and share with us, so we can understand, to help you if need be."

"Yes, Ben, please *help us* to understand," added Mark with an expression of genuine concern.

"I'm so sorry," Ben continued.

"What was so horrible?" asked John, reaching out gently to touch his shoulder.

"They started to hurl taunts," Ben slowly replied. "They said a pathetic Jew like me didn't deserve such a desirable Jewess, especially one with long legs...and hair... and...I leaped toward them."

"And what then, Ben? What did they do?"

"The largest of the three held my wife while the others tied me to a tree. I was screaming. One of them hit me in the head with a rock. I passed out. When I opened my eyes, my wife was hanging from an olive tree, screaming and fighting while they ravaged her. Then one of them hit me...again."

"Oh my god in heaven," John whispered.

The others were silent.

Moments passed.

"When I awoke again, they were gone. I'd been cut loose. So had she. We were lying together, in sand, dark with blood."

All sat in stunned silence, staring at Ben. Speechless as he wiped streams of tears away from his cheeks.

"I crawled over to her. I touched her. Her soul had departed. I wrapped her in a blanket and held her for two days and two nights. I prayed that God would take me too. But it was not to be. Early on the third morning, the wind was blowing hard. I awoke to her soft hair caressing my face. For a moment, I thought we were home, that she was alive again. But I soon realized, God had surely taken her. I found a small cave near a spring and carefully placed her there on a bed of palm leaves. Much later, I bid her farewell then protected the entrance of her resting place with a wall of large stones…then turned away…following my feet… walking west toward the sunset."

Chapter 8

As Boudica continued to observe the activity around the Trinovantes' campfire, her muscular body responded with instincts of a predator full of deadly volcanic energy, ready to explode. Her eyes reflected the glowing firelight as she focused on the most threatening of the five figures, the one standing, casting a huge silhouette across the foreground of the circle. His back was turned toward her as he faced the others, who were sitting on the far side of the fire. Their faces were clearly visible, eyes fixed on the flames.

A low growl rose from her throat. Boudica had discerned the solution. Take the giant down from behind, then deal with the others. Her body stretched, spreading her weight between her hands and feet. She felt the chill of dew on the wet grass between her fingers. Her lips gave way to a catlike grin. She would make good use of her cold, wet claws. Boudica gripped her sword firmly. Her elbows and knees were flexed like bows. When she was ready to launch her form, the warrior queen of the Iceni leaped into the light and sprinted toward her prey.

With three bounds and an electrifying shriek, Boudica pounced upon the giant from behind, splitting his skull with a downward stroke of her sword as the weight of her flying torso smashed his spine and drove him, facedown, into the fire.

The impact of her attack blew a shower of red-hot coals over the heads of the others who were frozen in a paralysis of stark terror, knowing they were next. Before they could react, she rose from the smoldering hulk beneath her, grabbed a burning tree limb with her moistened free hand and hurled it into their midst. Two forms were attempting to rise, blinded and screaming, as she cut them down with swift strikes from her flying sword.

As Boudica whirled to confront the remaining Trinovantes, a gray-haired man sitting next to a boy threw up his hands, shouting, "Sir, we yield to Roman justice!"

Boudica's instinct prevailed. Using both hands, she raised her sword over her head and stepped forward while glaring down at him to ask, "Are there others of your ilk in my domain?"

"I swear," replied the elder, "my grandson and I are all that remain."

"No outriders, scouts, pickets, or spies?"

"None. I swear. There are none."

"Very well," she responded then peered into the darkness. "Isolda and Fiona," she called, "it's safe!"

When she saw her daughters emerging from the darkness, Boudica plunged her blade through the necks of the dead Trinovantes lying at her feet. The survivors cringed under a shower of blood. Boudica returned her sword to its scabbard, freeing her hands to grab both heads by the hair and toss them nonchalantly into the fire. As the flames rose, she pivoted to face her horrified captives, untied the knot in her abundant red hair, and let it fall freely over her shoulders. With her hands still wet from the blood and sweat of her combat, Boudica opened the front of her purloined Roman tunic from neckline to slender waist. Both captives could see the blue tattoos on her chest. They were rising and falling over the ruthless heart of a woman now clearly identified as *the* Iceni queen.

Chapter 9

Ben's narrative of the horror he endured had touched the hearts of the men who were gathered around him. After a pause for reflection, John said, "I believe Barnabas and Mark will agree. We owe you an apology for the way we urged you to reveal the intensely sensitive information you finally divulged. But please understand our motive. Given the danger we face anytime we are outside a diminishing number of relatively safe places, we're compelled to be wary of *any* new acquaintance. You might have been a clever spy sent out by the Sanhedrin, the Romans, or both, in order to expose us. Those factions have been known to use every subterfuge imaginable to identify believers like us and deliver them to martyrdom in gruesome ways, often without recourse to any civilized matters of law. In light of the persecution some of our brothers have experienced, and the horrific deaths that have resulted within our circle of believers, we were bound to question you further before fully accepting you and your offerings as trustworthy."

"We seem to be kindred spirits in one way, Ben," added Barnabas. "All of us have lost much, yet we also have much to gain. We're therefore offering you an opportunity to hear some wonderful news about *liberty* for all who choose to listen. So will you walk with us tonight, rest in our quarters, and hear more about the new covenant with our Almighty God and Creator?"

"I will. I surely will," Ben replied immediately, bowing his head humbly in a gesture confirming his complete submission and sincere appreciation.

The remainder of the evening had passed. Ben awoke from a restful night. He was alone in a very large room. His robe and sleeping mat were soaked with sweat. The heat was unbearable. He recalled an unusually pleasant dream, a distant memory. He wondered where it came from, what it might have to do with his dilemma, if it might have some prophetic significance. Regardless, it was the first night of healing slumber since the death of his wife.

The lingering residue of the dream caused an infusion of new energy badly needed by his aching body. He stood unsteadily, recovered his balance and walked across a wooden plank floor to a long dining table surrounded by a number of large reclining pillows. As he examined the table and its surroundings, his senses suggested the pleasure of a communal meal. He smiled when the smell of cooking reached his nostrils. His mouth began to water. Ben thought of his home. He should send a message to his parents.

But his thoughts were interrupted by a woman's voice drifting up a stairwell. "Are you awake up there? If you're ready for something to eat, come down here and dine with us."

He responded immediately. His bare feet swiftly carried him down a flight of wooden stairs as he tried to remember his last meal. The thought perished at the sight of a woman standing at the bottom of the stairway, smiling with her arms opened wide.

"I'm Mary, the mother of John Mark. Welcome to our humble home. I believe you know the others. There's my son. We simply call him Mark around here. Next to him is Mark's cousin, Barnabas. Next to him is our beloved friend John, the son of Zebedee and Mary Salome, a hero in our faith. You came here with these fellows early this morning while I was still asleep. I'm delighted to finally meet you."

"I'm pleased to meet you too. I remember the others," he responded. "I appreciate your gracious hospitality, Mary. It's good to see all of you in the welcome light of a new day."

Ben acknowledged the greetings of the others, and as he did, he noticed they were all clothed in the customary attire of the working classes, plain and practical, with open-toed sandals, long robes, cloaks, and shawls of earthen tones. John was particularly distinct with the look of a man who had endured much in a relatively short lifetime. His gray hair and beard framed strong features lined with wrinkles that spoke volumes. Barnabas could have been John's twin, if it weren't for his larger size and the bulk of his legs and lower torso. Mark was easy to distinguish with his shorter stature and youthful appearance of an early adult whose skin was not yet ravaged by rugged outdoor life and the familiar signatures of monumental stress that showed on his wizened companions.

Ben was finally seated on the dirt floor, close to the fire, cross-legged and shoulder to shoulder with the others in a tightly knit semicircle. He acknowledged their remarks with civility but otherwise remained silent as he devoured a bowl full of cereal, warm with fresh goat's milk.

"Benjamin, I hope you're not disappointed with your breakfast," Mary said. "You must have smelled my lamb stew on your way down here. But don't worry. It's in the big kettle on the coals there. You'll get plenty tonight when it's done. If the heat gets too much for you, just sit back farther from the fire."

"I was boiling in the upper room, but all is well now," said Ben. "I'm blessed to be with you."

While he ate, the others started to laugh and playfully mock his ravenous attack on the contents of his bowl each time Mary refilled it.

"Watch out, Mother. He almost bit your hand off last time," said Mark.

"Indeed," added Barnabas. "Hit him with your wooden spoon if he lurches at you again."

"On the contrary," Mary replied. "Do I look like a woman who would harm such a fine specimen of a man? Shame on you, Barnabas, for even suggesting that. You should know better by now." The room resounded with a loud chorus of ribald hoots and howling laughter.

As the noise subsided, a sense of tranquility began to rise in Ben's troubled mind. He felt its presence in body and soul, like a tiny flame beginning to challenge the darkness within him. Sunlight was streaming through an open window. He was stimulated by the uplifting glow. It reflected off the others while they interacted happily. Ben was feeling a new vitality unlike anything he had known previously, even in the lavish comfort of his home.

These good people are genuinely fond of me, he marveled. *They have quickly extended their charity to a stranger who might wish them harm. In this era of insecurity and potentially grave danger for them all, they have chosen to place my well-being ahead of theirs.*

When he had finished eating and appeared to be satisfied, John said, "We had a chance to talk while you were asleep, Ben. We've considered all that you shared with us last night…in the garden…and on our way here. We discussed your background, your recent suffering, and your increased curiosity about Jesus of Nazareth. We have a plan. We'll answer the questions you asked and try to ease your spiritual discomfort so you can make some important decisions about how you wish to proceed with your life, in light of all that's happened. We thought it would be best to use the backdrop of our Passover rites to pick up where our ancient scriptures left off…at the beginning of a new covenant. We commonly refer to it as the *new testimonial.*"

John paused for a moment, glanced at Barnabas, and continued. "The coming of a Savior, as foretold by our prophets, brought words *directly* from our God. It was Jesus who finally appeared and presented the new, referring to it as the fulfillment of the covenant our people had previously observed. I've asked our brother Barnabas to begin the narrative because he's more articulate than I am and also has extensive experience with our new brother, Paul."

"Very well. Thank you, John," Barnabas responded as he turned toward Ben. "I appreciate this opportunity to speak earnestly with you. It's interesting that John mentioned Paul. You remind me of Paul, when he was much younger of course. I don't want Mary to think she's the only one who appreciates the beauty of your youth."

"I'm flattered," Ben replied as everyone joined in laughter.

The humor made all in the gathering completely at ease in a meaningful exchange among men with nothing more to lose yet found value in goodwill among comrades who were dearly bound in a cause of utmost importance.

"We first heard of *Jesus* through John the Baptizer who was martyred by Herod Antipas," Barnabas continued. "God's plan for continuation of the *divine process* had been revealed to John. Before his death, he spoke of the imminent arrival of 'someone mightier than I'…a being foretold by prophets throughout the history of Israel. John's baptisms were performed in preparation for this important arrival."

"I have seen references many times in our ancient scriptures," Ben responded, "and I've recently heard of the Baptizer. I've also seen many references to a 'Messiah,' a new king in the line of David, who would come to save Israel from its enemies. I recently heard that John had indeed been baptizing with water to cleanse and prepare the multitudes for the coming of a savior."

"Yes, very good," Barnabas continued. "And on the day *Jesus* came to the River Jordan, our dear Peter's brother, Andrew, was present, along with his friend Nathan. They were standing on the west bank of the river at a place not far from its drainage into the Dead Sea, near Jericho, a day's journey east of here. John had been baptizing at that location for some time. Not for forgiveness of sins against God's moral absolutes, given to Moses in the Ten

Commandments, but rather for awareness and repentance in an act of spiritual cleansing and initiation into a very special group of virtuous believers who would join together in remission…like the curing of a physical malady or disease…then subsequently support, encourage, and sustain one another in a healing process that would create spiritual health and vitality in a community of caring brothers and sisters, who were, in effect, *taking the cure,* together."

"I understand," Ben responded with a smile.

"The Baptizer had gathered a large group of such followers and many others seeking God's true wisdom in troubled times. At one point, the crowd of onlookers, and those awaiting baptism, parted to make way for a diminutive figure with long hair and beard who was robed in radiant white cloth. He entered the water from the east bank, just like the Israelites did when they came back into the Promised Land at the end of their exodus. When John saw the man, he stopped baptizing and stood fully erect. According to Andrew, John looked at the man and said, 'Master, I need to be baptized by *you*.' But the man stood fast. He focused on John. His eyes were burning with overpowering intensity. He commanded John to baptize *him*, and John did. At that moment, the clouds parted. A voice from the heavens called down to all present, saying, 'This is my beloved Son in whom I am well pleased' and a visible downpouring of energy, like a waterfall of dazzling mist, cascaded over the man, ruffling his wet garments and sending glistening ripples across the surface of the river. Everyone witnessed and heard the words, including Andrew, who said he and others very close to him also saw a splendid white dove hovering directly over the *miraculous event*."

"I'm feeling intense exhilaration. I can easily imagine that Andrew, Nathan, and the others must have experienced so much more during those *incredibly moving* moments!" Ben speculated with unrestrained exuberance.

"Indeed," Barnabas replied. "And later, when Andrew and others approached the man, he hastened to identify himself as 'Jesus of Nazareth' who came from Galilee and would return there in forty days to begin his divine ministry. He was unlike any of the prophets, wise men or reverent rabbis, whom Andrew and the others had experienced in the past, so they took up with him when he came back to Galilee, after a retreat in the desert."

"Yes," said John. "It was a *wonderful time!* After calling Andrew's brother Peter, and my brother James and I, Jesus settled with us in Capernaum on the Sea of Galilee where we'd been living and fishing most of our lives. Before long, there were twelve of us who took up traveling, sleeping, and eating with him. His preaching of the *'good news'* in the new covenant filled us with the *love* he projected. The new hope for the *new life* he revealed enthralled many who joined in our ever-expanding group of disciples. However, there were many others among the Judaic fundamentalists who refused to heed his words because his prescriptions for living a holy life were not in complete agreement with some aspects of the Mosaic Law. As you're aware, Ben, *the law* was delivered during the time of the Exodus. It was designed to wean our ancestors from the sinful comfort they found in the pagan practices of their Egyptian captors, who turned them into slaves. Our God and Creator wanted his children to be saved by turning their allegiance back to him, and that would require the kind of discipline we find in the books of *Numbers* and *Deuteronomy* in our ancient scriptures."

"Yes, and that's where most of the rites and ritual details were embedded in our culture and our government *as laws*," Ben interjected.

"That's correct, Ben," John responded, "Jesus referred to those laws and their values *repeatedly*, during his ministry. Jesus also indicated that he was, in effect, an aspect of our Godhead, begotten not made, one in being with our Father as his one and only son. One in Being with the Father through whom all things were made. Born incarnate of our blessed Mother Mary in a uniquely miraculous manner involving the infinite power of God's Holy Spirit. He came to speak *the words* of God's wisdom with us…wisdom that is based on love of God and love for one another with charity, mercy, and forgiveness rather than strict observance and meticulous adherence to the many details of Hebrew laws and traditions that have evolved dramatically over time, as our faith progressed in the hands and works of men. His words and his claim of Divinity as the Son of Man and Son of God eventually enraged our religious hierarchy…those who generally lived good lives ensuring obedience to the law, yet often turning their backs to the less fortunate, whom they considered to be unclean. During a sermon, Jesus gave to a large crowd gathered on a mountainside, he expanded on Our Father's message by affirming the *basic rules* of the Ten Commandments and describing those blessed by God as the sick, the peacemakers, the merciful…those loving God above all else, and the humble, the weak, and those who hunger for justice, those in despair, and those who serve others in acts of selfless charity. After that day, from time to time, we noticed that Jesus would, upon request, perform acts of mercy and healing that were *absolutely miraculous!* Those acts were bestowed upon those described in his sermon and on those who came forth humbly with immediate needs. He focused most of his attention on those I described, specially the children, and treated them with kindness, respect, and unconditional love. And I must tell you, it was abundantly clear *to us.* His healings went beyond those of John the Baptizer. He forgave the sins of the afflicted, then touched them, and they were healed *instantly!* We witnessed many of these miracles. When doubters attacked him for blasphemy, saying, 'Only God can forgive sins,' Jesus enlightened them saying they were right! He was *one in being* with the Father and therefore held that *power* eternally, with no restrictions regarding matter, time, or space."

"Was this healing a result of the *grace* we speak of?" added Ben with a questioning gesture.

"We weren't sure about what he was referring to, at first, Ben. But we earned later that the power to heal and perform other miracles was *in fact* the preexisting, eternal power of the Godhead's Holy Spirit, promised by Jesus and delivered to us on Pentecost exactly fifty days after *His resurrection* from the dead. Jesus's tomb had been sealed with a huge stone. It was open! The guards could not explain why it was empty. His Resurrection is *unquestioned* among us. Our Godhead had proven that *his Holy Spirit* truly had the power to make all things and do all things! Given the evidence we found, there was no other *rational* explanation. Jesus appeared several times during the forty days he was with us…before *his ascension!* He had a glorified body we recognized immediately. He was able to do unimaginable things. We touched him, talked with him, and ate with him! Much about Jesus is still a mystery, to be cleared up in time. However, there was absolutely *no doubt* that *he was* what he repeatedly claimed to be! He died for us in order to pay the cosmic penance for all sin, for all time. He opened the way to forgiveness of future sins…by loving God and living according to God's will. This was articulated and demonstrated repeatedly by Jesus's example during the time he was with us. *God became man because he loves us!* There was no other way to save us from our sinful nature, so we could enjoy the grace to live good lives here, in *the church* Jesus founded. We helped to build that church… His mystical body on Earth…to sustain believers as they prepared to go on living even better lives in accordance with his will now and forever in the presence of God, in his kingdom to come."

"Amen! Thank you, John," Barnabas exclaimed. "And on the night Jesus was betrayed, He had supper with John and the other apostles upstairs in *the room* where *you* slept. He broke bread and gave pieces to everyone, then said, 'Eat of this bread. It is my body that will be given up for you so that you might live forever.' Then Jesus took the chalice, filled with wine, also blessed it, and said, 'This is my blood, the blood of the new and everlasting covenant. It will be shed for you, so your sins will be forgiven. Drink it in memory of me.' Later, over table, he talked more about the meaning of his words. John heard those words. He was there. So it's his to say."

"That night was the culmination of our many days with Jesus incarnate," John continued. "We talked a bit more in the garden known as Gethsemane, on the Mount of Olives, where we met you. He often went there to be in prayer with Our Father. Mark was there with us, until the temple guards came to arrest Jesus. Everything he said that night was *amazing!* Jesus said he was '*The Word*' mentioned in the beginning of the creation story in the *Book of Genesis*. And by observing that simple act of eating consecrated bread and drinking the wine as he demonstrated, we would be taking him, his words, all he is, and all that he did, into our being…nourishing our souls and our spirits…and by consuming the essence of God's Word, his soul and divinity…we *would* receive *the grace* we needed to go on, to take the right path in our quest for holiness, following in the footsteps of Jesus by living in accordance with his example and embracing the truth in God's will with the love he created in Jesus Incarnate…who was God but born here as a man, so we could relate to him as he *showed us* the way to salvation.

"Now, in the light of reflection and subsequent events," John added, "it's all very clear. The hard part for us, going forward, will be to describe our experience with Jesus in a way that will last the test of time and convince others we are simple, truthful witnesses. We were called by an incarnate aspect of our God to help him deliver the greatest of all riches to mankind, in the form of a living example of unconditional love with the assurance of divine justice forever, for people of goodwill."

Then John paused, cleared his throat, and summarized, "So Jesus's primary mission, as the incarnate Word of God, was to reveal the Father to us and give us his promise of eternal life with him, in his heavenly Kingdom. He also gave us what we would need to establish his kingdom on earth and gave Peter the mission to be our leader and build it on a solid foundation, so 'the gates of hell would not prevail against it.' And Peter began that process by sending many of us to be bishops in the surrounding territories. Thomas went to India, Phillip to Ethiopia, Mark will eventually go to Egypt, Simon has gone to North Africa, Jude went to Armenia, then Persia, Bartholomew went to Asia Minor. Matthias, who succeeded Judas, has gone to Armenia, replacing Jude, and Andrew went to Byzantium, then onward to Russia. Linus is ready to succeed Peter as the bishop of Rome and head of the *Church*. He will continue our work, and the process of succession will go on until Jesus returns at the end of time, as *we* understand it."

"A truly amazing story, *the greatest of all*," Ben exclaimed. "You're passing it from mouth to mouth now with those bishops, their disciples, and many others, just as you've done with me. But will that be *enough*?"

"It will not," John replied. "We have an oral history regarding our time with the Christ, the Anointed One. But we recognize the need for more to ensure survival beyond us. We've already begun that work, and Mark will reveal what we have done thus far."

"Thank you, John," Mark began. "I've made copies of many letters dictated and written by Peter and Paul and have copies of all I have written in my testimony. I also have all of Matthew's work, and what I have written thus far in my notes from my own experiences with Peter and Paul, and the extensive notes I took during my interviews with Peter, in Rome. Our brother Luke was also with Paul and others for many days, and I have copies of everything

65

he has done up to this point. John is well along with his writings. And I imagine he will talk with you directly concerning those, Ben."

"I will, Mark," John confirmed with a smile. "I plan to make time to continue what you've suggested. I think it's obvious that Ben's concerns will be well answered as we continue our work. It also appears that your urging of Peter and others, and the great progress you've made on your own book, along with your work during the time you spent with Peter and Paul, will *help greatly* to produce the written building blocks of the early history of our church. Our Creed and the help of God's Holy Spirit will also be of lasting value to Linus and the others, who are already gathering in Rome. Mary, the Mother of Jesus, is gone now. Her husband Joseph is long gone. As are Mary Magdalene, my mother Mary Salome, my brother James, our Stephen, and many others. All heroic, all gone. I've been poisoned, yet survived. Today has been a good day for me. I hope it's been the same for you as well, Benjamin."

"It certainly has," Ben responded with a smile. "I'm grateful beyond telling."

"Good," said John. "Then I have a suggestion."

"Please reveal it," Ben requested, leaning forward with anticipation.

"I must travel from here to Ephesus very soon, to ensure Mother Mary's dwelling and property have been properly cared for by the members of Paul's community there. I also need to find some seclusion. I want to finish my testament for Mark along with some letters. I know my work will be edited as everything is, over time, but the fundamental message Jesus left us *must not fade away.*"

"*Amen!*" added the others.

"If you come with me on my journey, Ben," John continued, "you can help me. And you will learn much more, if you do."

"I am honored you should ask, John. I will help you as much as I can."

"Then it's done," John replied with a satisfied smile. "I've also been thinking of something your mentor and teacher Gamaliel said to the Sanhedrin around the time of the persecution of our Lord and Savior. It was something to this effect. 'Be careful. If this movement is by men, it will pass. If it's God's, it will last forever, and you will have, in fact, persecuted our *Almighty Godhead.*' That statement reflects great wisdom. You've been blessed, Ben, by the time you spent with such a great mind as Gamaliel. By the time you and I part, you will know all you really *need* to know to go on. What you do with that knowledge is of course up to you. But if you concentrate your mind and your time and effort on all you *should* know, your decision will be obvious. Do it, and you will live."

And with that, the first day's meeting adjourned. They broke the bread, gave thanks in memory of Jesus, and shared Mary's stew.

Chapter 10

Boudica and her daughters continued to stare at their captives while they prayed, fearing their lives would not be spared, believing there would be no mercy. For them, death was imminent.

When the elder wrapped his arms around the boy, Boudica extended her hand toward her daughters. Both lowered their weapons and stepped back as she asked the elder, "Do you recognize me?"

He gazed up at her. His eyes blinked. He was shaking. So was the boy, a rather innocent-looking lad who was nearing the age of the startled guard Boudica bludgeoned to death in the Roman camp.

"Please have mercy…if not for me…at least for my grandson," he stammered.

"I've asked you a question!" she barked. "Stop convulsing like a constipated dog. Give me an answer *now*, or I will rain death upon the both of you with *one stroke* of my sword!"

"I'm shocked and confused," the old man responded. "You're dressed as a Roman with a Roman sword, but reveal an Iceni queen…speaking as a woman…with a great warrior's skill."

Boudica threw her head back, roaring with laughter, even surprising her daughters.

Her response came quickly. "I'm the widow of your enemy, *Prasutagus!*"

"Then…you…*are Boudica!*"

"*Queen Boudica!*"

"Queen Boudica. How is that possible?"

"My husband is dead. I mourn, as do my daughters."

"The Romans?"

"Yes, in part," she replied.

Her revelation sparked a rapid response from the old man.

"*Those bastards!*" he screamed.

Boudica and her daughters exchanged glances, then slowly relaxed as the gray-hair recovered and revealed he was a direct descendent of Addedomarus, the onetime leader of the Trinovantes. As such, he was respected, thus able to convince the majority of his tribe's surviving leaders that great justice could be won by wiping out the Romans, who had taken advantage of their client arrangement to extract huge taxes, pillage their land, and confiscate their property. Having accomplished that critical objective, he had been traveling with his surviving grandson and their escorts to conduct a reconnaissance of Catus's encampment to determine its suitability as a next-step target for an attack to overwhelm the Roman garrison there and provide a stunning victory to inspire his Trinovante warriors. It would raise their confidence and generate a strong desire for greater victories. Boudica's assault on his small party had foiled that plan, but certainly not his purpose.

After much discussion, the old man and Boudica reached an understanding of the common interests they shared, then came to a mutually agreeable set of terms for planning and decisive action to counter the treat presented by the Romans. The two agreed that any attempt to go against the Romans in battle required a superior force and a carefully devised plan in order to succeed.

Like-minded Celts must unite to banish the Romans. And Boudica quickly recognized the need for a powerful coalition formed around her tribe and the Trinovantes— united and joined with unwavering support from their Druid priests. After getting her new consorts and her daughters back to the protection of her tribe, she would launch a journey, from one meeting hall to the next, beginning with her Iceni, moving on to the Trinovantes and even the Brigantes and Silures, if necessary. Then she would proceed westward to the sea and the sacred grove of the Druids on the Isle of Anglesey. Once there, tribal leaders and their Druids could offer human sacrifices to the goddess of war, discern the future, through examination of their victims' entrails, and receive a series of ritual blessings from the High Priests of the Druidic Cult.

Boudica knew her warriors loved to fight and were not afraid to die in battle but hoped that divine intervention might save the day, if they were outmanned or suffering from unforeseen disadvantages that might result in a defeat and associated consequences of enslavement for the rest of their lives, or excruciating pain and suffering in a slow death by torture.

Chapter 11

After Ben's first day with John, Barnabas, and Mark, he attended more meetings with the trio and visitors who described their personal encounters with Jesus. The results were amazing. They inspired him, beyond words. Ben felt blessed. *He believed.* His knowledge of the testimonies, and revelations they contained, left no doubt. Reason, common sense, and trust would be impenetrable barriers to any form of repudiation. He had discovered the paradox in multitudes of mind-boggling details, words, expressions, and images. He had discovered the mere simplicity of his emerging faith. That was its essence—the simplicity. *Why did my teachers make it so hard?* he mused.

Ben would fully embrace the values of faith, hope, and charity and learn more through experience. He was rapidly gaining wisdom regarding the value of a spiritual life in the present, as well as the next. He realized the value of the words, actions, and examples of love, redemption, and *resurrection* that Jesus had demonstrated, as well as the value of those recently gathered around him, who had been reliable direct witnesses. His existential anxiety had vanished, replaced by the confidence of knowing and trusting that by following the example set by Jesus, and the words that he spoke, his own life would not be wasted. It would not be in vain. Jesus had clearly proven that life after Earth was real.

His life, death, and resurrection showed *the way,* so others might follow.

During the days and weeks after Ben's initial gatherings, persecutions of believers in Jerusalem increased dramatically. Meetings became less frequent and only possible at night, when one or two people would appear, share what they most wanted to say, then quickly disappear in the shadows. Ben knew there might be trouble.

On a still-dark morning in the spring, he awoke to John's urgent whispers. "Wake up quickly. Gather your belongings and come downstairs quietly. Dire peril approaches."

Ben hurried to ready himself, with loincloth, long tunic, shawl, cloak, and colored headband, then strapped on his sandals, stuffed his few remaining possessions in a carrying bag, and went down the stairs.

John motioned for him to take a seat near the fireplace. He could make out the forms of Mark and Mary, in a dark corner of an adjacent room, hastily packing scrolls in a bag. Ben's abdomen convulsed. The air around him felt heavy, hard to breathe.

John grabbed his arm and whispered, "Can you leave *right now?*"

"Yes," Ben replied and was suddenly outside, on the cobblestone street, not fully awake, clutching his bag and running as fast as he could, following John through the darkness.

When John slowed to a brisk walk, both were able to catch their breaths, then continued darting from one shadow to the next, waiting, listening, and running until they passed through the *Porta Salaria* and were well beyond the high-wall surrounding the city.

As the two left the outskirts of Jerusalem, the darkness was lifting. They began to walk with caution following a stream that meandered through a secluded valley. When the morning sun's rays lit the high slopes of the barren hills on the west side of valley, Ben realized he and John had turned and were walking toward the northeastern shore of the middle sea. The contrast between the tans and browns reflecting from hillsides' sparse vegetation became apparent as he followed John on a winding path near a stream that was flowing through a carpet of green grass under a canopy of palm trees. From time to time, they would stop to take water from the stream to satisfy their thirst and maintain their strength and overcome the heat they would eventually encounter as the day passed and the sun's rays intensified. Ben began to notice that John was constantly scanning their surroundings and examining the surface of the trail each time they stopped. His curiosity finally exhausted, he asked John about his reason for the seemingly obsessive caution.

"I've learned the hard way," he responded. "I'm one of the twelve who's still alive and not yet on trial. I've much work left to do, Ben. I can't die *now*. There's danger everywhere, from places and people we might never expect. Fellow Jews have killed many of our disciples, sometimes without warning. And in these hard times, there are bandits and zealots and cutthroats in abundance. And the Romans are everywhere. Always the Romans, ready to do the killing to maintain order in their interests, like they did with Jesus at the urging of our high priests."

"Always the Romans," Ben repeated. "I think the people who surprised me on the last night of my journey might've been Roman soldiers who left their posts to hunt for travelers like me, anyone lost or injured or dying from exposure, easy prey that might have items of value."

"Certainly," John replied. "I've also encountered some of that, and I'm curious to know if you're wondering why we left Mary's home in such haste."

"I am," Ben admitted.

"The threat was even greater than I thought," John admitted sadly. "While you were sleeping, an informant came to warn me about a group of Romans and Jews, together, who were striking at night in places where disciples might be meeting, hiding, or sleeping. Much like the thieves you encountered, they are packs of wolves who feed on us and the zealots who have little to do with us and our cause. They're politicized Jews, militant nationalists who've gathered a great following. I fear there will be much destruction because of them. Only one of our twelve has had an association with those rebels. That one is our Simon. But it was long ago. He was a friend of Barabbas, who was freed instead of Jesus by Pilate, the Roman procurator. Barabbas is still a zealot, out there running wild. But Simon has changed, just like Paul. His contact with Jesus in the public baths quickly convinced him that violence isn't the best path to freedom. Simon was an iconoclast who became a fierce, rebel firebrand. His change to espouse peace and goodwill was widely regarded as another of our Savior's many miracles…something *He alone* had the power to perform. As a result of that miracle, Simon truly came to love Jesus, but when Simon joined us, many believed we were revolutionaries as well. That's another mistake we suffer from, greatly. Killing and stealing from Christians and zealots is quietly supported by Roman justice, so it's flourished. The informant who came to Mary's early this morning is a trusted sister. She risked her life to let us know a pack of those Jackals was about to attack *us*."

"I had no idea!" Ben exclaimed.

"That's true, Ben. You truly have no idea. That's one of the reasons I wanted you to travel with me. I don't wish to be cruel. Quite the contrary. But honesty and transparency are always best. We decided to give you charity because it's the way Christ taught us to follow. But with you, there was more, another reason. You're a good lad, a lot like Paul turned out to be, in many ways. You have much to offer this world if you'll wake up and discover the reality. Your soul is good. We're kindred spirits. In my opinion, the difference is this. I see *you* as a young man shielded and favored in a life of luxury, seldom exposed to the darkness that prevails deep in the hearts of many. You have recently suffered, but you still have no concept of the specters of demonic evil that are regularly manifested in the world beyond your father's gate. Now you've been tossed into the intensity of some of its cruelest manifestations and have witnessed the hideous torture and destruction of a loved one, not to mention scores of others. Now you want to run away, to go where there are no Romans, so you can follow Jesus and find yourself. It's not going to be that simple. We must talk more, Ben. But for now our survival is *not assured*, so follow me closely."

As they moved on in silence, Ben had time to think about John's words. When night fell without moonlight, they camped without a fire. John broke their bread and prayed. They consumed it along with some salted meat and drank the life-sustaining water continuously replenished by a nearby underground source.

After they finished their meager meal, John turned to Ben and said, "There's something else you must understand, Ben. You're an exception in many ways. You're a rich Jew who *does not* think the followers of Jesus are lunatics, heretics, blasphemers, or zealots. You also know our religious hierarchy has much to lose if we succeed. They're leading the people against us, just like Saul of Tarsus did as a Pharisee. Our Saul, who held the cloak of another at the stoning of our beloved Stephen, is an example of the viciousness of the attacks on us. Those attacks are fueled by fear and self-interest. Saul was among the worst, until *Christ* risen confronted him directly on the road to Damascus. What a change to behold! Jesus chose him. Saul became our beloved Paul, and he will, no doubt, be martyred himself for sharing the good news about love, mercy, peace, and redemption. I know you have heard this before, Ben. It's a good thing to remember. It could happen to any of us."

Ben's thoughts about Paul's conversion and potential martyrdom were provocative. He was beginning to feel an attraction to Paul and his work. "I also know of the baptism given to Jesus by the Baptizer. Was Paul also baptized, after he was changed by Jesus?"

"Yes. He was baptized by disciples in Antioch, as confirmed by Barnabas in his testimony."

"I remember now," Ben responded. "Barnabas also said that Paul had been like the rest of you at one time, a devout Jew, committed to Judaism, but quickly converted to follow *the way* after meeting Jesus. His baptism must've given Paul the additional strength he needed to carry out his new mission with such dedication."

"Absolutely," said John. "It's the same for all who've been martyred thus far. But John baptized with water. The strength of God's Holy Spirit descended upon Paul when he met Jesus. It came with fire and blinding light carried by wind, just as it was for the rest of us in the upper room during the ancient harvest feast of Pentecost. On that day, the *power of the Spirit* flowed through us. It was morning. We *weren't drunk* as some have suggested. We ran down the stairs you used many times, then went out, into the street, and on to the temple where there was cleansing water in abundance. We used it to baptize hundreds. And we've since passed that authority on to *our* disciples. The feeling was impossible to describe. It all came together on that miraculous morning, just as it did for Paul, when he was blind, but heard '*Saul, why do you persecute me?*'"

John paused. His countenance radiated. His eyes were glowing. Ben could feel the energy that exuded from him as he continued.

"I also want you to know that I've been with Jesus from the beginning of his ministry, when Andrew brought him to us in the synagogue in Capernaum, and we walked to the shore of Galilee after he preached to us. We met Peter and my brother James and many others who were there fishing. We heard the Word of God, *words of love and eternal life*, coming directly to us from his lips. He was exceptional. *He was amazing!* He was *not at all* like a normal man. He was not like us, not like the many we knew in the past. He told us to drop what we were doing and follow him, and we did so *immediately*. There was nothing else we could do. Where else would we go after that? He had the words of eternal life for our souls! I was with him body and soul when he raised Lazarus from the dead, and when he healed a man who had been blind since birth. I was with him the night of our last meal, when he was betrayed. I stood with his mother along the way as he carried his cross and while he was crucified. I heard his words that final day as he suffered horribly. I know he was referring to the *Twenty-Second Psalm* when he asked why God had forsaken him. But the psalm goes on to say that those who trusted God in their hour of need were not disappointed. Jesus had taken on the sins of the world. God is sinless. He hates the sin but loves the sinner. He turned his back on the sins Jesus was bearing, as his *only Son* died to repent, do penance for *all sin,* and thereby enable future redemption with the same love and forgiveness for all who would return that love doing what is best for *their souls* and others, and living according to his will, just as Jesus had demonstrated during the time he was with us, his death, and his *glorious resurrection!* He made all of that possible for *us,* and *he even forgave those who crucified him!* I saw the open tomb and the burial cloths He left behind. I was there when He appeared in His gloriously resurrected body. He spoke to us clearly on all of those occasions. *All of us heard him.* He told us to wait ten days for the special help he would send, then go forth as evangelists to spread the good news he had shared, out of love, *not by the sword.* Those appearances and the coming of the Holy Spirit left no doubt. Our fear and confusion ended. Our Godhead was with us and always would be.

He had given us faith and redemption with the strength to persevere gladly for the sake of the world. I've seen it all. I was there. *It is real!*"

Then John was still, suddenly silent. He seemed to be listening.

Ben could hear the sounds. Men were coming toward them, carrying torches. There were voices.

"She said they were headed for Ephesus. I can see their tracks. Two men."

"Do you think she might have deceived us?"

"After what we did to her? Are you joking? I couldn't endure what we did to her. Do you think she would lie, knowing we might come back and do more, if she lied to us?"

"But you killed her anyway."

"I know what I'm doing. She might have told others about us. Keep moving along the stream."

John looked at Ben. "It must have been *our* Mary, Mark's mother," he whispered. "May God have mercy on her soul…and be with Mark as he mourns while protecting the writings he's gathered."

Ben recalled the sack Mark was packing with Mary's help, then whispered, "Let's crawl up to higher ground. They'll have a hard time tracking us there."

When the light of dawn began to illuminate the canyon, Ben looked down from their hiding place. He could see a group of men slowly moving along the path. They were well beyond the water source where he and John had camped. Ben emitted a sigh of relief.

"What is it, Ben?" asked John.

"I think we're safe now," he replied.

John crawled forward from his resting place and joined Ben in his vantage point.

"Good," he said. "We'll use a different route from here, Ben. Mark and Mary were the only people who knew I planned to end up in Ephesus. I didn't tell you until the last minute. Now you know why."

"I do," said Ben.

"Good. Let's proceed."

They went northwest on a path some distance inland from the sea, more secluded, and avoiding other routes normally used by Romans, bandits, and hostile Jews. The day was sunny, no clouds or strong winds. John was more relaxed.

As they continued to walk side by side, both were silent, engaged in their own thoughts, until John turned toward Ben and said, "I *didn't* want to discuss certain matters with you in the presence of the others. I have a feeling you'll eventually go beyond my limits in your efforts to rid yourself of the Romans. So you need to know more about Peter and Paul. I've reached a conclusion. Of all of our brothers in Jesus, *they* will be remembered as the two who *did the most* to ensure our movement sustained the strength it needed to survive and continue to prosper."

"But you are held in the highest regard by all of those in Jerusalem I've encountered," Ben responded with obvious consternation.

"Only because my brother James was our bishop there and has already been martyred. James the brother of Jesus has assumed that responsibility now, and Peter and Paul have since gone to Rome. I seem to be the only one of our original group left in the inner circle of the Jerusalem community."

"That brings me to ask why Peter and Paul went to Rome. It seems that city might be the most dangerous place of all," Ben surmised.

"Neither of those great men have any fear of being there," John replied. "It's the crossroads of the civilized world. To them, it seems logical. It's the best place to be in order to spread our *good news* to the many who travel from there to the far reaches of the Roman Republic as it becomes a world empire, expanding in every direction. We have a community of converts in Rome that is rapidly growing. There are many displaced Jews there as well. Peter feels that he should be our bishop in Rome, our universal leader. We all agree. After Paul had some heated discussions with James and Peter regarding relief of Gentiles from onerous kosher and circumcision rules, Peter confirmed Paul as the best qualified to deal with them. He's proven his worth in that *very* important mission."

"Does Peter have authority to be the leader of the universal church Jesus founded?"

"Yes," said John. "It was clear to us when we traveled to Caesarea Philippi. As you may know, it was named for Phillip, the father of Alexander the Great. The Romans have a high regard for what the Macedonian Greeks brought to this part of the world. While we were there in Philippi, Jesus asked us who we thought he was. All responded saying various things. Then Peter said, 'You are the Christ, the Anointed One, the Messiah, the new King of Israel, the Son of our Living God,' thereby *confirming* that Jesus was *not* another in the line of our prophets."

"How did Jesus respond to Peter's answer?" Ben inquired.

"He said, 'Blessed are you, Simon, son of Jonah, because no man has revealed this to you.' That moment was the definitive affirmation of Peter's divinely given insight."

"I wonder how Peter knew it above *all* of you."

"Of course, we all knew that Jesus was not like any of the others who had come before. But Peter's perception was *extraordinary!* It came not as a result of his intelligence, his education, or his depth of knowledge of ancient scriptures. It could only be the result of a *divine chrism* of the Holy Spirit…a divine grace given directly by our Godhead."

"So Jesus bestowed a very special honor upon Peter."

"Yes, indeed! He said, 'I will call you Cephas,' in Aramaic. The same meaning as *'Petros'* in Greek meaning *rock,* as you know, Ben."

"I do," Ben replied. "It's hard to follow at times. No wonder people get confused by all the languages brought to us with place-names changing, men's names changing from Hebrew, to Aramaic, to Greek and then Latin…and the names of Greek gods changing to Latin equivalents after the Romans adopted them."

"I agree. It *can be* confusing," said John, "and Jesus went on to say, 'On this rock I will build my Church and the gates of Hades *will not* overcome it…' And with that came the keys to the Kingdom of Heaven, eternally."

"So, God's Church on this earth will rest on that grace Peter possessed."

"Yes. We think of it as Christ's mystical body on earth, with one knowledge, and that is *the love of God.* I also think Jesus used the words 'will not' because it's not only united in the work of Peter, and the rest of us, but also in the work of those who will come after us, adding to our foundational knowledge by continuing the inspired work Jesus commissioned at the beginning, until it's completed when heaven comes down to Earth in Jesus's glorious return."

"And all of you will also continue to work on the writings that Mark and the others have discussed as part of that effort?"

"Yes. *Absolutely*," John replied. "And as you know now, Ben, I was very close to Jesus in love and friendship, but Peter succeeded me from the beginning in regard to his perception of Jesus…his love of Jesus, and his very strong response to *the reality* of Jesus's resurrection. In summary, Peter did so much to inspire others during a very turbulent time. He was totally committed to Jesus and the work he left for us to do."

"What did you observe about Peter that caused you to come to that conclusion?"

"I remember a day when Jesus approached Peter. He was angry. He'd been fishing for a long time, but caught nothing. After Jesus ordered him to go out and lower his net again, Peter found it full of fish when before there were none. Peter kneeled before Jesus and said, 'Lord, I am a sinner. Lead me.' From that point, Peter was with Jesus at every, key event. My brother James and I were there as well, at the wedding in Cana where he turned water into fine wine, at the *transfiguration* when we witnessed Jesus talking to Moses and Elijah on the mountain and during the storm when Peter walked on the water until he took his eyes off Jesus."

"And there was a message in that," Ben interjected. "As long as we keep our eyes on Jesus and *trust him*, we can navigate the stormy waters of this life and follow his example of true love into the next life, just as Jesus *has already done*...and you have witnessed!"

"Yes, Ben," John continued. "Precisely! As I mentioned earlier, Peter was also with us at Caesarea Philippi near the Heights of Golan. He was there on the dark night of our final meal with Jesus, and in the morning as well. Peter denied Jesus three times as we were waiting in the courtyard of the high priest's home, where Jesus was being tried by the Sanhedrin. Peter was also present for the events that followed Jesus's resurrection, including the day when we returned to Galilee as Jesus said *we should*. We were fishing. We saw Jesus on the beach. When Jesus called to him, Peter was mostly naked, fishing near the shore. When Peter saw Jesus, he covered his own nakedness, just as Adam and Eve did when they realized they were no longer innocent... because they had sinned. When Jesus asked, 'Simon, do you love me?' Peter responded, saying, 'Lord, you know I love you.' And the Lord said, 'Then feed my sheep.' Then again, he asked, 'Simon, do you love me?' And Peter said, 'Lord, you know I love you.' And Jesus said, 'Then feed my lambs.' Then he asked a third time, 'Simon, do you love me?' And Peter said, 'Lord, you know I love you. You know everything.' And with that, Jesus said, 'Then feed my sheep.' Peter had denied Jesus three times on the dark night, and three times Jesus had compelled him to confirm his love and his loyalty."

"So Peter realized he had sinned by denying Jesus three times and needed forgiveness. Jesus wanted to make it perfectly clear that love is the essence of his message. When we love in the way Jesus did, we'll be aware of the needs of others, and *not* deny them in *their* hour of need."

"Exactly, Ben. You've revealed the *heart* of our faith! Believe in Jesus, love Jesus, and come to love others just as Jesus loves us. Our purpose, our reason for *being*, the meaning of our lives is found in love and the joy it brings to others. God is love. Jesus loves us. Together, they've assured our contentment. We can feel their love and know *we are loved by the greatest of all*, here and beyond."

"So at the moment you describe, Jeshua confirmed that Peter was a believer of a very special kind, a mere man who truly loved him in the same way he revealed to us, with his sacrifice on the cross, *on our behalf,* to take all sin away, through His sacrificial death, and thereby give us the ability to be forgiven and thus, be redeemed! And Peter would be a man who would also continue to be a strong witness to the love of God that enabled Jesus's humiliating death and the *victory* of his glorious resurrection! Jesus won, and we can too! We can rejoice in our victory, now and forever."

"Absolutely, Ben. And Peter and I were the first to reach the tomb that morning after Mary Magdalene came running back with the news of her discovery. *There was no doubt about it!* There were no guards. They had returned to their barracks at first light. The stone that sealed the entry was rolled back. The entrance was open. His burial cloths were there, neatly folded, in plain sight."

"Do you know who rolled the stone away from the entrance?"

"There's been much speculation about that, Ben. Those who've the most to lose by his rising blame *us.* But there's no doubt in *my* mind. The power of love rolled the stone. The same power that created us, and our Earth, rolled the stone. The Holy Spirit delivered by God through Jesus was *with* Jesus, and *within* Jesus. And by that alone, it was easily done, even in silence, in the dark of night, or early dawn, after the guards departed," John replied.

"Of course," said Ben. "It seems so simple, unless one's reasoning is obsessed by denial due to fear of the consequences, or being too proud, or too inconvenienced by what it takes to follow in his way, loving God. For me, it's the final proof, confirmed by his appearances, as it was for Thomas. Perhaps others less fortunate might still be in doubt, but for us there is none."

"Yes," John replied. "It stands to reason that others who have *not* been touched by the Holy Spirit might not be aware of the magnitude of Creation, the *unlimited power* and the incredible force that was necessary to produce fire with heat sufficient to melt rocks and cast light so far that it illuminates everything in the absolutely miraculous and incredibly beautiful results we see, hear, and touch all around us. Men without prior knowledge or past experience with such phenomenal outcomes are often dumbfounded and react with denial in the face of majestic happenings. On the day of *his ascension,* Jesus said, 'You will receive *the power* when the Holy Spirit comes upon you, and you shall be my witnesses both in Jerusalem and in all of Judea and Samaria.' And we watched in awe, as he rose ever so majestically until we could see him no more. He had vanished. We were lost. As we walked down the mountain to begin the task he gave us, we were stunned, in disbelief. He would actually leave us in that manner. We were terribly confused, afraid of being in the absence of his irreplaceable leadership."

"I can understand that," Ben said. "You had been with him so long. You were within the circle of his power, then suddenly realized you were on your own, to do as he commanded, under commission, to complete a daunting mission, *without him!*"

"Yes," John affirmed. "It was hard to imagine that we could be successful in his absence, but all of that began to change for me when Peter broke the bread in his memory. I could feel him within me, body, soul, and divinity. Then, ten days later, during the Feast of Pentecost, Jesus sent us the help he had promised. The Holy Spirit descended upon us in the upper room where *we* were in hiding and *you* have slept."

"I know, everything changed at that point," said Ben.

"It did. *It was amazing!* It was the birth of our church. We were filled with *grace,* the unmerited favor of God. We had no fear! We ran outside, a crowd had gathered, and Peter spoke in a loud voice, saying, 'You Israelites should listen to what I have to say. Jesus of Nazareth was attested to you by God with deeds of power, then was handed over to you according to the definite plan and foreknowledge of God. You had him crucified, but God raised him up, therefore, let the entire House of Israel know that God has made him both Lord and Messiah!' Everyone, the entire audience was cut to the heart. We took hundreds to the temple to use the water there in baptizing. Some testified that Jesus had also appeared to *them,* soon after his death."

"Amazing!" Ben exclaimed.

"And so it was," John affirmed.

Chapter 12

The night had passed peacefully. Ben and John had camped in a secluded spot and were well rested. They resumed their journey at first light. The sun was directly overhead when John paused, pointed toward to the west, and told Ben they were passing to the east of the port city of Sidon. Peter and Paul had apparently stopped there during their seaward passages to Rome. John mentioned that Paul's undertakings had made significant inroads with Gentiles, along the same route to Greece he and Ben were traveling. Paul had been the first to establish churches in Greece and started others throughout the lands of Syria, Anatolia, the graveyards of Troy, and throughout Asia Minor during the same time John and Peter were doing the same in the region that included the Judea and Samaria.

Ben acknowledged John's remarks with a nod and said, "This land we've been walking across, following in Paul's footsteps, is a place that's seen tremendous conflict in the past. Now it's the Romans, before that the Greeks including the Trojan War, and the conquests of Alexander the Great. I recall that *our* United Kingdom of Israel was divided long ago into the Kingdom of Israel and the Kingdom of Judah. The northern Kingdom of Israel and the Kingdom of Judah developed civilizations that were different in some ways because Judah was smaller and mostly rural. The tribe of my namesake and the Levites eventually joined with the tribe of Judah, and the Davidic Line began in the south. The Assyrians conquered the northern kingdom. Then came the Babylonians who took many of our people back to *their* homeland where Abraham was born. And the Persians eventually conquered Babylon. By then, our people were scattered, even before the Greeks came. And *now* many are fleeing from the Romans who call what is left of our homeland *Palestina*. It's all very interesting."

"Yes, Ben," John responded with a smile. "It's all very interesting, and it's all very sad. It seems we've come full circle. I think back to the time when our ancestors were fighting the Philistines and some Canaanites. Now the chosen people have been scattered four times, perhaps like God's seeds in the wind. So my brothers, like Paul, might find some degree of kinship, charity, or understanding, during their travels, and travails, far and wide. But that too might turn into irony."

"That reminds me," said Ben, "we've talked long about Peter, which I much appreciate, John, however, at this point, I feel like I'm more inclined to follow in the direction of Paul. Perhaps, going even farther than he has. Thus, I hope to hear more about him whenever you have time."

Both were feeling more secure, beyond pursuit. John began to speak in a more relaxed manner, slowing his pace as they continued to walk side by side.

"Gladly, Ben!" he responded with obvious delight. "Paul was born in Tarsus, southeast of here, the child of diaspora Jews who lived in a mixed culture of Jewish and Greeks. He became a Roman citizen, much like you did, thus was a man of three cultures and well qualified to pursue his present vocation. I'll not forget the day Barnabas brought Paul to Peter James, and me...when he returned to Jerusalem after his conversion. Paul had been alone in the desert for a very long time, then started evangelizing on his own. We'd been worried about others who might do the same, perhaps confusing those they encountered. But Paul was clearly, miraculously, *one with us!* What he told us and the questions he answered so precisely proved that, beyond a doubt. He was overflowing with *divine* revelation. He'd been chosen by Jesus, just like Peter and the rest of us. His time in Jerusalem with your former mentor Gamaliel steeped him in Judaism, its rites, liturgies, and history recorded in our scriptures. Paul also had a complete knowledge of Plato, Aristotle, Homer, Sophocles, Euripides, Aeschylus, Pythagoras, and Homer, just as you have. However, it was his intimate knowledge of every aspect of the same teaching and experience we received from Jesus that convinced us. It was astounding, clearly beyond coincidence and *truly miraculous!*"

"No doubt?" Ben responded.

"None," John replied. "The results of Paul's encounter with Jesus have been amazing, the ultimate confirmation. He once breathed murderous threats about us. Now he's a leading advocate, dedicated 'til death. His many letters to the churches he founded tell it all, especially those he sent to his converts, Jews and Gentiles alike, who had gathered around the many crossroads leading to Rome. His approach to the Gentiles was approved by Peter and James. I felt the same and was delighted by their decision. They were right! Once that was done, Paul garnered scores of believers everywhere he went. But he's paid a high price to do it. He has been hounded by Jews, Romans, and a host of heathens. I didn't mention this to the others before we left, and Barnabas and Mark will know soon enough that our Paul has been *taken* to Rome, under arrest for a trial of his own request. Paul has the rights of a Roman citizen, and he is convinced that his testimony during the trial will would be heard and recorded and might help our cause by clarifying misconceptions and lies of others, who want to defeat us, for all the wrong reasons. Those who hear and read his God-given words will finally know the truth about our movement and the reason, the purpose, and the meaning of Jesus's mission."

"God help him," Ben added.

"Amen, Ben. And let's pray God will also help young Mark," John added. "I wonder if he's received the tragic news about his mother."

Both were silent as they continued to walk.

John eventually resumed their discussion.

"My thoughts have returned to Paul, Ben. As he was when we knew him as Saul of Tarsus. I can imagine how he felt along the road to Damascus on the day of his encounter with our Lord, when he was blinded by the light that struck him, then heard *the voice* calling, and inquired, 'Lord, who are you?' Then received the reply, 'I am Jesus, whom you are persecuting. Get up and go into the city. You'll be told what to do,' and so Paul did, with a great deal of difficulty. It must have been overwhelming."

"I think he was probably wondering what in the world had happened to him," Ben remarked. "He'd been on his way to punish others, then was knocked to the ground, blind and being ordered by Jesus. I assume he must've been shocked and confused, humbled at least, in the presence of God's overwhelming power."

"Humility in a heartbeat," John said with a chuckle. "Yet Jesus *did not* exhibit the full measure of his *own* power, as he could have when he first came to Israel, like the Messiah portrayed in the scriptures, the mighty warrior king we expected. Instead, he allowed himself to be humbled as a lesson for us. It took Saul…who assumed the name Paul…a very long time to know Jesus and grasp the *whole truth*. But Jesus was patient. How great it is that our Lord and Savior *loves us!*"

"Amen, Amen!" Ben shouted in response, raising his arms and holding them high above his head, his eyes on the sky.

"Yes, brother Ben!" John exclaimed. "And like us, our old Saul knew he must reconsider everything he thought before, given the blinding light and other aspects of his encounter with our Lord and Savior. Paul realized that his new mission was to declare the coming of a new king who would fulfill all of the promises made to our people. Paul has traveled many thousands of meters by perilous sail and passing through danger one step at a time, to endure jails, beatings, and incredible abuse in order to succeed in his perilous mission."

"I understand," said Ben, "and I hope to do the same."

"I have prayed to hear that from you, Ben. And *that* being the case, I will help you to complete the preparation required for your mission, and we'll do that in Ephesus," John promised as he embraced Ben then placed an arm around his shoulders.

"After that, you'll decide how far you want to go. You must know that when Paul went to Greece, he was bringing our church to the underbelly of Europa, to the region we refer to as the West, and perhaps, as you said earlier, someday you could carry the good news there too."

Having said that, John moved faster.

Ben was smiling as he followed close behind.

Two days later, they were tiring when Ben spied a stone dwelling on the outskirts of what might be Ephesus. He could see it looming in the darkness as John motioned for him to stop.

"That's Mary's home, Ben. We've been guided right to it! We should make sure there's no one hiding here, waiting to harm us. You walk slowly in a large loop to the right side of the house. I'll do the same, walking to the left. Be on the alert for potential danger and signal if you need help. We'll meet on the far side, one way or another."

When the circle had been closed without incident and the two were together again, John moved toward the entrance of the dwelling, with Ben following close behind. The door had been removed. They could see inside. John entered without hesitation.

"This is where I brought Mary, the mother of Jesus," he said. "I want you to see it and touch it, to experience it, just like you did in the upper room and in the garden, to allow all your senses to bathe in the reality my family and I experienced with Mary and Jesus and all that transpired when we were together. Then think of me. Ask yourself... why would my friend John tell me all these things if they were *not* true? And why would my brothers and I, and many others, die horrifying deaths for this if we knew it was a fraud, that we made it all up…that it was a hoax, a sham, or a lie? If we had removed the body of Jesus from the tomb and still pretended he had been resurrected, would you think that could be possible? And if someone claimed he was not really dead when he was placed in a tomb, do you think his Roman crucifiers would allow that…at the price of their own lives…would you think that was possible? And if the Roman guards allowed someone else to move his tombstone and escape with his body while they were on guard, do you think that would be reasonable? They would also be crucified if that happened! And do you think the stone could have been moved by human beings, and the guards *would not* know it? The guards left the tomb at first light while the stone was still in place. A short time later, the women came to the tomb and found it empty. The stone had been rolled back. The number of men needed to do that were nowhere to be found. And they could not have done it and escaped with his body in the short time they had. You already know what Peter and I found when we arrived soon after the women ran off to tell us. I was there! The tomb was empty, except for his burial cloths, neat and carefully folded. I do think there's a chance that young Mark and a couple of caretakers might have passed through the scene, at some point, around the time Mary and Mary Magdalene where there, but no one else was in sight the entire time Peter and I were there. There's more… much more, but we'll get to that later, Ben."

"Thank you, John. I'm stunned. It's is all so real to me. All that you do is more than enough. I'm ever so grateful for the great honor of this precious time with you. Your words and your witness are so inspiring! Others should be so fortunate."

"You're most welcome, Ben. And I'm enjoying it as well. Can't you tell?" John concluded.

"I've noticed you're certainly more relaxed, walking, here in the desert," Ben responded. "Perhaps feeling the threat to you is less than it might have been or could be elsewhere?"

"You're right, Ben. I also have time to think more and I've been thinking of the Trinity. You should do the same. Meditate. Pray about it, Father, Son, and Holy Spirit acting as One in love and communion. One God, in three persons you can relate to…beings, aspects, or integral parts of the Godhead…if you wish, and it enhances your understanding of the certain knowledge Jesus revealed, whenever he talked about the Holy Trinity as Father, Son, and Holy Spirit acting as One in divine love and communion with the saints like Mary and other faithful believers. It's a key, just as his resurrection was and the Holy Communion, with the bread and wine…his body and blood…we did not understand at first. And then there's the prayer he gave us in answer to the question, 'How should we pray, Lord.'"

"I'll gladly embrace all, in their entirety," Ben promised. "And I understand our custom of giving all to the first son. It's so obvious. Our culture was the base from which the new covenant came, and Jesus coming from the Father in his image and likeness with the power of the Father's Holy Spirit is understandable. When we think deeply about it, pray about it as you have suggested, and use the intellect, the ability of rational thought, and the logic and common sense God gave our first parents, it all comes together, enabling us to believe and trust our Creator, all he truly is, and all that he has been, *eternally*."

"Yes, Ben, and please remember what Moses said so long ago in answer to the question 'What is the meaning of life?' and 'What must I do to inherit eternal life?' Can you remember what I told you when we were in Jerusalem?"

"I can," Ben replied. "Jesus tells the scholar the same thing using his own words. *'Don't ask me. Tell me yourself what you know it to be. The man answers. You shall love the Lord, your God, with all your heart, with all your being, with all your strength and with all your mind, and your neighbor as yourself.'*"

"That is the essence," John confirmed. "And Jesus adds the words used by Moses in a similar situation, saying, 'Do this, and you will live.' You learn well, Ben, and there's something else I just remembered."

"What is it?" asked Ben.

"It's about the place where we found you, in the Garden of Gethsemane…the place where Jesus knelt and prayed to Our Father on the night *before* he was crucified. Your presence there, at that hour, gave us a start. At first, we thought our Savior had returned for the last days. I think it was a foretelling, from on high…more than a coincidence…a confirmation that our meeting was meant to be."

"I can imagine," said Ben. "That would have been a wondrous conclusion! I was drawn to that spot. I felt something very special, just as I do now, the same as I did in the upper room in Mary's home. I thank God every day for our meeting, John, and I'm so sorry about Mary's suffering. She was so kind and so real."

"This Mary, the mother of Jesus, was 'real' just like Mark's mother. She was truly divine in all that she did…in her joy, her suffering, and her sorrows. I pray that her role will never be diminished nor forgotten by future generations. Two of our Mary's have passed on now, like Joseph and some of the others…to be together again with our Savior in God's loving embrace. I can feel the *joy* of their *blessed* reunion."

Ben's eyes were overflowing with tears. He noticed that John's eyes were clear, gazing into the night sky, while John smiled from ear to ear.

After that night, the two stayed together for many days surrounded by disciples who lived in the region. Ben took testimony from John, added it to what he had written in his own hand, and created copies on paper, in Greek. John read and approved all the copies before they were polished, then rolled, and bound them together in scrolls.

One afternoon, as the process neared completion, Ben approached John.

"You seem to be worried," he observed.

"I am," John replied. "I think our work is progressing well, but I feel like I should add more, something in the way of letters, like those Peter and Paul have sent to our new communities, like the one here in Ephesus. The faithful gather in home churches seeking the truth. I've talked to some of the believers who've helped us. There's one point that appears to be essential. It must be regularly clarified for those we embrace in our efforts, lest other notions detract from the essence of our message."

"What is that?" Ben inquired.

John opened a scroll of papyrus and began to read. *"What was from the beginning, what we have heard, what we have seen with our eyes, what we looked upon and touched with our hands, concerns the Word of Life for the life was made visible. We have seen it and testify to it and proclaim to you the eternal life that was with the Father and was made visible to us. What we have seen and heard, we proclaim to you, so that you too may have fellowship with us, for our fellowship is with the Father and with his Son, Jesus the Christ. We are writing this, so our joy might be complete."*

"It is profound," Ben marveled. "How will you use it?"

"I intend to place it at the beginning of the letters I plan to write. Please make a copy. I will include it in the satchel of documents that Mark and I have prepared for your journey."

Ben thanked John and did as he asked.

During the days that followed, more dictating, writing, and translating was completed with the help of trusted disciples. John gathered the copies he had promised Ben, placed them together with some other items Mark had prepared and rolled them into an oilskin-wrapped bundle that fit neatly inside Ben's satchel. When he was done, John told Ben that he and some others were going to carry similar documents south to Qumran, near the North Shore of the Dead Sea where they hoped to find Mark and his Essene companions.

Ben and John had talked long. John had shared everything, answered all of Ben's many questions, and added some fatherly advice.

"Before you leave here, I must tell you that *wherever* you go, there is one thing that will help you, and another that will plague you along the way. The first is this. *Please remember these words.* 'Just as Moses lifted up the serpent in the wilderness, in this way must the Son of man be lifted up in order that everyone believing might have in him life eternal. For in this way, God loved the world, and so God gave the only Son in order that everyone believing in him might not parish, and rather, have life eternal for God did not send the Son into the world that he might judge the world, rather that the world might be saved through him.' Jesus showed me. He is *our advocate*, and he will do what is right to prepare us for God's embrace in his Kingdom, whenever his will be done."

"I will always remember these words, John," Ben replied.

"They are the essence of our good news, Ben, but man's nature will plague and confound you with *hypocrisy*. I think Jesus did his best to demonstrate that terrible fault. One day, when we went to the temple from the Mount of Olives, where we had spent the night, we encountered a group of men who were preparing to kill a woman using stones, just as they did to our Stephen. They were scribes and Pharisees. They had taken the woman in adultery, claiming they caught her in the very act. They confronted Jesus asking Him if the punishment for that act should be stoning as prescribed by Mosaic Law. Jesus ignored them, kneeling to write something on the ground with his finger. He was writing names of the sins the men themselves had committed. They challenged him again, and he told them that 'the one who is without sin is the one who should cast the first stone,' and they departed, leaving the woman alone. Jesus did not condemn her, rather told her to 'go and sin no more.'"

John paused for a moment, then said, we knew those who soon departed. They had done the same things, some of them even with her. Jesus had unmasked their hypocrisy. Even in great cultures that draw their laws from the principles inherent in their religious beliefs, many are hypocrites, and it corrupts the *politika* the Greeks wrote about. The word means 'affairs of the cities,' the governments their ideas formed to provide control and good order in their societies...from families, to clans and tribes, with common laws binding all citizens like ours and those we have seen with the Greeks, the Romans, and others. But the nature of men must be realized in the evolution of laws, and reality should be the guiding control on their content. Laws made without that understanding *do no good*. The hypocrites will take advantage of them, and their corruption will breed injustices of great harm to well-meaning citizens and faithful believers alike. And lastly, remember that Jesus told us to render unto Caesar what is his and to God what it his. The meaning is multifaceted, like many things Jesus said, and mere men will need time to understand better. But dividing what is spiritual from what is material will be a test for generations to come. You must know that as well."

Ben had experienced enough. He understood. "Your advice comes from the love we know, John. I cannot repay you properly for all you have done on my behalf, but I will do the best I can to consume your wisdom and share it with others, in words, and in deeds."

"That is enough," John said, smiling.

And on the day of their parting, John baptized Ben with water, saying, "I now baptize you in the name of the Father, the Son, and *most powerful* Holy Spirit that proceeds from them, to cleanse you with the living water that will sustain your body and spirit and welcome you into the community of the mystical body of our Lord and Savior Jesus Christ on this earth. May you live in the eternal Spirit of our Almighty Godhead and Creator and perfect your soul, thus as a child of our loving Father you will be renewed and ready to return to his embrace in the new life to come. Go now and *do your best* to sin no more while sharing your love with others in need, *just as Paul has done.*"

Then John laid his hands on Ben, imparting the gifts of the Holy Spirit, the same gifts as those Paul had received during his encounter with Jesus on the road to Damascus.

The two embraced in silence.

Ben turned and started walking back along the same way he and John had traveled together.

When he paused to adjust the shoulder strap on his satchel, Ben looked back once more, but John was out of sight.

Chapter 13

As he continued walking south toward Sidon and the sea, Ben was deep in thought. He and John had discussed the best route to use to escape the Roman curse going north. Ben agreed with John's assessment: avoid the mass of Romans marching to Gaul by using the sea route that bypassed them. There would be danger, but not as much as there could be along the paved road from Rome to the interior, or paralleling it to take advantage of the cover and concealment on both sides of the road, where bands of cutthroats and thieves were hiding. There had been numerous reports of thievery, enslavement, and murder along that way, as well as aggressive recruiting by Romans seeking replacements for their dead and wounded. The sea route was used by a diverse blend of spice and silk merchants and traders from regions East and West, thus the better choice.

During three days of slow travel, Ben had been cautious, hiding and resting as necessary, along the path he and John had followed earlier. As he turned west toward the port of Sidon and inhaled the familiar scent of the sea, Ben welcomed the wind that carried it. Upon reaching the top of a high sand dune, he stopped to enjoy the panoramic vision of the angry sea and a fishing boat being dragged out of reach of waves pounding the shoreline that extended north and south as far as he could see. Three men were struggling with the boat. They were dressed like humble fishermen he had seen on other shores. And without hesitation, Ben strolled down to meet them.

"I'm a lone traveler seeking directions," he shouted over the sounds of wind and waves.

One of the men heard him and turned about. "Come forward!" he yelled. "You look rather harmless."

When he reached the boat, Ben received a warm greeting from the crew and asked, "Can you tell me if I'm near the Port of Sidon?"

"You are," responded the most forthcoming of the three. "It's a short distance to the south. You'll see the city from afar along the shoreline. It's the main port in this area. It's been fortified for many years. The Romans control it now, as they do everything and everybody, *everywhere*."

"To be sure," Ben responded, smiling. "I'm curious. I've seen many boats like yours, but I see no nets here. What manner of fish do you seek?"

"We dive for these," said the man nearest the boat as he held up a spiny sea snail about the size of his fist. "The Greeks started to call us 'Phoenicians' from their word for the color purple, because we make purple dye from the entrails. We're actually Canaanites, descendants of Ham, Noah's son. Our city is named for Canaan's son, Sidon."

"I see," Ben responded with a nod.

"And I suppose you're a rich Jew descended from Noah's son Shem, a *Shemite* if you will."

"I confess to that," replied Ben with a chuckle. "You appear to be a very wise man."

Upon hearing that the man's companions began to reel with laughter.

"He's neither a wise man nor a true Canaanite," said the man holding a murex. "He's what we call a *Canaanized-Celt* because his father was a crazy Celt and his mother was a lovely local girl."

"It's true," said the amused brunt of his comrades' jabs. "These ruffians have taken me into their fold because I'm such a fine figure of a man who attracts young women to our group. Both of them scavenge the least beautiful after I've picked the best. My name is Ian, and yours?"

"I am Benjamin, from Damascus."

"And what brings you to this forsaken wilderness, Benjamin, from Damascus?"

"I'm a searcher," said Ben. "I have come by way of Jerusalem and Ephesus, having been treated badly by the Romans and kindly by some Jews, who now follow Jesus, the Christ."

"You mean the Savior, the Anointed One, who visited us in Sidon in years past?" asked an older man who was packing a pile of sea snails in sacks.

"The same," answered Ben. "He's been called many things, like those of us who've struggled with three or four languages during our lifetimes. One very close to him has recently walked with me from Jerusalem to Ephesus. His name is John."

"Of course. Our Peter spoke of John the last time we saw him. He was on his way to Rome by boat and stopped in Sidon for a brief visit with us."

"I feel like I've known Peter for a long time," Ben replied. "John and the others have told me about him. Are you a friend or a follower?"

"I'm both," responded the older man with a spontaneous smile, his eyes wide with a rush of enthusiasm. "Peter is my friend, and I will love and follow the Savior he serves, forever. There are many in Sidon who feel the same as I. But we have to be careful. There are many among our people, and the Romans as well, who don't share our belief and would kill to advance their point of view or their pocketbook. We've found that a few of the Bedouin descendants of Ishmael, Abraham's son by Hagar, are particularly ruthless in that regard."

"As a matter of fact," said Ian with a chuckle, "we who claim *no* religion find these conflicts quite curious, and often quite deadly. I'm not one to dabble in such matters. I simply want to break even. To survive as best I can, to save *myself* for as long as I can, and strive to find happiness in all that I do."

"And what *do* you do?" asked Ben.

"When not drinking, fighting, or hustling pretty women?" Ian laughed, as his companions jostled him and joined in the merriment.

"Yes," Ben replied, "and when you're not harvesting sea snails and getting roughed up by your friends."

"I'm in the business of merchant sea trading," Ian responded. "My crew and I have made port in Sidon to off-load a bit of cargo while I'm visiting my mother and cavorting with these louts. I have a feeling you and I should talk more. The sun is getting low. Let's pack up our catch and head for the docks so we can sell our haul and enjoy the evening."

It was dark when they reached the home of Ian's mother in Sidon. She was asleep and the two settled outside at a wooden table. Ian started a fire in the nearby cooking pit, hung two fish on a spit over it, placed a loaf of bread, two cups, and a large vase full of wine on the table and took a seat near Ben on a bench.

After they had each downed a cup of wine, Ian poured another and said, "Ben, I feel like I've known you for a long time, but in fact, we're strangers. I have no dog in any of the fights that take place in this world. But I've been compelled to learn to defend myself. My father taught me the ways of Celtic warriors who have spread their culture far and wide. His lessons have saved my life on a number of occasions. When I saw you approaching us alone, I thought you must be a fool who had lost his way or lost his mind. Not even the best and the bravest can survive out there alone."

"At times I feel like I'm all *but* brave," said Ben.

Ian was silent.

Ben studied his face. It was fresh and full of life, handsome yet capable of ferocity and surrounded by thick hair of a reddish tint that hung over his broad shoulders and large biceps.

"I need a good man I can rely on," Ian continued. "But before we get into that, I would like to know what you're up to at this point. Where are you headed, Ben? What is your plan?"

"I'm like a lost child," Ben replied. "I've had some hard times recently. I want revenge against the Romans. But more than that, I want to live in harmony with my Creator's will and rid myself of Roman domination of my spirit. I wonder, will revenge satisfy my soul, or is it best to forgive? I want to open my mind to learn the truth about this life we share and be a free man who can live with that *truth* and die well with assurance of certainty. I've seen many…including my wife…who were murdered by the Romans without knowing the answers I seek. My wife wasn't sure. She had hope, but she lacked certainty. If they had murdered me as well, on that day, I would have died with the same frame of mind as my wife's, however, I've recently been given a second chance with a new philosophy, a compelling revelation born of an ancient religion. The first to embrace it went to their deaths willingly, without hesitation. It has captured my imagination and caused me to feel I've discovered the definitive answer, the key to the gateway for a better life *here*, and the best *far beyond*."

"I'm very sorry about your wife and understand your desire for retribution," Ian responded. "And it sounds like you need to find a place where you *can* pursue a better life? All of that, without fear of unending persecutions by new hordes carrying better swords and new ideas, sweeping through your peaceful valley and burning down your little house in the secluded woodlands?"

"Yes. You're mocking me, but that's it, expressed in the simplest of terms," Ben retorted.

"My friend, I've found that in this world there's nothing simple about anything, and it's only going to get worse before it gets better, if it ever does," said Ian with a smile. "I can tell you right now, if that is your dream, your vision, you'll have to fight in order to realize it, unless you're willing to compromise, one way or the other. Therefore, it's this I must tell you: I *also* have a dream. Mine is not so noble as yours, yet in following it I might be able to help you, if you're willing."

"As I've tried to tell you, Ian, I'm torn between my need for lasting certainty in my faith and my lust for revenge against the Romans. Regardless of what I decide to do, it will be with profound hope that I might discern my Creator's true wisdom as I continue to wander. And I will fight if I must, in order to accomplish that end."

"I understand," said Ian as he looked about to confirm the two of them were alone. "You are a seeker. You seek clarification. There's nothing new in that. You're also a man of good character, one I can trust. I didn't want to share this with my local companions, but I *will* share it with you. I transport and trade many things…silks, spices, oils, dyes, and food. However, it masks my principal interest in commodities of *silver and gold*."

"Silver and gold?"

"Yes."

"I never would have guessed," said Ben.

"That's precisely the point," said Ian. "My Phoenician-Celtic heritage called me to the Middle Sea. I eventually ventured out to the great ocean, then up the coast of Gaul with my crew. We were caught in a storm, had to haul in our sails, and were at the mercy of tide and current for days. Early one morning, we finally saw land. One of our mates recognized it as the coast of what he called *Erieu*, and he gave us to understand it was named in honor of a Gaelic god, or goddess. Lately, I've discovered that it's referred to as *Hibernia* on Roman maps and charts. We made a landfall on the west coast of the place and soon encountered a tribe of Celts who were involved in mining gold and silver. They were businesslike and rather friendly, much to our surprise. We quickly concluded that all could benefit from expanding the trade of this value, and we began to move the ore from there to the island of Anglesey on the Britton coast where local Celts had earlier learned how to refine the ore into bullion. We now have a trading relationship along a route that extends from here to *both* of those locations. Our business is flourishing, and the lode we discovered on Hibernia has yet to be fully exploited. The locals in both places appreciate our service in the trade lanes because it brings them high-value items and commodities they can pay for with gold and silver, to provide comforts otherwise not available to them given the backward nature of their culture, compared to us and the Romans."

Ben listened intently, enthralled by Ian's revelations. "Do the 'natives' you speak of have anything to do with the Romans?" he asked.

"Nothing at all, Ben. That's where you might find interest," said Ian. "I've been told that the Romans have no interest in the place. It's somewhat small and barren. They have so much else in their growing empire in Britton and the mainland that adventures into places like Hibernia would be a waste of their time."

"I see," said Ben with a thoughtful glance at Ian. "So you travel great distances. You go to a place rich in precious metals and do what?"

"I sail with a load in my hull, covered with grains, wood, coal, and other cargo, making ports along the way. The first is on Hibernia, then easterly across the channel to the small island of Mona on the west coast of the grand island of the Briton Celts. The Roman charts have marked the larger island as *Albion*, but there is little detail otherwise. A handful of settlements, including *Londinium* in the south, a few roads…but little else. On the northern tip of that island, they've marked the land of the *Picts,* but nothing more."

"It seems I might sooner be rid of the Romans by going with you along the sea route, however, I know little of travel by water and the hazards that go with it."

"At this time of year, the weather, currents, tides, and winds are as good as they get. I've had no trouble with pirates, Roman or otherwise, in my last two trips. It's up to you, Ben. I sail with or without you on the second night after this."

"Very well," said Ben. "Tell me about your boat and your crew."

"Walk with me to the harbor and you can see both. We have no time to waste. I can hear the call of the Siren of Sligo as she looks upon a lap full of gold, in her cave in West Erieu."

Five nights passed safely, and Ben was standing in the bow of an Arab dhow, sailing west across the Middle Sea. The sun was at his back, and the sea spray caressed his face with moist kisses, cool and inviting. The ship's bow was gently rising and falling as it cut through the ripples that moved across the calm, mirrorlike surface, reflecting the features of high clouds with shifting shapes, gliding easterly toward the mind-breaking mysticism of the Orient.

Ben was happy, sailing west. His face was radiant, burned by the sun in a healthy glow. His lips were pulled tightly into the smile of a man who found freedom so ephemeral he thought it was priceless. His mind was transformed by the idea and the vastness that surrounded him. It was another of the Creator's miracles, a reminder of his presence in a relationship with *the* Almighty that was intoxicating. He was weightless, with the power to rise, overcoming his sadness, yet causing him to weep as he heard the call, "Come back to the rudder!" It was Ian.

Ben regained his composure, grabbed the rail, and made way to Ian's station, in the stern.

"I can see that you're sharing the rush, Ben. That's good," said Ian with a grin. "Now grab the rudder handle. Keep the bow steady, guide on the high rock formation directly to your front. I've heard there are bones of our most ancient ancestors buried in caves at its base. That massive rock marks the passage from this sea to the great ocean we'll sail across during most of our journey. Once we turn north, I'll pass this job to the crew, then *you must* learn the common language of the Celts to perfection. With that and the sword and dagger on your waist, you'll have some of the tools you'll need to survive. I'm going down to check cargo now. Blow the ram's horn if you need me."

Ben's nerves tingled. He gripped the horizontal arm of the rudder with both hands and squeezed down hard so the others would not notice his hands shaking violently.

How could Ian abandon me here? I've never done this before, he mused.

As Ben surveyed his surroundings, what he saw was a revelation. His throat tightened. The other members of the crew, an array of ragged garments from loincloth and headband to long coat and turban, were beginning to smile, then shout, and waive their arms with gestures indicating their approval. They had been watching closely, and they liked what they saw.

Such rapid acceptance by those hearty men was a tonic to Ben's spirit. The warmth it exuded swept through his body like morning sun burning through the fog from a dark night clouded with terrifying dreams. He felt gratification with the progress made thus far. The vessel he was guiding had passed a number of important checkpoints since sailing west from Sidon on the Phoenician coast west of Damascus; and passing to the north of the island of Patmos, then Samaria, and the city of Caesarea, a provincial headquarters in what the Romans called Palestine, including Jerusalem and the former southern kingdom of Judea as well, then continuing on a westerly tacking, south of Cyprus, south of Rhodes, and north of Crete looking farther north through the Aegean to *Byzantium* and the Black Sea passage, then south of Achaea and the Isthmus of Corinth, south of Roma and the islands of Sicily, Sardinia, and Corsica, past the port town of *Massallia* and on toward the southwestern point of the coastlands of *Hispania*.

All but the Iberian Peninsula had come and gone, and all were etched in Ben's memory. He had left much behind, fading away in his wake, washed away in a baptism, liberating him with new scenes that seemed to renew all his senses. He thought of his parents, his wife, and times past. In spite of his lingering sadness, he was beginning to enjoy a heightened sense of something new and exhilarating, a conviction that stemmed from his time with John and the others. Ben *knew* there was much more to come. For the first time in his life, he was completely open, confident, ready to imagine it all, and was looking forward to all it might be.

As he continued to revel in the birth of his zest for spiritual exploration and worldly adventure, Ben noticed a dark object on the portside horizon. The object drew nearer. It was a vessel with two masts like his. When it turned rapidly to intersect his path, Ben's eyes narrowed. His jaw muscles tightened. He grabbed the ram's horn. Two blasts and Ian was at his side.

"What do you need?" he asked.

"Look there." Ben pointed. "Off the port bow. Coming out of the horizon. It must have seen us. It changed course suddenly and appears to be closing."

"Yes, I see it," said Ian. "They're pirates, perhaps Berbers. All hands!" he shouted. "Secure your knives and sword belts, boys. Conceal your lances along the port rail. *We're going to be boarded!*"

As the crew rushed to follow his orders, Ian turned to Ben. "That scow is from the South Coast. I'm certain they're pirates of some kind, hunting for bounty. We'll try an entrapment. It's our best hope. We can't outrun them, so we'll simply stay our course and play the helpless victims. You stay at the rudder. Keep her steady and move closer to the shore as you go. If we've got to swim to save our necks, we won't have far to go."

Ben's fear had turned to exhilaration. He was a free man, running with the wind. The sea spray hit his face. He was refreshed, smiling with his teeth clenched. His wife's face flashed before him. She too was smiling. Her long hair was blowing in the wind, swirling around her shining image as she led him through the crashing waves and salty mist.

"By God, we're going to make it, Rachael! *One way or the other!*" Ben screamed.

The pirates were upon them. The scow slammed into the dhow's port side. Five forms brandishing swords leaped onto the rail. All but one were skewered in midair by Ian and his crew hoisting their Roman lances. The lone pirate who escaped the fate of his comrades charged directly at Ben, waving his sword and screaming as he came. Ben let go of the rudder. The dhow swung hard to the starboard, knocking the pirate off balance. Before he could regain his footing, Ben charged, driving the point of his dagger into the man's left eye and burying the blade up to its hilt. The pirate's body collapsed beneath him and went limp as Ben continued to plunge his dagger into a lifeless face, until it became a bloody pulp.

He heard the sound of Ian's voice. "Yield, Ben! You've killed the bastard *enough!*"

"*Rachael! Rachael!*" Ben screamed, ready to plunge again. But this time his hand was forcibly restrained. Ian's stare met his, eye to eye. There was recognition, then roaring laughter exploding from both as they felt the thrill of their own death postponed and the rush of a victory fairly won.

"It's a good day!" Ian shouted. "We've all done well. Let's make haste to dump these swine back in their boat and give them a fiery funeral to begin their journey to the nether world."

As shouts from the crew subsided, the crackling fire became a roar. Ben stood watching while the pirates sailed away in their blazing coffin, fully engulfed in flames like a cosmic fireball at sunset, slowly disappearing below the horizon.

Several days passed quietly. The encounter was not forgotten but lay far behind in memory and distance. The dhow had passed through the mouth of the Middle Sea, sailing north along the coast of Gaul.

The quiet time gave Ben and Ian the opportunity to talk and train. Ian exposed Ben to his history as a Celt whose tribe had fled the Roman expansion into territories along the Rhine River, then dispersed into Asia Minor following his birth. They spoke their native Gaelic and eventually Greek following Alexander's Macedonian expansion into lands once held by Germanic tribes, Babylonians, Persians, Assyrians, Israelites, and Egyptians. With the onset of the Romans, his people became fluent in Latin.

Ian described the Celtic way of war, attacking in large undisciplined masses. He speculated that the discipline, tactics, and advanced technology of the Roman forces would eventually overcome the Celts in their native lands, as well as those they adopted in their vast migrations.

Ben thought about that. Given all he had learned from the Romans who frequented his father's home, he had to agree. The Romans would prevail, at least for the foreseeable future.

With the exception of religious matters, Ian and Ben felt the same about most things of real value to their respective cultures, including the best way to deal with the Romans: by avoidance. It had served Ian well thus far by allowing him the opportunity to bypass them and connect with some friendly, like-minded Celts on the islands of Hibernia and Albion.

"We work around the Romans," said Ian. "This route we're taking is one of the best examples of how to do that. In time, the Romans will expand to the point of inadequate control just as other great empires have done in the past. They too will eventually fall back of necessity and leave more room for folks like us to tinker around the margins. Empires like theirs, which cannot control their borders nor sustain strong economies, will eventually be doomed, infiltrated, and invaded by others *from within and without.*"

Ben hoped it might be so. He held fast to an emerging belief that there would someday be evidence of a place on earth where a man could live outside Rome's tyranny, in a place where good people could lead a simple life of self-sufficiency with the freedom to pursue happiness in a philosophy and faith they could easily embrace. The Greeks had done that with their city-states for a time, so it might be possible again, somewhere, someway.

Some degree of independence and privacy had always appealed to Ben. He was not concerned that, in spite of his own efforts, and urging by Ian, he was unable to be close with other members of the crew, all the time. They worked well as a team plying their trade. But like Ben, at other times most seemed to prefer being alone, taking full advantage of limited opportunities to pursue their personal interests. Ben was actually quite pleased with the relationship, since it satisfied all his needs and left him time to continue his training with Ian, speculate on what the future might bring, and pray for the grace to endure all things happily.

When the second moon of the voyage was on the rise, Ian gathered his crew to advise them of a change in his plan. Ben had received prior notice from Ian and understood it to mean that instead of first going to the Sligo Gold Mine in Hibernia, the captain had decided to drop their cargo earlier, as a better course of action. So Ben sat silently, with the rest, as Ian began to speak.

"Based on my calculations from our last trip and the wind and tides we're experiencing now, I'm convinced it will be best for us to go direct to the Isle of Anglesey, off the west coast of Albion. We can drop our entire load of goods there, then take half the time it usually requires to row and sail farther west, to the west side of Hibernia. We can then spend *two months* in the mines, instead of one. With all of us pitching in with a few Celts, we could have enough gold and silver ore to reach our cargo weight limit including ballast. We can trade with them to satisfy their needs, and the winds currents will be with us when go east to return to Anglesey. We can help our Celt partners there to refine our share of ore into bullion, then load it first, and cover it with cargo bound for Gaul. Our partners on Anglesey will be twice as happy this time, because we'll be leaving them a split of ore that's twice as big as the one we left them on our previous visit. In addition, we'll sign a contract with them for an even greater share of gold next time, to ensure they don't cut our throats while we prepare to depart. Those Celts are smart... They know the ancient rule...*it takes gold to get silver*...and since we do our own unloading in Gaul, we should be in and out of there fast, with payment for delivery of goods and twice as much bullion left in our hold as we had last time. With good winds and favorable currents all the way down to Malta, our return home should be swift."

Ian paused for questions. There were none, so he continued. "This run is very important for two reasons. I have a feeling something is about to explode with the Romans in Palestine. It's something that might have a wide range of ramifications, with dire consequences for our region. The Jews are on the verge of revolt. As Ben knows, the pressure has been building for some time. This might be the last time we're able to unload and exchange some of our bullion for Roman coin on the black market, before the regional chaos begins. We have people to care about there, and our timely arrival with the additional wealth should ensure our success in moving our loved ones and their shares of coin and bullion to safety."

The crew was silent, exchanging glances.

After allowing adequate time for his men to reflect, Ian asked, "What say you to my plan?"

"You've always steered us right, Captain," said the hand at the rudder. "We're with you all the way!"

"Aye!" shouted the rest in unison.

When the gale hit their dhow at first light, the blast tore off the foresail and shattered the mast. The crew was upside down and underwater while some were still sleeping.

Ben had been at the rudder and was blown over the starboard rail, down into the raging sea. He remembered stories about fishermen overboard on cold nights, who would suck a full draft of seawater into their lungs, then dive for the bottom in hope of hastening the end of their agony.

The waves hit hard and fast, pushing him under each time he tried to breathe. He had to kick and claw upward with all his might, then take a bite of air before the next downward plunge, again, and again, until the weight of his freezing arms and legs pulled him under.

Chapter 14

Ben awoke to a blinding light, facing upward, suspended. His wrists and ankles were tied together over a pole carried by two strangers, one at each end. Four others were walking along, two on each side, and speaking in a Gaelic dialect he struggled to understand. "Good fortune for us!" a stranger on his right exclaimed, causing a flurry of raucous responses.

The captors eventually grew silent as they rotated through the front and rear carry positions and walked alongside to take breaks, stretching their arms and legs to relieve stiffness and tension. Ben's head bounced up and down, his splitting headache was unbearable, but he must not make a sound. His wrists and ankles burned like white-hot flames circling around them. It seemed like ages in the agony of a tortuous confinement, with up-and-down motion, as his captors carried him over rocks and fallen tree limbs scattered on the ground by the storm.

As they pressed on, Ben noticed these men were different from any he had ever seen. All were mostly naked. Their fair skin was painted with faded bluish dye. Over that were various adornments, like primitive artwork, painted in blacks and whites to form circles, animals, and strange symbols that could be words constructed with an alphabetic code he could not break. Some heads were shaved.

Others had long brown or red locks. All were average-sized men, fiercely savage, carrying swords and other weapons that marked them as warriors of the Briton Celts of Albion, whom Ian had described.

The realization brought a gasp of fear that Ben quickly silenced, as they entered what appeared to be a village, partially hidden in a grove of unusually large trees. Circular dwellings covered by conical thatched roofs appeared in the distance, some larger than others, with one structure toward the center of the cluster dominating the rest. Animals were scattered throughout. Cows, sheep, goats, dogs, and chickens were everywhere. Ben saw a wide variety of racks and tables and benches made of rough-hewn boards and tree limbs, some being used as workbenches, chairs, and racks for hanging meat, furs, fish, and other items being prepared for food, clothing, or bedding. Dark smoke from numerous cooking and warming fires rose and collected over the scene creating shapes in ominous clouds seemingly poised to release a downpour of impending doom. It could be an omen, Ben thought, as he prepared himself for the worst.

Night was beginning to fall as his captors removed Ben from the pole and tied him to an oak tree in a standing position, with his back to the bark. He was facing the center of a common area, with the dominant structure standing on the far side. Halfway between his position and the large building, at the center of the open area, was a circular fire-pit with an iron pole the height of a man firmly planted in the middle. Ben noticed men stacking logs around the pole, then setting them on fire with flaming torches taken from those placed throughout the area, so numerous their collective inferno was rapidly replacing the fading light of day.

Ben also noticed a large group of men and a handful of women beginning to gather near the fire, with their backs to the large structure, facing him and appearing to look directly at *him* with eyes that reflected the rising flames, burning brighter with eager anticipation.

When the crowd started to part, creating an opening in front of the entrance, the large wooden doors of what Ben thought of as the big house opened outward. Four men emerged carrying what appeared to be a long table with stout legs. The men were wearing black robes with hoods. Their faces were partly obscured by shadows as they moved to the beat of drums and the eerie whisper of high-pitched wooden flutes. The sounds combined with moving shadows in a haunting yet stirring rhythm heralding images of a horrible but heroic dance of death. Women began to chant in high pitches. Their voices sent shivers through Ben's spine. The skin on his back scraped painfully over tree bark. He felt blood trickling down the back of his legs.

Then Ian came into view, spread-eagled, naked on top of the table, facing upward, his hands and feet secured to the table legs by ropes. His face was horribly contorted, eyes bulging, mouth wide open, lips moving in a babble of sounds, like words without meaning.

The table was placed between Ben and the fire. The men in robes formed a circle around it, spaced far apart, to allow the crowd to see Ian staged to become one of the ritual victims in a Druidic sacrifice like those he had described to Ben during their voyage.

When one of the Druid priests raised a torch, there was silence. As another priest began to speak, Ben could make out the *Gaelic* the priest was speaking to describe the celebration of an alliance under one of their leaders. The ceremony about to begin would mark the beginning of a war on the Roman occupiers of the Celtic lands of Britton. That effort would be led by a Druid Priestess and Warrior Queen of the Iceni Tribe. Her name was *Boudica.* Ben would not forget.

The crowd roared approval as one of the hooded figures removed its cloak and parted its long robe to reveal a woman unlike any Ben had ever seen. He was stunned. His fear subsided. His mind concentrated on her image. She was tall, in a colorful gown that clung tightly to her form. Red hair cascaded over her shoulders. She carried a sword on a gold-buckled belt. A brooch hung from a chain around her neck. She looked directly at him. Her glance met his for a moment, passed quickly around the crowd, then returned to examine him thoroughly with an electrifying, hypnotic gaze.

Ben jerked upward, erect in his full height, feeling transfixed, and responding to a jolt of raw emotion. His heart beat faster. His blood boiled, streaming new energy through his battered frame. When she began to address the crowd, Ben was reeling from the aura of her persona as he felt the power of her words.

"On this night, we begin total war on our Roman oppressors. No quarter will be given. Our revenge will be complete. We will join in a revolt against Rome as one people united by common interest in a common cause against a common enemy. Our past differences forgotten, our past offenses against each other *forgiven!* In the morning, we will follow the path our high priests divine tonight from the vital innards of these sacrifices to Andraste. With the instructions and blessings received through them, in return for our sacrificial offerings, I will lead your chiefs, *my seconds,* and the warriors they will muster. We will combine our strengths. Our forces will wipe out every Roman on our sacred isle. When we are done, your dwellings will be adorned with Roman treasure and Roman heads. We will live forever, knowing that we are the chosen ones. No others can change our sacred destiny. Onward together, *in victory!"*

As the crowd shouted its approval, she turned to look back at Ben. This time, the firelight revealed the curiosity in her expression, brows knitted, eyes squinting through slits lined with molten magma striving to illumine the depths of his being. Her lips parted in a mysterious whisper as she slowly turned away. Ben strained to hear in vain as she vanished—consumed by the roaring mob.

As Boudica disappeared in the crowd, the remaining priests took charge of the ceremony, shouting instructions to groups of warriors gathered around them. One group surrounded the table where Ian lay while another entered the big house and soon returned with a man wearing a Roman toga torn into bloody rags. When the third group started to move toward Ben's position, he could hear the voice of a man who must have been the Druid high priest.

"Attention," he commanded. "Now lift your heads and turn your faces to the sky, where *Andraste,* our goddess of war, dwells. In honor of her, we will offer three captives as sacrifices. One will be impaled on the stake and burned. The one on the table will be flayed and fed to our dogs, and the last one will be skinned alive and gutted for entrails examination and divining, as our queen has requested. It should amuse you to know that the first is a Roman who participated in the brutal rapes of Queen Boudica's daughters. The second is Gallic, descended from the Averni tribe. His father was a follower of Vercingetorix who killed many Celts in the territories surrounding his and caused others to flee here to Briton where they have waged war against us in attempts to steal our belongings, our women, and our precious land. The third is a worshiper of a foreign god. He came here to take our gold, our silver, and our spirits. From his entrails, we will divine more about his brand of evil, just as we've done with others of his ilk."

The crowd was roaring mightily as the priest's introduction concluded, and the group around Ian split him from breastbone to genitals with a hooked axe, then slowly peeled filets of flesh from his arms and legs with their knives. He was shrieking in spasms as one of the Druids started tossing the bloody carvings to a couple of wild-looking dogs gathered around the table. When Ian's screaming reached a spine-tingling crescendo, it was obvious to all. He could see the dogs eating his flesh. The onlookers relished the spectacle. Their thundering chants, derisive taunts, and howling laughter rocked the arena like an earthquake.

Ben could not bear to look. Instead, he turned his head, closed his eyes, and began to shout in Aramaic, "*Abba, Abba*, please have mercy on us all. Free your children from this hell!"

The men around him started to remove what was left of his clothing and prepared to use their knives. One of them grabbed a handful of his hair and turned his head toward the firepit where four Celts were impaling the Roman. As the flames began to devour his spasmodically jerking legs, the Roman's repetitive screams of agony intensified, causing thundering rounds of approval from the wide-open mouths of a chorus of human faces hideously contorted in all manner of demonic ecstasies.

Ben began to inhale rapidly in short breaths. His body heaved with the effort. His heart was pounding. He thought it might burst. As the first Celt dragged the point of a knife down the length of Ben's thigh, a strong arm smashed into his wrist with enough force to break it. The Celt's knife flipped into the air, then landed point-first in the dirt.

"*Cease!*" demanded a voice with authority. "By order of Queen Boudica, this man will come with me. Pick up your knife, cut him loose, and take the second Roman instead."

Ben let out a gasp and looked up to see four Celts dragging a man in Roman garb out of the big house and through the parting crowd. Blood squirted from a ragged gash in the man's crotch, as four Druids nailed him to the tree where Ben had been tied.

The high priest's voice thundered out to the crowd.

"The Roman now nailed to the tree is our substitute. He was also at the site of the rape. He was captured at the same time as the other. Queen Boudica remembered him. He's *the one* who scourged her before joining the others in the tent where her *children* were moaning and begging for mercy. Our queen wanted to deal with him after her speech. As you can see, Boudica has removed the instrument the Roman used in that atrocity, and she will present *it* as a gift to her daughters."

The crowd noise, especially from the high-pitched voices of the women, was so loud Ben no longer heard the screeching of his nearby replacement, much less the sounds from the other victims. He was being led out of the circle and hurried into the darkness where he crossed a narrow span of water on a log raft and spent the rest of the night bound and bleeding, staggering through the blackness of a mystical forest, remembering the oil-skin bundle John had given him, and realizing he'd lost everything but his life.

Chapter 15

Ben could feel the presence of Celts moving all around him. Escape was not an option. Even if it were, he *would not* take the chance. He wanted to find Boudica. He sensed she might be near, so he plunged onward through the darkness until ambient light began to show through the thick vegetation, and he felt the chill of fog lying low along the ground. As the morning sun spread its warmth, mist began to rise, creating the shapes of shades, like spirits leaving graves in search of their destiny. Ben thought of his wife. He remembered the members of his crew, thinking of their souls rising from the earth like the phantom mists driven by their spirits as John had described while watching Jesus ascend, fading out of sight, lost in the clouds, gone but still present in John's mind, touching his heart with a spirit undeniably *still alive* and transcendent, in an everlasting presence.

Ben stopped suddenly. His thoughts were interrupted. Forward movement had ceased. The nondescript forms around him were standing still, now visible through a thin layer of mist. All were heavily armed. Some wore helmets, some wore leather caps, others were bareheaded, a few had lime-washed, spiked hair. He saw homespun tunics, trousers, and cloaks made of colorful tartan among other forms, stripped to the waist, or wearing nothing but loincloths. In many respects, this group appeared much like the others he had seen after he was captured. They were one people, one race, however diverse as individuals, in a wide variety of uniquely different ways. Some had blue dye on their skin, along with a variety of symbols painted in black and white. Some had shaved heads. Others had flowing red hair down to their shoulders. All wore leather belts with knives, daggers, long swords, clubs, and battle-axes attached. Several carried oval body shields made of wood, with metal boss and decorative ornaments. A few also carried spears, bows, and arrows. Several in the group had arms and necks adorned with gold bands, chains, and torques. Footwear varied from leather boots to sandals to bare feet, all together a motley crew of individuals, ready and willing to fight side by side until victory or death. He was among the iconic warriors of their culture, and his life was theirs to spend.

Ben felt a contraction in his gut as he turned to see three men emerging from the group and moving fast toward him. Other Celts standing along the grassy path between him and the advancing trio were stepping to the side in silent deference. Ben was about to do the same, until the leader halted, directly in front of him.

"Come with us," the man commanded then turned to walk briskly back in the direction he had come. Ben fell into step behind him, and the two guards followed closely. They were moving along the path of the night's travel toward what appeared to be the front of the column, passing others now seated, out of the way, eating, drinking, and kindling small fires. Their weapons were ready on their belts, or nearby within reach. Some noticed Ben's passing with dour expressions of scorn, curiosity, or indifference. All were savage warriors in a wholly uncivilized land, ready, willing, and able to protect their kin in a miserable existence. Ben had noticed this elsewhere, in other cultures. Those who had little wealth, and little else to lose including their lives, seemed not to dwell on their deaths. They showed no fear, no anxiety, only acceptance as a part of their lot, a fact to be dealt with during moments in dire peril, but not before.

Ben spied a large fire. His escorts were turning toward it.

"Wait here," said the lead walker. "I'll motion you forward when she's ready."

Ben perked up. He could follow the Gaelic dialect well enough and was thankful to Ian for that. How tragic it was that a man such as Ian should have so brutal and lonely a death. But Ben knew he was about to meet Boudica, and he began to prepare for that imminent and potentially life-threatening event.

When the guards motioned for him to follow the pathway to the fire, Ben could see a group of warriors standing in a semicircle, facing toward him. In front of them, seated on a large boulder, arms and long legs extended toward the flames, was Boudica. She was frozen in a pose so compelling he came to an awkward stop, admiring the vision until one of the guards pushed him forward to stand in the circle of fire. Like some mythical goddess, too divine to notice him, Boudica continued to stare at the flames.

Ben gazed at the scene slowly unfolding in front of him. Boudica raised her arms toward the sky and began to turn her head toward him until her chin came to rest on a bare shoulder. Her eyelids were half shut, long eyelashes curved upward toward her eyebrows, perplexed by some inward meditation stolen from the chaos of life and death that swirled around her. Her face slowly turned upward. Her eyes widened slightly with a hint of surprise, then narrowed to an icy blue-green stare that caused Ben to hesitate briefly. He stepped back in awe, then stood helpless, once again, in the path of her paralyzing presence.

Her lips slowly parted. "Who are you?" she inquired in a voice so soft it caught Ben by surprise.

He hesitated.

She raised her voice. "Can you hear me?"

He was completely disarmed.

"Can you *not* understand my language?" she continued. "Have you been struck dumb at the sight of a warrior's breasts?"

"Yes," Ben responded, averting his eyes.

"Yes, to what?"

"Both," he replied, looking up at the crowns of towering oaks standing around them.

There was silence.

Ben's eyes darted back to Boudica. She had pulled up her tunic. It hung loosely around her shoulders. She was beginning to utter a sound Ben well remembered, last heard long ago yet unmistakable. It was the uplifting music of a woman. The Iceni queen was giggling in an affair of innocence, then laughing, arching her back and throwing her head backward under an arc made by flowing red hair. Her robe fell from her shoulders, coming to rest in folds around her waist. She was unbridled, like a wild mare, unrestrained, her white teeth bared. Then she settled back with a muffled sigh and a coquettish stare from eyes wide open and beginning to twinkle in anticipation of joyful emotions from stimulus in a game of playful mischief.

"You make me laugh," she said. Then motioned to her guards. "Fall back," she directed, "and leave us alone."

The guards responded immediately. But their leader kept looking back for assurance that all was well. After he redeployed his charges in a wide circle around them, and beyond the range of Boudica's voice, she turned to Ben.

"How are you called?" she asked, facing him directly.

Ben found himself in an awkward position, standing while looking down at her face-to-face less than an arm's length apart. She seemed quite at ease. He was not.

"My name is Benjamin, Queen Boudica. It isn't right for me to look down on you. May I sit?"

"You may if you wish," she responded with a sensuous, catlike smile as Ben repositioned to a place near her. "You speak our language in an amusing way. You're not a Celt, at least not from any of the bands we know."

"That's true," Ben replied. "I'm from the land of Judea. It lies on the western extremity of a region the Romans conquered and named Palestine."

"Do they control it now?"

"Yes. Completely. And it's happened before."

"Others have done the same?"

"Yes, many. Babylonians, Persians, Assyrians, the Macedonians of Greece, and now the Romans. Before all of that came to pass, my people abandoned the land to escape a terrible drought by going south to Egypt, where they were enslaved for many years by the Egyptians, then returned after a harrowing exodus."

"Except for the Romans, I've never heard the names you give these people. What are *your* people called?"

"It's a *very* long story," Ben replied. "The father of our religion was called Abraham. His son was named Isaac, and Isaac had a son named Jacob who was later called Israel because he wrestled with our God one night. Israel had twelve sons. They became the leaders of our twelve tribes. One of those tribes was prominent. It was led by a son named Judah, and from those we became known as Israelites, Judeans, or Jews. I'm a descendant in the lineage of Judah. My parents named me in remembrance of our northern tribe of Benjamin, which fell from our God's favor due to the sins of its king Saul."

"So I could say that your people are called Israelites and you are a Jew. Is that right?"

"Yes, it is, Queen Boudica. That's the way it stands. Our religion is called *Judaism*, also from Judah. And one might say *your* religion is *Druidism?*"

"Yes. I might say it that way. And did your people fight to defeat or escape the people who dominated them?"

"They defeated many in ancient times, then escaped from the Egyptians later, and came back to their land after forty years of wandering in the desert. But they did not have the number of warriors they needed in order to defeat the new invaders. There are many of my people who still live in our land, and there are just as many scattered widely in many directions, living as they can in the lands of their conquerors."

"Will those left behind fight the Romans?"

"I believe there are some who will try, but it will be futile. The Romans will prevail. I fear that our land, our

Holy City of Jerusalem, and thousands of our people who remain there will soon be destroyed in a slaughter of apocalyptic proportions. Those who survive will be scattered for the last time, and our homeland will be contested forever."

"Did your priests make sacrifices to bring help from your gods?"

"We have *One God*, and our priests did make sacrifices to him."

"Only one god? What sacrifices did that god require?"

"Sheep, lambs, mostly," Ben replied.

Boudica was stunned. Her expression changed dramatically, frozen, perplexed. Then came more laughter, roaring, in waves, finally disappearing behind tightly closed lips.

"Is this true?" she asked in a tone reflecting complete disbelief and astonishment.

"It's the best I can tell you at this point, Queen Boudica, given my limited use of your language."

"You've done well for a foreigner," she responded. "Are there Gaelic speakers in Palestine, from whom you learned?"

"Only one I knew well. He lived in a land that Celts had reached in their migrations to escape Germanic tribes, Romans, and Bedouins."

"And he taught you?"

"Yes. He did."

"Where is he now?"

"I fear to tell you more about him," Ben responded sheepishly.

"*Why?*" asked Boudica.

Her brows knitted again with an expression of recurring concern. When Ben withdrew in further avoidance,

Boudica shifted her position and leaned forward until he could feel the warmth of her breasts and the heat from her breath. Her face was less than a hand's width from his. Her lips were parted, teeth bared. Ben looked into her eyes and inhaled sharply as a filmy gray curtain closed over the white pools around the blue-green eyes that once shined brightly, through shadows beneath her brows. Ben recalled the shark, attacking through shallow water while Ian's crew pushed the dhow across a sandbar near Sidon. The creature rolled to its side as it was about to strike. Its jaws opened. Ben could see the protective covering slide over its eyes, an instant before Ian delivered a blow with his iron rolling-bar, disabling the shark and sparing Ben's life. But Ian couldn't help him anymore.

Ben was on his own, and Boudica tore into him. "Listen to me, *Jew*, and mark my words," she hissed. "I have no time for weaklings. If you can't engage in straight talk and would rather pout like a child, what good can you be? Your people obviously cannot fight your enemies and win. You run to other lands and act like cowardly weaklings. You offer sacrifices of lambs instead of people. You have only one god, and you give him lambs? No wonder your enemies make slaves of you and chase you out of your lands. People and their heads are what we sacrifice, and we have many gods to please. We have taken so many heads from our enemies our gods delight, even when we take some heads for ourselves to decorate our dwellings and summon our strength for battle. No wonder your god frowns upon you Israelites. You are *babies* and he wants his children to be men and women who are warriors in his service. *Get up!* Go with my guards. Do not approach me again until you deal with me like a *man* who is worthy of my time and attention. I need help, not weaklings. If I see you again, as you are on this day, there will be *no mercy. I'll sever your head from its moorings without regret!*"

Ben's mind was reeling as the guards escorted him back to his original position in Boudica's order of march. His confusion and consternation were apparent to one of the escorts, an older man who looked familiar. Ben had seen him before in one of the many rotations, as the guards changed around him, after his rescue from Druid mayhem. The man could be a grandfather. He had the marks of many years in time and turmoil across his wizened countenance, yet his moves and mannerisms reflected those of a much younger person. His gray hair laid heavy on his head. His countenance appeared to be gentle. His eyes were tired from too much trouble and not enough sleep. After Ben glanced at him several times, the man moved closer and began to speak in a low voice.

"I don't know who you are or what you did, lad, but I think you might need some advice. Keep looking straight ahead and listen carefully."

Ben acknowledged the man's instruction, kept his head up, and continued to walk.

"I could get into serious trouble for communicating with you under these circumstances. If Boudica decides to dispose of you for any reason, or I appear to be too friendly toward you, I could go down with you, especially if there's the slightest indication that I attempted to help you, or even spoke to you. Do *you* understand?"

"Yes. I believe I do," Ben affirmed.

"You couldn't understand all that's going on around here, but that's good enough for now. Just keep your head down, your mouth shut, and do as I say," replied the man. "I'm known as Kale. My sons and I have been walking and watching near you, since we left the Druid Grove on Anglesey. Various guards, escorts, and others may come and go, but we are tasked to stick with you, one or all, at all times."

"My name is Benjamin, and I wonder who gave you that charge."

"Boudica, in secret. Don't ask any more, nor reveal my answer to anyone. I'm an old friend of Boudica's dead husband, Prasutagus. We grew up together and remained friends as he clawed his way into the monarchy as a clan leader, second, tribal chieftain then king when others on the mainland adopted that title to identify a position at *the pinnacle* of political power. There's intrigue around the throne now. It's complicated by relationships among priests in the Druid circle and constantly competing families, clan leaders, and seconds who are *never* satisfied with the amount of sexual favors, power, and wealth they acquire. The more they gain, the more they want and the more trouble they create for those of us who simply want to live out our lives in good order and leave some measure of respect for our families when we finally go under."

Ben turned toward the sound of Kale's voice but stopped as he recalled the caution. *At last,* he thought, *a kindred spirit in this band of savages. Someone who might even share a common bond. And perhaps a ray of hope in this dark, dirty, and utterly depressing prison without walls.*

"Now the first thing you must know is when a leader goes down, there's change," Kale continued. "It makes everything harder to bear than it otherwise might be. People fear the change. They sense it immediately. The power struggle, the taking of sides, the deals, the rush to spoils, who will win, who will lose, and what it might mean for *every* man, woman, and child, affects everyone in a troublesome way that's debilitating. Someday we might have a smoother transition, but now it's particularly hard for Boudica, as a woman. She's under tremendous pressure. She has much to consider, and much to fear. She cannot trust anyone at this point, except for her daughters and me. The internal conspiracies and consistent pressures from surrounding tribes are sometimes as great as the threat from the Romans. Boudica has to deal with it. She's become cynical and suspicious as a result of many disappointments. However, there's something about *you*, lad, something Boudica's intuition has revealed. She's on the edge. But she's a good girl who has suffered much in her young life and endured some unspeakable abuses. Reflect on *your* experience. Think about what *she* is trying to tell you. Pray for discernment. But for now, be still. These guards will be stopping soon. *You'll need all the help you can get!"*

Chapter 16

Since his shocking encounter with Boudica and subsequent meeting with Kale, Ben had gone far and learned much. He knew Boudica's retinue was returning to the village that housed the Iceni throne in the east central region of the great island. Boudica's primary residence and throne room were located there along with quarters for all who served and protected the monarchy. Included in the group, by tradition, was a cell of Druid priests who advised the queen and serviced spiritual and ancillary needs of the Iceni inside the fluctuating boundaries of the claimed tribal lands. Raids, guerrilla warfare, and periodic set-piece battles for more land and plunder were the norm among the various tribes including the Iceni. The larger battles consisted of masses of warriors attacking each other in mobs that hacked, bashed, and clawed until one side retreated from the battlefield, and the other declared victory and divided the spoils, often including captives who could not escape the prospects of a torturous death or a lifetime of humiliating slavery. With those expectations, warriors often fought to the death against all odds or cut their own throats to avoid the alternative. Battlefields were abandoned by the losers, leaving their dead to be mutilated and beheaded for trophies to adorn the victors' homes.

Ben's learning continued when Kale quietly gathered his sons around him at rest halts, food gathering, and scouting ahead. The goal of this effort was to enhance his rapidly growing base of knowledge by familiarizing him with tribal customs, mores, values, laws, and traditions while taking full advantage of the underlying thread of Ben's ability to communicate in the Gaelic vernacular. His eagerness to engage in hand-to-hand combat with Kale's son Rand soon produced another opportunity for success in his assimilation. Ben had been through a good deal of Greco-Roman wrestling and weight training as a youth, and his strong body and motivation to use it in a wide variety of activities proved to be of significant value. Rand had a reputation for being one of the bravest and most effective warriors in the entire population of fierce Iceni raiders and fighters, and the Iceni respected Ben's ability to hold his own, especially during hand-to-hand combat training when Rand would use the basest of dirty tricks to punish with vicious kicks and eye-gouging, until Ben was nearly blind and suffering debilitating pain. In mock combat with dagger, club, and sword, Rand would cut or bash Ben's ears, nose, and private parts then howl hysterically when his opponent fell to the ground with raging shock and pain. But Ben would never yield and soon became Rand's equal.

One evening when they were in a secluded cold camp near a Roman garrison's location, Kale took the time to have a long talk with Ben. It was the first time the pair had been beyond hearing range of Kale's sons, who had taken up their positions guarding the perimeter of the Iceni camp. Without fanfare, Kale finished his meal of smoked beef and fresh water, looked around to make sure they were alone, then turned toward Ben and said, "I know you've been anxious to hear more about your status and why we're working so diligently to bring you into our culture in a way that might enable you to go beyond mere survival in the constantly changing situation we're struggling to overcome. Much of our motivation in regard to your training was motivated by selfish interests. However, there's another aspect of our behavior you should now be aware of."

"I thought as much," Ben replied, "and I've wondered how long it might take for you to trust me enough to take on more risk by going beyond what you've already accepted."

"I've reached that point," Kale confirmed with a nod. "As I told you earlier, I was a close friend of Prasutagus until his tragic demise. I've known Boudica since she was an innocent little girl who was pledged to him by the royalty of a rival tribe, when they realized he was destined to be our king. It was strictly a political move to seal an alliance with blood. There was nothing she could say about the arrangement given the customs and traditions related to the power men have over the lives of their daughters. I imagine your people might have similar arrangements involving power, territory, heredity, and great wealth controlled and shared, especially among elites worthy or not. As much as I admired Prasutagus, I'm compelled to tell you the truth. He was a brute. I think it's tragic that a man's ability to destroy other men and their families, and even brutalize their own children, often becomes the key to the selection of our leaders, both secular and religious, yet this is the life we know, and you must accept it for now just as

Boudica has been able to do with an extraordinary degree of grace and fidelity."

"I think I'm beginning to understand," Ben responded.

"That's good," said Kale. "Now in regard to alliances, I think you should also know that Boudica is painfully aware of the historic animosity of a number of tribes that surround her domain. It's one of the many threats she must deal with at the same time she's attempting to build and hold together an effective alliance against our common enemy. Many of our Celtic allies might benefit from betraying us to the Romans whenever they sense an opportunity to prosper. The only thing preventing that is the fact that the Romans under Nero have recently betrayed a confidence with us, and several others. So as long as Boudica provides whatever causes other tribes, our people, and our Druids to cast their lots with her as their best hope, she will survive. If not, even her closest seconds won't hesitate to destroy her and keep looking for the next opportunity to serve their own selfish interests. Some among them have even played all sides against one another simultaneously. It's a very clever, ruthless, and lethal game of deceit. As you might imagine, it could be fatal to trust anyone now that the Romans have reentered our *extremely dangerous* mix."

"I know from my own experience," said Ben. "It seems to me you've described much the same as what's happening in our former Jewish kingdoms of Israel and Judea. The Romans control everything with an iron hand and seem to fear the unity our religion creates. It has tightly bound my people together for two millennia or more. The Romans savagely persecute anyone who might revolt, but as long as religion is not at the roots of rebellion, they seem to tolerate our beliefs and practices. The irony there is that many of our *own* people view converts to the new way of Jesus as blasphemers who must be dealt with in the cruelest of ways. Those Jews have recently been more of a threat than the Romans. They've even used Roman leaders against us in their treachery. In fact, our religious leaders even did that with Jesus. The Romans did not see Jesus as an existential threat, but cooperated in his persecution to appease the religious activists in order to maintain law and order. Many of those activists are actually Zionists, who fervently want to end Roman rule. Those who follow Jesus are innocent of *any* intrigue or sedition. Their way is one of peace made possible through love of God and their brothers and sisters in faith, who are created to be children of our Almighty Father, whose apostles and their disciples are *not* at all like the Druids. The difference between those I lived with and Druids such as Salan is like daylight fading to darkness in the gloom of a terrible night. I think the next Romans that come here will know that, and they will seek to end the Druid influence on your people."

Kale thought for a moment. "I overheard our highest priest at the recent Druid rite. I'm curious about something he said, about *you*."

"I think I know," said Ben. "It's about my religion, my beliefs and values, and the danger I might represent, with attempts to destroy your souls and steal your gold."

"That's it," said Kale, adding a chuckle. "Is it true? Do you plan to do that?"

"Not at all," Ben replied with a spontaneous smile. "Your Druid high priest was simply using a fantasy to turn you and your people against me, just like *our* high priest did when he suggested to the Romans that Jesus had come to drive them away and therefore was guilty of sedition."

"Tell me more," Kale requested, "about your god and the *Jesus* you speak of."

"I do worship the one God, the ancient God of Israel. My people have a long history with that God, our Almighty Father and Creator, who has spoken to us directly in the fullness of our time. I think his frustration with our continuing cycles of sin and supplication caused him to try one more time, by showing his love and giving us the solution to our dilemma by offering the sacrifice of an *incarnate aspect* of his eternal being, in the form of Jesus, who would pay the cosmic price of atonement and reparation for all sins, past and present. Then lead us to a better way of life *now* through the example of Jesus…and all that he taught and his *divine promise* of everlasting life in the world beyond. Jesus demonstrated that miraculous fulfillment in the presence of reliable witnesses to his own death and rising, and subsequent ascension to God's heavenly kingdom, forty days later, after appearing to those same witnesses and interacting with them on a number of occasions. The word 'kingdom' was used by Jesus because Jewish history included a series of 'kings' people could relate to in their understanding of the *grand majesty*. He was a *stark reality*, not mistaken by any who were there. Those among the witnesses who have not yet been martyred are writing their recollections as a legacy for all who might read, learn, and *believe*. Jesus also left behind the gift of God's earthly kingdom in the universal church he founded, so faithful believers could share the blessings of a spiritual relationship with

God while still here, preparing for the next life, to be born again, in the infinite renewal of springtime eternal."

"It's a powerful message you bring, Ben," Kale replied.

"It certainly is, Kale, and I believe it might also contain the *most* powerful mystery of all."

"And what is that?" Kale inquired. His eagerness was reflected in forward leaning posture, his expressions changing, eyes focused steadily on Ben.

"For us, solving that mystery requires the use of the *free will* our Creator gave us because he loves us," Ben continued. "That *gift* gives us the freedom to make choices *and* the liberty to choose from a wide variety of alternatives that have been created for us in this world. And the choice I have found to be the most important in relation to the essence of our *purpose* in this life, simply stated, becomes this. Is there a Creator, a God, or is there no Creator, no God? What *we decide* in choosing between those alternatives might well determine the quality of our lives *here* and, perhaps, the destiny of our immortal souls, *forever!*"

"So our souls have the ability to go on in being, beyond this life?"

"Yes, Kale," Ben replied. "John and the others convinced me. Jesus assured them. Our souls are everlasting. They live forever once created. Our Father intended happiness and complete satisfaction to be their ultimate goal. But he also wanted us to be *truly free*. To have the choice and use that gift wisely to embrace the love and beliefs stemming directly from Jesus's example, then demonstrate the faith those beliefs define for the good of others...helping *them* to choose wisely and achieve contentment for themselves, not only in their present circumstances, but also 'til the end of time. Just imagine what this world would be like if everyone simply did what God created us to do, what He has repeatedly asked us to do…to seek, to understand, and to try our very best to live according to his will in our daily lives. It reveals the true meaning of our existence. It's by far the most important aspect of our lives. Think about it. *It's real*, Kale. It's worth trying. We can prevail. God is ready to help us. Think about all He has already done. We must know that. We must examine the evidence, use the minds He has given us in His image and likeness, and be wise enough to simply say *yes…to give Him a chance to prove His love and divine sincerity!*"

"And what must we do to obtain happiness, *forever*?" asked Kale as he leaned forward assuming the posture of an intelligent and vitally interested man, intent on hearing Ben's every word.

"We must choose to respect our Godhead and the love He has shown for us through His creation of mankind and the sacrifice of Jesus Christ, *Our Savior*. We must strive to live as Jesus did and choose to embrace a relationship with Him, rather than turning our backs. We must do our best to live according to His will every day we are given and share with others the *good news* Jesus brought and validated with *His fulfilled promise of resurrected life*, in the greatest of all victories."

"There is much to understand in all you have said so far," Kale responded. "But how will our minds remember and repeat all you've said so we can recall, react accordingly, and strive to live in harmony for the rest of our lives?"

"I had some of the original written words with me when I came here, but lost them at sea," Ben replied. "If

I could read those words to you regularly, in your language, it would help you to understand and reflect on the sacred mystery I'm trying to convey. But for now, I must simply try my best to answer your questions with words based on my experience with the apostle John and others like him, including their disciples such as Mark and Barnabas, who are collecting the words to prepare a new testament to supplement the ancient Hebrew scriptures of the Old Testament, while at the same time helping to raise the church described as '*Katholikos*' meaning 'universal' in the Greek language. It's commonly used in our writings. The writings of the new covenant testament will include all of the church's history, thus far. The church was founded and commissioned by Jesus. He entrusted it to his apostle Peter and confirmed it at the time of his ascension into heaven, forty days after his return from the dead. It was born during a Jewish celebration fifty days after his resurrection, during the Passover holiday, when God's Holy Spirit descended upon Peter, John, and others gathered in the upper room of a home in our Holy City, just as Jesus had promised. And from that day, those brave men have gone out to begin work building Christ's Catholic Church, to last for all time."

"I understand the difficulty you portray, Ben, and the writing and building process that's ongoing as well, but I need clarification in regard to the 'resurrection of Jesus' and what those words mean to you," Kale responded.

"It means that Jesus was crucified by the Romans and rose from the dead to be seen alive several times in a renewed but recognizable form, before he ascended into heaven to *rejoin* with our Almighty God and Creator. He has blessed us with the *Church*. God's kingdom on earth. He sent the Holy Spirit to the apostles in order to strengthen and enable them to continue their mission of spreading the good news that *God loves us* and *gave us* his divine power to persist in a holy life here and upon our passing, to awake in the *eternal spring* of renewed life, with love everlasting, and complete fulfillment in the glorious beauty of God's all-encompassing presence."

"Your words have tremendous power and raise many questions. I wish to speak with you more about this Christ. Would you be willing?" Kale asked.

"Most joyfully," Ben responded. "In the meantime, please remember what Jesus said directly in response to your question, when it was asked by another. *You must love your Creator, and you must love your fellow man, as I have loved you.* It's the essence of our calling, Kale. Love and respect God and do for others what you would want them to do for you. Take care of them and do your best to bring them the peace and happiness desired by those who are made in the image and likeness of our Creator."

"And Jesus *did* die for *us*, so we would have a better life here and forever?"

"Yes. It is *real*. I'm a believer myself as a result of his causing. My beliefs reflect the godly principles, the cardinal virtues that I'm striving to achieve in my lifetime. But it's not my intent to convert you to my beliefs, nor did I come here to steal your treasure. I came here seeking the freedom to worship my God, seek his help in my way, and live free from Roman tyranny among good people who show kindness and charity toward others. If I can do that before my life on this earth is ended, and help Boudica along the way,

I'll depart this kingdom a truly happy man, expecting to awake in the next."

After Kale departed to return to his sons, Ben continued to think about their conversation. It revealed much; however, he regretted that his own contribution had left much to be desired. He was beginning to feel the same concern that John expressed. He recalled that even John, as a direct eyewitness to Christ, had trouble articulating his experience in a way that would help others to feel the same as those exhibited by John and the others.

Ben also worried about his own inability to find all the right words, the *new* words needed to express the true majesty of the mystery, the miracles, and the overpowering presence of a resurrected Man-God's persona. Ben hoped John's completed writings might overcome in time, by providing the details in well-chosen words that would reflect the passion in John's own presentations, *and also* convey the emotion John himself had radiated while speaking in those inspirational moments, when they were together.

Ben had tried his best with Kale, not in vain, he hoped, but more was needed in his discourse. Like John, Ben would pray for help, recognize his human limitations, and keep trying to reflect the perfection and charisma Jesus projected.

But Ben's reflections ended abruptly as shouting and screaming erupted in front of him, where he last saw Boudica. They had traveled only a short distance since the dawn. It had been calm. He had no idea what the source of the commotion might be.

Some of the Celts around him were also surprised. Their security seemed to be compromised. They started to run forward, toward the commotion. Others began to scan the flanks and rear, to look for signs of movement. Ben sensed imminent danger.

Then he saw the Romans.

They were mounted, on horses, using swords, hacking their way through the Celts in front of him, spearing them with lances, and crushing them under hoofs of raging horses that were kicking, biting, and trampling fallen bodies.

Like a bolt of lightning, shock paralyzed Ben until he saw Boudica fighting in the center of the maelstrom, holding her sword in both hands.

He sprang into action without thinking, running forward, grabbing a sword from the hand of a fallen Celt, then hurling himself into the flank of the nearest Roman's horse with such force that the horse's hindquarters collapsed. The Roman rider's leg was trapped beneath his horse. He was screaming until Ben sliced off his head with a single blow of his sword, then quickly grabbed the head by the hair, clenched the horse's reins between his teeth, mounted, and rode the plunging beast directly into Boudica's attackers, waving the bloody head. Before they could react, Ben drove his horse's flying mass into them, bowling their mounts over and sending the riders crashing to the ground.

Boudica was there instantly, hacking them to death before they could recover.

The tide of the battle had turned. A dozen Romans were on the ground, overwhelmed by the mass of Celts who were finishing them.

Ben heard Boudica shout his name. He turned his mount toward her.

"Get the one who's fleeing. *If he escapes to warn others, we're doomed!*"

Ben dropped the Roman's head at Boudica's feet as he thundered past her, taking firm holds on the reins and his sword, grinning and yelling like an unhinged madman. Chunks of earth and grass kicked up by Ben's charging mount landed around Boudica. She dodged what she could and stood smiling, as he hastened to obey her command.

Ben was gaining. He urged his mount on. As he closed on the Roman rider, Ben could see him, looking back, in a panic. *Good*, he thought. *This is exactly what we need. Romans fleeing, in fear of losing their lives.*

A few moments passed. Ben was galloping alongside the Roman who was trying to handle a javelin and stay on his mount. With a single downward blow of his sword, Ben severed the man's forearm and sent the javelin floating up in the air. He clinched his own reins in his teeth and grabbed the flying javelin with his free hand. The Roman anticipated what Ben had in mind. With his remaining hand, he yanked his horse's reins to pull out of range, then noticed too late that his javelin had been returned, when its point popped out of his chest. Ben quickly reached out, grabbed the reins on the Roman's horse, and brought it to a halt while the rider was still in his saddle. Ben swiftly gathered both sets of reins in one hand and swung his blade clean through the Roman's neck in one sweeping movement. The Roman's head bounced off the ground, rolled, and finally came to rest in a patch of grass with its eyes frozen in horror, still fixed on Ben.

Ben secured his sword, dismounted and returned to his saddle with the severed head in one hand and controlling both horses with the other as he slowly rode back to Boudica.

When he reached Boudica's position, he reined in, stopped next to her; calmed the Roman's mare, and presented the Roman's head and his horse's reins to Boudica without saying a word. Then he bowed gallantly, turned slowly, and rode back to his appointed place in the line of march.

Kale met Ben with a look of amazement.

"You've confounded me, Benjamin. Not long ago, you spoke about peace and hope and love for our fellow man. What would your Christ say about you now, after watching the spectacle of your rage, your wild riding, your killing, and your obvious rebellion against his words?"

Ben thought for a moment then said, "Kale, my madness came from love. When I saw those Romans trying to destroy Boudica, I remembered my wife and hundreds of others of my race who were also terrorized by mounted Romans. I couldn't stop myself. It was over as fast as it began."

"It was!" Kale agreed. You were a fearsome beast in a horrific storm of speed and slaughter. But that *must have* been one of your sins. Will you need to make restitution, at the time of your inevitable passing?"

"My God only knows, Kale. At this moment, I feel like I did what I had to do, out of love."

"So you would risk the loss of glory in your eternal life for a sin?" queried Kale.

"As I've told you, Kale, I only want to find a place where I can live in peace, love my God, and be all he wants me to be. But on this day, the Romans were once again trying to destroy that dream for the sake of their worldly gains and the infernal greed that possesses them."

"Your God has placed you in the middle of a dilemma, Ben. You seek to be with him in a special place here and beyond, yet to be there in this time of butchery, *you must* sin in order to love. With *your* god, it seems that sin is unavoidable. With *our* gods, we kill and *they're* happy. It's easier. There's no sin!"

"Perhaps not enough love, as well," added Ben. "With my God, it might've been the same for a time, but a better way seems to be clear *now*. Perhaps the best we can do in this place is to strive for the new way of love and let God judge us according to what he sees in our hearts and our minds."

"Perhaps," said Kale as he wrapped the horse's reins around a tree trunk. "Let's eat while we can, hope for the best, and pray we'll somehow survive the evil in this world as it is *today*."

"Amen!" Ben responded.

Chapter 17

In the dark of the following morning, Ben was startled by Kale's urgent whispering. "Wake up, Benjamin. Rise *now* and follow me."

"What is it?" Ben asked, shaking his head to release the residue of a troublesome nightmare.

"All I know is it's urgent. Boudica wants you *now* while the Druid, her seconds, and others of high rank are still sleeping," Kale answered. "Be silent and follow me."

Moments later, the two were at Boudica's side. She was seated on the ground with her back resting on the trunk of a fallen oak. It was obvious. Boudica had moved outside the ring of guards that normally surrounded her.

"Please go back now, Kale," she whispered.

When Kale was out of sight, Boudica turned to Ben.

"Sit next to me," she commanded.

When he was settled, she faced him. "Tell me your name again," she demanded.

"My name is Benjamin," he replied.

"But Kale calls you, *Ben*."

"Yes. He usually does."

"Move closer to me, Ben."

Ben reluctantly obeyed. He could feel her warmth.

She moved closer. "Do you find me desirable?"

As passing clouds uncloaked the moon, the light revealed her perfection. Like other things he recently discovered, Boudica's sensuality was powerful, and disarming.

"Do you find me *desirable*?" she repeated impatiently.

"Yes," Ben responded. He feared her but could not resist. His throat tightened. "How should I call you?" he croaked.

Her lips retreated in a smile. "Call me Boudica when we're alone, Queen Boudica when we're not."

"Queen Boudica...Boudica," Ben stammered, clumsily trying to resist without offending her. "I'm not sure how to say this, to make it clear in your language. Please be patient. I must tell you *the truth*, no matter how difficult... so you can trust me."

"Trust is what I need most," she replied earnestly.

Silence followed. The moon continued to move on its celestial path, traveling westward. Both followed its progress, deep in thought. Ben wondered what Boudica might be thinking. His eyes slowly moved between the vision of her loveliness and the mystery of the moonlight caressing her from so far away. It could be the gaze of a pagan god beaming down on a goddess far superior, yet temporarily bound to earth, and so different from those the Sumerians, Egyptians, Persians, and Babylonians the Greeks repudiated as they fashioned their own gods with art in the image and likeness of higher human forms imagined to be *their* deities and demigods. They were models in classic forms that inspired thoughts of humanity's potential to reach beyond animals and objects, to grasp powerful ideas and amazing accomplishments that distinguished their being from the rest, as they traveled far beyond their mortal limitations in soul and in spirit, rising above their natural fate, to approach the majesty beyond intellect hidden in the mystical heights of Mount Olympus.

Chapter 18

As the evening passed and the moon continued its journey to the west, Ben and Boudica were still together as the night of their second meeting continued with silent contemplation.

The need for trust they discussed earlier became the catharsis of their emerging relationship. Both seemed to know it. Their long period of silence reflected the discovery; and each needed time to consider the consequences. Ben realized his fear of Boudica had turned into profound respect for her fortitude and faith in her judgment. She was truly remarkable, in every respect. His adoration was mounting.

She was the first to speak, openly and comfortably sharing her thoughts as the two resumed their conversation in a caring and collegial manner. Any lust between them seemed to cool as their verbal interaction continued, bringing them together in a more meaningful way, speaking softly as the birds awakened, chirping their greetings to a new day.

As the light of dawn appeared, the couple was surrounded by mist, in a frame of mind that suggested the budding of a unique relationship that might grow and survive unimaginable circumstances. Their brief encounter with intimacy had been an enchantment. They shared their hopes and dreams with a familiarity that bound them in trust; and both wanted more.

As their intimate exchanges continued, Ben shared his concern about the surprise attack by the Roman cavalry patrol. He expressed his anxiety about her future safety. She told him the truth. Boudica knew her security was lax. She wanted him, rather needed him, to help her.

When he heard the sounds of others stirring as the sun began to rise, Ben carefully and more formally responded by offering advice. "I must risk your ire in order to do what I feel is right for *you*, Boudica. I know about the Romans. Their leaders in my land were guests of my parents on numerous occasions. I listened while they talked about their conquests. I talked with them and asked many questions. Those you're about to fight have perfected the art of war, and their science has produced a formidable arsenal. I dare say they might destroy you, unless their economy collapses from wanton corruption and extravagant waste of their treasure. That and their arrogance, believing that the sons of former enemies they brought into their ranks will remain loyal as Roman citizens and *not turn* against the empire, might destroy it from within."

"I think I understand what you mean, Ben. The thing I cannot imagine, the thing I cannot understand, is the reason why your parents brought Romans into your home as guests," Boudica injected, frowning in her disbelief. "The only reason we spoke to Romans without anger was to avoid or postpone the blatant intimidations they eventually brought upon us, when they got the upper hand."

"My father was a wealthy merchant," Ben responded. "They needed him, and he needed them. So *everyone* in my family was obliged to become a citizen of Rome. For *us*, the result is this. With my experience and my Roman citizenship, I might be able to help you learn more about how the Romans fight and what you might do to be more effective against them."

"You saved my life, Ben. I want you. I mean…I need you…I need your help."

"*You* saved my life as well, my queen. I'm honored to serve, in spite of the fact that *you* and *your* warriors move like you're taking a leisurely stroll in the sun."

"I've hoped that someday you might *like* how I move, Ben."

"I much admire the way you move, Queen Boudica," Ben responded with a grin, "but *not when* Romans are near and about to attack *you!*"

"That's better," she responded, feigning a serious squint, her lips cast in a smirk.

"When you're moving with a small detachment like this one," Ben continued, attempting to stifle another grin, "I hope you will have outriders placed to your front, flanks, and rear, all the time. Those outriders can be walking or riding, as long as they are moving at the same pace as your main body."

"I thought you no longer wanted to dwell on my body," Boudica remarked with a wicked glance.

Ben laughed. His eyes revealed his fondness and genuine delight in reaction to Boudica's comments. Her ability to play and be humorous in such perilous times was immensely endearing and the sign of an inspirational leader.

"As I might've admitted earlier, I'm not well spoken in your language. Perhaps I should have said 'the larger part of your formation, on the march.' What I'm desperately trying to say is, when *everyone* is walking at the same speed and remaining alert at all times, you and your warriors will have time to react quickly with enough force to repel an attack. And when you're *not* moving, every other person *must* continue to be alert, watching for signs of enemy activity, in rotation, while the others rest and take time to tend to themselves, their weapons, and their equipment. If you had outriders in place today, they would've given you early warning of the Roman's approach. You would've had more time to defend or hide in ambush to strike them as they rode by."

"I understand, Ben, and I *will comply.*"

"Good! How many men died because those precautions weren't taken?"

"As many as the fingers on my hands."

"I'm sorry."

"I understand. They died bravely…Please continue."

"As soon as possible, we should send a small detachment forward from your main body. The detachment should carefully move in the direction the Roman cavalry came from, in order to determine if there are more Romans in front of us. Their cavalry acts as scouts, provides security around the flanks of their infantry, and performs other tasks during battles. They also carry messages with superior swiftness. It minimizes the risk of interception and ensures timely delivery. This group you and I are with is at a disadvantage. At the moment, we are the only ones who have horses."

"So you and I will be our own cavalry scouts. I'll leave my second in command here."

"That's the best we can do, under the circumstances," Ben added. "Your second should move the rest of the group along a different route, to the place where you want to meet when we're done. You and I should begin our reconnaissance as soon as possible."

Boudica did not hesitate. She called for a warrior to bring their horses, briefed her second, and the two proceeded with Ben in the lead, moving quietly and searching the ground for hoof prints and other evidence of Roman activity.

When he halted, dismounted, and led his horse back to Boudica, she asked, "What is it?"

"I just wanted to tell you that from now on, I'll be dismounting from time to time to listen and closely examine any tracks or other signs of activity we might come across. In the event I'm attacked, don't wait for me to recover. Turn and ride for your life."

As he turned to remount, Boudica whispered, "I will, Ben, but with regrets."

Ben acknowledged the tender response with a nod, then mounted, and rode on.

The sun was directly overhead when he reined off their path and motioned Boudica to advance.

When she was beside him, Ben said, "It looks like we've found a Roman encampment. Let's dismount and crawl forward to take a closer look."

Both dismounted and moved to a higher vantage point, lying flat, side by side, and peering over the low grass that concealed their position.

Boudica flinched, then inhaled with a start.

Ben leaned toward her, searching to their front to determine the cause of her reaction.

"What is it?" he asked, squinting into the distance along the same line of sight as Boudica's.

"It's that bastard, Catus," she whispered then turned to Ben. "Move closer to me."

As he did, she gave him a gentle nudge. "You've done it, Ben. Now we can plan our first attack!"

Ben confirmed her sighting. They drew back silently, remounted, and rode back to meet the main body.

Along the way, Ben occasionally stopped, then rode back along their trail to see if anyone was following them. When he did so for the last time and returned to Boudica's side, it was late afternoon.

"The cavalry must've been taking a message to someone," he reported.

"How would you know?" she asked.

"I was just thinking. There was a very small space open in the cavalry corral in that camp, just enough for the mounts of the group we encountered."

"So what?" Boudica inquired.

"It means that after the attack on us, the surviving Roman horses didn't run back to the camp. The camp is quiet, and routines are being followed."

"What do you surmise from that?"

"Those in the camp don't know we've wiped out their comrades. A patrol would contain more riders than we encountered. I'm thinking the small group we encountered was on a courier run. There might be good news in all of this."

"Good news is always welcome," she said. "What is it?"

"You might have the element of surprise to your advantage when we come back to get Catus. You might also enjoy the very timely benefit of some helpful information. If I'm right, one of your men has a courier pouch in his plunder."

The two exchanged knowing looks, then rode on, side by side.

In the gloaming, they entered the welcome seclusion of a darkening forest. When Boudica told Ben she recognized where they were, he dropped back, and she took the lead, riding up a ravine toward the top of a hill. As they reached the crest, Boudica waved to a figure coming into view from behind a large oak. It was Kale.

He welcomed them with a look of relief and guided the pair to the top where a group of Celts had gathered. Boudica dismounted and led her horse toward them without looking back.

Kale took the reins of Ben's mount. They could hear voices raised in anger, expressing concerns about Boudica's long absence with her unfamiliar companion.

Kale continued to lead Ben and his horse. The voices faded into silence.

When he and Ben arrived at the center of a hollow surrounded by an array of large bushes, Kale tied the reins to a leafy branch, and Ben's horse began to devour the leaves, as he dismounted.

Kale turned to Ben. "Don't worry," he said with assurance. "Boudica looks great with confidence on this day. You've done well. She's defending you. She'll take care of *them,* as well."

"I'm sure she will," said Ben. "Now, *we* must ensure her victory."

Early the following morning, Ben and Kale began to discuss a plan for attacking the Roman camp. Kale knew the Celts. Ben knew the Romans. Their knowledge of friend and foe was complete. They also knew that Boudica's time would be spent winning the confidence of her key subordinates and finding the Roman dispatch.

There had been a delay in the continuation of their movement toward Boudica's village. The reason was obvious. She had chosen a good location and was allocating time for them to begin their detailed planning and preparation for what was sure to be the seminal moment in the birth of a bloody rebellion.

"I think we should draw a picture on the ground to use as the outline for our plan," Ben said as he began to clear a patch of grass large enough to outline a square three meters wide on each side, in the dirt. Then he cut a sharp stick and used it to inscribe the key aspects of the terrain, including the Roman camp and the disposition of the troops he had seen. At the center he drew a circle around Catus's approximate location and marked it with a triangle to indicate the distinct leather tent Boudica had identified.

"It would be best to give Boudica a span of control of four," said Ben when they had finished. "Each of her four seconds would have enough warriors to overcome the Romans on each of the four sides of the camp."

"I agree," said Kale. "All flows naturally from there."

"Boudica should attack with four groups at the same time, hitting each of the four sides of the encampment and driving toward the center," Ben continued. "The ragged line I've drawn outside the square represents the tree line of the surrounding forest. The distance between that and the edge of the square indicates the amount of cleared or open ground the four attacking forces would need to cross silently, before striking the first line of the Roman defense. Their movement to the edge of the forest would begin after dark. All would be in place when the first light of dawn appears, and ready for Boudica to signal the attack with a blast of a horn or by lighting a torch near her position facing the weakest part of the Roman defense. The leading edge of the group Boudica's with, will hit the cavalry corral straight on, overwhelm any opposition and move directly to the leather tent. Half of her following force will secure the Roman horses and move them back to the tree line while the other half secures a path for her to ride directly to Catus's tent. She'll be protected all the way in and arrive at the leather tent close to the moment when Catus is taken alive, struggling to awake from his last sleep before *Hades*."

"What a grand moment that will be!" Kale shouted.

"Yes, indeed," Ben agreed. "Boudica has told me much about the night horrors she still suffers from her last encounter with Catus's tent. By the time she finishes with him, and the attack is over, there should be enough day-light to ensure the successful recovery and removal of our plunder. The bounty will be a fine reward for Boudica and her warriors as well. The same force that attacks the corral will mostly be mounted at that point. It can act as the rear guard for the main body as it moves on to the location Boudica has chosen for her rallying point."

"Your plan is brilliant in its simplicity," Kale remarked when Ben finished. "Even an undisciplined mob will under-stand and execute this plan to perfection. The surprise and shock effect of our ferocity in close combat should easily overwhelm the Romans. It's a wonder. Where did you find this wisdom?"

"In my father's home, with Roman centurions and generals who played war games and drank good wine while lusting after my mother," Ben said with a wink.

"And just in time," responded Kale with a satisfied smile. "Here she comes."

Boudica approached with purpose and wasted no time. She focused on Ben. Her tired eyes revealed signs of affection and respect. Kale noticed, glanced at Ben, then looked down, deep in thought.

"I've explained my position in regard to the both of you," Boudica began. "Our Druid priest has doubts, but he's yielded to my judgment, for now. I must show him and the others the results of your support *and* my leadership. I believe the time has come. We need a plan for a stunning demonstration of my power. The camp that holds Catus is the objective. We'll use it to accomplish that end. What are your thoughts?"

Kale glanced up at her, then turned to Ben. "Tell our queen what *you* have to offer, Benjamin."

Ben stepped forward. "Queen Boudica, please look down at your earthen battlefield, and I'll show you *the way*."

It was late in the day when Ben concluded his briefing. He had answered Boudica's questions and acknowledged her comments. She rose to her full height and began to walk away.

But after a few strides, she stopped, turned around, and faced Ben. "I must think further as we complete our journey to my village. Destroy what you've done on this ground. Have another like it on the floor of my throne room on the evening of our return. By then I hope to have the Roman dispatches and other items to consider, before we complete your excellent plan."

When Boudica was out of sight, Ben turned to Kale. His eyes were clear. His look was conclusive. His smile removed any doubt.

Ben nodded then hastened to destroy the evidence.

Chapter 19

Ben and Boudica were riding together as they approached the outskirts of Boudica's village. "We're home, Ben," she announced.

Ben nodded as he surveyed the area around them, surprised by its simplicity and lack of anything approaching what he had experienced with Oriental and Middle Eastern cultures. Compared to what he knew about the era of Israel's King David and the palatial grandeur of his son Solomon's estate, Ben found Boudica's royal equivalent less than inspiring, primitive at best.

The hard-walled circular dwellings with conical thatched roofs were like those he had seen in the Druid village, arranged in concentric circles with narrow footpaths separating each ring. The spaces between dwellings, and those in common areas, were crowded with frameworks and platforms for preparing hides, meals, and other items typical of daily life in a subsistence-level society adapting to more civilized methods. Smoke rose from open doorways and through holes in the peaks of conical roofs. Scores of raggedly clad men, women and children moved about in a slow, pulsating rhythm that belied the surrounding danger of the time.

The only security precaution that was permanent, and seemingly reliable, was a continuous berm of an average man's height surrounding the outer circle of dwellings, with a gate where he entered, and another on the far side of the village. Two men with weapons stood at each entrance, another pair walked casually back and forth along the berm, occasionally turning to scan the surrounding fields and forests.

A greathouse constructed of timber stood in the center of the innermost circle. When they reached it, Boudica motioned for Kale to enter, then she and Ben tied their mounts to a post near the doorway and entered while the rest of the contingent hastened to their dwelling places. The double door entry opened to a room large enough to hold thirty or so at meetings around a large firepit in the center. Cubicles with draped entrances lined the outer walls. A ladder placed against the far wall led to an overhead loft. There was a long banquet table to one side of the fireplace. A raised platform stood on the other side, facing the fire. The platform apparently acted as the stage for a throne, distinguished by a massive chair in the center, with lesser chairs on both sides. All were easily accessible using wooden steps on either side of the platform. The arrangement suggested flexibility for a number of activities with all situated to place the key leaders and their immediate subordinates in positions of honor that facilitated interaction.

As they entered, armed guards on each side of the entrance bowed as Boudica passed. A warrior carrying two sacks followed her to the banquet table, placed them on the floor at her feet as she was seated, then bowed, and departed.

As Boudica settled in her chair at the head of the table, she motioned for Ben to be seated on her right side, and Kale on her left.

Kale took notice. Ben was seated to the right of the queen in the favored position. Kale stared at him with a comical smirk.

Ben acknowledged with a condescending grin and a wink.

A woman entered with food, wine, and water and they began to eat.

Boudica was famished. She spoke between pauses to eat.

"I wanted to get the three of us alone, before I include the others," she said. "Benjamin, I want you to take the sack nearest my foot when you leave here with Kale."

As she paused to eat again, Ben asked, "May we know the contents of the *other* sack?"

"Not yet. I want to examine it myself. Perhaps then," she responded and continued to eat.

Ben understood.

"The sack I want *you* to take contains the pouch the Roman courier was carrying. Go through the contents and come back before dark with your findings. When you come, allow time for some discussion and enough time for you to make the battlefield likeness by the firepit, so it can be seen by the four group leaders I've selected, their seconds, and our Druid priest, Salan."

When they had finished their meal, Ben and Kale departed. Ben unhitched his mount, and Kale led the way to his humble home where his wife greeted them, offered more food and drink, and did her best to make Ben comfortable.

The couple reminded Ben of his parents. A pang of sad remembrance overtook him momentarily. Kale noticed Ben's distraction, and his questioning led to a full disclosure of Ben's past. Kale and his wife were touched by Ben's sorrow, and from that point, the relationship took on a warm glow of common hardship shared by three good souls in a hostile world with no borders to patrol and secure, in order to protect their territory, themselves, and their loved ones from daily peril, hostile invasion, and clandestine infiltration.

As Kale and his wife continued to talk, Ben excused himself and carried the sack to a quiet corner. He opened it, reached in, pulled out the pouch, and opened the dispatch. It was a lengthy document in three copies, written in Latin and addressed to each of three legion commanders.

The sender was Gaius Suetonius Paulinus, a Roman general and new governor of all Britannia. Each copy began with a summary of Gaius Julius Caesar's early expeditions in Gaul and *Germannia* and went into some detail regarding a more recent penetration of the island of Britton by his successor Claudius Caesar, some set-piece battles that had been won by the Romans forty-three years after the birth of Christ.

Seventeen years since, and here comes Paulinus, Ben reflected. *He's taking advantage of the successful conquest of tribes on the mainland, releasing legions not needed there and ordering them to cross the channel with a mission to end the rapidly rising Briton Celt resistance.*

Ben also noticed the documents mentioned the Romans' success in establishing a southern province on the island; their conquest of the Trinovantes and the establish-

ment of settlements in *Londinium*, along the big river out-
let to the sea, *Camulodunum* to the east, and *Verulamium*
to the north. It appeared that Camulodunum had become
the permanent Roman capital. Its colony contained a
large number of Roman veterans and their families. Client
arrangements with other Celtic chiefs brought to terms
were also mentioned, including those of the Iceni and
Brigantes. Rome wanted these successes exploited by sending General Paulinus with the unity of command and the
assets he needed to get it done, including three legions: the
IXth *Hispania*, the XIVth *Germania*, and the XXth *Valeria*.
Paulinus would report directly to Emperor Claudius,
who had personal interest in finishing the conquest he
began. Claudius saw Venutius of the Silures as the prominent leader of the Briton Celt resistance, however named
Boudica's Iceni and the Trinovantes as the most likely to
strike given reports of recent complaints from those tribes
regarding perceived Roman injustices. The Druid influence in the resistance was also mentioned. It appeared that
Paulinus would be heading west to put a bloody end to the
uniting influence of the Druid priests by slaughtering all of
them and wiping out their settlement in the Druid Grove
at Anglesey. The next step would bring the same fate to
Boudica and others who might rebel in her name.

The news was bad. Ben sighed. He had first learned
of General Paulinus from his conversations with Roman
soldiers in Damascus.

Kale overheard his reaction. "What have you found?"

"The Romans have moved three legions across the
channel from the mainland. They're going to launch a

major offensive to wipe out the Druids and subdue or kill the rest of us. We must warn Boudica, *immediately*!"

When Kale and Ben arrived Boudica was pacing back and forth in her throne room.

"Enter," she called. "I fear bad news."

"Yes," Ben replied. "We must talk."

When the three were seated Boudica's eyes focused on Ben's, casting a shadow of doubt, then fading to the vision of a tortured soul struggling with a burden no honorable person could escape. She was trapped in a hellish inferno of anxiety and desperately hoping for mercy.

As he completed his ominous report, Ben recognized Boudica's dilemma. She was duty bound to serve her people, as a matter of conscience. Her agony was exposed, Ben felt the mind-numbing fear that raged behind the mask of her bravado. His search for meaning ended. His purpose was finally revealed. He would sacrifice *everything* for the sake of an earthly trinity that included Boudica, her children, and their everlasting souls.

Ben's earthbound life and his passion for mercy would be spent to save them in remembrance of another who rendered the same unto him.

Chapter 20

As the time drew near for Boudica's meeting with her sub-ordinates, Ben and Kale made haste to prepare the great room. They reconstructed the sand table on the floor near the fire and made certain there were enough logs and torches to provide heat and light.

Boudica had departed for errands elsewhere in the village.

When she returned, she was accompanied by two young ladies. On seeing them, Ben gasped. One looked like Boudica, younger but with the same beauty, bravado, and grace that was out of place in her environment. The other was smaller, frail, and timid yet striking in her way. Both had red hair and were wearing long robes of sheer cloth, hanging loosely around their forms.

When they approached Kale, he laughed then embraced them without hesitation. As the taller of the two embraced Kale, Ben could see she was much more than a girl. He blushed, ran his fingers through his unkempt hair, and rose to his full height, painfully aware of the deplorable state of his long-neglected appearance.

When the tall one released Kale, she lowered her chin slightly and looked straight at Ben through long lashes. Her green eyes surveyed him with a wanton gaze. The hint of a smile touched her lips.

"Kale has known these girls for ages, Benjamin. They're my daughters. Fiona is the bold one, and Isolda is bashful. I've told them about you," Boudica added.

Ben nodded. The realization entered his mind. *The girls brutalized by the Romans. Both alive and still beautiful.*

"We've much to do, girls," Boudica said fondly, reflecting her admiration. "Please retire to your places and have the guards bring whatever comforts you desire."

Both turned and moved toward the ladder leading to the upper chamber.

Ben could not take his eyes off Fiona's muscular, long legs and petite bare feet as she climbed quickly and quietly out of sight.

His concentration was interrupted by the sound of Boudica's voice.

"Kale, will you make the rounds and let my seconds know we'll gather in here, after I'm finished with Benjamin?"

"Gladly," Kale replied.

As Kale turned to depart, Boudica moved to the corner table.

"Come here," she beckoned.

Ben walked to her position. Both took seats.

Boudica reached down by the side of her chair, lifted the sack seen earlier, and laid it on the table.

"The warrior who had the courier's package, also had this," she said. "He found the contents on the shore the day you were captured. He'd been carrying it ever since, waiting for an opportunity to bring it forward."

"That fellow must be a hybrid of pack rat *and* hound," Ben remarked.

"Yes, and he's added great value as both," Boudica responded with a chuckle, her eyes brightening when she pulled out the contents.

Ben thought he was going to faint. He was stunned, in disbelief.

"I found strange marks on these documents, perhaps some language. I thought you might know."

"*Oh my god!*" Ben exclaimed. "You've found the bundle of documents that John and Mark prepared for me. The writings are in Greek. I've been praying for a miracle. Somehow…someway I would find them." He grasped Boudica's hands. "Your hands hold the greatest of treasures! It was lost, perhaps forever. Now, it's found, safe in your hands. Please trust me, it's a sign of good things to come. I will save and protect *all* with the power it brings to my spirit, just as I will do unto *you*, my queen."

Boudica's expression changed. Her eyes were filled with tears. Her words came softly as she released the prize and its contents into Ben's waiting hands.

"Of course, it's yours," she whispered. "Do with it and with me, *whatever you wish.*"

Chapter 21

As darkness descended, Ben lit the torches at the entrance of the great house.

Boudica's seconds were gathering to hear her final words before moving their warriors into position for the attack on the Roman bivouac. Each would have a hundred well-armed men under their control. They had scouted their routes and were ready, when Boudica appeared in the light. Some stepped back in surprise. All were amazed. She was their queen adorned with long boots up to bare thighs and a short tunic with an open collar gathered below outlines of her breasts and fastened with the Iceni queen's brooch. The emerald at the center of her golden brooch, its circular setting, her torque, armbands and wristbands radiated green and gold, pulsating in peaks and valleys, dancing in the light of the flaming torches that were flickering in a gentle breeze. Her long red hair blazed, creating a halo effect around her striking countenance and radiant blue-green eyes. Her weapons were in place, shining and ready as her voice sliced through the silence.

"I've one thing to add before we begin our movement. My counselor Benjamin, whom you met last night, when we discussed my plan. He has volunteered to help with our signal to attack, to ensure it is coordinated, so we'll *strike together* at the most advantageous time. When all of you have sent runners to my location to confirm your warriors are in position, he will crawl forward across the open space, to a place near the horse corral, where he will wait, watch, and listen. If he sees the Romans are lax and the camp isn't properly guarded, he'll crawl back to me and I'll light the torch at my position, to begin our attack. When you see that signal, run your men as silently as possible and crash *through* the barriers to do as I outlined last night. But if Benjamin is discovered prematurely, he will cry out in their language, saying he's a lost Roman who has escaped from the Trinovantes. When they let him in, he'll throw off his robe, grab one of *their* torches, and start waving it. That will be the *alternate signal* for us to attack. You've had time to relay my plan to your subordinates. I know you've rehearsed the actions you'll take after breaching the Roman defenses. Do you have any questions?"

"Yes, Queen Boudica," said the Druid, stepping forward. "You discussed the Benjamin issue at our meeting last night. You revealed his Roman citizenship and your many reasons for trusting him in spite of that. However, I continue to think his strange beliefs and his status with the Romans *do not* bode well for our cause. What now do you say to the possibility that he might spoil the surprise of our attack by giving warning to the Romans when he is nearest to them and fleeing to enjoy their protection?"

Boudica turned to Ben and nodded as he stepped into the light.

"I know you by sight, but not by name," Ben said, glaring at the Druid while squarely facing him.

"I am Salan," the Druid replied with a malevolent sneer.

"For you and for all present, I say this, Salan. I *never* pledged allegiance to Rome. My status came as a result of my father's choice. I will never see my father or my mother again. My wife was tortured, raped, and murdered by Roman cavalry. Thousands of my people have been crucified by the Romans. Queen Boudica saved my life. I have pledged my life, and my honor, to her. If I'm a traitor to Boudica as you think I might be, you'll know it forthwith. But one way or another, our attack will succeed because of the power *she possesses* in her spirit and the superior fighting skills of the brave warriors she has allocated to her plan. Our odds are twenty to one at the Roman camp. Our queen has also ordered hundreds of her warriors to stay here, to secure Iceni homes and families. What else do you want?" Ben concluded, as he stepped back to join Boudica.

"Go silently to victory on this good night," Boudica commanded as her warriors saluted and quickly dispersed.

Only Salan remained. "Why didn't you allow me to speak again?" he demanded.

"You asked a question, Salan. Benjamin gave you the answer," she replied. "What more could you possibly want?"

Chapter 22

Having silenced the Druid, Ben and Boudica mounted their horses and rode through the darkness in silence, each dealing with their respective thoughts. They were traveling with the contingent of warriors that would attack from the west side of the Roman camp, where the horse corral was located. Ben was pleased with the discipline of the column. It was moving expeditiously with scant noise and no light. If each of the four columns performed as well as this one, victory would be assured. He knew their plan was good yet continued to experience a gnawing sensation in his gut. He had been bold to volunteer. But he had prayed and was certain that, with God's help, surprise in superior numbers would win the day. He was fluent in the dialect used by Roman leaders. In the worst case, he could use that skill to some advantage. He could also run like a deer and wrestle like a bear, so his chances of escape, short of success, were acceptable.

Salan worried him more than anything. He had a strong instinct when it came to identifying potential evil, and evil was precisely what he saw in the Druid. The man reeked of it.

Ben was also concerned about Fiona. Her mother said she was bold, partly in jest, he assumed, but he sensed there might be trouble with her. At their first meeting, Fiona presented something Ben remembered about the harlots who plied their trade in the Byzantine bazaars. They were beautiful, comely, and scantily clad women who would belly dance until they spied a man of means lusting for them. Then they would stare back with seductive intensity until the victim reached for a soft hand that would lead him to an unexpected fall. Temple guards and others in government to maintain law and order avoided areas offering such attractions, where victims of collusion, corruption, or extortion were often at their own peril. "Proceed at your own risk" was the word on the streets. Ben had accompanied his father to many business meetings in the bazaars. Each time his father would warn Ben about those women, telling anecdotal stories about men he had known personally who were addicted to perversions ending in death or despair. Ben had been a target of these women on occasion and knew he could be tempted despite his religious objections and the constant warnings he heard during Sabbath Day preaching and teachings. Fiona might be hard to resist.

Then there was Boudica, a mystery to be sure. Ben had an attraction to her, like none he had ever experienced nor imagined before. He was well aware of it. He was simply enchanted, perhaps crazy about her. From adoration to sinful desire, his feelings and emotions raced wildly during every close encounter with Boudica. He would try to be careful, perhaps not enough. Perhaps he should talk with Kale about tribal marriage customs and traditions. There might be a way, without resorting to the Druid's influence. But how could that be possible? Boudica's obligations and Salan's secular and religious influence over all things life and death in their barbaric Celtic culture, and its long-standing traditions, might be an insurmountable barrier to the liberty to love and be happy under current conditions, wrought with tyranny—especially when a choice of religions entered the mix. The spreading of Christian values would take time; certainly more than *his* life span might be.

Ben's thoughts were interrupted when Boudica stopped. He reined in, dismounted, and approached her.

She looked down at him and whispered, "We're a short distance from this group's position for the attack. Those with horses must dismount and secure them here. All of the Roman horses we captured and any prisoners of value will be brought here as well. Pass this instruction back to those behind us."

"I will," Ben replied.

"*Our* dismount point will be farther forward. The guards will muzzle our mounts as you suggested."

"Good," Ben responded. "Will the Druid be with us?"

"No. I sent him to the group on the side of the camp farthest from ours. Your beliefs are in conflict. I fear you might kill him. If you did, I would have to find another priest. As you can see, I'm already quite busy," she whispered.

"Bless you, my queen," Ben responded.

As Boudica slowly turned to ride on, he noticed the white flash of her teeth. *She was smiling at me*, he marveled. *In a moment of dire peril, she's found humor.* His spirit was rekindled. He remounted and hastened to relay her message.

When all was ready, Boudica came to his side, touched his lips tenderly, then pointed toward the Roman camp. Ben inhaled deeply and began to crawl. "Dear God, please have mercy on my soul," he murmured.

After what seemed like an eternity, he came to a suitable vantage point and began to survey the camp. He was amazed. There were no barriers between him and the horse corral. He squinted, counting the number of horses. Only half remained inside the enclosure. Where had the rest gone? It was a concern. He would report it…if he lived long enough to see Boudica, again.

There were five sentries he could see in the torchlight—none were moving. All were seated and remained in that posture as he continued to observe them. When the silence was broken by the sound of snoring, Ben turned to crawl back to Boudica.

He found her just inside the tree line. "It's time," he said. "The five guards on our side appear to be asleep. Some of the cavalry mounts are missing. Does that trouble you?"

"Yes. I remember the last time I saw Catus. He was riding away with a cavalry escort. The guards are asleep. It makes sense. We should plan for his absence and capture his second if need be. Let's go, and may your god be with us."

"Amen," Ben added then moved toward their mounts. He untied both muzzles, checked the saddles, and led the pair back to Boudica.

She turned to her torchbearer. "Open your embers pot and light the torch."

As soon as the torch was lit, Ben could see the figures of men on his left and right flanks, moving silently toward the Roman encampment. When shouts erupted, he and Boudica leaped into their saddles. Ben urged his horse on. Boudica was right behind him. They reached the corral at full gallop, passed to the right of the wooden fence, and followed the path marked by cheering Celts and Roman corpses. When he saw the leather tent, Ben yanked his horse to a stop, dismounted, and grabbed Boudica's reins. She leaped from her saddle, sword firmly in hand. Her cape was flying, like the wings on a fire-breathing dragon. When she hit the ground running, her image in action was embedded forever in Ben's mind. And when he spied several of her warriors approaching the entrance of Catus's tent, he pointed the way and Boudica dashed past him.

He hitched their horses to a post, unsheathed his sword, and ran as fast as he could to catch her. When the tent flap flew up, he was right behind Boudica, until they were inside, standing together in front of two warriors holding a dazed man wearing a loincloth.

Boudica confronted the man, grabbed him by the hair, and yanked his head upward.

"*It's not Catus!*" she shouted over the roar of the chaos outside.

"Who are you?" Ben threatened, holding his sword close to the Roman's throat.

"Quintus, the proconsul to Catus," he responded in Latin.

"Speak Gaelic," Ben demanded.

"*Where is Catus?*" Boudica shouted, her spittle flying into the Roman's face.

"He's gone to a meeting. In Camulodunum."

"When did he leave?"

"After dark."

Boudica released his hair and stepped back. "Just as we thought, Benjamin." She sighed, masking her disappointment.

"Benjamin? You're...a...Jew?" the Roman inquired with trepidation.

"I *was*," Ben replied, glancing at Boudica. "We should leave this man to be guarded and return to the battle, Queen Boudica."

"Follow me," she replied as the Roman collapsed in the arms of her men.

Outside the dawn was breaking. They could see the day had been won. Scores of tents were blazing. Some Celts were already withdrawing to their starting points with captives, horses, and plunder well in hand. Dead Romans were scattered around the camp.

Boudica's group second reported success in his sector. She acknowledged and ordered him to withdraw to the rendezvous point and advise his counterparts to do the same. As he departed, Boudica recovered her sword in its scabbard, then turned to Ben.

"Hold me," she demanded.

Ben hesitated. "What will the others think?"

"I don't give a damn!" she barked, shaking violently, then weeping as she was received and held by gentle iron, in the arms of her trustworthy companion.

The two were reluctant to step apart. The Roman captive in the leather tent needed to be vetted. He was there when they arrived together, restrained in his bed with two guards watching over him.

"Has he talked?" asked Boudica.

"Not since he fainted after hearing your name, Queen Boudica," one of the guards replied with a grin. "When he finally opened his eyes, they stayed as they are now, looking up at the roof of the tent and mumbling something that sounded like it might be a prayer."

"Very well. You can go outside," Boudica commanded. "Have someone bring me a flaming torch. There's a nasty chill in the air. I think this Roman needs fire, so he'll be warm enough to avoid the deadly plague that's been going around."

Ben turned away to hide his delight.

The Roman's breathing came in gasps.

Boudica laughed. "Relax, Quintus. We don't want you to die before your time."

"I'm sorry for anything I might have done," said the Roman breathlessly, turning his eyes from Boudica to Ben.

"Catch your breath while we wait for the torch," Ben muttered.

"I've done nothing since they sent me here from Jerusalem. You *were* a Jew. You might understand my dilemma," the Roman replied.

"Speak. You've nothing to lose but your life. You and your Roman brethren have already made many lives worthless, or extinct," Ben retorted.

"I fear all I can't control. If I tell you the truth, *you'll* kill me. If I tell her the truth, *she'll* kill me. If I tell my own people the truth, *they'll* kill me, or do worse, by banishing me forever to another faraway place…without my family."

Ben turned to Boudica. "I think we should take this man with us, Queen Boudica. I believe he may have a story worth hearing."

"He's yours, Benjamin. Bring him and the torch. We must go now and meet with the Trinovantes. We have much more to do."

When they were outside, Ben put the torch to the tent. All watched while it burst into flames. As the leather tent collapsed in the midst of the inferno, he turned to the Roman. "You're blessed to be out of that *Hades*."

"I thank God for your mercy," Quintus replied.

"And which of your cohort of gods do you thank?" Ben asked.

"This might be my last word, but it's the truth. I thank the God from whence Jesus came to save me, my family, and our servant."

Ben looked at the Roman, in disbelief. "Fear not, Quintus. If Jesus is in your heart, and truly on your mind, we'll know it soon enough."

Chapter 23

Ben and Boudica had much on their minds as they rode back from the victory. The vetting of the Roman captive and a timely meeting with the Trinovantes were foremost in their minds. They knew it would not be long before Catus got word of the slaughter at his northern camp. Their next objective must be defined soon in order to maintain some degree of surprise.

Of the score of Briton Celt tribes, the Trinovantes and the Iceni had suffered the most from Roman occupation. It began with Julius Caesar, was continued in earnest by Claudius when he became emperor, and was presently being consolidated and exploited by Suetonious Paulinus at Nero's behest. Nero had tightened the reins on the Britons, so much that even those who had been strong clients in the past were in doubt about future returns on their loyalty. Boudica knew most of the Trinovantes were ready to fight; however, recent changes in their leadership prevented certainty about their reliability.

As soon as they were safely back in the Iceni capital and recovery was complete, Ben went to Boudica for clarification regarding his next role.

She was waiting at the entrance of her throne room when he arrived.

"As you can see, morale is high, Queen Boudica. Your people are celebrating in earnest. Their confidence in your leadership is *soaring!*"

"All is well at this point, Benjamin," she replied. "However, I think we both know that my seconds, our Druid, and perhaps some others, will soon come forward demanding to know my next step. We must start in earnest now, to answer that question."

"Yes," said Ben. "I've talked with our prisoner, Quintus. His story fits well with the contents of the dispatches we intercepted. Paulinus has taken the bulk of his force into the west to subdue the Druids at Anglesey. He knows many of the Druids are drawn from the aristocracy and realizes how much the social, political, and administrative life of the entire island is bound up by them. Their control over the religion of the masses is especially troublesome for him. Paulinus regards it as the glue that might keep your people together in times of external threats, in spite of their history of internal feuding. If he annihilates the Druids and destroys their sacred center, that threat will be mitigated. Quintus said the Romans in Palestine have decided to employ the same strategy around Jerusalem, against the Jews, whose zealots have united politically. Unfortunately, the new Christians will suffer as well, even though they generally have little interest in overthrowing Roman rule themselves. They simply want to spread the good news, seeking to know and serve God in peaceful ways, like Mark and Barnabas who, as disciples, are continuing the work begun by Peter, James, John, and others, including Paul, an extraordinary man, I hold in highest regard as the *thirteenth apostle.*"

"One way or another, it seems innocents suffer the most when religion is used and abused, and peace never lasts for the ages," Boudica observed. "When men continue to seek opportunities for plunder through power, taking from others to benefit themselves, it spreads like a disease with little hope for a cure. We either give up or we fight, and the Romans have given us no choice but rebellion. The *greatest tragedy* of all is that we'd still be fighting among ourselves if the Romans weren't here, again, trying to sub-jugate us in order to bleed off our bounty and fuel their all-consuming fire of imperialism."

"It's truly *tragic*," said Ben. "However, if you can drive off the Romans this time, other tribes might see the advan-tage of uniting across the land with a common identity that puts an end to the historic squabbling and *protects everyone* from foreign threats to your sovereignty. With Paulinus ostensibly out of the way for some time, I think you have a rare opportunity to succeed now, to *try* with the Trinovantes, then add additional support you can count on along the way as you move south quickly to attack the Roman provincial headquarters in Camulodunum. It could be your only chance to gain momentum and unite your people in a common cause."

"That would make sense," Boudica replied. "More than anything, the Trinovantes want their old capital back. The Romans took it by force. Now they tax those dis-placed, who have to pay for all the building the Romans are doing, including the temple of Claudius. It's a continuing reminder of their subjugation. The Trinovantes are being turned into slaves by the Romans and all of their elitist sycophants. The shoddy treatment the Trinovantes receive

from the Roman veterans, their families, and Celtic collab-
orators who occupy Camulodunum is *outrageous!*"

"It is, and it seems that your insight regarding the
Trinovantes has revealed where the strength of our numbers will lie for the foreseeable future. Is that true?"

"Yes. They are the key."

"Whose trust do you need among their leaders?"

"That is the question," Boudica responded. "Their king
was Addedormarus some time ago. His son Dubnovellaunus
succeeded him, then ruled for several years before being
supplanted by Cunobelinus of the Catuvellauni."

"So the Trinovantes you rely on *now* are in fact a sub-
tribe of the Catuvellauni?"

"That's my understanding."

"Then Cunobelinus is in effect the Celtic king of the
south?"

"Yes. But there might be *others* more directly controlling the Trinovantes *now.* Change happens rapidly, and
often, especially in times such as these."

"And where does Cunobelinus stand regarding the
Romans?"

"Since the invasion by Claudius, he's been strong
for them. He still is, as far as I know. But we did have an
encounter not long ago with a Trinovante who claimed to
be a descendent of Addedormarus. He was with his grandson and three other men. I killed the three and captured the
two, not knowing who they were. I spared them to find out
if they were in my territory to prepare for an attack against
us. We've long been in conflict with the Trinovantes. The
nominal border of our tribal lands is the dense forest we
passed through on the way here from Anglesey. We've been

raiding each other across that *meaningless* boundary for as long as I can remember."

"Did your encounter end well?"

"It did. I felt like he could be with me, however, both he and his son might be dead from conflict by now. His grandson was a lad. But it seems that the young of our tribes become men and women at an early age now, so I'm not sure if a grandson, a son, or someone *unknown* until now might be our consort today."

"We *must* find out," Ben replied. His expression was blank, reflecting consternation.

"It would be far too dangerous to go south at this point without great numbers," Boudica responded with obvious concern.

"I will do it for you. *I must*," said Ben. "I can ride from here through the forest and across the boundary by going straight down the Roman road. As a Roman citizen, which I am, I would need the proper clothing. I could find some as I travel, or after entering the city at night. From what you have told me, Camulodunum should be large enough and diverse enough to allow me to blend in and perhaps find someone who might be willing and able to help. At the onset, I could claim to be a Roman veteran's offspring visiting from Rome then later assume some other guise in order to find my way to the leader of the Trinovantes, extend your greetings directly, and present your proposal."

"Let me think," Boudica responded. "I want to be sure before you depart alone on a task that might take your life."

Ben understood and was silent, listening with sincere appreciation for her caring.

"There are two superior tribes in addition to ours and the Trinovantes," Boudica continued. "The Catuvellauni, under Caratacus and the Silures who offered strong resistance against Claudius and Scapula. But they were eventually defeated. Caractacus fled to the Brigantes, who controlled the north, but he was betrayed by their queen, Cartamandua and her husband, Venutius. Both were loyal to Rome at that point. Later, she and Venutius divorced, and he took up arms against her. But she was well defended by the Romans. They supported Cartamandua throughout the first rebellion, and she was able to hold her ground."

"Why were they divorced?"

"When we met, Cartamandua was lusting for Vellocatus who had once been her husband's armor bearer. She was talking about making Vellocatus king, to officially replace her vanquished husband with a bedservant. I departed in *disgust*. I think she might be attacked *again*, by Venutius. His manhood has been wounded so gravely he would rather have revenge against her than join us against the Romans."

"So the Catuvellauni *and* the Brigantes are awash in corruption, hence not worth pursuing. And the Silures?"

"After their last defeat by the Romans, the Silures retreated to their homeland in the southwest. Now that Paulinus is here, they're probably hiding among their coastal rock piles, licking their wounds, and totally cut off from us by Paulinus as he marches through their territory on the way to destroy the Druids. We would be foolish to count the Silures in our numbers."

"So you and your Iceni would *perhaps* have the majority of the Trinovantes and an unreliable scattering of dissatisfied others, possibly including some small breakout groups from the Catuvellauni, Brigantes, and Silures, that would fragment into your ranks from various subtribes, and remain beyond your span of control?"

"I'm afraid so, one way or another," Boudica replied. "Thus the question of reliable control shifts to the majority of the Trinovantes, and becomes *the issue* we most need to resolve."

"*My God, Boudica!*" Ben exclaimed in disbelief, wishing her departed husband might return for a moment, to impart some key wisdom he must have had, but obviously elected to take with him to his funeral pyre.

"You keep calling on your god, Ben. I'm bound to mine and must invoke Andraste and others because of our Druid tradition. The only unity we've had comes from the hope they give our people and therein lies much of our strength. But I think Druid power is fading. Only those of us who've been wronged by the Romans have the will to fight, and those who do fight have no other powers to call upon. That, coupled with the well-entrenched Druid influence in politics, law, and administration of government, still provides at least a chance for a fragile unity. Indeed, I'm confused. I think there must be something more."

"We should talk more about that," Ben replied. "I've much more I would like to explore with you…about your beliefs and mine. How different they seem to be. You and I came together under seemingly impossible circumstances yet so natural, so much *more* than coincidence, so right in the midst of everything that feels so wrong. Our Roman captive, Quintus, has much in common with us, and so does Kale. We seem to share a calling, something we might address together around the bundle you returned to me. It contains the writings and experiences John the Evangelist shared with me before we parted. Quintus was a Centurion in our Holy City, and in Capernaum on the Sea of Galilee. He too had direct contact with God's messenger. Like John, Quintus experienced his divinity and so have I because of that testimony. We all feel like better men, once dead, but now alive, touched by the Holy Spirit sent down by Jesus to empower all of God's children with the strength to keep trying, doing *our best* to pursue righteousness in defiance of evil."

"You *are* the best man I've ever known, Ben. I'll await whatever you wish to share."

"I'm delighted by your words, Boudica. I will live for that time to do more, but for now, I'm compelled to beg your leave, so I can find the leader of the Trinovantes before Catus gets word of your victory and is able to anticipate what you plan. Given the *uncertainty* we've discovered in these moments, your destiny rides with me, and to that I *must* attend."

"Then go now, Benjamin. May your God bless and ride with you and bring you safely back to me."

Night had fallen. Ben's horse was ready to run. The two became one, delighted by the freedom of running like the wind, feeling physical release, abandoning any need for control. Their flight was euphoric, and so they went, thundering through the grassy plain until both were spent. When they stopped to rest, Ben saw high ground ahead, spreading from left and right and covered with tall trees rising as far as he could see in the moonlight.

"We've reached the great forest, my friend," Ben whispered over his mount's loud breathing. The Roman stud needed rest. Ben stopped, dismounted and began to walk, leading his horse around huge tree trunks rising from a carpet of thick undergrowth. They were moving with the moon, to the west. Ben thanked God for the beacon.

Before long, they were on the Roman road. Ben was mounted and turning to follow it south, urging his horse onward, yet cautious, stopping to listen from time to time, watching for campfires and anticipating ambush attempts from both sides of the road.

As the night passed and the moon continued its westward ascent, Ben continued to whisper to his horse. Now more than an animal, it was a trusted companion in a strange world where phantoms were easily imagined and reality was the only thing to fear.

"If our information is good, Paulinus is far to the west seeing the same moon, moving toward Anglesey Island and his conquest of the Druid sanctuary. We must find out and be certain, for Boudica's sake."

As birds began to chatter above him and the roadbed beneath began to descend, Ben dismounted and led his horse back into the forest. Before long, he saw an opening, moved toward it, and was able to see Camulodunum spreading out below.

As the first light of dawn began to show along the skyline to the east, Ben found a good vantage point and hitched his horse to a fallen log. He sat on the deadfall, amazed by the panorama, now clearly visible from his vantage point.

The former capital of the Trinovantes had grown into a city that reflected the Roman architectural influence he had experienced in the urbanized areas of his homeland. There was evidence of a barrier around the city, obviously constructed by the former occupants but now neglected and apparently unguarded. Toward the center of the colony was a massive Roman temple with pillars and posts and an assortment of adornments, including a statue of Claudius that reflected the grandeur of the Greek and Byzantine art prominent in the temple area, but appearing to a lesser extent in the major buildings and dwellings throughout the city. Aqueducts were moving water through sewage and irrigation tiles along the roads, crisscrossing avenues that were laid out in a highly organized, familiar fashion. The place was alive with activity in a cosmopolitan atmosphere seemingly free of concern about the looming threat. Word of Boudica's recent victory and the intercepted dispatches must have been withheld or not yet received. It would be easy for him to enter the settlement at night. There were plenty of alleys he could move through, mounted or not, and many escape routes, including the ocean that was visible in a blue-gray stripe beyond the town limits to the south.

Ben ate, rested, and watered his horse at a nearby stream that tumbled down to the valley floor and entered an irrigation canal complex around numerous fields lined with hints of a wide variety of trees and bushes and plants bearing fruits, nuts, and berries. He could clearly understand how the Trinovantes were feeling about their loss of this special place and the harbor that surely provided a variety of commercial, trading, and security needs.

As soon as it was dark, windows in the colony glowed with candle and lamplight. Torches blazed along the main avenues. Ben made sure his mount was securely tethered, then walked boldly through the high grass, down the hill, and into the midst of the city. There were so many people moving around it was difficult to tell who were Celts, Romans, or otherwise. He looked at his own attire and realized he needed no adjustments. Most inhabitants were dressed alike, with long robes, pants, tunics, scarves, shawls, cloaks, sandals, and boots in various combinations that made the wearers comfortable in season, but otherwise defied uniformity and any sense of ethnic distinctions. Ben could detect every color of the rainbow, even in the dim light, and after he dusted off and straightened his short tunic, scarf and headband, he felt right at home. The feel of his sandals scraping the cobblestones and quarried rock surfaces of roads and sidewalks brought a relaxed smile to his countenance, and he began to acknowledge the nods and greetings of the many he passed. When he came to a group of men and women conversing around a firepit, he joined them without fanfare. Others were coming and going from what appeared to be an evening ritual of sorts, exchanging news of the day and discussing a wide variety of topics.

A woman standing near the center of the group was particularly animated. Ben moved toward her as she talked rapidly, employing a variety of hand and arm gestures to punctuate her dialogue. When she mentioned Suetonius Paulinus and how his absence had been welcomed in her part of the town, Ben moved nearer. When she said "good night" and began to leave the group, he followed, walking behind her at a safe distance of several meters and stopping occasionally to feign interest in places he was passing. He concluded she was not a Roman. Her gait was typical of local Celts. The language she had spoken in the group reflected a broken *Latinate* that indicated she might be approached in Gaelic, when the moment was right.

When she turned down an alley illuminated by low torchlight, Ben called to her in a gentle voice. "Pardon me, ma'am."

She stopped and turned toward him with a smile. She was lovely. When he noticed her long robe was plain, Ben remembered the same attire his family's servants had worn in Damascus. He hesitated, thinking about his wife, and the gentle people who helped them, so appreciated as servants because of their importance as part of a society functioning for the good of all God's children and their various abilities, respected and happy, sharing the comforts of his home and their culture. How different it was then and there compared to his life in the present. His people had also learned much from their Macedonian conquerors regarding the classical societies of the Greeks, and Ben empathized with people in other cultures that had failed to do the same. He felt just like John did. There truly was a difference between having slaves and having servants. Slavery was an abomination, but employing good people to provide services that contributed to their societies, by using the skills God had given them, and were compensated fairly for the value they contributed for the benefit everyone seemed fair. When accompanied by faithful kindness, love, and mutual respect, it made sense, but Ben was saddened by the realization that *this* young woman of goodwill was not so fortunate for obvious reasons. He regretted that her freedom and the liberty that should be hers had been stolen and might never be returned, at least not in *this* life.

"Sir, did you need something?" she inquired politely, still smiling, appearing to be an innocent young woman perhaps *too naïve,* who in the moment was feeling no fear.

"I'm sorry, young lady, I was just wondering if you might know where I might find a member of the Trinovantes tribe, one living here, or nearby, who could help me with a matter of customs in Celtic tribal marriage."

"There are many of us here who are serving the Romans elites in their villas," she answered. "I might be able to help you, sir."

Ben approached her. "I'm new to this place. You seem very kind, and I do not wish to cause you any trouble."

"What trouble could you cause me?" she asked. "I'm a simple person. A Celt whose life has been changed by the Romans. I have no regrets, but there are many who do, and they hope for relief to come."

"How do you think that relief might come?" Ben asked.

"I'm not sure. There are so many different people here, since the Romans arrived. It's hard to tell what might happen. Perhaps it might come from the Druids. But I heard tonight that General Paulinus has marched off to destroy them. So it might come from inside this place. Many Celts here are in touch with others outside and are trying to scare the Romans by putting dye in the river to make it run like blood. The Druids cut off the heads of some captives, removed their jaw bones to signal deathly silence, and piled their heads on the bank of the river in plain view, where all could see and heed an omen of horrible things to come.

But all of that is just one aspect of the chaos that constantly swirls around us. It's the life here…always strange things happening every day. We get used to it and go on. Now let me take you to the person who probably knows something of *real interest* to you. Is your woman someone I might know?"

"I doubt it," Ben replied with a smile as they continued to walk down the alley toward a much-older man sitting on a bench, smoking a long pipe, and staring into the sky crowded with twinkling stars.

"Wise elder, this man needs help," she said as the old man turned toward her. "I forgot to ask his name."

"I'm Benjamin. Thank you, young lady, and please take care."

"I will. Good night," she replied.

Ben paused to watch her glide gracefully out of sight. His face reflected a sadness cast in doubt and foreboding about her future, as he turned to confront the man on the bench.

"So, Benjamin, what is it this old man might do for you? But wait," he interjected. "Where do you come from?"

"I come from far away to ask for the hand of a woman I met in Gaul. I'm a Jew. She's a Celt," Ben replied. "I think she's with the Trinovantes now. I want to find her and determine what we might do to join forever in a proper rite of marriage."

"A Jew. I should have known. You people always talk in terms of forever while you rob us in the trade you've started here, since the Romans came. I thought you might be from the west of here. The Celts there are dark, like you. I think they might've come from the distant south, perhaps *Iberia,*

Hispania, or whatever it's called now. I know the leader of what's left of the Trinovantes. His name is Cogidubnus."

Ben remembered. Boudica had mentioned the name.

"You can thank your lucky stars, my boy. If you wish, I can take you to his camp tonight. Right now."

"*Now?*" Ben responded, surprised by his incredibly good fortune.

"Yep. But as we get close, I might have to blindfold you," the old man warned. "I overheard the girl as you approached. I think you can appreciate the need for caution."

"I do indeed," Ben replied, "and I'll be glad to proceed with whatever precautions are necessary to protect you and any others I might meet through your good offices."

Thus the two began the hard climb out of the lowlands surrounding the colony. The old man had to stop several times to catch his breath. By the time the eastern sky showed light, they were at the crest of a hill. The old man stopped again, to sit on a rock, breathing deeply and stretching his shaking legs.

"Young man," he panted, "as soon as I can catch my breath, we must talk."

Ben waited, still thinking about the girl who had so graciously helped him, and the potential for many like her to be caught in the middle of a tragic outcome he was helping to orchestrate. He could see the expanse of Camulodunum in the early-morning light and realized there might be hundreds of innocent people still sleeping there. But the sight of the Temple of Claudius, a god to the Romans and the source of constant misery for the Celts, brought empathy with irony. It must have been an outrage of the kind a stranger could appreciate, he imagined, a bleeding breech of justice that could not be tolerated forever by those who were so grievously displaced. Perhaps the Trinovantes had endured enough and were enraged enough to accept and execute immediately the plan for their freedom he was about to suggest.

When he heard the old man cough and begin to speak, Ben turned to kneel beside him.

"I know you have *lied*," he snarled, facing Ben squarely. "The girl who brought you to me also knows. She's very wise for her age and can see things others miss. We've discerned that you could be the one we've been hoping for. Surely, you're *not* on a mission for marriage, so before we go any farther, I must insist that we be truthful to one another. At my age, I have nothing to lose, however, I must protect others if I can. So I must confirm your identity before you meet with the Trinovantes, those who've suffered most from the coming of the Romans who have killed many of us. They've taken our land for their veterans, a reward for them and a curse upon us. They treat us like we're animals. They want us to worship their gods. If you're aligned with them, you must kill me now, before I call for help. I've been sitting in the middle of the colony for many days, watching and waiting while spying and sending word by night through runners who take what I've seen and heard to those you want to meet. So hasten to tell me the truth behind your story and, thereby, determine our destiny."

Ben quickly related his background and purpose. The old man was satisfied, and the two continued to walk, until he spied some Celts who were rising from their positions around a small warming fire.

One came forward, smiling. "Welcome, wise man. What do you bring us this morning?"

"I bring you a man of goodwill who's on an earnest mission from Queen Boudica, of the Iceni."

The man stopped smiling. His expression was stern. He looked at Ben.

"Do we meet face-to-face now in a common cause, after *so many* years of hatred and conflict between us?" he asked.

"We do," Ben replied. "Queen Boudica sends regards and requests an audience with the present leader of the Trinovantes in order to discuss with him a plan for an attack by our joint forces on the Roman colony that squats in the middle of your tribal lands."

The man's smile returned. "It's about time. You're the good news we've been waiting for! You're most welcome. Come. I will take you to Cogidubnus, our king."

Now we are certain, Ben thought, as the elder turned and started walking back to his bench in the colony.

Ben's encounter with Cogidubnus went well. The new leader of the Trinovantes was young. He was condescending, coy, and exceedingly crude in speech and mannerisms. His arrogance was unsettling; however, he accepted all that Ben presented and revealed that Paulinus had reached the Druid grove on Anglesey. His soldiers had killed all the Druid inhabitants they could find. A small group of surviving priests had made it back to Cogidubnus's lines carrying a report of horrible slaughter, the torture of men, women and children and the burning of their sacred grove. The Druids who managed to escape wanted revenge in the form of Roman prisoners to offer up to Andraste as their sacrifices, and they were already helping to gather thousands of displaced Trinovantes for immediate retaliation in the hope that Paulinus and his men would be too far away to react effectively to an attack on the colony in Camulodunum. Cogidubnus also confirmed that he had sent his Trinovante spies southwest to Londinium and north to Verulamium in anticipation of their subsequent attacks on Romans and their Briton sympathizers in those settlements.

The meeting lasted much longer than Ben anticipated; and he departed in haste, anxious to bring news of good fortune to Boudica and express his reservations about the loyalty and trustworthiness of her recently revealed Trinovante counterpart. He decided to follow a shorter route by cutting across the trail he and the old man had taken earlier.

When he stopped to gaze down the hill toward Camulodunum, Ben was shocked. He dropped to the ground, squinting through the rays of a rising sun. A group of men, wearing Roman attire, were hanging the old man from an oak tree, shouting and laughing as they penetrated his writhing body with their giblets. Ben thought of his wife. He felt the outrage, but there was nothing he could do. He had to keep moving surreptitiously, as rapidly as possible. So he quickly bypassed the area, located his mount, and galloped up the Roman road to deliver his report.

When Ben arrived at Boudica's doorway the next morning, he could see her inside, meeting with Salan and her seconds. Her daughters were seated in the rear of the room, listening intently, as he passed the guards and entered.

"Greetings, Queen Boudica, I bear good news from the Trinovantes," he interjected. "May I speak?"

"By all means," she responded, showing him a seat at the table. "I've prayed for your safe return, Benjamin, and my prayers have been answered. Be seated…and we will attend."

"I've been fortunate indeed," Ben said as he took his place next Boudica. "It must've been due to your prayers. It was *so easy*. The world around the colony at Camulodunum is in a state of entropy. I'm certain Catus is somewhere in that area, but there appears to be no continuity of command. The city is wholly unguarded. If Catus has received news of your raid on his camp, it wasn't apparent to me. There *is* some concern among the people about tricks played by spies and Druids, who've sent frightful omens to the population, but there's no organized reaction at this point. The city appears to be yours for the taking. Cogidubnus *is* the leader on the Trinovantes side."

"At last, *we know!*" Boudica yelled, leaping out of her chair.

"Yes, my queen," Ben replied with a smile, as Boudica sat down slowly, her eyes still fixed on him. Her ardor apparent to all.

"Paulinus has destroyed the entire Druid stronghold where you saved me," Ben continued. "He's slaughtered hundreds there as well, essentially eradicating Druid influence in most of Britannia. But he's still far away, marching at thirty kilometers a day. It will take him several days to respond effectively to whatever you do in the region that includes Camulodunum, Londinium, and Verulamium. Thousands of Roman veterans have been settled in those colonies after their discharges, but they're not well armed, nor do they appear to be ready. Even when Paulinus gets close enough to respond, we'll have well over a hundred thousand men against his three legions, each with a strength of around five thousand legionnaires and officers. Paulinus might also roust some auxiliaries from veterans and indigenous volunteers, but he'll still be fighting against odds of at least five to one. Some of the surviving Druids are with Cogidubnus now and helping to gather as many of his people as possible, to be ready to attack Camulodunum in a day or two. Cogidubnus agrees with your plan to hit the colony from the northeast and west simultaneously, so we can quickly overwhelm the city and trap survivors with our chariots if they flee down the river to the sea. Cogidubnus agreed to keep his warriors in their present positions, to the west of Camulodunum, until you arrive from the east. He'll be ready to attack when your warriors are in place, and he sees your signal."

Boudica was elated. Her seconds shouted their approval. Salan was morose as always and sat quietly digesting the news.

Fiona jumped to her feet and ran to Ben. She embraced him with both arms, then fell upon Boudica, expressing her joy. "Mother, please take us with you!"

Isolda remained seated, her eyes downcast.

Chapter 24

The great room was empty. The meeting had ended. Only Ben and Boudica remained, gazing at one another across the table.

Boudica was the first to speak, following an uncomfortable period of silence. "I think we're about to begin an undertaking of such magnitude I cannot comprehend it. I'm seeing the numbers, moving into position. There are thousands of people spreading across the countryside out there. I can't see the extent of their mass in any direction. I feel my control is fast slipping away. We've never had anything like this to compare. Salan is certain. The signs are ominous. I have doubts about his ability to see and understand the reality gathering around us. His divining is often wrong. He explains it away by pointing out things *we did* to cause the gods to abandon us in our hour of need. Then he calls for more sacrifice and atonement to win back their favor. His power seems to be adequate for lesser things, but we need a greater power now. I fear he and the others in the Druid cult do not have the answer. I certainly do not."

"So you feel that his power to help with magic, rituals, and sacrifices isn't strong enough to summon your gods for the task ahead?" Ben inquired.

"I think it's more than that, Ben. Our Druids have led us to some successes, but this is different. Suetonius

Paulinus knows it as well. He struck at the heart of our religion and apparently wiped out an unthinkable number of priests who commune with our gods and tell us what those gods need to be satisfied with us. Now our priests have been reduced in number, and their sacred grove has been decimated. They couldn't protect *their own* when facing the Romans. Any power they might muster could be further reduced, giving us only a pittance of what we'll actually need to survive against our enemies, even if those enemies were raiding bands of Celts, just like us. My mind has always led me to accept what I was told about the Druids. But at this moment, I feel they have only been serving themselves with the practices they've recently employed. They hold their power over us and expand it to politics, government, and other aspects of our lives, more for their benefit, less for the welfare of the people they should serve and protect in harmonious relationships with the *'divinities'* they approach on our behalf."

"But, Boudica, you are one of them...a priestess."

"I was part of the royalty of a tribe that came here from Gaul. I was mated with Presutagus to form an alliance. Now that I'm a queen, I've been included in the Druid society, so they have better control over me...so I can be used more effectively to serve their interests."

"It sounds as if your experience in close proximity to the Druid hierarchy has caused you to doubt their integrity."

"Yes, it has. But it's developed into much more than that. I'm also questioning the legitimacy of the entire system, the tenets of our faith, the laws drawn from those beliefs, and even the gods we worship. Those *'gods'* have largely come from superstitions and simple explanations for things *no one* truly understands. I believe the Druids might've created those gods to fill specific needs with answers we can live with, in order to explain our nature and how we fit into the world around us. They developed rituals to keep us aligned with those gods and their power by appealing to the evil within us…our basest delights. When the Druids torture and kill others in horrible ways, it entertains, amuses, and makes our people feel more powerful. Their comfort reinforces the amount of support the Druids receive. But the Druids have proven they're powerless without the people they manipulate. I've been acting as if I'm a true believer in all they bring. At times of comfort, it is easier to do. But we're not fighting other Celts anymore. On this day, we march to meet Romans."

"It's profound. I'm surprised. What you have revealed is a source of great encouragement," said Ben. "I've had a similar experience. It brought me to this moment. The Romans in my land called us 'Pagans' because we did not, and would not, worship gods similar to yours. Now the Romans are in your land attacking the heart of your ancient religion, to destroy what unity you have, then conquer, and dominate you with a tyranny that expands the power of their secular empire by using religion as another weapon in their arsenal. Some of our highest priests in the Sanhedrin cooperated with the Romans and even used them to retain their power with the people, many of whom were inclined to follow Jesus and His teaching about God's will for peace and brotherly love. The behavior of our Sanhedrin demonstrated their self-serving corruption and hypocrisy with egregious extremes, much like their counterparts in the Roman senate. I saw that. It strengthened my commitment to find something that might rise above that, to inspire me with true wisdom, blind justice, and virtue worthy of respect. It was the hierarchy, the elites, who confounded me most. Those I expected to be better failed the test. Of course, there were many good people who silently suffered throughout our domain, tormented by establishment elites yet remaining ever faithful for the sake of their families, and continuing to pursue true love, hope, and happiness in spite of their circumstances."

"So we *do* have much more in common than I thought," Boudica replied. "Romans *kill* our Druids on the one hand but *help* your religious leaders on the other. Our religious leaders and yours do essentially the same, *whatever it takes* in order to maintain their power over us. And on this day, you and I sit here, facing one another, sensing there is something bigger than what we've been trained to uphold by men of authority who lead us in mysterious ways. But in reality, they should be serving something much greater than us, something greater than them. So we struggle to reach out to whatever it is that *we* need, but are unable to find it because of our limitations. But you and I have realized it and are coming to grips with the fact that our highest priests are failing us miserably in *their* representation of all that is truly divine."

"Yes," Ben replied. "Exactly! And we're also finding that even our highest priests can have much in common with the Romans. They conspire in tyranny. The outcome is sad. Many good people suffer as a result. They become slaves rather than servants, not having other choices with the freedom and liberty God intended for all of his children. It's taken away by selfish men who should be *praying* for God's forgiveness rather than *preying* on those who provide all they need. Yet get *no* just rewards for their service, working hard under miserable conditions, with unconscionable treatment."

"What is it that causes them to do such things to others?"

"They are *men*, human beings just like us," Ben responded. "Their nature calls them to use us and even each other to advance their selfish interests *above all*."

"So, Benjamin, how does a Jew reach the place where you stand today, here with me in this hour of need?"

"In my case, it began with the story of *Creation*, how we, and all we sense, came into being presented in simple ways that rational minds can understand and accept without further proof. I am in awe of its power and majesty. I saw the amazing results every day. I felt our creation *could not* be an accident, that it just came out of nowhere, happened as a coincidence, and produced a miraculous *result, without a cause*. It was a colossal, cosmic event, when all of us and all we know came out of absolute nothingness. I could *not* believe that some supreme organizing and guiding power *did not* transform that beginning into an ongoing process, now evident in everything we experience in the vast complexity of *our* nature and the nature that surrounds us. Our minds have the ability to feel the presence of something, or someone, much bigger and more powerful than we are. Animals don't seem to agonize over thoughts of that kind. We do. And there is a reason for that. Consider the thing we call *religion*."

Boudica interrupted in need of clarification. "So in your head, your mind, and perhaps in the minds of your earliest ancestors, there's been a notion about all you say, a guiding influence *there*, at the very beginning?"

"Yes. Something eternal, that has always been there. Simply stated, as a guiding power, the preexisting Godhead that implanted in us, at some point, the ability to realize and communicate over many centuries with my people, made in his image and likeness, who passed on an oral history, then used written words to describe the countless times the Godhead spoke and what resulted. It's the oldest written record of an emerging religion I know of. It was documented in scrolls marked to portray symbols and images and concepts that we could understand, using words much like you saw in the Roman dispatches."

"I can neither read nor write, yet I'm an aristocrat in my land," Boudica interrupted.

"I know," said Ben, with a look reflecting genuine empathy.

"So, Ben, when you were a little boy, your people used those words and told you and taught you things that described a way of life, the way you would live, in the life you would be living?"

"Yes. Perhaps the same as for you, Boudica. I know the Greeks and the Romans have done the same in their way. For me, the climax occurred with the arrival in our land of an aspect of the Supreme Being, a Messiah, a savior foretold in prophetic writings much like your Druid divining, but describing someone who had been sent by the Creator, the Godhead, who had existed forever, eternally, and was still in existence and would continue to be in existence, *forever*. That Savior came to us in a form we could recognize. He was born incarnate, named 'Jesus,' and looked and acted and talked just like we do, but he was quite different in an amazing way, and he *proved it!*"

"So did this *being* move among your people…to do this proving?"

"He did. He knew all things better than anyone, like he'd been with my people though all time. He walked far with a group of followers that eventually numbered twelve. He selected men with good hearts, salt of the earth, simple people of my faith at the time. I was with one of those twelve before I came here. His name is John. The bundle you found contains some of John's writings, his evidence, and his *own* testimony as a direct eyewitness of Jesus while he moved among the people. The bundle also contains some writings from other witnesses with whom Jesus lived and traveled during the two years he was with them. They all saw the same things. Quintus, the Roman we captured, was also an eyewitness to the man-god. Quintus knew my friend John as well and has talked with Kale and with me about his witness. We believe *him* as well. The things Quintus described to us are very much the same as what John observed when Jesus healed Quintus's servant and scolded the priests about how they had strayed from the will of the Father in their practices. He told them what they *must do* in order to live according to the Father's will, to have a better life here and an everlasting life beyond, an afterlife, in the glory of God's heavenly kingdom."

"What else did Jesus say?"

"He talked of a 'great commandment' to love our Godhead above all things and love one another as he loved us, just as he evidenced through his many blessings in words and in deeds."

"And what is the *love* Jesus described?"

"To put others before self and be gentle and caring and kind to them, to treat them *justly*, just as we want to be treated. We want to be loved. Others are much the same. We should always remember that simple fact."

"And how would we know if we were doing the Godhead's will?"

"We would feel it in our minds and in our hearts, throughout our being, our body, soul, and spirit. Doing God's will would be hard to uphold in *this* world, but it would give us joy and satisfaction like no other and the opportunity to live a good and truly happy life here and forever. Many of the priests at that time, especially some of their key leaders, disdained the poor, sick, and troubled people; however, those who followed Jesus in his way learned that the unfortunates and downtrodden were the ones he reached out to most often, along with the children. Always the children. And above all else, Jesus wanted all of God's people to have a way to be forgiven for their recurring sins, to rise above them and have a sustainable way to live a holy life. All of this must be done with God's help. People had shown in the past, they *could not* do it alone. In order to please God with their goodness and renew strength in their efforts, to remain pure in heart…and be ready for God's loving embrace Jesus allowed himself to be crucified by the Romans, with the help of some Jews…for speaking God's Truth and showing the way to live within the boundaries inherent in that truth. Jesus died on his cross, but rose again, as no other incarnate being has *ever* truly done, then went back to our Father, our Creator, after telling his believers to heed his example so they could join with him and the

Father and their Holy Spirit in their heavenly domain. He later sent the Holy Spirit to help with the same power that created heaven and earth. God's Spirit was with him and with the believers, thus they had the power and the courage to go out as he commanded, to tell others the good news that all who believed in God and his Word would be forgiven their wrong doing…their sinning…*if* they were truly repentant. He paid the eternal, cosmic price, the ransom for all sins resulting from God's gift of our free will, and the choices we make among the many we have. The Greeks thought and wrote about those gifts as *freedom and liberty*."

"But why was he killed?"

"Because some of my people felt he was a blasphemer and a potential threat to the power they'd gained over time by obscuring much more important God-given beliefs with a myriad of compulsory laws of their *own* creation. Many of those laws involved arcane ritual details that overshadowed the key values that Jesus emphasized and clarified in his teaching. He was quick to point out the error in their ways. Rather than focusing the minds of the people firmly on God's will, the tendency was to subordinate God's will to man-made minutia and behavior that reeked of hypocrisy. Their actions were contrary to the Creator's intent. Happiness for his children had been the goal. Good order, true happiness, and lasting satisfaction can only result from obedience to God's commandments and the moral and ethical absolutes they defined. Our religious leadership had intentionally distracted the people from the essence of the truth. Many were *using* the people to make themselves rich and powerful in material ways, instead of ministering to their spiritual needs, addressing their misery and setting a proper example for men of their calling, who *should* behave in the roles God intended for those who take care of his children. In effect, they had forgotten that they too were God's children. Some corrupted their God-given mission to make gods of themselves by placing their needs before those of our God. Loving God and his children above all things was their *first* commandment. Jesus revealed the corruption in their practices. They were outraged by his remonstrations. Jesus's sacrifice on the cross, for the benefit of mankind, became the ultimate example of what God meant."

"And did his followers *actually* see him alive after he died?"

"Yes, they *did!* They *all* saw him in the same way, and they *all* agreed in their individual testimonies."

"If one man sees something, that is one thing," added Boudica. "If twelve men see the same thing, *that's more than enough.* But I cannot imagine why *anyone* would kill such a man. We must talk more. I need certainty at this point in my life. I'm willing to listen. Will you pray for us to this God of yours?"

"I will, Boudica," Ben promised, "and I will also ask that he be with you and send his spirit to guide you, to protect you and help you understand the *great mystery,* as well as the rational things we must recognize in order to believe Jesus *is* who he said he was. Then follow his example and accept what he has offered through the *power* of our Creator. He wants us to seek the good life here on earth, then go on as Jesus *did,* back to the loving embrace of Our Father in the eternal beauty, truth, and renewal of life in His everlasting home, we call *heaven.*"

"Thank you, Ben," Boudica softly replied after pausing for reflection.

"It's my pleasure to serve you in any way I might, Queen Boudica," Ben replied, "and I would ask only this. Before we leave here today, will you please take time to meet with Quintus, to hear the story of a former Roman centurion and the experience he had with Jesus, and how it's changed his life as well?"

"I shall. Bring him to me, now, along with Kale, and my daughters."

Chapter 25

Ben obeyed Boudica's command for another meeting. The group she requested was gathered in the firelight.

"So Quintus," Boudica began, "Ben has told me about you. There's no need for you to be fearful about your circumstances. Benjamin has vouched for you and explained the cause of your exile in our land. In a strange way, you've become an ally, in our time of great need."

"Again, I thank you for your mercy, Queen Boudica," Quintus responded. "As Benjamin and Kale know, I'll do whatever I can to help, especially in the spiritual matters associated with your struggle. I've been on both sides. I *know* the truth."

"Very well," Boudica responded. "Now rest assured and tell me about your experience with Jesus."

"The first time I saw Jesus, *I knew* intuitively. Many Romans think of our emperors as gods. I have known three of them in my life, so far…Julius, Claudius, and Nero. All of them are men. Jesus is beyond all of them, in every way that truly matters. Emperors are men who get their power over the people they rule from marriage, heredity, trickery, and murder. *Caesar* is a derivative of our word that means 'hairy' in our language. I cannot reconcile '*hairy*' with either the name or the power I experienced in Jesus Christ, nor can I feel the same about our cold, dictator gods whose power comes from the people who worship their statues. They are icons *imagined* to be in their likeness, by the men who carved and chiseled them into existence from dead wood or lifeless rocks. The power in Jesus is clearly supernatural and comes from him to his people for whom he cared and shared everything including his most precious life. He looked like a man but was surely from the God of Israel, incarnate by a miracle. I saw him heal several in Jerusalem and Capernaum. I listened to his words, and I spoke at great length with his friend John and many others. Everything made sense to me and touched my heart like no one else could've done. When my servant fell ill from paralysis, there was nothing our physicians could do. No magic, no occult, nor eastern mysticism or medicine could relieve his agony. I went to Jesus in the market place and asked him for help. He said I should take him to my home immediately so he could see my servant. I deferred based on my profound respect for Jesus. I was not worthy that he should enter under my roof. I asked him to simply say the words. I believed his words would carry the power of *creation*, and surely heal my servant. Jesus praised my faith in front of all present. He told them they would do well to follow my example. He said it should be easier for Jews to believe, given their history. It was all there, direct and simple to behold. He told me to go and find my servant healed. As I bowed and turned to leave, some of my legionnaires came running with good news from my wife. Our servant had risen from his bed and was walking and saying he was ready to return to his duties. I'm a man of authority hardened in the ways of my culture, and *no fool. Jesus is real!* He healed my servant! I can feel his presence daily, through all my senses. In my mind, in my heart, through the spirit that energizes my soul and connects me with God's Holy Spirit. It's hard to explain. It's a *miracle!* I can feel the power. There's nothing else to compare. It's unlike anything I've ever hoped for, or dared to expect. It's *real.* It's all good!"

Boudica was silent. She had listened attentively. The attitude of her form was relaxed. She was resting in peaceful surroundings.

"I want to know more of this," she said. "What do you think, Ben?"

"We'll have time while your warriors continue to gather. I should bring the bundle John gave me and present some of the items from the contents that I've reviewed thus far."

"Yes," said Boudica. "We should *all* be aware of these things."

The group was still engaged in animated conversation when Ben returned. He hastily opened his pack, removed the bundle, and unwrapped it.

"There are four key items here," Ben announced. "The first is a *creed* assembled by my friend John and the other followers of Jesus. It's a set of beliefs that are based on Jesus's teachings…a summary of ideas…the beliefs that form our faith and give us the hope and the love we need in order for us to carry on together. Next is a prayer to the Father. Jesus repeated it to John and the other followers in response to a question about how best to pray. According to John, it's an outline of prayer in daily discussions with God. Next are some extracts from one of the many letters Paul the apostle wrote to the Gentiles who were converts in the communities he touched after his own conversion by *the risen Christ.*

And there are John's recollections of his own experiences with Jesus over the course of the two years he spent day and night as a trusted and beloved apostle. And lastly, there are a handful of brief texts to be shared and discussed as we progress."

"That's good, Ben," Boudica affirmed, with obvious enthusiasm, smiling as her eyes beamed reflections of firelight.

"I think John's examples of what Jesus conveyed to his apostles might be the best place to begin. They're things remembered over time and recorded in spite of extreme duress, because they stand out in the mind of the writer as having the greatest importance. The one that strikes me most is John's expression of Jesus Christ's mission in a brief statement that I will paraphrase as 'God so loved the world he created, and the people he made and placed upon it, that he gave up his only begotten son, incarnate, so that others could overcome their tendency toward bad deeds in sin, then be forgiven in their sorrow and *redeemed* for good living in this life...while preparing for an eternal life in a heavenly paradise, following Jesus our Lord and Savior, surrounded by God's trinity, in communion with the exquisite joy of an eternal spring, bringing life renewed in everlasting *true love.*'"

Boudica reflected on Ben's comment and replied, "So in John's view, in what he wrote about the things Jesus said, and the things that he did, there's an eternal Godhead in *three* aspects that I might refer to as 'persons'...the ancient God of your people and two others who together deliver his word and his supremely powerful spirit to people like us, those *made* in his likeness, who inhabit his earthly creation, living here now in a kingdom made possible by the words and actions of the *One he sent*. And his people…his children…are trying their best now, to do what his love requires in order to go on, after this life, to join in his heavenly kingdom with many others who loved, worshipped, praised, and petitioned him for his own sake, and the gifts Jesus promised, that you have revealed in our discussions."

"I'm amazed by your insight, Queen Boudica," Ben replied. "You've reached the core of my understanding, at this point in my spiritual journey. What John wrote was not of his own invention but a summary of the essence of what Christ himself had revealed during the time they were together. John's experience also revealed that as we embrace these things of the spiritual life with our *minds*, within our immortal souls, we change in a good way, growing in fortitude, temperance and prudence to understand and embrace the justice in our existence that ultimately comes from God, through the love he has shared with mankind. And we must remember that God is a spiritual being, who consistently reminds us that material things become secondary as we strive to achieve his ultimate goal. Reaching that goal is the most important of all our pursuits in the brief opportunity we have to attain eternal salvation and the joy of complete satisfaction that it brings to those who acquire true wisdom by following the path God has created for us, and hopes we will choose using his love inspired gift of our *own free will*."

"It's complicated but simple, I believe," said Quintus. "We've been given a choice and the ability to make it. We either accept, or we don't. I've seen what acceptance can mean. After meeting Jesus, it was the only way I could follow. Living as I did as a Roman, seeing how we struggled, and what little it meant, I realized what God intended in the beginning, Queen Boudica. I believe we now have the chance to live a better life, and we should do our best to embrace that life for the good of all in humanity. Even if *we cannot* accomplish it universally, in our lifetimes, through our example, perhaps others might learn given more time and create a place where life is better, where many will come and sustain it until heaven and earth become one, existing forever in the season of living water, for people of goodwill, who want their souls to be purified and ready, when they're called *to meet their Maker*."

"The way will be hard, just as John and the others have demonstrated," added Ben. "There will always be those who try to stop us. But our search must continue for as long as it takes. The Roman civilization and many others have been lacking and cannot survive forever. We must provide for the ages those things God's children need most in their lives."

"And we must confront that *truth*, one way or another," added Boudica, "and along the way, we must *first* confront ourselves. We're spiritual beings in a temporal world who seek what we may *not* find, as we march away today. Perhaps we'll be surprised by what we *do* find in our quest for freedom and divine truth…to guide us spiritually with open and enlightened minds."

"Amen," said Ben. "We hear your words, Queen Boudica. We're ready!"

"And we're prepared to accept *whatever* the outcome might be!" Fiona added as she leaped up and faced the dawn outside the doorway, brandishing her gleaming, razor-sharp sword.

Chapter 26

As they left the great house and mounted their horses to begin the march to Camulodnum, Ben could *not* believe his eyes. He and Boudica were being followed by a horde of human beings too numerous to measure. He noticed warriors mixed with women and children, wagons, carts, and animals of various types under a host of flags and pennants that identified a mind-boggling range of kinship strata, grouped into subtribes, clans, and families. The horde stretched for as far as he could see on the far side and was disappearing in a massive dust cloud that was drifting toward the rear.

Ben was concerned. He rode up to Boudica. "Please turn and look back at this mass, my queen, especially the large number of women and children and the beasts, wagons, and carts moving with them," he added to draw her attention. "They're mixing with the rank and file of your fighters and destroying their cohesiveness."

"It's the way we've gone to war for ages," Boudica responded, smiling. "Don't fret. It's a tradition. Just accept it. I couldn't stop them if I wanted to. We're all fighters, and the women want to stay with their men to help in any way they can. The beasts and the fowl are what we eat, our rations. Each family brings their own food. The women prepare it. The warriors return when they can join in meals and visit with their families. The women and children love to see the fighting. They watch and listen as the Druids urge our men on with their horns blaring and high-pitched whistles blowing, and they sometimes join in the howling and chanting that's meant to inspire our men and frighten their opponents."

"I've heard of camp followers, but never in such magnitude, blending in with their warriors on the march," said Ben. "Aren't your warriors concerned about the safety of their women and children?"

"Yes, they are. But apparently not as much as you. Their women know how to fight. They sometimes enter the battle themselves. The same is true for their children. From now on, the warriors will rotate outriders on our flanks, rear and front as you recommended. They will alert everyone to peril, in time to react effectively. And as we near our objective, the warriors will move to the front. The rest will find vantage points where they can safely observe the battle."

Ben rode on in silence. An expression of grave concern shadowed his countenance. He would say no more about this revelation. Henceforth, he would pray for deliverance from the unthinkable, especially for the women and children.

When thoughts of her daughters began to recur, Ben moved faster, came alongside Boudica again, and asked, "Where have you placed your girls?"

"They're far to the rear with Kale and Rand and some women I trust," she responded with a questioning glance. "Why do you ask?"

"I'm worried about them," Ben replied. "I can't stand the thought of losing them in the chaos that's already closing around us. If I had to find them, even now, it would be difficult. Look behind you."

Boudica turned in her saddle. "I understand," she responded. "I too have never seen a mass of people so large. It's overwhelming. On the one hand, it gives me comfort. So many are ready to join in this great cause. However, I share your worry about the means of control for such a large body of independent minds. They're apt to turn to their own devices when the fighting begins, especially when it's hand to hand and each man must fight for his own survival and the plunder that awaits him among the dead."

"I understand," said Ben. "The melee will erupt the moment you signal the charge into the colony, if not before. I'm not sure about Cogidubnus. But if we can control the timing of the attack, and your location at the start, you and your daughters will be safe, out of harm's way. That could also enable you to meet with Cogidubnus at a known point he could reach immediately after your victory, so you can plan and execute your next move while the two of you still have the upper hand in initiative, mass, and momentum."

"And what do you propose?" asked Boudica.

"There's a bald hilltop on this side of the colony. You'll be able to see it clearly as you approach. You should move directly to that location as fast as you can. Have at your side a ram's horn and banner. When your warriors are in position and ready to attack from your side of the colony, you can blow the horn and wave the banner from side to side. I'll move to the rear now, find your girls, and bring them to you on the hilltop. After I'm sure they're safe with you,

I'll leave to join Cogidubnus. I know exactly where he'll be. I'll skirt the colony to reach him. I'll *make sure* he holds short, at the ready, on his side, and waits for your signal to attack at the same time. I'll also tell him to join you on the hill, when the outcome of the fighting is known, so you can make the decision to pursue or withdraw. Overwatch and communication methods like I'm describing have been used by the Romans to conduct what they refer to as 'coordinated attacks,' and their leaders I spoke with in Damascus said they used similar tactics and techniques to their advantage during their fighting in Gaul, where the terrain is much like we have here."

Boudica's expression revealed growing confidence and relief in Ben's caring on behalf of her daughters. "Very well. Go then," she commanded without hesitation.

"I'll return as soon as I'm able," he promised.

"Good!" she snapped.

When Ben turned to ride away, Boudica assumed the posture of a smiling, confident leader, riding tall in her saddle, shouting instructions and inspiring those who gathered around her. Ben looked back and smiled as he continued toward the rear of the surging mass of humanity.

As he guided his mount through narrow passages in the crowd, Ben encountered Celtic warriors in huge numbers, dressed for battle in their widely varied attire. They were brandishing their weapons of choice and looking without exception like brave men elated to have an opportunity to strike not just another clan or tribe but against the Romans who had so long and so blatantly defied them. Ben was overwhelmed by the depth and breadth of the thousands of souls moving gallantly toward their destiny.

Ben continued to ride through the oncoming tide, searching through a cloud of blowing dust, until he heard shouts and saw several arms waving. He finally spied Kale with two of his sons and the girls. As he neared, Ben could see all of them beginning to smile and noticed that Fiona's smile was by far the most visible.

"Welcome to the rear of the beast!" shouted Kale over the din. "We hoped you hadn't forgotten us in the chaos of this slow-moving menagerie."

"I could never forget you, Kale," Ben shouted back, "especially when you and your sons are far behind and over-watching such beauties! I was afraid you might abscond with them to a kingdom worthy of their grace."

"And you were right, but not before I found a suitable chariot to whisk them away in royal comfort. We should find one for them, Benjamin. And we will. Just wait and see. Look at those smiles. They agree. We will soon tender to our princesses the service of noblemen."

"Kale, you are a gentleman to be sure. As you have suggested, we must exchange their horses for a chariot immediately to ensure that our lovely charges will travel in a style and comfort befitting their station."

Ben watched as Kale made the move to a nearby chariot. He was delighted to see the smile on the Fiona's dusty face as she and Isolda were settled in their new conveyance, driven by Rand. Their mounts followed closely, reins held by Rand's mounted brother and another able handler. Ben knew the chances of them getting lost in the chaos had been unacceptable. He breathed a sigh of relief. Having Boudica's daughters under Kale and his sons' control reduced Ben's anxiety to a tolerable level. He turned his horse and led the way, moving toward the place that would be their temporary safe haven. He was pleased with the progress, moving with the tide, and smiled when they reached the crest of the bald hill. The day was still filled with light. He would be able to reach the Trinovantes and their leader long before dark.

When he was assured the girls were safely in place with Boudica, Ben rode down the hill, skirted the colony wide to the north, then turned southwest until he saw the location where Cogidubnus and his seconds had gathered. As he advanced toward them, Ben glanced eastward. He smiled. The dust of Boudica's march was not visible. The wind was carrying the huge cloud away from Camulodunum and into the sea. The defenders of the settlement would have little early warning. He praised and thanked God for the gift, then dismounted as soon as he saw Cogidubnus looking toward the east and smiling at the sight of a favorable omen.

"It's good to see your horde coming and bringing *no dust*," Cogidubnus greeted him with a cackle. On this day, he looked disturbingly evil, appearing smaller than Ben remembered, but the size of his ego adequately compensated. His smile was crooked. His beady eyes signaled deception. Cogidubnus could not be trusted. Ben decided to humor the little serpent until Boudica could meet him face-to-face.

"It's good to be with you, Cogidubnus. I've brought word of Boudica's progress as well as some final thoughts about ways to enhance the impact of your attack here, and hasten our advance toward subsequent victories."

"I look forward to hearing all you have to divulge," Cogidubnus replied with a sinister grin. "Let us proceed to a suitable location where we can speak with assurance of privacy and not be disturbed."

As soon as their exchange was complete and Cogidubnus had briefed his seconds, the two moved to a vantage point overlooking Camulodunum. They could see evidence of Boudica's approach and the dispositions of Cogidubnus's Trinovantes. The formations were deep and wide, ready to attack. It was obvious. The veterans and others in the colony were becoming agitated by the spectacle unfolding to the east. They were hastily making final preparations to defend both sides of the settlement.

Cogidubnus moved closer to Ben. "My spies have been watching for some time and noticed preparations on this side of the settlement beginning two days ago. There's no way of knowing for certain, but something stirred them up a bit, causing activity beyond their normal routine."

"It might have been the result of news about our capture of a Roman courier's pouch, or our victory at Catus's camp finally reaching them," Ben replied. "There were no Romans along our way here, so I doubt there could be other sources of alarm or an early warning for Paulinus at this point."

"It doesn't matter, one way or another," Cogidubnus responded with an arrogant smirk. "Paulinus is out of our way for a few more days, and the Roman veterans here are poorly armed. I think we'll see a slaughter approaching annihilation in a victory that, until this day, we could only imagine. If it goes the way I expect, my warriors will want time for celebration and plunder. Londinium will come into their minds as well. You should be aware of that. They've been wronged beyond *your* comprehension. Their revenge may turn into madness before we're done. In any event, I'll do as you ask and ride to Boudica's location for a meeting, as soon as the outcome is certain, and I've sensed the will of my fighters."

"I too have been wronged by the Romans, but revenge uncontrolled could eventually lead to defeat," Ben replied. "For now, we must pray we'll overcome our lust for blood and treasure and instead spend our good fortune on what's best for those we are honorably bound to serve and protect."

"Your words have power at the moment, Benjamin," Cogidubnus replied. "However, the time for words is over. Can you hear my men? Can you see them brandishing their weapons, straining for release with the Druids behind them chanting for blood and holy sacrifices?"

"I see it all from here," said Ben, "including Boudica's line, standing in silence on the far side of the colony. Her signal to attack is near."

Before Cogidubnus could answer, a ram's horn blared above the din. Boudica's banner was waving from the hilltop.

Successive waves of thousands of fierce warriors crashed through the barriers on both sides of the city, then raced on, running and raging through the streets. The Roman veterans were being inundated by the sheer force and magnitude of the onslaught, going down in a chopping, slashing, stabbing, spearing, and clubbing stampede that rolled over mangled bodies and drove survivors back to their last resort, inside the Temple of Claudius.

Behind the first wave came the second and the third, now moving slowly on the Trinovantes side, stabbing chopping and maiming the wounded. Ben was shocked. Some of the Trinovantes began tearing down wooden huts and shelters, igniting piles of wood, and hurling victims into the roaring flames.

As the first wave of the Trinovantes met Boudica's Iceni at town center, the two forces melded into a leaderless mob. Captives, the wounded, the innocents were all slain while begging for mercy. Piles of wood began to grow around the temple. Fires were raging. Ben could feel the intense heat. He thought it must be like fires in the Greek legends of *Hades* for those inside who sought shelter from the massacre outside in the streets. When the walls of the temple began to crumble and the shrieking and roaring overcame him, Ben turned to confront Cogidubnus. But the leader of the Trinovantes was nowhere to be found.

"*Dear God!*" Ben screamed. "*Please bring an end to this horror!*"

But there was no end in sight. Both forces were engaged in irreversible butchery that reached levels of savagery defying description and further witness. Ben sprinted to his mount, jumped into the saddle, and raced toward the hill where Boudica stood transfixed by the flaming horror that raged below her.

As he approached, Ben could see her clearly, perfectly erect and regal. Looking down the hill, in utter disbelief. He wrenched his mount to a sliding stop, leaped from his saddle, and dashed up the rise, into Boudica's field of vision. When she saw him, tears poured down her cheeks. Her expression changed from shock to relief.

Chapter 27

The sun was setting over the scene of grisly death and smoldering destruction. Boudica was standing next to Ben. They were looking down at the remains of a Roman colony wiped out by a lust for blood and revenge unparalleled in the minds of those gathered around them. Thousands of mutilated bodies were scattered across the landscape. Around and above stood the rolling hills, reflecting the reddish glow of hundreds of fires extended upward to touch the oncoming clouds. The fading rays of the sun reached farther, into the heavens, as if to attract the attention of divine Andraste as a witness to the most unholy sacrifice mankind could ever devise. It was another of the many mind-bending contradictions Ben had struggled with, God's gift of free will, given out of love, and the choices subsequently made by men, colliding in a paradox, numbing his mind and confounding his soul.

When Boudica quietly turned away and departed with her entourage, Ben glared into the darkening firmament.

"How could this be?" he cried out. Again he asked, then answered without speaking. Men had taken a blessing and made it a curse. The love that was God's motivation for Creation has, once again, been turned into sorrow, like death on a cross for the best of men in order to pay the universal price of cosmic justice needed for past and present trans-

gressions, to end heinous acts such as this with the redemptive power purchased for salvation with eternal life for even the basest of men, who might believe and repent with a simple change of mind, to end these never-ending tragedies by following the way of our Creator's true wisdom for the rest of our days, here and beyond. It had all been revealed. Ben was convinced. God's *Word incarnate* had come to do that. Jesus had died in the hands of jealous, ambitious, and selfish men, *but rose* to reveal the ultimate proof of the triumph of eternity in the unselfish sacrifice of an incarnate form of our God, who would humble himself to save us *from ourselves*. What little this brief life on earth compares to the light of eternity revealed in God's power to create, and his willingness to forgive, with love and tender mercy.

"I must go on with this," Ben whispered. "I must understand the beliefs that define my faith and provide *hope* that inspires me to love and pray for the souls freed from this field on this day…for something good to be revealed and remembered in their passing. From the blessing of hope we derive from our faith, we can receive the grace and strength to carry us forward in spite of hardship and disappoint. We will follow the light, and it will guide us forward through the darkness to join others of like mind in changing the world we have inherited into a better place, a place that's as close as we can get to the new world to come. In doing so, we can benefit others and redeem those who perish in that noble process. Thus, I must never abandon my faith in spite of the constant temptations born of the men who surround me. I must believe in the good and continue to struggle in the fight to achieve it, so those who go down believing in what has been *proven* will in their last breath go on in the comfort of knowing they are loved by the greatest of spirits and the life of the Spirit is the life that's real, and the only life where true freedom and liberty is complete with justice, fulfillment, and satisfaction that *never needs more.*"

Ben felt truly free for the first time in his life. He was standing alone, speaking out loud. "What lies below this hill is simply matter, pieces of flesh and bone, the human remains of people whose names were given by parents whose Creator gave *them* the ability to bring new life to earth for brief moments in the time line of eternity. Now their spirits have been invested with the strength to over-power damaged matter, to free their immortal souls from human bondage, to leave the enslavement that held them, to fly away, and reach the heights of their Father's home-land, to be welcomed by his loving embrace. But for *some* who still live the dark life and go forward here on Earth, the answer will be to continue the pain they've chosen to inflict on others. And for others, the answer will be a glo-rious response to God's love, by forgiving debts and the trespasses of others, serving their Godhead and sharing his love with their children, their brethren, and others, alike."

Then he paused, distracted by a sound, but continued. "And for those who keep on killing to impose their way, their cause will ultimately fail, for it's the way of man. But the way of Almighty God will not perish. Instead, it will stand forever in a land promised to those pure in spirit who reflect the divinity that brought love to earth with his gift of Creation, and still yearns for our choice to *return his love* and demonstrate respect for him in acts of goodwill unto others."

"Ben, are you listening?" a voice called out.

"Oh, yes, I'm listening to what I *must do*, Kale" he responded, shaking his head, in a trance.

"Ben, are you with us in mind? You seemed to be talking to yourself."

"Yes, Kale. My attention is yours now. Tell me whatever you need."

"Cogidubnus is here along with his seconds. Boudica has gathered hers. They're about to meet. She's called for you to join them."

Ben rose and quickly followed Kale to the top of the hill.

Boudica welcomed them with a nod as Cogidubnus said, "I hear your words, Queen Boudica, and I respect your position. I too am horrified by what I've seen. Now *you* can see my seconds standing next to me on this hill. They represent the men below who caused a bloody but overwhelming victory against the invaders who've celebrated our downfall for many years. They have treated us like dogs, and Andraste has given us an unmistakable sign. Our warriors have seen it. They will *not* agree to anything other than total war and annihilation of the Romans in the lands of the Trinovantes. Our warriors are supremely confident and ready to move on to Londinium. They won't respect, nor will they obey any leader that gets in their way, including *you*."

"The truth is, *you've* lost control of your people," Boudica shot back, "and now *you* want us to follow their example in Londinium and Verulamium, and on to battle Suetonius Paulinus, *wherever* he decides to stand."

"We *must* exploit this routing while we can," Cogidubnus responded. "The consequences of resistance will be death for *anyone* who tries to interfere."

"I agree with Cogidubnus," added Salan. "The signs are right now, and Andraste demands satisfaction for the good fortune she has heaped upon us. She has given us two decisive victories, but that is not enough. She demands the blood of the Romans on our alters. The majority of *your* seconds agree. Can't *you* see?"

"Yes, Salan. I see. We spoke at length before your arrived. I must respect their wishes. But I must tell you, and tell all, my heart *is not* in this butchery. My seconds also told me, and I have seen with my own eyes, that until your Trinovantes crashed into my Iceni warriors they were killing only those with weapons who stood in their way. When the Trinovantes intermixed with my Iceni, the battle changed to ruthless butchery and vengeful retribution. Our men *followed* into the fray. It was wanton murder and much, much more. They were behaving like crazed animals, not men. Now there's no turning back. I understand that. I must yield. But *you* must also understand that, henceforth, the Romans will surely do the same."

"Very well," said Cogidubnus, stepping in front of Salan. "Your compromise reflects your wisdom. We'll deal with whatever the Romans bring. I suspect my scouts are already moving southwest on the road to Londinium looking for signs of Paulinus's reaction. We know the majority of his force is still west of here, marching back from the destruction of the Druid base."

Ben stepped forward. "Queen Boudica, as you also know, Paulinus's Ninth Legion is northeast of us. As we move toward Londinium, that legion will be on our right flank and might be coming fast, if a rider from Paulinus has reached them with an order to reinforce. I recommend we allocate a portion of your force to hold back the Ninth Legion and deflect any attempt to hit us on our right flank or rear, where most of our women and children are traveling."

"I agree, Benjamin, absolutely," said Boudica, "as you suggest. We'll arrange to do that *immediately* after Cogidubnus and his seconds depart."

"I'll be ready to move my main body toward Londinium by midmorning tomorrow," Cogidubnus added. "I presume you'll follow with your main force. I'll hold my men short of the city and meet you along the road when you arrive. Unless Paulinus intercepts us, and we go to battle immediately, you and I can complete our plan for Londinium based on the information my spies and scouts bring back from their observation of the colony and its defenses, *if any*," he added with a chuckle.

Boudica was speaking with one of her seconds. She turned to Cogidubnus. "Our meeting has concluded, King Cogidubnus. As you suggested, I shall meet you along the road to Londinium as our destiny unfolds."

Cogidubnus bowed and departed with his seconds.

Ben began to think. *He's surely fooled me. The little snake is truly wicked and deceptive. Even Boudica might not be able to overcome his evil. If he carries her along in this scheme, it could lead to her ruin. If he were a Roman, Cogidubnus would be a Nero, a madman with murder on his mind, but clever in his influence in crafting the basest designs. He's set a sinister*

*trap. God help us if he succeeds. I must warn Boudica again,
as soon as the moment is right.*

After discussions of internal concern regarding the
order of movement going forward, the Londinium attack,
and a potential Roman incursion where Kale would be riding, Boudica released him and her seconds, to resume their
preparation for the march to be continued at first light.

Ben remained with Boudica. They walked to a high vantage point on the hilltop, sat next to one another in silence,
and looked down at the burning ruins of Camulodunum,
until Boudica finally succumbed to the darkness in a deathlike slumber. While she slept, Ben watched over her and
prayed until the sun began to rise and reveal the full extent
of the carnage.

When she awoke, Boudica looked past him, down the
hillside.

"Ben, we must go down there," she whispered.

Sickened by the thought, he rose without speaking to
ready their horses, then paused for a subtle distraction, a
gentle tug, a hint that someone was watching. He took a
few steps, then looked up. It was Fiona, standing naked in
the dawn on the highest point of the hill, sword in hand,
looking down at him, smiling, with an attitude of complete abandonment reflected in her posture. She seemed to
be reaching out to him, presenting herself, offering herself
wholly and silently with a penetrating gaze. Her red locks
were caught up in a gentle breeze, swirling around her head
and shoulders. She was radiant in the light of a new day, an
uplifting symbol of resurrection.

Suddenly, alive with youthful vigor, Ben's steps quickened. His mind was clear. Renewed and refreshed, he

returned to Boudica. Both mounted and rode down the hill, surrounded by escorts. When they heard a voice calling from above them, both looked up. Both could see Fiona, glaring directly into the sunrise and waving her sword. The fullness of her beauty was revealed in the light, a regal beacon of hope, shining brightly, boldly facing the supreme challenge of another horrific day in her brave but very young life.

"She loves you, Ben," Boudica whispered.

They exchanged glances. Then Ben looked away, hanging onto his silence. As the two rode through the smoldering hell of Camulodunum, they were surrounded by hundreds of wagons and carts piled high with plunder, including the severed heads of men, women, and children with bloody faces, stuffed into gaps, peering outward without eyes. One was a young woman with dark flowing hair. Ben leaned over in his saddle vomiting in loud barks.

"What's wrong?" Boudica asked, her eyes wide with surprise.

"Everything," he replied, wiping his face with a forearm as they turned west along the Roman road to Londinium, following the masses, never looking back.

Chapter 28

As Ben and Boudica pressed on, toward Londinium, they looked back and noticed a small cloud of dust rising behind them. It was a single rider, spurring his horse like a wild man, moving toward them along the road from the east and weaving through the throng that followed them. They halted, reined their horses around, and continued to watch.

The rider closed the distance between them with the speed of a lightning bolt, then slid to a stop in an explosion of dirt and dust that temporarily obscured their vision.

When Ben could see the rider's face and was certain, he asked, *"What is it, Kale?"*

"It's the Ninth Legion, Ben. Our outriders have seen them. They're coming toward us from the northeast, down the Roman road. At the rate they're moving, they could hit our right flank by morning."

Ben turned to Boudica. "We've anticipated this. I recommend you continue on, my queen, to meet with Cogidubnus and deliver *this warning*. Paulinus must be headed our way from the west and has called for reinforcements. His advance must be accounted for as you finalize your plan for Londinium."

"It will," said Boudica. "We'll send scouts out to the west and anticipate his appearance at some point as we continue the march."

"Good," Ben replied. "We must stop the Ninth immediately before it closes in on us. Kale can lead me back to the covering force you've assigned for that mission. We will help your seconds there to move their groups into ambush positions tonight, along both sides of the road the Ninth will follow as they continue their march toward us. We'll win the day and bring the victors back to rejoin your forces long before Paulinus can threaten you and Cogidubnus."

"Done," said Boudica. "Neither you nor Kale need to worry about my relationship with Cogidubnus. Last night I remembered hearing my husband's recollections and his opinion of the man. Prasutagus told me that in the days when Claudius led the Romans here a few years ago, Cogidubnus's father gave up. He quickly discerned what was best for *him* and sold out to the Romans. For that, he was admired by Claudius. However, as time passed, other leaders in his tribe became outraged by the treatment *they* were getting from the Romans. They told him he would have to go *against* the Romans if he wanted to remain in power. Otherwise, they would overthrow him. So here is his son *now* joined with us. Like the father is the son. We cannot trust him, and we must expect that Cogidubnus will find a way to survive and prosper, one way or another. If we lose, I think he will find some way to blame me and side with the Romans, and if we win, he will find a way to destroy me and consolidate our tribes under *him* as king, perhaps in a confederation with Cunobelinus, who is of the same ilk and might speak *well* for him, with the Romans. I'll proceed with that firmly in mind until we meet again along the way to Londinium. But you must know, above all, I must do what I think is best for *our* people."

"And I should have known," Ben said, "you have discovered the nature of the serpent, and you will do what is best while I'm gone."

Then he saluted Boudica, turned his mount, and soon vanished with Kale, galloping into the massive cloud of dust and smoke that hung over the path to their first encounter with a mighty Roman legion.

The two rode close to one another along the way and soon left the road to avoid the oncoming masses. Before long, Kale sighted the location of the designated seconds. He rode directly into their midst and dismounted. Ben followed. A large group formed around them. Both seconds appeared, each representing divisions of about five thousand fighters in a combined force twice the size of the Ninth Legion's five thousand. Ben felt comfortable with the two-to-one odds. The number was adequate for an ambush, where the elements of surprise, shock, and instantaneous hand-to-hand combat could be employed. The closeness, violence, and speed of their initial assault would eliminate the Roman advantage with long and intermediate-range weapons and drive many legionnaires to ground before they could draw their short swords, thereby limiting the effect of Rome's most lethal and effective weapon.

The plan Ben outlined for the seconds and their subordinates was simple and direct. He would lead one division up the west side of the road, and Kale would lead the other up the east side, with each division moving in a single file formation behind their seconds, one warrior behind another until they spanned the same distance that a marching legion would cover along the road while moving in a line of cohorts comprised of four or five formations of centuries, one behind another. When the appropriate length was reached, Kale and Ben would halt their respective files, face them toward the road, then move them forward in the direction of the roadbed until they reached the point where both lines would be close enough to see each other, when looking across the road. At that point, they would stop and begin preparing their individual hiding positions. The lines would be long enough to ensure the Romans would be hit from both sides of the road at precisely the same time. None would be given the opportunity to escape. The entire legion would be surrounded the moment the ambush was sprung. The Celt warriors would adjust their positions in the lines, so they could not be seen from the road, and the ambush force would be firmly set in place. Mounted Celts would back up those on foot in the lines closest to the road, by riding back and forth behind them as the ambush was initiated, then overtaking and cutting down any Romans who managed to escape the onslaught. Ben and Kale knew from their experience that the trees on either side of the road were far enough apart to permit mounted mobility, yet close enough to conceal the ambush force from discovery by Romans coming down the road, even in daylight.

Ben and Kale had traveled down the same road on their way to scout Camulodunum. It was obvious. Their knowledge of the terrain and their clever plan left little to chance. Aided by moonlight, their movement into position was flawless. The trap was set; the men settled in. A night watch was activated to ensure nothing slipped by in the darkness, and the remainder of the night passed without incident, quiet except for the sounds of nocturnal animals and birds.

At sunrise, Kale and Ben adjusted their positions slightly to ensure they could see one another across the road. The seconds and their subordinates moved along both lines to make sure their warriors were well concealed with their weapons ready to charge, running in full force across the short distance between them and the Romans along the road. Kale had a ram's horn ready to blow when the last elements in the Roman column had passed his position and could easily be eradicated by the ambush force charging out of the forest and into the sides of the unsuspecting Romans as they marched down the road in formation. If the leading elements of the Roman column were about to march past the flanks of the ambush position on the far end, before that portion of the ambush force heard Kale's horn, the seconds *there* would initiate the ambush with a blast from *their* horn. Kale and Ben would then order required adjustments to compensate on their flanks by using mounted Celts held in reserve to attack any Romans who had not yet entered the death trap.

As the sun rose and beams of light began to penetrate the forest, the natural sounds increased. Word was sent down the lines to be particularly cautious and avoid any movement that might alert the oncoming Romans. Soon after the final preparations were completed, Ben and Kale began to feel the ground tremors and heard the increasing noise of foot and hoof falls coming from the anticipated direction of the Romans' approach. Final adjustments were made, and silent signals were relayed up and down the lines to alert all hands to the impending arrival of the leading Roman unit.

Then it came. The first Roman element. A group of five men moving slowly, looking carefully over the surface of the road for telltale prints or marks and stopping occasionally to listen for sounds of movement, unnatural noises, or deadly silence. Shortly after the point element passed, the first century of the first cohort moved into view, in close formation of four files abreast, with each file containing about twenty-five soldiers, one behind the other in full battle dress, carrying shields and javelins. One after another, the units passed, some including horses in gaps between units and all with weapons that Ben knew were typical of a light legion. When the ten cohorts of five centuries each had passed, a fully outfitted mounted unit came into view. It was Roman cavalry at its finest, a hundred men on horses in two files of fifty each.

Tension built as the riders passed. No ram's horn signal had sounded from the far end of the ambush.

Ben's heart began to pound.

He feared the Romans might hear the sound.

He held his breath.

When the last two horses were far enough down the road to be well inside the ambush, Ben rose slightly from his position and gave the final signal. Kale rose slowly from his prone position, raised the ram's horn to his lips, and blew a mighty blast that was quickly silenced by the deafening roar of ten thousand Celtic warriors running, screaming, and shouting as they crashed into the Roman column from both sides of the road, like the Red Sea of the Exodus rolling over the Israelites' Egyptian pursuers, upending, smashing, trampling, and crushing the legionnaires along the roadbed, horses and all, then slashing, stabbing, hacking and bludgeoning them to death.

Ben was on the road in a heartbeat, finishing downed Romans one after another without mercy until there were none left to kill, and his bloody sword was slipping from his grip. He stood fully upright to look down the road, now an endless field of mangled humanity, under the feet of Celts in swarming masses climbing and crawling through mounds of gore, finishing anything that moved, cutting and hacking plunder from the butchered bodies of five thousand young Romans, all dead or dying and covering the road bed with bloody corpses, for as far as Ben could see.

"My God and his wrath," Ben murmured, as he dropped to his knees, exhausted. "A massacre in moments, like locusts falling on a wheat field."

Chapter 29

Boudica saw two riders approaching in the twilight. Their horses were barely moving, plodding toward her along the road from the east. Both riders appeared to be dead or asleep. Their heads were bending low and bobbing. When their horses stopped in front of her, Boudica recognized the faces, stained with streaks of muddy blood. Her eyes opened wide. A smile touched her lips. She inhaled deeply then sighed with relief and rejoicing.

"It was a massacre," Ben whispered, lifting his head to face her. "We've destroyed the Ninth Legion…except for some cavalry…a few riders…might've escaped the pursuit of *our* mounted warriors."

Boudica paused to regain her composure, then responded, "So Suetonius Paulinus is left with two legions he can count on, some cavalry, a long-range weapons support group, and any auxiliaries he might be able to round up along the way. Is that it?"

"Exactly," Ben responded. "Have you heard any more…about him and his plan?"

"I have. He reached Londinium with his cavalry, then hurried back to the west, after warning the colony we were coming. He apparently understands he can't defend the settlement given our numbers. Its commercial value is growing, but not enough to justify the risk at this point. Both

Londinium, then Verulamium to the north, are ours for the taking. After that, we'll have to find Paulinus and deal with him in what I hope to be our final battle. It seems he won't try to stand in our way until his remaining forces are nearer to ours, perhaps north of Verulamium. The inhabitants of that city are primarily Celts who've been won over in client arrangements. The Trinovantes hate them as much as they hate those who occupy Londinium. Both places might be turned into hellish blood baths, but there's nothing I can do to prevent that. My people are too confident after what we've done. They won't want to stop until they have driven the Romans into the sea that surrounds us. I can't bear to see any more slaughters like the one in Camulodunum, Benjamin. My plan is to remain in close proximity to our main force, with a small security detachment for my entourage, so I can be close to my seconds, until I know what to expect from Paulinus. I believe we've lost many warriors to the looting. I estimate we can still count on a force of two hundred thousand, or so, going forward, split evenly between our warriors and those of the Trinovantes. We'll strike together, side by side in both Londinium and Verulamium. Our Iceni forces will stay to the east of the main road, the Trinovantes will stay to the west, as we approach and attack both of those settlements."

"I think that's wise," Ben observed. "It should prevent our forces from intermingling with the Trinovates like they did during the attack on Camulodunum, and it should also enable your seconds to better control their warriors as they march and move into their assembly areas. Control will be even more important when our scouts report we are close to contact, and our clash with Paulinus is imminent. Cogidubnus will probably have his way when we strike the settlements, just as he did in Camulodunum. At this point, we're compelled to let that be. But our meeting with Paulinus *after Verulamium* is the one we must be especially well prepared for. In that encounter, we'll be engaged with a well-armed and well-trained mass of cohesive and disciplined Roman soldiers. If they outmaneuver us at the onset, we could be destined for defeat."

"I agree," said Boudica.

"If you no longer need him here, Kale should go rest now."

"Please proceed carefully, Kale," she replied as he departed in silence, waving farewell.

When Kale had disappeared in the distance, Ben turned to Boudica.

"I must gather and prepare some volunteers with horses to ride back through Camuldunum," Ben continued, "to make sure no one is following you and reinforcements aren't coming across the channel to Paulinus, from Gaul. We should send that mounted force out at first light. At the same time, I must go northwest to find Paulinus, so he doesn't catch you by surprise as you concentrate on Londinium and Verulamium. At the rate of march we calculated for the majority of his forces, I believe I'll find him outside of striking range, north of Verulamium. You should be safe, up to that point."

"It's wise, Benjamin. Do what you've proposed. But one thing more. I want to spend this night with you before you leave."

Ben hesitated. Never before had she looked at him as she did then.

"It's not what you think," she responded.

Ben attempted to mask the passion revealed in his gaze. "What I think wouldn't be proper to say."

"I'm flattered, Ben. However, I understand what you value. Perhaps later for us. In the right way that you follow. But for now, it would be enough if you would read, and tell me more, about the writings you hold in your care."

He stared into her eyes, into the depths of her soul. Boudica had seen hell, and she needed to know more about heaven.

"I understand, Queen Boudica. I'll be close by, awaiting your call."

Ben had just dozed off when a soft voice awakened him. It was Fiona whispering in his ear. Her breath aroused him. He raised himself on one elbow. They had never been this close. He gazed at her. She had come to him as a woman, much more than an excited girl. He was captivated by the power of her attraction. He pulled back with a lurch that surprised her.

"What's wrong?" she asked. "Did I frighten you? It's only me, Benjamin. Just Fiona."

Ben recovered and sat upright. "Believe me, Fiona, I know it's you," Ben replied after forcing a cough to hide a nervous quiver in his voice.

"I'm sorry I disturbed you. My mother wants you, and so do I. Isolda is also waiting, along with Kale and Quintus. The Druid has left to meet with others in the Trinovantes' camp. Please take my hand and follow me closely."

Ben grabbed his pack in one hand, grasped Fiona's hand with the other, and followed her form as she led him through the darkness to the circle of firelight where Boudica waited.

When all were seated around the fire, Boudica looked around the circle, greeted each with a nod, and began to speak.

"We march west to Londinium tomorrow. Then north to Verulamium, while Benjamin rides northwest to find Paulinus. I'll take Fiona and Isolda with me. Kale will drive our chariot. Quintus will stay with us, helping with his knowledge of what the Romans might do in the aftermath of the onslaught that's launched our rebellion. If our success continues beyond Verulamium, other tribes will join us. That could bring Roman reinforcements into our land to stop us, or it might bring total victory in a united effort, especially if their emperor decides to abandon the conquest here for better opportunities elsewhere. The tide of battle is taking us to Londinium and Verulamium where the Trinovantes have scores to settle with the Romans and other client Celts who have robbed their lands and abused them terribly. Our early move to a client kingdom forestalled the same treatment for us, but it's lately come back in full force under Nero's rule. If we can win this round and beat Paulinus in the next, we'll take back the south. There are existing client arrangements in the north that might then turn to us, as soon as our victory over Paulinus is known. If we can wipe out Paulinus together, our island will have few Roman soldiers remaining. At that point, we can consolidate and repel Roman reinforcements if they come. I feel that we're on the evening of a shift in the balance of power. The coming days will decide the fate of our land and our people for *a very long time.* I also feel we need some special power as we approach this trial. That's why I've asked Benjamin to talk with us tonight, so we might not only know better how to deal with our Druid leanings with prayer and sacrifices, but also determine what help might be available to us as a result of what Ben can bring through greater knowledge of the power that *his* God has given him. He seeks the will of his divine instead of relying on his own, when attempting to get good outcomes for those who are in desperate need. The Romans are after Ben's people just as they are with us. We may be able to join in a worship that could bid well for Celts and Jews alike who are resisting the Roman expansion into their lands and their attempts to dominate, enslave, or annihilate us in the process."

Ben had listened carefully to everything Boudica said. He knew he had a challenge. He asked himself how it might be done and prayed for guidance as he waited. It would take time, but there was no other way. Time would end with the coming dawn, and those gathered around him might be dead by the next.

"I'm thankful you've asked me to speak, Queen Boudica. In times like these, we *do* need to consider this thing we call religion. And since some of you haven't been present for *all* of the discussions we've recently had, I'll try to repeat ideas and key aspects you might've missed."

Then he paused for a moment, gathered his thoughts, inhaled deeply, and continued.

"To me, religion is simply a set of beliefs concerning the cause, the nature, and the purpose of our universal experience, particularly when considering the Creation of it all by a transcendent, supreme power, and our inherent sensing of a need to relate to that supreme power through devotional and ritual observances, and a moral code of conduct for our relationships with that power and our fellow human beings. Most religions seem to have much in common; however, my religion is rather unique in that my people have, for thousands of years, recognized only *one* supreme power, a Godhead and Creator who's the Father of all of us, *his children*. We believe that our Father is spiritual. He dwells in an ideal place, beyond the limits of our ability to comprehend, and beyond the limits of our universe. When I look out at the stars, and all else that surrounds us on this night, I naturally contemplate. I think about things that seem to be connected to that Being, and I feel Its presence deep within me. That presence reaches me through its power, its Spirit. It's the power that created all things visible, like the stars, and some things we might *not* be able to see, like our minds. Let's just say, all we know and all that we do not know. It's infinite and everlasting. We have called it 'God' and refer to that God as 'him' as a result of my peoples' tradition of placing ultimate responsibility on men, whose God-given nature included unique attributes, including the seed that produces the breed and generation of the children of women who are equal in all things that truly matter and superior in some ways that *truly matter* most in the mind of the preexisting being *that connects 'his' Spirit*...his power to do and create all things that animate our essence...*to the 'souls'* we men and women are created with, along with our bodies. Our bodies *contain* our souls while we're here on earth. When we *die,* our soul continues to live. It's everlasting. God's will for us, for our souls, is all about loving him and our fellow human beings. My people recognized him, but they strayed from him many times, because of the free will he gave them to choose between right and wrong. When times were good, my people chose to turn away. They felt they didn't need him. They began to sin against his will by violating a set of rules, 'Commandments' he had given them, to respect and follow. To *not follow* those rules was to 'sin,' meaning, behavior to be avoided. For example, one of those rules involved the love we've been given to share with God, the giver, and with others around us. Another word for that *love* is *charity*. Charity calls for us to help others, to treat them with kindness and respect. The sins of my people, their lack of charity, their straying to other gods, that encouraged them to kill or harm one another in reprehensible ways, and their seeking of other evils to satisfy themselves, were terrible mistakes! Those *diversions* actually took away their happiness and caused pain and sadness. In their distress, they would turn back to God for help, promising that if he did as they asked, they would be faithful to him, they would love and respect him and follow his rules in return. But when they continued sin without love, God decided to show them the ultimate act of love by sending them an aspect of himself, in the form of an incarnate divine we call 'Jesus Christ,' the Anointed One, the Savior. That savior, that 'Messiah' was foretold by our prophets for thousands of years and recorded in a library of Holy Scriptures my people have read and followed throughout their history. Jesus *was* that Savior. He was born to a woman by the power of God's Holy Spirit and lived with my people for some years. During the latter part of that time, he told those who gathered around him about God's words. Jesus reminded his followers to obey the *Ten Commandments*, which I will read in detail to you later… and to love one another as God loves us. He then gave his life, made *a sacrifice for us,* by allowing himself to be turned over to the Romans by our high priests, and be tried and crucified by the Romans, with the help of some of my people who *did not* believe in him and were afraid he might try to usurp the *power* they had accumulated over the course of many years."

"Excuse me, Ben," said Boudica. "It sounds like they were much the like our Druids."

"Precisely, Queen Boudica. Jesus *was not* what he was accused of. He was not a blasphemer, a Zionist, a rebel, or a person who would encourage sedition against the Roman Empire. He said repeatedly that his life would be a sacrifice for us in order to pay for all the sins committed since the beginning of our time, and he would be our advocate for forgiveness of future sins, if we *repented* by admitting and being truly sorry for those sins, be redeemed, and spend the rest of our lives doing our best *not* to repeat them, and loving one another as he loved us. Then he would lead us to everlasting life with God, the Creator, the Father of us all if we would *simply* follow his example and live according to God's will for our *happiness!* Jesus also performed many miracles, as described by John in the bundle I have, but the greatest of all was after he was crucified for love of us. He died and was buried but rose from the dead to be alive and seen again several times by John and his other close followers, called Apostles. *No one else has ever done that!*

"Jesus was sent by God to *show us* that our souls were everlasting and would live beyond our material, earthly bodies when they perished and our souls where freed to return to our Creator. He was killed on a 'cross' that was invented by a people know as Phoenicians. The Romans used horrifying death on those two pieces of wood to punish and frighten their enemies. People who follow Jesus refer to it as the Tree of Everlasting Life, and I've learned that many Greeks, and other people who live far to the east of my land, embrace essentially the same beliefs about their souls and the afterlife. When Jesus had completed his mission, he *did not* tell his apostles to fight the Romans to get revenge for his death, or to persecute the Jews for their role in causing that outcome. Instead, he gave them a commission to share with all people everywhere 'the good news' he brought, then said farewell, he would see them again and ascended into heaven, to return to our Father, the Godhead, as they watched him leave this world and fade away in the distant blue sky. Jesus also said he would send our Father's Holy Spirit to them, to be with them always, and even help *us* if we *asked for his help*. Those men and others, including me, have received the Holy Spirit, alive and working in our spirits, as a result of our belief in Jesus and the Godhead who sent him. I'm now referred to as a follower of Jesus Christ, the Anointed One. I' m therefore a Christian…as we have been called by others in Syria… and I have been 'born again' out of Judaic roots from the same Godhead, living with Jesus and God's Holy Spirit, according to his will as it was revealed by Jesus in his *words* to guide us to a new and better way. I no longer fear death. I will try my best to help whomever I can. I know I will live a better life on this earth by seeking the power of the Holy Spirit to help me avoid temptation and live according to God's moral absolutes to go happily from this life to the next, just as Jesus did *and promised for us.*"

Then Ben paused, deep in thought. He had talked long, but all were still with him, eyes on him, listening intently. They too realized this might be their last night together.

"I know that I've said a great deal," Ben continued. "However, it seemed to be necessary. Some of you *had not* heard those words in the past. I repeated them for you as carefully and as thoroughly as I am able to do as a man…at this point in *my* journey. Perhaps I should stop now."

"No! No apology is needed, Ben," Boudica protested. "It's exactly what we need at this time in our lives. These are things we should know and consider very seriously as we go forward from this place. I have realized the kingdom of your god is beyond all I previously could imagine. I am a queen. My husband had a kingdom. He is gone. It is mine now. It is small but important. I'm sacrificing and suffering a great deal for it. But it too will be gone someday, and so will I. Please proceed as you wish."

All nodded in agreement, without any hesitation, and Ben proceeded.

"I think I should emphasize that my people have worshipped one God since the beginning of their time. I had no choice when I was born. I was the first son of my father, and by custom, everything they owned would be passed on to me when they died. I would be responsible for everything, including the protection of my siblings, my wife, and their material and spiritual welfare. I've lived with my religion, called Judaism, all of my life, just as you have with your faiths, Queen Boudica…you and your daughters, and

Kale, with Druidism, and you, Quintus with Roman poly-theism. I was raised on the notion that the Godhead, the Great Spirit, was also our Almighty Father and Creator. For me, that means I believe God created us and all that we see around us. *Everything!* And I believe like the Greeks that every result has a cause. In other words, to me it is rational and logical that we, along with all we know and see, must've been caused by a preexisting power unlike any-thing *we've* actually experienced. So I must ask. Do you think it's an *idea* you might consider? Could it be possible that there's a transcendent Being who has existed forever, eternally, and has the power to cause the results we see, hear, touch, taste, smell, and know in our minds, *or* do you believe there was *absolutely nothing* and out of that nothing, all of this just happened? If you believe that something can come out of nothing, it might be impossible for me to take you beyond that belief given my human limitations, at this time. Perhaps it might be a waste of *your* time to listen fur-ther to anything I have to add."

"I'm open to the possibilities you're suggesting," said Boudica. "As you know, we have many gods. They were *given power* by people like our Druids. Then came the Romans who believe their king, their emperor, is a god. In light of all that and what your actions have shown us, why would I *not* consider what you have to say, Ben?"

"Very well, my queen," Ben responded.

"Queen Boudica," Quintus interjected, "I think my emperors recently decided *themselves* that they would be gods. For example, Nero has declared Claudius to be a god and had a temple built in Camulodunum to worship him. Claudius was a man. He has died. He has *not been* resurrected. His temple has been destroyed. Jesus referred to himself as a temple. He told those who threatened him that if they destroyed him, he'd be rebuilt in three days. That is exactly what came to pass! He *was* resurrected, in three days' time."

"Amen," said Ben.

"Nero is a man, only a man," Quintus added. "Nero set up Claudius as a divinity so that he could be his successor, *to be himself a god of his own making.*"

"So you don't believe Nero is a god-man, like Jesus?"

"No, Queen Boudica. I do not. Men decide who their next emperor will be. Nero is the emperor because Claudius was his uncle. Many believe Nero, or his mother, poisoned Claudius. If the latter was indeed the culprit, it would mean that Claudius was killed by his sister. Nero proclaimed that Claudius was a god and then claimed that he was therefore a god as well. Claudius hasn't risen from the dead, like Jesus did. Nero will not. Roman emperors are men selected by men out of a corruption that cannot last forever."

"I think the same, Queen Boudica," said Ben. "I find it quite amusing that in the Latin language, the name 'Caesar' comes from the word for *hairy.*"

"That is true," added Quintus, "and *none of them* have created anything! Other men do the work. Just as it was with the Egyptians."

"My people were slaves of the Egyptians," added Ben. "They built many things for the Egyptians. The Egyptian gods did not help *their* people, but the God of Israel did indeed help his, during their escape from slavery. What do you think about all of this, Fiona and Isolda?"

"I'm not sure about the Egyptians," said Fiona. "But I *do not* believe that something can come out of nothing, *without a cause*. My mind will not accept that."

"I'm the same as my sister," said Isolda, "and I'm unsure about our gods. I can't understand why, when the Druids do all they do for our gods, those gods would allow what's been done to us by the Romans. I know what happened to me was not your fault, Quintus. You're different. Even our Druids do horrible things, and many people think it's right and good."

"You're right, Isolda. I'm a different man *now*," Quintus responded. "I've compared the Jesus we talk about to my emperors. What they think is good often becomes *an abomination*. Jesus exceeds them in ways that appeal to my soul, my essence, my heart, and my mind. I was and still am a witness to Jesus and a true believer. Jesus healed my servant, and I have *seen* him do the same with others. He also spoke the words that rang true for me. If we were all like him, things would be much different. He talked about the God who sent him and derived his power to heal and perform many miracles. He spoke directly about the Father's will for of his children. Jesus did it all in ways that went straight to my mind, my heart, and my soul. He did it like no others. No others I've seen or imagined. Can you imagine what this world would be like if everyone did what he asks? I wish others would dwell on that and compare it to what we have *now!*"

Fiona rose to her full height. She looked at Quintus. Her eyes reflected embers glowing in the dying fire. "Are you saying that *you're* one of the direct eyewitnesses, like those Benjamin knows?"

Quintus looked up at Fiona, smiling in reply. "I am, and I know of many others who are, but are too afraid or too proud to admit it."

Fiona stood firm. She continued to stare at Quintus, then turned to the woodpile and replenished the fire. As the flames burst into new light, she stepped into her place without a sound and was seated.

Ben was certain her soul had been touched.

He glanced at Boudica. She and the others were silent as well.

"Quintus mentioned the soul," Ben continued. "I'm wondering if you have a concept of that. My people believe that there's a body and a soul. Many Greeks believed the same. The soul is what matters. It's the spiritual part of us and the vessel of our being. Once created by God, our souls live forever after our bodies die and await resurrection. Jesus showed men that. After he was crucified by the Romans, he was buried but rose again to be seen by my friend John and many others. Nothing like that has ever happened in the history of my people. For thousands of years, their prophets predicted the coming of such an indestructible being, *to save them*. Jesus was the *One*. But most did not realize it fully, until all of these things happened. John was with him in all the great things, the miracles and the mysteries, until he rose into the heavens to return to the Father. John and the others were there as well. They were simple men who received the power of the Father through Jesus and were willing to die horrible deaths gladly professing their *absolute belief* in their Godhead…the source of the Holy Spirit's power to create, to make, and do all things."

"I ask you then, Queen Boudica, Fiona, Isolda, and Kale. Do you think these things could be possible?"

"I've always felt there was a power, out there in the void, that was so much *bigger than me*," said Boudica. "I think the notion was part of me and dwelled in me from birth. When I began to be schooled by the Druids, my parents, and others, I was told of our gods. Their words accounted for much and satisfied me for a time. When I had my children and fully realized what they'd been born into, what the Druids urged us all to do in the name of the religion they practiced daily, and saw the results, I began to doubt. Right before he died, my husband was beginning to feel the same. He told me about his sadness regarding all of the sacrifices, the torture, the hideous things like the Wicker Man they crowded human sacrifices into and burned."

"I think I know," Ben interjected. "It was after my wife's death and the mass crucifixions I witnessed. It came to me. 'How can this be?' I asked. And the answer was that God gave man free will. Mankind chose to know about evil at a time long ago when everything was good. God had given them fair warning. That choice was passed on from generation to generation in a tragic legacy. Some chose evil of the kind we discussed, *the sins*. Many who made that choice have created a hell of sorts for others who chose good and tried to live their lives in a different way, like Jesus talked about and demonstrated when He was with us."

"What did Jesus say about that way?" Fiona asked.

"He spoke for the Father of us all, Fiona, as if he was a brother," Ben responded. "He said the greatest of all things we can do is to love the Father, Our Creator, the Godhead, above all things, as he loves us and love one another as Jesus did in his example, by putting others first and being charitable toward them…by being kind and helpful and doing what's best for them, helping them to avoid the bad things that cause harm. He also held up the ancient law of our people, the Ten Commandments I've mentioned, telling John and the others not to kill, not to steal, and not to be jealous of others who might have what we *do not*. He said that those who inherit the Kingdom of God are the poor in spirit, those who mourn, those who are meek, those who hunger and thirst for the right, those who are merciful and clean of heart, the peacemakers and those who are persecuted for the sake of righteousness. All of those would have eternal life with the Father. He spoke words from the Father as the Father's only Son, who inherited the power of the Great Spirit of our Father and Creator. It's as though some of the things I was required to do by my parents as a good citizen, and what you do as a good Celt, and all those things I tried to do in order to be a good Jew, were in conflict with much of what Jesus advocated," added Ben. "As a good Jew, I followed the details of the law to the letter, but lived in luxury and looked down upon those Jesus wanted to help the most but were avoided as unclean by many of the highest religious leaders. Some of them even helped to get Jesus crucified as a blasphemer and revolutionary, a threat to Roman authority. If Jesus and his followers were truly rebels, it was not in the temporal sense. The Jewish religious leaders probably thought of them as rebels simply because they were not afraid to share the truth Jesus was speaking at the behest of the God of Israel. One of the wisest was the mentor of Paul and *my teacher* as well. At the risk of his own death, Gamaliel the Elder told them they best be careful lest their persecution of Jesus turn into a persecution of their own God, the same God whom Jesus represented when he continued to emphasize that strict obedience to the laws of man is not what saves us. Men will make many laws, but abiding by God's law of faith, hope, and love is the only law with the power to save us. Jesus was sent by God in order to set the record straight and help us prepare for the journey of everlasting life."

"Yes, and what if everyone lived like that, like Jesus, whom they persecuted? Look at what the Romans did to me," said Isolda, opening her robe to show her scarred back. "I've been destroyed by men who do just the opposite and from that they gain satisfaction and power for themselves. And look down there, in Camulodunum. See the remains of women who suffered horribly from our own Druids, and others, with lust for revenge, *on my behalf.* It was *the last thing* I wanted, but they persisted, and others joined in, even some of our women participated because they thought it was the *right thing* to do."

"But that is the rub, Isolda," said Ben. "Upon hearing what you just said, I'm reminded of the sorrow I have felt for people, especially women, who turn to evil as children...those who are born with innocence, with a blank slate in their tiny minds, and do not have the advantages I did as a Jew with the long history of my people. I've been searching my mind and realized, for as long as I can remember, I have always had a feeling about what was good and what was bad. When I did things that were bad, I think *I knew* they were bad, at some level. But if my parents did not correct me, I would do the same thing again because it satisfied an urge I had. It bothered me somewhat, but it also excited me. It gave me a feeling of pleasure I wanted to repeat…until my parents, or one of my teachers scolded me. Then I would feel even worse, because I wanted them to like me…to love me. The feeling, the sense I got from their intervention stayed in my mind. It reminded me. It confirmed that the pleasure I enjoyed had consequences I wanted to avoid in the future. So the next time my human nature caused me to have the same urge, I would stop and think about what I was about to do. I *knew* it was wrong, and the memory of the consequences I suffered the last time helped me to overcome the urge because the consequences were more than I wanted to bare. Just think about the less fortunate child who does a bad thing and instead of suffering the consequences is rewarded continuously, and in time cultivates a mind-set that hardens and overcomes any feeling of guilt. Even a healthy mind will eventually submit and go on feeling pleasure, seeing good in what is truly, terribly bad. The real power and the true wisdom are lost to them. When we realize God is our Father and we are his children, it's a good thing for us and everyone we touch.

"What then is the real power?" asked Boudica as she hastened to help Isolda cover herself.

"It's to make our souls free to soar with energy from the Holy Spirit and *not* be slaves to the things that are bad for us and for others. Always consider the other man, the other woman. Do only what is good for you and for others, and like Jesus, you will rise from the dead and live forever with him and the Father in the glorious heaven they have created for all whom Jesus mentioned in his beatitudes. Those who will be truly free men and women on earth, because they are free of sin and full of God's grace, his *promise*, and his power. They seek the true happiness God created for us to enjoy, the true happiness that can never be realized fully and sustained during the external quest for image, status, and money. Instead they seek internal peace. They know their souls will live forever, just as Jesus promised, and they will be taken up to the Godhead in the end of this life because he loves them, and they have returned his love by living the best way of life, in accordance with his will. It is best for him, and it is best for us. Those who choose *not* to love him in return could *be risking* their eternal lives… never experiencing the joy of forever being in the splendor of his presence…*instead* dwelling in the darkness we see in the evil that's allowed to exist in this world, except in those very rare places where we *might* be able to preserve God's internal graces for those of his children who seek him. In order to do that, we must change by seeking to be in places where we can be 'the children' God wants us to be, *not the alternative*. Even on this earth, we can avoid temptation by focusing our efforts on spiritual virtues like those in the beatitudes… The attitudes we can cultivate for the sake of genuine happiness truly everlasting, enriched by a closer relationship with Jesus, walking in his footsteps, following his example, to the very best of our ability."

"I hear your words regarding what others who've been with Jesus have passed on to you. Your words fill my heart with new life," said Fiona. "People have told me that I'm high-spirited. I think that means I have a big life force in my body. I want that force to be strong enough to help me grow right as a woman, help others of like mind to do the same, and fulfill my life with them.

"It would be a good path to take, Fiona," Ben replied, with an expression reflecting his agreement, and a hint of pleasant surprise at her revelation.

"Thank you, Benjamin," Fiona responded. "And I also hear you saying I can have an even-greater life force in my everlasting being, a force that's alive in my soul, enabling me to be with this loving God, his Son, and their Spirit, inside me forever, with complete satisfaction and contentment and *joy*?"

"Yes," Ben replied. "That is what I truly *believe*, Fiona. You've just described the life with the Holy Trinity, three divine aspects of our Godhead in community, acting as one in love and communication in a beautiful relationship for all who believe and go on living the life *you* desire. Life as it should be. And in times like these, when we are compelled to fight, we seek God's mercy and his willingness to forgive. In this moment, we are preparing to face the unknown. We wonder, what will the outcome be? We don't know the answer at this point in our lives. But we will go forward to find out. And the best we can do when we face the unknown is to maintain the strength our faith gives us and trust in God, come hell or high water, so one way or another, we'll be with him at the end…be that today… tomorrow, or *whenever* he calls us, to come home."

"That is what I want!" Fiona cried out. "Even if I have to leave my home here and go to another land to find and preserve a place where I can do that. I'm young. That is what I want. If I have to escape evil by fighting through it, I will die trying to find the right way in a place I can seek to be virtuous and strive to be holy for the rest of my life!"

The firelight was fading, its warm glow replaced by the chill of a new day's dawn.

"I agree," said Kale as he stood up and departed quietly, to put a saddle on Ben's trustworthy servant in waiting.

Chapter 30

As Ben rode west, he was thinking. It seemed to be a life-time or more since Boudica had saved *his* life. Now he was going back toward the Druid Grove to locate the remaining Roman legions and discern Suetonius Paulinus's intent, for her sake. She had been one of the unfortunate children he talked about in their recent meeting. She wanted to have that meeting, knowing it might be her last. And Ben might not return from this errand. But that did not matter to him. His thoughts would be spent wondering how best to help her. He must face the unknown and find the answer to a number of very important questions in time to save her. Had General Paulinus received news of his decimated legion and the massacre at Camulodunum? Had he sensed that more massacres were imminent? Had he completed his mission at the grove, as Cogidubnus reported? If so, how long would it be and how many men would Paulinus finally muster before he decided it was time to face Boudica's fury?

The Roman general must know he would be vastly outnumbered given the present strength of his forces in Britton. There had been no indication that reinforcements would arrive from the mainland in time to join the inevitable showdown, as far as Ben knew. So what terrain would Paulinus select for the battle? Where could it be, and what might it look like? And what tactics would he employ to offset his numerical disadvantage? Ben was also wondering about Boudica's ability to control her forces when arrayed against the Romans. He had the gnawing feeling that in spite of the precautions she had discussed, the Trinovantes would set the tone for Londinium, and subsequent encounters, just as they had done at Camulodunum. If that happened, Boudica would be responsible for the outcome, but Cogidubnus and his seconds would, in fact, be controlling the action when the engagement began and the mayhem started.

On the other hand, the Romans had the discipline, the protection, and the weaponry to prevail against savage hordes outnumbering them. They had proven it repeatedly wherever their empire chose to expand its influence. Ben began to feel the nausea. A stark reality was emerging in his mind. It was affecting his nerves. His mind was plagued with visions and various possibilities, all portending dreadful consequences.

He reined in his horse and dismounted out of sight from the road. Light was beginning to filter through the boughs of the lofty hardwoods. The forest was still.

"Dear God, our Almighty Father and Creator," Ben prayed out loud. "Please stay with me." His lips were trembling, his brows knitted in a curious reflection of his fear, anxiety, and uncertainty about everything that was closing around him and a handful of imperiled people who had grown to trust him and were depending on his help. They hoped he would come to their aid like a savior, with plans and actions that enabled them to continue with some degree of confidence that their efforts might not be in vain, and something good might be their reward in the outcome.

"I praise you," Ben continued. "I thank you, Father. I return the love you have shown unto me. You have enabled me to survive thus far, thereby proving you *do* care. So please send your Holy Spirit into my spirit. Raise me to the level of this challenge, so I might serve well those I care for most. Allow me to adequately care for them, thus, their lives will truly be in your hands, and their souls will survive to soar beyond this life regardless of outcomes in the foreseeable future, according to your will. And allow them to someday realize the dream articulated by Fiona, last night, before our parting. For all of this I say, and for all of this I pray in the name of our Lord and Savior, Jesus Christ, in the glory of the Holy Spirit, who comes from you through him who died, so that they might be redeemed and delivered safely, whenever *their time* arrives."

In retrospect, Ben thought it interesting that he had mentioned Fiona. He had marveled at her impassioned statement. She was truly willing to die, trying her best to find the *right* way. Her words had touched his heart, casting her as a kindred spirit. *How strange it was,* he mused, that his initial impression of her was reforming in his mind. Something deeply subconscious was now rising to the forefront in words that had been formed spiritually, fully present in his thoughts, and ready to activate in conscious awareness.

As he ended his meditation, Ben felt the presence of another. He turned to look back along the roadbed, and saw a shadow, a fleeting movement. Someone, or *something*, was stalking him. He dismounted hastily and led his horse farther away from the road.

When Ben was deep in the protection of thick vegetation, he parted the branches of a small oak and could see well beyond his location. There was a small clearing illuminated by sunlight. If his follower entered that space, he would be able to see clearly and discern the best course of action, to fight or take flight.

After a reasonable time had elapsed, Ben concluded that the stalker had avoided the open area and was circling around it, to cut his tracks and continue to follow him. He swallowed hard. The follower was surely a very good scout. With more respect and keenly cautious, Ben tied his horse's reins around a tree trunk, left it to graze as a decoy, and began to seek a better vantage point, hoping to regain sight of his follower.

When a branch snapped behind him, he turned toward the sound. A blue flash, the weight of a flying body hit hard, on his side, knocking the air out of his lungs and propelling his left shoulder into the hard bark of an unmoving tree. The impact spun Ben's body around. He fell backward onto soft grass. The body was on his chest, muscular, pressing him down. He must escape, wrestling with flying arms and legs, preventing his escape, holding him down. The skin was smooth, moist with perspiration, covered with blue dye. Perhaps a Celtic warrior. But grappling, with breasts, beneath a soft neck, and broad shoulders. His rage was inflamed. Days, weeks and months of anger, abstinence, and tension exploded in a frenzy, pulling him into the seamless contact of two bodies, in the heat of battle, and the overpowering rush for survival, then heat joined in passion pounding, joined, until the moment of paralyzing pleasure and release in a new state of consciousness, oblivion, without a sound. Every ounce of energy was depleted. Two bodies finally separated, slowly, lying silently side by side, blind, and struggling to breathe back all that was lost in the spontaneous chaos. Two minds grasping the implications of the complete satisfaction and peace.

Their eyes met, in recognition. Neither moved, locked in a daze, feeling euphoria, in near disbelief of the power unleashed in their desperate attempts to control one another. Their intent at first contact, the fear, the instinctive struggle of predator and prey, was fading, leaving them alone, but still together, alive, and basking in an aura of contentment, restrained, until Ben began to laugh softly, then louder and louder. Fiona's lips extended to a grin, then a smile. She began to giggle, as soft laughter bubbled from deep within her, bursting in a torrent of shrill howling, a sound that could only made by a feral woman, again and again, then embracing, *both* laughing in the throes of an all-consuming splendor, giving everything—mind, body, soul, and spirit—in complete surrender.

In the gloaming, they were at rest. She in deep slumber, her limbs still entangled with his, her face resting on his chest. A chill was in the air, but her body was warm. He, in a state of wondrous bliss, wanting to remain there, forever.

As she began to stir, looking up at him, still smiling, Ben began to deal with the reality. *She was Fiona.* The mystery of their joining in such an impossible, unimaginable way was weighing on his mind as he slowly returned to conscious awareness of place, time, and circumstance.

"Fiona?" he whispered.

"Yes, Ben," she responded through moist lips, moving lightly over his chest.

"My God!" he exclaimed. "It *is you!*"

"Yes…it is, Ben. Have I caused you to sin?" Fiona asked, with obvious trepidation. "If it's a sin, I am…*so sorry*. It was *not* my intent."

"How could *this* be a sin?" Ben responded.

"You don't know?"

"I'm lost, Fiona."

"Then please hold me, at least until you know. It's all that I need."

As the darkness of night closed in all around them, Ben sheltered her in his arms and silently prayed to his God, until a question formed in his overworked mind.

"Why did you follow me, Fiona? Why did you stalk me and take me down like an animal on the kill?"

"You left me no choice, Ben."

"What do you mean?" he uttered, looking down at her with an expression of complete confusion, a puzzlement, that left him struggling for some understanding of the young savage he was trying so hard to know, for a reason so difficult to comprehend.

"I'm not certain about what I've felt since the first time I saw you, Benjamin," Fiona finally whispered as she moved her body to gaze directly into his eyes. Even in the darkness, he could see the glow of intensity in her eyes, a blue-green radiance, hypnotic, completely open, and inviting, with transparent depth, haunting, yet drawing him into her immortal soul.

"When you rode away to face the Romans, for my mother and me, I realized I could not live any longer…

without you. I had no choice but to follow you and find you, and be with you, even 'til death. I *know* my death will come soon. But it cannot be without you, far away from you, able only to think of you, to wonder if you still lived…if you could rush back to me *alive,* so I could see you one more time, to perhaps find some way to tell you that everything I am and everything I have is yours for the taking, *forever.*"

Ben was losing something of himself and his way. He was desperate, struggling to retain all he thought he was, in the midst of a profound confusion that was beginning to challenge the core of his very existence, his identity, and all that he believed about himself.

"So you tracked me into this hell, to say *that?*"

"Yes. When I thought you knew I was following you and you might escape and I would lose your trail, I panicked. I had to do *something.* I had to act. It would be my last chance. When I circled and saw you waiting, I went for you fast, to stop you, *any way* I could, but with *no intent* to harm you."

"Shush, shush," Ben whispered. He was moved, beyond words, unable to speak.

"I'm sorry, Benjamin. I couldn't help it. I've caused you to sin. And now you mourn. I can feel your tears, falling on my hands, as I touch your face. Please forgive me."

He reached out to her, as gently as he could. His hands were shaking, as his fingers carefully stroked her hair, touched her cheeks, and felt her soft breath. As their lips touched again, Ben felt a flood of warm tears mingling with his.

There were no words in any language to describe the dynamics lifting Ben's spirit. It was rising and reaching, soaring in a state of spiritual joy he could only imagine before. It could only be *the love* that Fiona had shown for him in the revelation of her perfection as an iconic embodiment of everything God must have felt and intended to portray, when he first uttered the word *love* at the completion of his most blessed and beautiful masterpiece.

Chapter 31

The morning light was filtering through tree limbs, landing softly on two forms entwined as one on a bed of meadow grass. Birds were greeting the dawn with enthusiasm, causing Ben to stir. His eyes opened, then closed, blinking to reveal an awakening he would rather avoid, feeling Fiona, still on his chest, her breathing rising and falling, peacefully sleeping. He was touched by her stillness, captured in a compelling vision too wonderous to disturb.

"Fiona, the day awaits. We must go," he finally whispered. "I'll bring up our mounts, then find a stream where you can bathe, and we can water our horses."

"That would be good," she responded.

"Do you have any clothing in your saddlebag?"

"I do," she replied, rubbing her eyes and drawing her hair away from her face.

Ben gazed upon her form. Serenity, adoration, and a sense of lingering pleasure was reflected in his smile. She was stunning in the worst of circumstances. He was drawn to embrace her. Then remembering his mission, he frowned, dismissed the thought, and reluctantly rose to prepare for the grim reality in another day's dawn. He found their horses, untied Fiona's bag, and opened it to examine the contents, smiling as he unrolled her ground-cloth to find a short tunic and knee-length leather boots neatly tucked inside, along with a hair brush, headband, and soft loin-cloth. *So little in such a hostile environment*, he thought. She had followed him like a Celtic warrior, riding naked except for the weapon buckled firmly around her waist, as if she was nature's only child with no qualms about exposing herself to it all, relishing the joy of the liberty she so wildly and innocently embraced, feeling the sunlight, breathing fresh air in the caresses of breezes, bringing falling leaves and life, touching her skin, so vibrant with good health. She was radiant in response to communion with all of God's aspects stimulating her senses and inspiring her spirit to awaken her soul, to rise to the new heights revealed and now possible to reach.

How wonderful, he thought, *and so sad her high-spirited and beautiful soul could be the victim of anyone, or anything as it soared over the surface of a world replete with unthinkable evil.* Ben felt an overpowering urge, a deep determination to do all he could to protect this lovely child of God and preserve her life by using all the courage and skill he could muster. He began to pray that God would help him with the blessing of strength and the tenacity of spirit he would need to deliver her safely to a better place.

The sound of water flowing over stones caused him to change direction. He found a perfect stream, widening from bend to bend, forming pools for bathing and watering. He tethered the horses. They began to drink deeply, their tails wagging, from side to side, reflecting the welcomed refreshment and their energy renewed. Ben smiled. He too was feeling renewal as he returned with Fiona's kit, stopping suddenly, as a sunbeam captured her form rising in its glow. The light lingered, warmly embracing her as she stretched, reaching for the sky with her arms fully extended in the captivating dance of a body recovering from exhaustion, prolonged passion, and a deathlike slumber to be awakened at the chill of dawn by a life-giving light like that on the glorious morning when Jesus was resurrected.

In spite of his growing anxiety, and his haste to get on with their mission, Ben could not take another step, nor could he restrain a chuckle as it sprung from his lips, reflecting endearment for a spectacle of beauty, joyously alive again, revealing a behavior so genuinely human yet also divine. Ben could not hide his reaction. When his sigh rose to the level of a laugh, Fiona whirled to face him with a glare that caused more delight. When she placed her hands on her hips, assuming a stance that communicated her displeasure, Ben fell to his knees, convulsing with bursts of roaring laughter amid overwhelming joy.

When Fiona opened her mouth to shout out her anger, Ben recovered quickly and ran toward her. Before she could react, he grabbed her slender waist with both hands and lifted her up as high as he could, then lowered her while braving vicious kicks and pounding with fists until her pursed lips and extended jaw were level with his. Then he pulled her closer, until their lips met. His kiss was tender. Fiona's protests were silenced. As her flailing limbs went limp, Ben loosened his grip, and her feet touched the ground.

"Oh, Fiona," he whispered. "I can't help it! You've cast a spell over me, girl. I don't know what to do except hold on and hope God will help us. But you must put on some clothing. Your smile alone is enough to make me weak.

When I saw you moments ago, I couldn't control the happiness I felt as I watched you rise from your awakening."

"Oh, Ben, that's beautiful. Whatever you say. I'm yours, but so dirty."

"You don't look dirty to me!" Ben responded. "Quite the opposite…but I've found a good place…if you *really* want to bathe?"

"Good!" she exclaimed, then paused. "During the night, I could feel your tenseness. I know you're getting anxious to move on. Let's *try* to do that now. And soon be on our way."

"We should do as you suggest," said Ben. "However, I'm still amazed that we could be laughing at a time like this. It's so *good*. I would do anything to stay here forever with you…in this heavenly place."

"Ben, please stop. You're making me cry. I feel the same. But we cannot allow ourselves to dwell."

"Very well. We must return to our duty to your mother," Ben replied, his jaw set and eyes narrowing in a clear transformation to the man he must be, in order to create a proper destiny for the women he adored and respected so much, whose courage had shown him the way.

"You're a puzzlement, Ben," added Fiona. "One moment, you're a silly child, and the next, you stand before me with the stature of a warrior who inspires me with the confidence I need to be at your side, as a second, bending my will to join you, without hesitation in whatever you determine to be the best way to live and the best way to die."

"*Amen!*" Ben replied, as the two walked side by side, following the sound of clear water flowing, until he said,

"Step into that pool, Fiona, and I'll scrub the blue dye off your back."

Fiona complied, and Ben continued to speak as he attended her. "When you finish bathing and are ready, please dress with this long robe and tie your hair up with your headband. I want us to appear as much as we can like Roman clients or the like. When we leave here, we must be bold. We'll continue on the main road. Paulinus will no doubt send his scouts forward on it, as he moves his legions southeast toward Verulamium. If we meet head on, my first reaction will be to hail them as friends and respond from there to determine their intent. One way or another, we *must* get word back to Boudica as fast as possible. So we need to change mounts before we leave here. Mine has Arabian blood. You'll be light as a feather on his back, and he'll outlast the Romans in a long pursuit. If you do have to run, direct him with your reins and heels and hang on to his mane with your strongest hand, so you *do not fall off.*"

"I will do as you say, Ben. Now you *must* finish, then leave me alone, so we don't get distracted again."

Ben nodded as he set aside the long curls that lay along the graceful curve of her back. Both were smiling as they shared the delightful implications imbedded in her words.

Ben quickly completed his task to her satisfaction, went to ready their mounts, and returned wearing a short toga, headband, and boots. His sword was securely held in place around his waist by a leather strap. The hilt of a dagger showed above one of his boot straps.

Fiona paused to stare at him, then readied herself as he had described.

The two continued to survey one another while they fastened their saddlebags, adjusted their stirrups, and prepared to mount. When Ben noticed Fiona's coy smile, a vanity entered his mind. *Perhaps she finds pleasure in my appearance as well*, he thought. Then with ease, the two swung upward, into their saddles, entered the Roman road, and began to ride in a single file, with Ben in the lead.

The pathway on any other day would be ideal for two lovers on a lark. Hardwoods lined both sides of the road creating a tunnel formed by leaves and branches, allowing sunlight to pass through gaps and splash in bright patches along the darkened surface of the pathway. The effect was soothing but also distracting. *An ambush here would be fatal*, Ben concluded as he motioned for Fiona to fall back until she was separated from him enough to escape cleanly, yet near enough to maintain visual contact.

As they continued, Ben stopped from time to time to listen. He dismounted and put an ear to the ground along the surface, then faced Fiona, smiling when there was no hint of ground tremors to signal the approach of Roman formations on the quick march or mounted.

During one of the halts, Ben noticed surface imprints that showed hoof marks leading in the direction of their travel. He signaled for Fiona to join him. When she was near enough to hear, he whispered, "It appears that Roman cavalry came through here at a gallop. It's quite possible that Paulinus sent them ahead of his main body to determine the disposition of your mother's main force. It also appears that they've done that and are hurrying back with the news."

"How do you read the results?" Fiona asked.

"It's hard to tell for sure, but I think this confirms that Paulinus knows he's vastly outnumbered and there's nothing he can do to protect Londinium, or any other settlement in the region. I suspect we'll meet his lead legion before sunrise tomorrow, moving slowly, attempting to find and engage with your mother, whenever Paulinus thinks he has a decisive advantage. We should proceed with *great* caution until we know more."

"Is there anything we might do to confirm Paulinus's intent once we've determined his location?"

"That's a good question, Fiona. Like everything else, I think we have to go to great lengths to do our best and confirm for *ourselves* certain key elements of intelligence *before* we believe in their truth and reliability. At this point, it's like a puzzle with some pieces that don't fit perfectly. I hope to have an answer to your question *soon*. But for now, the only thing I know for sure is that safeguarding you is the earthly purpose of my existence. How are you doing?"

"I'm fine as long as I can see you and hear those words," Fiona replied with a radiant smile.

"Very well," said Ben as he turned to remount. They traveled on, going slowly and quietly, without incident, until Ben stopped suddenly.

Fiona joined him. "What is it?" she whispered.

"It's a sound. A horse snorting. My mount flinched when he heard it. Stay on your horse and hold my reins. I'll walk ahead and listen."

Ben dismounted and walked to the point where he was about to disappear around a gentle curve in the road, then stopped. He waited and watched, then turned around suddenly, and started running back to Fiona. She reined in and held fast. When Ben was near enough, Fiona positioned his horse, so he could vault onto his saddle in one leap. Out of breath and eyes wide, he grabbed his reins from Fiona's hand.

"It's the lead element of Paulinus's army. They've entered a long stretch of road just around that bend. They're going slow, watching for tracks along the road's surface and looking to the sides for signs of an ambush."

"What now?" asked Fiona, leaning forward in her saddle with a look devoid of fear and poised in readiness for instant response.

"We'll ride toward them. But first, do as I do," Ben said, then unbuckled his sword belt, raised his tunic, rebuckled the belt around his waist and dropped the tunic over it so both belt and sword were covered and concealed. Fiona did the same, and the two rode on.

"We'll ride up to the point where my boot tracks end," Ben continued. "Then ride forward slowly from there, until the Romans see us. There are three in the lead element. You'll see one in the middle of the road, and one on either side of him. Look surprised, but not shocked, and slowly rein in your horse when I come to a halt. Stay a bit behind me. Be ready to wheel around and ride back to Boudica. I'll give you a signal. Let your mother know where we found their advance party. I'll return as soon as I can to report their intent and anything else I might gather."

Fiona looked worried. "Will you promise to come back and find me?"

"I will find you on this side or the other, Fiona, and I'll ride through hell until I do," said Ben as he turned grimly to face the Romans, reining in his horse with his left hand and raising his right hand to signal recognition and respect.

"Hail, brothers!" he shouted in Latin. "I'm a citizen of Rome with news of great tragedy."

"What have you to report?" the lead Roman inquired, moving ahead of his companions and motioning both to halt in place.

"Camulodunum has been destroyed and thousands slaughtered by the rebels," Ben responded. "We've heard that the legion that was hurrying to reinforce that colony was destroyed by an ambush. The rebels have reached Londinium with intent to commit another atrocity there. We fear they might try to ambush *you*, if you continue down this road to intervene."

"We've already heard all of that, from our spies and loyalists. Our general will choose the ground we fight on. And we'll continue down this road until he tells us to stop. But *do* come closer, friend, so we can talk more while surveying the attributes of the maiden who follows you so closely."

"They're going to rush us if we go any closer, Fiona," Ben cautioned with a whisper, as he continued to look directly at the three Romans. "I've also seen movement coming toward us inside the tree lines, along both sides of the road. You must escape and ride back along the road as fast as you can, Fiona. Tell your mother all we know, and especially what we just learned. *Hold tight*, until I make the first move."

"I will, Ben, but you *must not* take the path of certain death," she whispered.

Ben nodded and continued to face the Romans.

"I'll do what I must. God speed to *you*, my darling," he whispered. Then he shouted out to the Romans, "I'm glad to join you! But my companion has urgent business to attend. Therefore, with my most ardent blessing, she'll take her leave, *now!*"

Ben's charge toward the Romans took Fiona by surprise. Her horse was spooked. She yanked the reins as it reared, then spun it around, and bolted in the right direction. She flattened out on her horse's back, with her hands locked on its mane, and her heals raking its flanks, too engaged to look back, to see Ben with his reins held between his teeth, freeing his sword and dagger from their concealments, and guiding his galloping horse with his knees and heels to crash into the lead Roman's horse with enough force to drive both horse and rider to the ground, then wheeling into the others using his sword to slice off one's arm at the elbow, then plunge his dagger up to its hilt between the wide-open eyes of the other. The speed and ferocity of Ben's attack froze the mounted Romans in in their tracks. Those on foot, circling through the forest to surround Fiona, were too disorganized and confounded to prevent her escape.

Ben took full advantage of the shock effect from his mounted lightning strike. He reined his horse off the road and plunged into the forest at a gallop. When the vegetation thickened enough to cover his retreat, he allowed his horse to canter then secured his weapons and used both hands to guide it through the bushes and trees that concealed them.

"Well done, good friend," Ben said while he and his horse caught their breaths and moved on in silence.

As the twilight faded to black, blending into an overcast sky, Ben stopped to water his horse and listen to the evening sounds emerging from the natural ebb and flow of nocturnal creatures and soft breezes. When his nerves began to calm, Ben's thoughts settled on Fiona. He repeated a series of silent prayers for her intentions to be realized and began to develop his best course of action in the light of what they had gleaned from the encounter with the Romans.

It seemed certain that Paulinus had given up any effort to save Londinium and Verulamium from their inevitable demise under thousands of Celtic swords. Paulinus no doubt counted his options and was seeking first to find terrain that might favor his vastly outnumbered force and take maximum advantage of their superior discipline and weaponry. Ben had reviewed a number of battles with his father's Roman guests and had a good sense of what those factors might be. He had passed through the local midlands enough to know that the high hill and forest belt separating the lands of the Trinovantes from those of the Iceni was not far from Verulamium. There was a river valley to the east of there, and a river might serve as an obstacle for an attempted crossing by infantry. If Paulinus could find a narrow defile in the western valley wall, steep enough, with a forest barrier to the rear on its uphill side, and a water obstacle to the front, he might have all that he needed to maximize the killing power of tightly interwoven, fully armored, infantry cohorts with their flanks protected by remaining cavalry. If the legionnaires were all carrying their basic load of javelins with both light and heavy weights, and different effects at various ranges, thousands of those sharp-pointed spears raining down on an assaulting force would be a significant advantage. It could break the spirit of the bravest, leading chargers and send a wave of panic into *rear* ranks, demoralizing, if not destroying, the effectiveness of the entire attacking force. The horrifying effect of those weapons, and the advantage in their use, might even turn a far-superior Celtic force into an uncontrollable stampede of souls desperately trying to escape the Romans as they counterattacked with their shields and short swords, at the same time the Celts were trying to avoid cavalry sweeping around the flanks of the Roman formations to protect their lightly armed auxiliaries, stop Celtic chariot penetrations, and annihilate fleeing Celts by running them down on horseback, or with chariots.

Panic gripped Ben as he thought his way through the tactics he'd learned from Roman officers. They had talked freely about Paulinus and others who had used these methods, these tactics, and these techniques successfully in other lands, and they would probably employ them again with a set-piece stand that the Romans might resort to, under current conditions. Ben concluded that he must scout the Roman line of march carefully, determine beyond any doubt the location Paulinus would select for what might well be his last stand in Britton, and give adequate warning directly to Boudica so she would have time to react, decide, and deliver a decisive response.

As he continued to think and doze fitfully, Ben began to notice a red glow rising above the treetops to the southeast. At first he thought it could be the sunrise, but reconsidered when the intensity of the glow increased dramatically. The gentle breeze that continued through the night was beginning to gain strength. Leaves were fluttering on branches of vegetation that surrounded him. He rose, took the reins of his horse in hand, and began to walk uphill to find a better vantage point. When they reached a suitable location, Ben stopped.

Strong gusts of high winds were beginning to blow around him. The red band grew, distinct, pulsating along the ridgelines of the vast expanse of rolling hills to the south. His horse began to raise its snout, showing signs of distress, scraping the rocky ground with its hoofs and snorting in ever-increasing blasts. It was fire! Ben could smell the smoke.

"It must be Verulamium," he concluded. "Boudica has completed the conquest of Londinium and is moving on to her next objective."

It was time for increased urgency. The ravaging was coming like wildfire in high winds, moving in his direction, and soon would arrive. Ben mounted and continued downhill toward the Roman road to Verulamium. Scores of flickering lights began to appear below toward the West. He presumed they were cooking fires the Romans were using to prepare morning meals before continuing their southward march. It was a good sign. Ben felt relief. The knot in his stomach began to unwind. His breathing was punctuated with series of reflexive sighs.

When he was out of the woods, feeling the even surface of the road, Ben dismounted. The dawn was beginning to show directly east, confirming his orientation along the lie of the roadway. He was on the right road, headed southeast. As the light increased he discerned shod hoof-prints going in both directions. One set was fresh, pointing to the northwest, and widely spaced. The other set pointed southeast, closely spaced, and partially obscured by the first set. He noticed the same number of prints with the same type of shoe in both sets, all standard issue for Roman army horses. It was clear. A detachment of twenty Roman cavalry mounts, all that was left of the Ninth Legion stock. They had passed, moving slowly toward Verulamium, then back *later*, on the run, traveling in the direction of the cooking fires Ben detected earlier.

"The Romans must know about the fate of Londinium. Perhaps Verulamium as well," he muttered. "What now?" he asked his stallion. "You must be as frightened and confused as I am. If I had a mirror, I could see my own face, placed between your wandering ears."

Then guessing rapidly to reach a logical conclusion, Ben deduced that Paulinus had, *in fact,* given up on both settlements and was slowly moving forward to determine his next move on the board, to find favorable terrain for a victory-or-die showdown not far from the road and somewhere between his location and a to-be-determined distance north of Verulamium. Such a location could provide all the advantages needed by the Romans and be close enough to the northwestern fringes of Verulamium for scouts to confirm the settlement's fate and also provide early warning of the direction, distance, rate of movement, and size of Boudica's army. Ben knew what to do. He mounted and continued to ride south toward Verulamium. The Romans would also be moving slowly and cautiously in that direction. He could stay well ahead of them and have time to give Boudica all she needed in order to move from wherever she might be into a disposition that would enable her forces to react effectively to the intelligence he would provide.

Ben turned to his God for help in a conversation that piqued his horse's ears. It sounded for the most part like a conversation between a loving child and a supernatural friend who cared enough to listen and would respond with transcendent power to solve a mystery that could only be resolved by something transformative, something akin to the ever-present and overwhelming *agapai* he was beginning to experience, and embrace, in his loneliness for Fiona.

Chapter 32

As he moved on, Ben was torn between his anxiety to make haste and his concern about the responsibility he had voluntarily assumed in the center of a maelstrom of horrific peril for himself and others he deeply cared about. He *must* keep his wits about him, remembering above all, if he hurried, deadly mistakes might be made. And if he tarried *too* long, he might *not* reach Boudica in time to provide the help she desperately needed. He recalled his recent surprise, when Fiona was able to sneak up on him. His first thought was one of Salan's Druids disguised as a painted warrior was attempting to assassinate him. But it could have been a jealous second of Boudica's who wanted him out of the way, or it could have been a henchman of Cogidubnus. Henceforth, he must be extremely cautious, and rely on God's help in this critical time of life's greatest need.

"Dear God," he whispered, "I'm yours, and I trust you. I have faith in you. You know what's on my mind. You know me. Please show me your will and send your Spirit to guide me along the way."

A comforting sense of calm settled over him. Ben was ready to proceed, aware of his surroundings and moving slowly, with other thoughts entering his mind. He was still confused by what he felt for Fiona and the undeniable gratitude, respect, and affection he held for Boudica. He had declined the intimacy Boudica had offered yet welcomed what he surprisingly encountered with Fiona, allowing him to go where he had never gone before, into a craving, perhaps lust at one point, yet discovered much more, with a woman who quickly responded. She was spontaneous, with no premeditation, willing to expose everything in the depths of her soul, opening the portal to her spirit for him to come in so completely, with no plan for the moment, not using him for hidden reasons he might not discern, rather fulfilling *his* every need, in a way he might never have imagined without her. In the act of that joining and the deep satisfaction it produced, he had discovered a void in his being, an emptiness bordering, at times, on the brink of despair, being lost in the darkness then saved, found, and fulfilled with internal satisfaction something so profound he could not turn away. He wanted to remain there forever in the joy of complete contentment. And when he had reached what he thought must be the height of all happiness, he found more and was held in a trance by the glory of it all, with a source now surely touchable, visible, there, and real, never leaving, so like him who loved and would *never betray.*

Fiona had come to him in a way that spoke of a complete death and awakening in another's life, so beautiful, so rapturous it could only be divine, holy beyond any holiness he had known on earth. Something that could only be reached in a great seeking without giving up, in a giving to all, especially the One who created him to love and be glad. To turn to another, who wanted to bathe in the everlasting spring, truly alive at the font of all existence, hearing the simple words at the final confirmation of *everything* the

Great Spirit intended to provide, in the joy found only in love everlasting, with fulfillment complete in divine satisfaction, never wanting more, and no fear of getting less.

As the lonely day wore on, Ben's thoughts embraced his rising anxiety. His search had not located the terrain features he was hoping to identify, but he did notice some footprints increasing in number as he neared Verulamium. He also noticed that most of the prints where pointed north, oddly leaving the roadway at various locations, then disappearing in tall grass on both sides of the road. He became more curious when the number of prints increased dramatically as he rode farther south. On rounding a bend, he saw what appeared to be a small settlement. There were no signs of life, other than the barking of dogs and occasional shadows appearing in a distant, darkened doorway, then vanishing before he could determine the source.

Ben decided it was best to move forward on foot, so he dismounted and proceeded, holding his horse's reins. The dwellings and other structures were a motley blend of circular Celtic huts mixed with crude imitations of Roman architecture. He assumed the arrangement reflected a cooperative arrangement that *did not* bode well for dwellers along the warpath of the vengeful Trinovantes and their Iceni counterparts.

When an old man who was obviously a Celt dared to step into view from behind a large oak, Ben halted.

"Are you a Roman?" the man asked with a tenor high-pitched and loud, belying a fear that was obvious to Ben.

"I'm a Roman citizen, now allied with the Celts," he answered.

"Have you come here to kill those of us who remain?" the old man quickly responded

"I have not," Ben replied, noticing the man bore the scars of a warrior, who might be able to help. "I've come to find a place where the Romans might stand between you and thousands of advancing Iceni and Trinovante warriors. And I'm wondering if this place is part of the settlement of Verulamium?"

"It's not," the elder replied, shaking visibly yet holding his ground. "We're of the same tribe as those in Verulamium, the Catuvellauni. We moved here some time ago by our own choice to be nearer our farms and fields. The Trinovantes hate us because we've cooperated with Roman settlers. They'll make waste of us, and all we have, if they get this far."

"Don't they recognize the common roots you share with the Trinovantes?" asked Ben.

"Trinovante, Iceni, Catuvellauni, Silure, or Brigante, we're all Britons… Briton Celts of the same stock who've come here from other lands, driven from those lands by other Celts who bore other names. We're in this land *now*, divided into tribes with many different names that have been raiding, butchering, and destroying each other for as long as any of us can remember. All of that insanity was caused by differences invented to justify the bloodletting fueled by elites called *Druids* who've invented a religion that feeds on hatred, appealing to the basest instincts of humanity in their ceremonies and rituals used to accomplish their own ends by gaining power they crave and pursue, in order to prosper in their own craven ways."

"I'm having trouble understanding you," Ben interrupted. "What is the dialect of the language that you're speaking?"

"We all speak the same language. The people to the west have named it *Gaelic* because in their variation of that same language, we're called *Gaels*…meaning, something that describes characteristics they observed to identify what's different about us. It made them feel superior in ways we do *not* understand nor appreciate. Then came the Romans with *their* language, doing the same here and on the mainland and elsewhere, I imagine. And so it goes on, confusing us in many lost identities and creating a plague of horrifying discrimination that comes and goes, but never ends. Today it creeps relentlessly toward us along this road, where we stand, to devour very living thing that gets in its way."

Ben stood still. He was confused by the old man and what he was saying, trying to overcome its impact while looking beyond him, remembering Fiona, Boudica, Isolda, Kale and his sons, Quintus, the lovely girl in Camulodunum, and Rachael, his wife.

"I see no others behind you," Ben finally uttered. "Are there more?"

"Yes, but only a few who are too old or too bound to their homes…like me…or too young and have mothers who'll *not* leave them in order to save their *own* skins. Perhaps the same as it was for other unfortunates caught in the middle of the madness in Camulodunum and Londinium, I imagine."

Ben flinched at the thought. "So the tracks I've seen on the way here were made by your people?"

"My people and many others who fled from Londinium and Verulamium after being warned by a Roman general who rode through here in haste two or three days ago."

"It must have been Paulinus," Ben replied.

"It was. He was going north, saying he could not guarantee our safety, but *would* return soon to put down the revolt in a victory over the horde of rebels moving toward us with their bloody mayhem."

"That confirms what I've gathered thus far," Ben affirmed. "I think he'll be looking for a place where he can get his back to the wall with his flanks protected, canalize the thousands who rush into his killing field, then surround and annihilate them. Paulinus has all the forces he can muster in a line of march to the north. They're coming down this road behind me, making thirty kilometers a day and trying to avoid a potential ambush. I'm going ahead to scout for suitable terrain," Ben added with calculated prevarication. "We're trying to locate a place that might fit my brief description. I hope Paulinus can reach it and stop the horde before it reaches *you*."

"I fought the first Romans who came here many years ago," the old man replied. "Our only success was in ambushes while *they* were in line of march, or in raids on camps occupied by small detachments. Otherwise, they defeated us handily until our leaders were all killed or captured and we conceded to Roman rule."

"I understand," Ben replied.

The old man paused, then added, "I know about the place you seek."

"Excellent!" Ben shouted, shocking the old man and causing him to wince.

"Yes…yes…I *do*. I know of such a place, to the south of here, on the right-hand side of this road. You'll know it when you see it."

"I will," Ben replied, "and may God be with you, my friend."

"God!" the old man shouted as Ben mounted and continued to ride down the road to Verulamium. "What god would allow these atrocities to happen to innocents who are caught in the middle between groups of madmen who show no mercy for anything, or *anyone* who gets in the way of their insatiable lust for revenge?"

Who could give a satisfactory answer to that question? Ben thought as he kept riding and scanning the contours and ridge lines of the hill mass that rose from the flat fields and farmlands along the west side of the road. The hills were in parallel with the road, for as far as he could see to the south, where clouds of dense black smoke billowed over the horizon and were rapidly obscuring the sun.

"It *must be Verulamium*," Ben uttered as his horse's head lifted to test the scent carried into its nostrils by a southerly breeze. "It's smoke that you smell, young stud. Relax and plod on. We'll still have some time before the Romans behind us get to this point."

Ben's thoughts returned to the old man, now waiting behind them. His fear and frustration, and the screed he delivered at their parting, had actually reflected a similar evolution the Israelites had experienced and documented in the books of their sacred scriptures, written in the Hebrew language from Semitic roots, named for a forebearer called Shem, a son of Noah, a patriarch in the line of Abraham, the father of three monotheistic religions. First, there was

Judaism, rising from Abraham and his wife Sarah's lineage of a son named Isaac and a grandson named Jacob, who was called Israel because he had wrestled with God. Then another rite emerged, embraced by descendants of Ishmael, Abraham's son by his wife's servant Hagar. Then, with the coming of Jesus the Christ, there was another.

"And what became out of all of that?" Ben asked out loud. The answer was clear: division and death ever since, among people essentially worshiping the One God in different ways. The ultimate paradox with an ongoing history of horrifying tragedy that might last forever. Ben continued to ponder, facing the answer to his question and the reasons for such hostility as he searched for the defile. In two or three days, it might determine the fate of thousands, spending or sparing their lives in the savagery of another conflict that defied reason yet drove men to mayhem in a swirling vortex of blood and tears, staining the earth for moments, remaining in the vivid tortured memory of a few survivors, for a handful of generations and then was forgotten by new multitudes who would damn themselves in their destiny by repeating the same mistake over and over again.

"The pandemic paradox and greatest of all tragedies," he thought out loud, "and here I go, plodding down this road, praying. Hoping man's free will would somehow choose a better day, with a better way that would mark the beginning of the end of the horrible cycle of destruction and death, that's our own creation. Instead, on this day, we have chosen to allow it to continue. And on this day, we'll find ourselves rushing into another of the fiery hells that are born of the evil that's been chosen by men."

Chapter 33

As Ben continued his search, watching and thinking about the evil surrounding him, he recalled that God's Creation included fire and brimstone. Even that might be thought of as evil, if it swept down a mountain and into a village, as volcanoes often do. As he knew well, water lashed by wind could also be fatal to those on high seas; however, he did not think of evil when he was drowning. To attribute evil to the Creator's nature seemed irrational and unfair. The same judgment seemed to apply to the knowledge of good and evil in the garden, with Adam and Eve. Their disobedience after God's warnings was met by consequences and correction. Feeling pain in birth, having to wear clothes, leaving the garden, and even death, seemed not so severe given all God had provided with numerous alternatives. It was man's choice to submit to his base-nature's callings, thereby causing or committing destructive acts that ended in tragedy rather than joy. It was a lesson. Human beings could behave like the animals God created to serve them, or they could rise to a much-higher level of existence. The choice was theirs. They were given the loving gift of an ability to make choices using their freedom to choose, and the liberty to select from a wide variety of alternatives. It seemed there was Divine justice in all of it, even in light of the fact that all men were *not* created equal. Some were brighter some were more beautiful, and some were better athletes than others, but the fundamentals were usually spread in a common foundation that could be improved by the user. Given freedom of opportunity and inalienable rights, all men could choose to do something that would benefit their societies, regardless of their belief, their race, or their ethnicity.

Ben's thoughts where helping to pass the time, but daylight was burning, and time was running out. When the smoke increased noticeably and the darkness got deeper, it reminded him that the daylight he needed would not last much longer. When his horse halted abruptly, Ben looked up. "That smoke you're smelling *now* is surely not coming from Londinium, young stud. It's much thicker and closer. We've got to move *faster.*"

Ben urged his horse on. The two went south at a gallop until they reached higher ground where Ben reined in, dismounted, and ran up to the crest of a hill, sucking in breath, then shouting *"It's Verulamium!"* when he saw flames, now clearly visible in the distance.

"It looks like a quick march from here!" Ben exclaimed as he dashed back to his horse and remounted. "We've got to find that place pretty soon. It shouldn't be much farther," he said while turning downhill toward the road to Verulamium, then cautiously moved south until he yanked the reins back suddenly stopping his horse.

"*That's it!*" he shouted.

The terrain he saw to the west of the road was exactly what he had visualized, including a narrow river that wound through the valley at the base of the defile. *Even that could be an advantage for the Romans,* he thought. *If the Celts use the wide-open fields on the east side of the road to mass for their attack, they'll cross the road going west when the attack begins. They'll have to cross the river, then reform before they begin their rush up the defile to the Roman positions. It will give the Romans some time to survey their dispositions and make final adjustments to improve their defensive posture as the onslaught continues.*

Ben estimated the width of the defile to be about five hundred meters. Enough to hold two tightly-packed legions, some auxiliaries, and cavalry. The defile widened on the downside enough to contain the attacking Celts, then narrowed going uphill, like a funnel. *Ballistae* and *Catapultae* could be placed to the rear of the Roman infantry formations to launch stones and bolts flying over the ranks of legionnaires, and down the hill, as the attackers regrouped after crossing the river. The javelin throwers in the infantry ranks and files, facing the oncoming Celts, would then be ready to bear the brunt of the initial impact and have the downhill advantage, as the charging masses struggled up the slope to meet them. The slope would become a decisive advantage for the Romans if they withstood the crashing impulse of the first wave's momentum and began to move forward relentlessly with their pointed-wedge formations, shoving their shields into the closely packed Celts and stabbing and slashing their exposed torsos with upward thrusts of thousands of razor-sharp short swords. Ben had heard these descriptions many times and could clearly imagine how it might look in the grand scale of a five-hundred-meter front crammed into a small canyon packed with thousands of converging, rising, and falling, waves of men moving over the piles of fallen bodies that would quickly accumulate. Ben was revolted by the thought of the carnage that would characterize the coming battle but was compelled to move on, in order to determine the status of the attack on Verulamium and estimate the distance from his location, near the defile, to the leading elements of Boudica's army. He needed to find Boudica, meet with her, and discuss the situation before she clashed with Paulinus and his formidable forces.

That did not take long. Ben had rounded two bends in the road when he saw a mass of human forms moving toward him. As the mob neared, he reined off the road and began to observe. Advancing toward him was a crowd of women, children, and old men running away from a large group of men on horseback who were slashing, trampling, and spearing what appeared to be a band of refugees fleeing from the holocaust in Verulamium. The smoke was so thick Ben could not identify the men on horseback, until they were two hundred meters away from him. Their horses carried marks he had seen before. The Trinovantes had reached the leading edge of the mob and were slaying anyone who moved north on the road. Behind them were scores of mutilated and trampled bodies scattered across the surface of the roadbed. Ben could also see more Trinovantes on foot, coming into view, running from one victim to the next, finishing those still alive with clubs, swords, and knives, and picking up plunder while the rampage continued.

Ben could no longer stand and watch. As the atrocities mounted, he rode directly into a group of Trinovantes who had encircled the refugees and were ruthlessly slaughtering those who managed to run fast enough to be farthest forward in their desperate retreat. Other riders were beginning to press on, in search of survivors and signs of the Roman advance from the north. When Ben came into view, the Trinovante closest to him raised his hand and shouted to his followers who were casting questioning glances at Ben as he continued to ride toward them.

"It appears that you've done well today, brother," Ben called to the leader.

"We have! And you?" he responded.

"Very well, thus far," said Ben as he reined in alongside the rider. "I'm scouting for Queen Boudica. I know the location of Paulinus and his army. I'm on my way to find the queen and render my report. Are you aware of her location?"

"I am," said the Celt. "She's on the next hill down the road, on the west side. She's overwatching our victory against the traitors in Verulamiun. Our leader, Cogidubnus, is with her."

"Good," said Ben. "I'll need an escort and safe passage."

"You don't look like one of us. How can I be sure?"

"I'm a Jew with Roman citizenship...by my parents. I hate the Romans. They've harmed me and my people greatly. I've pledged my allegiance to Boudica as my savior and my queen. I know her daughters well, and I wonder if they're with her."

"I don't know if her daughters are on the hill, but I do know someone who can help you find Queen Boudica."

"Well enough," Ben said as the man turned away.

"Laybu!" he shouted to a nearby comrade. "Do you want to escort this man safely to Queen Boudica's location while *we* go on to find the Roman army?"

The man called Laybu rode forward. Ben turned to the leader and said, "Be careful on your way, friend. Paulinus is not be far away. He has ten thousand well-armed soldiers."

"So be it," he responded. "It may take us a bit longer, but wiping out the Romans is assured given the practice we've had with these swine."

Ben acknowledged the man's bravado and turned his horse to follow his escort through the killing field, avoiding one body after another until he stopped to look down at the body of a woman.

"Why do you stop? What are you looking at?" asked Laybu. "We're in a hurry to find and finish the Romans, and I have a meeting with Cogidubnus."

"This woman's face reminds me of my wife's, after she was killed by Roman cavalry," Ben replied. He *did not* look down again, until they reached the base of the hill that was *his* destination.

As they left the road to begin the ascent, Ben noticed a Roman war chariot canted to one side along the road's embankment. Two stout horses were still harnessed and hitched to the tongue.

"Whose chariot is that?" he asked.

"It belongs to no one," Laybu replied. "Some of our men found it in Verulamium and brought it along as a trophy for Cogidubnus. He didn't want it, so we left it here."

"I think I can find a good use for it," said Ben.

"Then take it up the hill. I must go to Cogidubnus. Can't delay anymore."

And off Laybu went, waving his farewell. Hurrying to meet with his king, then plunge into the midst of another bloody nightmare.

Ben grabbed the reins on the chariot, and steered his horse and the two pullers upward.

When he got to the hillcrest, he dismounted, patted his horse on its flank, checked to make sure the chariot and its pullers were secured, then continued his search for Boudica.

Chapter 34

When Ben found Boudica she was standing alone on the southern crest of the hill, perfectly erect in her posture, hair down to her waist and wearing her colorful cloak, gathered on her bosom, beneath her gold-encrusted emerald brooch. She was holding a spear in her right hand, point up. Her form was concentrated on a widespread scene of blackened carnage and human remains that diverted Ben's attention. It was shocking, so repelling it caused him to stumble. As he regained his balance and looked up, Boudica turned toward him.

Their eyes met. "Ben," she uttered. *"You're alive!"*

"By the grace of God, Queen Boudica," he responded with trepidation.

"Come here," she commanded. Her countenance framed the familiar green eyes, wide-open, radiant, reflecting delight, and releasing her spear to clatter on rocky ground when she rushed to embrace him.

"Put your arms around me. Hold onto me," she whispered.

"I will, my queen," Ben responded as his voice faded in a sigh of relief. "I have much to share with you, whenever you wish."

"And I *with you*, as well," she replied as the two moved back from the crest overlooking the smoldering remains of

Verulamium together, sitting side by side on a large boulder, staring at one another, then turning to gaze across the horrifying spectacle of another bloody day.

"Camulodunum, Londinium, now this," Boudica began. "I've lost control in the madness, Ben. It's too much to bear alone. There were thousands down there who were mostly Celts just like us, including many innocents who were trapped in the horror, as you can see. This must be one of the sins you've talked about, and if so, I must accept the consequences. The half death of the flogging I survived with the ugly scars forever feeling and remaining on the backs of my daughters as well, and the death of my husband, the gross injustices of the Romans against my family and my people, Catus's camp, Camulodunum, the Ninth, Londinium…and now *this*…all combined to shatter the mind of a little girl made to be a queen by birth, but certainly, *not by choice*."

"I think, and I believe that the killing of innocents is always a sin, Queen Boudica," said Ben. "Especially for those participating in ceremonies cheering at the sight of bestiality inflicted on others by men who devised that evil and used it to their advantage to influence the masses and gain the power to control and intervene in every aspect of their lives and their deaths. The evil they celebrated and inflicted on others is surely a sin. I will mourn forever what they did to my companion, Ian, after you left the ritual on the night you rescued me. He was a good man. And those who accept such practices and encourage their children to do the same, it's a sin as well, I believe."

"So this Ian is the one you refused to talk about on the night I chastised you?"

"Yes. I did not want to burden you after you saved me. It wouldn't be right."

"So, I'm twofold or more in sin. I can feel it deep inside, as I gaze down this hillside and see the results."

"I believe it's true wisdom you speak, Boudica. There was sin, however, the sorrow I see in your being and the good conscience that troubles you now, can also bring you saving grace. Please think about it. *I beg of you.* But time is running out. First, allow me to tell you what I've found."

"I will, and you may," she agreed.

"The Romans are closing in on us from the northwest, coming down the main Roman road I followed. Ten thousand I think, under Paulinus."

"And what do you think they'll attempt to do in the face of our strength?"

"It could only be one of two choices. Retreat to escape, and loose face awaiting the arrival of reinforcements that may never come, *or* select a location that favors their strengths and fight to win, or die, with honor."

"And their strengths?"

"If they decide to fight now, their main strength will be the overconfidence of *your* warriors and those of the Trinovantes. They're mostly young and have never been in a set-piece battle against Roman legions with strong support. Roman artillery pieces are like large bows, mounted on wagons or chariots. They can launch stones and pointed iron bolts long enough to skewer five or six men at the same time when they're running in close quarters, one behind another. I've never seen a *balista* used, but the accounts of the Romans in my parents' home, who had used them on forces much like yours indicate that the effect of a hundred or so firing at once can slow if not break a charging mass of warriors. The same is true of the *pila* javelins their infantry use in closer quarters, throwing thousands of javelins flying into the masses, in a single launch. If that is not enough to turn an assault, the surviving chargers will then meet a wall of close-knit, armored legionnaires holding shields and stabbing oncoming warriors in their chests and stomachs with viscous thrusts of their razor-sharp short swords while protected behind their shields. After the initial charge hits the Roman line, the Roman infantry will start moving forward, pushing and knocking down subsequent chargers then trampling, stabbing, and climbing over bodies as they continue to press on. Their cavalry and lightly armed auxiliaries will be on the flanks harassing and breaking up chariot runs and other attempts to penetrate their formations from the flanks. Knowing they will all die if they fail, *every Roman* will go down fighting and *all of them*, standing together, will be very hard to kill."

"And what about you, Benjamin, what would you do?"

"I would do the same except for one doubt, at the moment of my last breath."

"And what would that be?"

"I *might* be thinking about Caesar, Claudius, and Nero, my Roman gods and the other gods and demigods my *people* have conjured up, like Jupiter, Mars, and Venus. I will be wondering what they will say to me if I join them in the afterlife, at their home on Mount Olympus, or where ever it might be."

"And if *you* die in the days ahead, fighting the Romans, what will *you* be thinking…if you're able to do that…at the moment you feel your last breath coming?"

"I *will be* thinking about the apostles, like John, some of whom are gone now. They willingly died, refusing to renounce their absolute beliefs and subsequent faith that Jesus Christ was who he claimed to be…an aspect of our Creator and Godhead, who was sent by the power of God's Holy Spirit to take incarnate form, and give us God's Word and his example of love and true wisdom. Those simple, humble men, who were martyrs, lived with Jesus and experienced Jesus in his teaching, his miracles, his death, and his resurrection. They were with him before his death and thereafter, when he returned to provide *tangible proof of eternal life*. They could see, hear, and touch him. He demonstrated beyond a reasonable doubt that he *had* achieved what he promised. He told them they could do the same. And after he left them, he sent God's Spirit to give them the power they needed to overcome anything while they shared his message with others. Thus, I would go into the afterlife believing in a loving God and Creator, asking for his grace, his mercy, and his blessings to bring me home safely, confident in his Being and hastening to receive his loving embrace."

Boudica was silent. Ben could see emotion, reflected in her quivering lips, and the tears welling up in her eyes.

"Just imagine a God who came humbly to Earth as a man," Ben continued, "who looked like us and talked like us and showed men and women alike that he loved them and wanted them to be saved from their own free will, to follow in his footsteps, overcome the death of their bodies, and go on to live the life of the soul in the grandest of places…where *he went* and still waits for us to join him after we live the good life he described, then died to provide for us. Just imagine this world, transformed by that kind of love, and *the hope it means for us all!*"

Boudica was sobbing. Ben moved closer. She turned to his loving embrace.

"I must hear and feel more of this love."

"Please wait here," he responded.

Ben went to his horse as Boudica watched him. He untied his saddle pack and returned quickly. He removed some neatly folded pieces of papyrus and animal hide that contained writing. "Please listen to the words of Paul, another like John, who described what the word 'love' meant, in a letter written in Latin and given to me by John, before we parted. I will read it slowly and stop to clarify if I think my translation into Gaelic needs more explanation. It's important for you to receive the full meaning of the writer's words and the symbols they create."

And with that, Ben began to read. "Love is patient… love is kind…It is not jealous…It is not pompous…It is not inflated…It is not rude. It does not seek its own interests. It is not quick-tempered…It does not brood over injury. It does not rejoice over wrongdoing but rejoices with the truth…It bears all things, believes all things, hopes all things, endures all things. And in my own words," Ben added, "and given time, *God's love* will bring out the good from what we first thought was bad."

"I've never experienced the love you describe, Ben. But it touches my mind, moves my heart, and quickens my blood. I have come from royalty, but *never* felt that love on the mainland or here, until I gave birth to my daughters, and again, recently, soon after *you* arrived here."

"I'm touched by your kindness, my queen. You seem very much out of place in this land, and its culture. You are beautiful, brave, and intelligent in rare exception."

"You are the same, as a man, Ben. You caught my eye, and my eye was good."

Ben blushed; moments passed in silence, until he raised his head, smiled at Boudica, and said, "I think we have two days, perhaps three, before the final meeting with the Romans. Our warriors are following their leaders up the road, and there are stragglers behind for as far as I can see."

"Yes, and there are many, still in Camulodunum and Londinium, and are taking their time to satisfy their lust and their greed. I've seen more and more wagons following, with wives and children, far back, behind their warriors, also enjoying the same satisfactions and looking forward to witnessing the slaughter of the Roman Army."

"They will be in great peril if the Romans prevail."

"The horror of all horrors?"

"Yes," Ben replied.

"Then I must continue to proceed along the way chosen for me, to do what I can to help. I cannot stop the Trinovantes, nor those of my people who've been seduced by them, however, I can encourage them to remain brave, do their best to stay alive and protect their women and children. The Druids will be encouraging them as well, for different reasons. There's nothing I can do about that. Perhaps it is *love,* that makes my decision to go on. Perhaps if anything *like love* ever prevails in this land, there will someday be a reason to say that evil has been turned into good."

"That is the hope we have, my queen. You're like our King David, and his son King Solomon. They were sinners like the rest of us, but they asked God to help them do good, to bring hope for their people. They did as much good as they could, and in turn, pleased God. With that same hope, we shall watch this unfold and even in our own deaths, find reasons to rejoice and be thankful."

"Yes. Thankful. And in the time we have left, I will be thankful if you'll read more to me."

"I will, and for myself as well. We should read the Ten Commandments again, as soon as we have time. It's a summary of our underlying values and a guide for us to use in our daily lives, for as long as we live."

"And for Fiona? Will you do so for her as well?" Boudica asked with a hint of guile.

"Yes. Of course. For her, wherever she might be," Ben responded in a manner that disguised his feelings of illusory guilt.

"Fiona is here, Ben. She's told me everything."

"*Everything?*"

"*Everything.* What you did to save her, what you learned about the location and apparent intent of the Romans… and what the two of you did, *together.*"

"My God!" Ben exclaimed.

Boudica paused, then added, "At the time Fiona arrived and reported, Cogidubnus was here, meeting with me. He told us he'd recently received news from a messenger about one of his seconds, a warrior named Laybu, who was heading north, beyond Verulamium with a band of his warriors, killing anyone not aligned with us as they went. This Laybu told the messenger he had seen you in their midst.

When Fiona heard that, she let out a wild cry of anguish and started running toward her horse. I agonized about her leaving before. I wasn't going to let her slip away again. I ordered my men to seize and bind her to the largest tree they could find. She's there, in a state of complete despair. We should go to her now. Come with me."

"What will you do with me?" Ben asked as he followed.

"We shall see," Boudica answered without looking back.

Ben wanted to jump ahead of Boudica to stop her, to determine what was going through her mind. He prayed and was struck by the notion that Boudica had found value in him. But her feelings for him were based on a need; and she had hastened to use him. If there was love, it had limits. Fiona was different. He breathed deeply. Ready to die. Ready for anything.

When he saw Fiona, she was sitting, legs spread, on the ground, her back was resting on the bark of an oak. Her head was down. Her eyes were closed. She was still wearing the tunic he brought her on the morning she bathed in the stream. When he saw that, Ben suddenly dashed past Boudica, running, then dropping to his knees, to slide between Fiona's outstretched legs. Before her guards could react, he drew his dagger, sliced through the rope that bound her, pulled Fiona away from the tree, and stood up, holding her face up, hair, arms, and legs dangling as he cradled her in his arms and cried, "Oh, Fiona, my Fiona… for God's sake…please rise and speak to me again!"

Over and over Ben repeated the words, until Fiona's long eyelashes began to flutter.

"Ben, Ben, is that you?" she whispered.

"It is, my love, *it is*."

Only her guards could see Boudica smile, as she turned and slowly walked away.

Chapter 35

Ben awoke in a cold sweat, reaching out for Fiona's warmth, feeling nothing but leaves covered with dew. He bolted upright, frantically gazing around, blinded by the early-morning fog around him. He panicked and jumped up on his feet, his eyes capturing the outline of a ghostly form gliding toward him through the mist. Closer it came. He unsheathed his dagger.

"Where in the *hell* am I?" he croaked.

"You're with *me*," came the soft response.

Ben waited in a crouch. The voice was strange yet familiar.

"Who goes there?" he asked.

"Whom would you *like* it to be?" came the response.

His eyes blinked wildly, revealing confusion. Her fingers touched his face.

"Fiona, thank God it's you," he groaned as they embraced.

"What's wrong, Ben?" she whispered. "You look like you just saw a ghost."

"I thought for a moment I *had*. Thank God, it's you, alive and so warm."

"Were you having a nightmare?"

"Not until I awoke."

He clutched her crazily, panting in short breaths signaling his relief.

"Ben, please relax," she pleaded. "You're going to crush me. I can't breathe." She giggled, wiggling and squirming, fighting for relief.

Ben raised his arms and cupped her cheeks with both hands. "Please don't leave me like that, never again. Wake me instead. Tell me where you're going, then take me with you."

"I won't leave you in a fog, ever again," she promised. "I might not find you when I return. It would be too hard to bear. Your embrace enabled me to deal with the rest of this day."

"You seem to be troubled now."

"I am. We must talk."

The two walked to a secluded location, found a patch of dry grass, and sat facing one another.

After some moments of reflective silence, Fiona began to speak.

"Mother has changed, overnight," she said. "I'm not sure why, so I must guess. I think she's quite disappointed."

"How so?" Ben asked with a perplexed look, his relief with Fiona's return fading briefly.

"She's more than fond of you, Ben. She knows about us. When she saw how you ran to me yesterday, she knew. Her hope vanished. My mother realized she would *no longer* have you in the way she wanted, in the way she had dreamed and desired."

"But...I," Ben stammered, confronting his troubling thoughts about Fiona's revelation.

"I know that you love her, Ben, but in a different way. She's realized it and so have I. Yesterday, when I awoke, you where embracing me, abandoning all pretense. My mind was quite confused, wondering what was really happening. I was astounded. My mind was reeling. My eyes were moving, *seeing everything.*"

"What are you saying?" asked Ben as he leaned forward in anticipation.

"She was stunned by your actions, but not like I was. At first, she showed mixed emotions, good and bad. She's my mother. I know her."

"And what does it mean to you, Fiona?"

"As she was turning to walk away, a smile touched her lips. I saw it. She knew it was good for us, and she knew what it meant *for her.*"

"What?" asked Ben. "What did she say this morning… about us?"

"Nothing."

"Nothing?"

"Not directly, rather subtle, perhaps as part of her plan."

"Her plan for what?"

"Her plan for our inevitable showdown with the Romans. Be still and I'll explain."

Fiona paused. She placed a finger on Ben's parting lips and continued.

"She's called for a meeting of her seconds and sent runners to bring Kale and his son Rand, Quintus, and Cogidubnus. She's planning to leave here and march forward, after the meeting, when the sun is directly overhead. She wants to drive our chariot. She wants Isolda and me to be with her. She also wants Quintus to be at the meeting, so he can add to what you've already told her about how the Romans fight, in order to provide a first-hand account from a former centurion who's seen it all. It's for the benefit of Cogidubnus and his seconds. Rand will be there as well, to get her instructions on what he should tell those who've stayed behind in our settlement…what they should anticipate in the event of her *defeat*."

"I *must* see her," said Ben. He began to rise.

"No, Ben, you should not," hastened Fiona, grabbing his hand and pulling him back to the ground.

"Why not?"

"It *would not* be good for either of you."

"I don't understand."

"You wouldn't."

"Why not?"

"Because you're *not* a woman."

"I still don't understand. We have another chariot. It's Roman. Much better. I must tell her, and you should be with *me!*"

"My mother agrees. She feels that it's best for you and me to lead her group to a vantage point above the plain, where the combined forces of Iceni and Trinovante will assemble before attacking the Romans. She wants Cogidubnus to hold there until most of the stragglers have arrived, then wait for her to address the masses and give the signal for the attack to begin. I didn't know about the other chariot. I'll tell her about that later."

"It's good. You're coming with me is good," said Ben his countenance softening with relief. "We can help her. But Rand should drive for her in the Roman chariot with Isolda. Kale should return to your village *now* to prepare those left behind. Quintus should be released to return to his people, before the battle begins."

"And what is your reason for those assignments?"

"You've seen the way Rand and your sister behave… when they think no one is watching."

"I have. They've tried to keep their relationship a secret. Rand is afraid that my mother will ban him if she finds out. But my sister doesn't care. I think she wants to die. I believe Rand knows that. He cares for her. Her scars are not a problem for him, and he has no interest in bringing children into this mess. Rand would go with Isolda beyond death if need be. He simply wants to be with her, one way or another."

"That's *true love*, my dear!" Ben exclaimed

"I know that, *now*. Because of you, Ben."

"I'm delighted you do," he replied, smiling broadly, then paused. "I'm sure you know that Rand is a good hand with horses. Isolda will be safe riding with him. He can easily handle two pullers, given the opportunity. I've secured the chariot and its horses along the path to Boudica's location. Please tell Rand he should feed and water them as soon as possible and check the chariot to make sure it's still sound."

"I'll tell him."

"And Kale is the perfect man to take his other sons away from here, as soon as possible, and lead them in preparing the rest of the Iceni for…*whatever* happens…after the battle."

"What are you saying?"

"I'm going to be very honest, Fiona. If the Romans win, and I think they might, the next round will be horrific."

"What do you mean?"

"They'll not stop until they wipe out or enslave everyone. It happened in Carthage, a city whose people attacked Rome and were beaten. The victory was not enough for the Romans. They wanted revenge. They launched an attack on Carthage that killed thousands outright, then went door to door, murdering everyone who couldn't escape through their siege line. Many thousands, women and children, were *murdered*. Then the Romans plowed sea-salt into the Carthaginian fields so that anyone left alive would starve to death."

"My God!" Fiona exclaimed. "They might do that to us?"

"Absolutely. So Kale must be told and have time to do what is necessary to save as many as possible if the Romans win. Winter is coming, and the Iceni haven't had time to prepare, given all that's happened. They must harvest their crops immediately and hide the food in the hills before the Romans can burn it."

"So be it," Fiona agreed.

"And Quintus has a family in Rome. He needs to go home. He and his wife and children have suffered enough. He should be released before the battle starts. If he and Kale both survive, they will spread the good news we've discussed. Perhaps it will inspire those inclined to believe in a better way with hope to sustain them, in the dark days ahead."

"As you wish. I'll do all I can to make my mother accept all your wisdom *before* we leave this hill. She wants me to be at her meeting. I'll meet with her privately around that opportunity. I must go now. Please pray for me."

"I will. The fog has lifted. I'll await your return."

Chapter 36

Ben sat patiently on the high ground waiting for Fiona. He worried about her yet appreciated the opportunity to gather his thoughts, pray, and prepare his weapons and equipment. His horse was nearby, rested and ready, as always in spite of lost sleep from the constant racket caused by people, horses, wagons, and livestock moving north on the road below. Hearing the seemingly endless din from the cavalcade was a comfort as well as a concern for Ben. The number of warriors would be formidable. He looked forward to seeing them gather on the plain, assembling for their attack on the Romans. But the menagerie of women and children was bound to be troublesome. He presumed Paulinus and his legionnaires were outraged, after learning their veterans had been slaughtered in the attacks on Camulodunum, Londinium, Verulamium, and the massacre of the Ninth Legion. Revenge might become a continuing motivation for the Romans, if they prevailed in the oncoming clash of arms with Boudica's warriors.

Ben began to have second thoughts about Boudica's use of the Roman war chariot. It must have come from Camulodunum where he'd seen at least three others like it and concluded that the Roman veterans had used them as mementoes of past glory. Seeing Boudica in that chariot might further incite the Romans and lead to some dire consequences once the battle was joined. But Boudica's appearance at the start, riding along the front of the leading lines of warriors in a captured Roman chariot, haranguing the masses, could become a decisive advantage by launching more inspired Celtic fighters into the Roman cohorts in the first waves of the assault. The Roman chariot was also larger, sturdier, and faster, with iron in its components and two strong pullers. It would be a significant advantage over the smaller wooden vehicles of the Celts that were pulled by a single horse.

Ben was about to reach a conclusion when he looked up, saw Fiona coming his way, and forgot about the chariot. He jumped to his feet and hurried out to greet her.

"It went well," she said with a smile as they discreetly embraced. "My mother accepted all of your recommendations. We're ready to move!"

Without further words, the two retrieved their horses, mounted, and rode to the front of Boudica's retinue. She was standing in the Roman chariot, issuing final instructions to her seconds. When Rand saw Ben, he smiled, then waved and started the chariot in slow forward motion with others walking or riding around and behind, some carrying banners and flags on staffs to signal Boudica's royal standing in command.

As they continued to line out and start down the hill, Ben and Fiona turned to look back. They noticed that Isolda was seated behind her mother in a comfortable space. Kale and Quintus were mounted, riding next to the chariot. *Good so far and a very impressive sight*, Ben thought, then turned to see Fiona riding close by his side, appearing regal and smiling as well.

At the base of the hill they turned north on the Roman road and were immediately surrounded by mounted warriors who encircled Boudica's entire party and began to clear a path through the crowd. As Boudica's chariot rolled forward, those she passed roared their approval, cheering and greeting her with words of encouragement and affection. Their warrior queen responded gracefully, much to their delight. Ben was moved by the spectacle, as was Fiona, who also attracted attention and responded appropriately.

"Fiona is as brave as they come," he uttered as his eyes rested on her, and his heart swelled with pride.

"Dear God above all, please allow me to be as brave as this woman I love more than life. Allow her to have all that is good, to live well, and have children to share the beauty of her being, loving and inspiring others, along the way."

As he peered through the road dust, Ben could see the hill that was their destination. The grassland to his east was flat and firm, and he turned his mount toward it.

"Please ride back to your mother," he called out to Fiona. "Tell her we'll turn off the road here and move parallel to it along the grassy plain until we begin our climb to the top of the hill."

"Why?" she called back.

"We'll get there faster outside this mob, and with the breeze blowing in from the east, we'll be up-wind from this dust cloud, able to see farther and breathe better."

Fiona smiled, nodded, and took off at a gallop as Ben led the queen's retinue off the road.

Before long Fiona was back, and they wound their way up the hill, reached the top, and continued to move until they were on the northern crest and could see a wide plain.

Both gasped. Below them was an expanse of colorful humanity unlike anything they had ever seen or could imagine.

"There must be at least a hundred thousand Celts down there!" Ben shouted.

"I can't believe my eyes!" Fiona responded.

"They're gathered in a huge bowl, to the right of the road," said Ben, "and that's good. It's precisely where they should assemble, and prepare for battle. Now look to the left, Fiona, on the west side of the road. You'll see the line of hills running north and south with a high escarpment on this side. Can you see the huge gash running down from the cliffs, toward the valley floor, the river and the road?"

"Yes. I can," Fiona confirmed.

"That's the defile!"

"I see it. I also see a group of riders on the road. They're slowly riding north."

"I see them too," Ben replied, "and I also see their leader, Laybu, the Trinovante we've talked about."

"So that's the evil Laybu whose message about you almost frightened me to death?"

"Yes, regrettably," Ben replied, "and it looks like his lead elements have stopped. They've apparently realized that this is *the place* where the battle will be fought. They probably suspect that the Romans are around the next bend in the road, just to the north of their position. *The stage has been set.* I can feel the tension. My heart is pounding. An epic event is unfolding in front of us."

"What does that mean?" she inquired.

"The 'stage is set' is an expression that comes from the Greeks. They raised hell in their time with the armies of their city-states. They even fought one another then joined to resist the Persians for many years. They finally defeated the Persians after many battles. If they had *not* prevailed, this world would be quite different in many unfortunate ways. The Greeks eventually brought us many treasures of mind and spirit. Their entertainment wasn't in a Coliseum, like those the Romans built to entertain and amuse their citizens with events often involving grandiose spectacles and bloody contests involving sacrifices. Greek performances were presented on a platform of sorts, a much smaller structure called a stage, adorned with art and other objects to create a setting for their entertainments called plays. So when 'the stage was set,' it was ready for the actors to act…to do what they planned for their audience. Now the stage is set here. You and I and the women and children, on the high ground to the east, are the audience. The action, the drama, is about to begin with our warriors on one side and Romans on the other, ready to respond as 'players' in whatever they've decided to present."

"I see," said Fiona. "So the Romans will be on the west side of the road, and we'll be on the east. If we're correct, they'll defend in the defile, facing the plain, and the 'play' will begin when our forces attack by moving across the road and river and into the frontlines of the Roman defense."

"That's it, Fiona, my general."

"I'm not a general, Ben. I'm simply repeating what you've told me and relating it to this terrain."

"You're too humble."

"You know that's *not* true."

"You're right, Fiona. I give up. You're the most *un-humble* woman I've ever known. Now, please tell your mother that her vantage point should be here, where we stand. I'll mark this spot, then move over to those trees to the left. I'll be watching for the Romans and waiting for your return."

"I won't be long," Fiona replied.

Ben watched as she rode back along the grass-lined trail to deliver his message to her mother. His thoughts were revealed by his words.

"You were right, Fiona. This play will begin with your mother's command. I'm certain its climax will have consequences so profound that neither the audience nor the players can imagine the impact of the outcome in terms of its lasting results."

Then Ben turned away and rode to his vantage point. There were no Romans in sight when he hobbled his horse and looked over the landscape. He could see Laybu and his Trinovantes near the bend in the road and watched as they rode around it, were out of sight to the north, then returned showing no signs of urgency.

Then Boudica and her escorts appeared to his right. She and Fiona were together. They dismounted at the spot he had marked as Boudica's vantage point and were looking down at the spectacle of an expanding mass of armed Celts covering the entire valley floor. The hills to the east of the warriors formed a horseshoe that opened in their direction. A growing crowd of followers were parking their wagons along the rim of the hills to form an amphitheater, herding their livestock into patches of meadow grass around them and lighting cooking fires.

My God, Ben thought. *This is beginning to look like a Roman Coliseum, filling up with spectators.* He marveled at their nonchalance, a bizarre contrast considering the nightmare about to unfold as Fiona appeared. She was riding toward him. He watched as she approached. When she dismounted, he grabbed her horse's reins and led the way to their secluded lookout. Once there, Fiona dismounted, embraced him, and held fast. Her head rested against his chest as they watched the colossal event unfolding. It was certain to be legendary in its proportions, too grand to describe with mere words, too terrible to consider the outcome and its implications.

Ben continued to hold Fiona and turned his attention to the west where bright flashes of light were appearing in the forest at the upper end of the defile. He squinted in an attempt to discern the source. Then exhaled with a burst of energy, causing Fiona to turn in the same direction.

"What is it, Ben?"

"It's them, the Romans!" he exclaimed. "They left the road *before* reaching the bend that the Trinovantes were scouting around earlier, hoping to catch the Roman's lead elements in line of march, before they deployed into battle formations. *Look!* You can see their eagle on the staff above the banner of the legion as it marches out of the forest, on the left side of the defile."

"*Oh God,* I can see it. Now look to the right side!"

"That's the other legion, Fiona. I can see their eagle as well. That confirms the legions. They are the Fourteenth Germania and Twentieth Valeria. We thought there would be two legions. So it looks like we were right. I can also see the horse-drawn wagons carrying their ballistae and coming into view from both sides."

As the lead centuries in each of the legions emerged from the treelines, Ben and Fiona continued to watch in stunned silence. The cavalry and chariots began to assemble in their staging areas, as the lead units of the legions marched down the defile in tight, rectangular formations. Bright reflections became more apparent as the first units continued to march, revealing all the legionnaires wearing metal helmets, body armor, and brightly embossed shields as tall as the men who carried them.

The formations of eighty to a hundred soldiers in each century continued to move into the defile one behind another, marching in cadence with the ominous beating of thundering drums, until the leading centuries from each side reached the bottom of the defile facing each other, about a meter apart, then halted. Subsequent units did the same until the defile was filled with a line of centuries covering a distance of five hundred meters. When trumpets blared, the legionnaires in ranks and files simultaneously turned to face eastward down the sloping defile toward the Celts that were massing on the plain beyond the river and the road. When trumpets blared again, a second line formed behind the first in the same manner.

As the Roman defense continued to deepen in cohorts, with two legions abreast, Ben looked toward Boudica's vantage point. He could see her in the midst of a group of onlookers, captivated by the same fascination as he and Fiona, not moving, not talking, simply fixated on the perfection and precision of a massive spectacle extending across an ever-expanding, awe-inspiring vista.

When Ben saw the Roman auxiliaries, cavalry, and chariots moving into position on the flanks of both legions and crews setting up their wagon-mounted supporting weapons, he turned to Fiona.

"This is going to be more than I want *you* to see."

"I know," she replied. "What should we do?"

"We must concentrate on your mother, your sister, and Rand along with those riding with them as mounted guards. I don't see Salan. Do you know where he went?"

"He wasn't at the last meeting. I think he might be mounted and off with a group of his Druid brethren, probably in the area of the wagons with the women and children, trying to get them organized to scream, yell and chant, beat drums, blow horns, and do whatever else they can to incite our warriors and distract the Romans. But I don't think there's any decisive thing they can do to drive them off."

"Nor do I," Ben replied. "Let's feed and water our horses and finish what little food we have. This will be a very long day. We must keep track of your mother, follow her closely, stick together, and *pray*. It appears that Kale and Quintus have departed to their own ends. There's nothing more we can do for *them* now."

"Amen," Fiona responded. "But I must tell you something, *now*."

"What is it?" he asked.

"My mother wants me to go with her."

"What do you mean? What for?" Ben inquired with a frown reflecting his grave concern.

"She wants me and my sister to ride in the chariot as she appears and speaks to our warriors, right before she orders them to attack."

"Oh my God," mumbled Ben, looking away toward the defile.

"You *must* understand, Ben," Fiona added. "She wants to show us to her warriors, to remind them of the suffering the Romans inflicted on the women of *their* royal family. She hopes to inspire and fill them with outrage and ferocity before they charge and fight well for family and freedom."

Ben thought for a moment, then replied with obvious reluctance.

"It's about love for them. It has made you *want* to do this. Therefore, it's right for you to go. It's a sacrifice, and I will ask God to bring you back safely. I'll be close at hand if you need me."

Fiona kissed him, then turned away.

Ben watched as she walked back to her mother.

When Boudica saw Fiona returning, she looked toward Ben. He'd seen that look before. He nodded and was about to turn away, when he saw Rand stepping down from the chariot and handing the reins to Boudica.

"*My God*," Ben uttered. "She's changed the plan! Boudica has decided to drive the chariot *herself.* She and her daughters will take the ride *alone.*" He thought for a moment, then realized there was nothing he could do, except to watch, as Boudica's plan turned into action.

Ben held his breath, exhaled, and began to pray.

Chapter 37

The sun was directly overhead when Boudica and her daughters appeared on the valley floor. They were following a mounted escort that had joined her along the way. The escorts were carrying her colors and clearing the way for their queen's Roman War Chariot to pass through the roaring crowd that lined the road. Ben continued to watch as Boudica drove back and forth along the leading edge of warriors who would soon begin their attack on her command. She had pulled down her robe so they could see her scars as she passed. Her daughters did the same. Iceni and Trinovante were cheering *together*, as the trio passed their positions. Boudica was shouting, urging them to remember the injustices that started their rebellion and fight hard to banish the Romans, protect their families, and defend their freedom.

After Boudica's last pass, she drove the chariot to the center of the leading edge of a massive body of two hundred thousand fierce warriors who were ranting and raving and waving their weapons, eager to enter the fight. Boudica lifted her spear, raised it over her head, then looked toward the defile. Suddenly, there was silence. The Romans were waiting. They were gathered together in one place, ready to be annihilated.

Boudica pointed her spear toward the defile. *"Onward to victory, my brave warriors!"* she shouted.

The horde of Celts, some naked, few with light armor, surged around her, rolled across the road, and plunged into the river, creating a thunderous wave that crashed against the far bank and continued to roar up the incline, carrying thousands upon thousands of warriors brandishing swords, spears, clubs, and crude axes massed and moving together, like a stampeding herd of wild beasts.

As the wave of humanity continued to roll up the defile, the Romans launched their first volley of artillery. Hundreds of large stones and long iron bars with razor-sharp points flew over the heads of the legionnaires, down the sloping defile, and into the forward running Celts who did not realize their peril until *they* were skewered, or saw several of their nearby comrades impaled on sharp-pointed bars, or crushed by flying boulders. But to Ben's amazement, the charge did not break. The mass continued to run over or around the dead and dying, drowning out their screams with shouting and yelling, until the next trumpet blast; and the second volley of stones and heavy javelins fell on *them.*

The attack faltered, but was renewed by those in the rear who continued to charge forward over the bodies of their fallen comrades.

Then came the first salvo of light javelins flying down the slope from thousands of throwers inside the legions' ranks. Hundreds of javelins hit their marks. The entire front of the charge faltered, then continued up the slope.

When the Celts were within twenty meters of the front ranks in their formations, the Romans launched the second salvo of light javelins, and thousands of sharp-pointed spears slammed into them. Ben could see piles of dead and dying Celts being trampled by those behind them, who were waving their swords and shouting as they pressed on, into the Roman front lines.

When the trumpets sounded again, the Romans quickly changed their line formations to wedge formations, forming a line of pointed triangles that created a saw-toothed, continuous line facing toward the Celts. Ben thought about the shark he escaped, and the lines of jagged teeth that could rip him to shreds, when the Celts ran into the pointed triangles, and were deflected to the sides of the *V*s, then crashed on Roman shields held firmly in place by tightly formed ranks of soldiers, shoulder to shoulder, in great depth, who were protected behind their shields and stabbing into the Celts' exposed chests, ribs, and abdomens with razor-sharp short swords.

When the Celts on the flanks of the charge tried to escape the saw-toothed maw, Roman auxiliaries, cavalry and chariots ran them down with lethal precision.

When the Celts entered the point where the defile narrowed, the steep inclines of the ridges on both sides forced them down further into the defile, where they were pushed, shoved, and packed so closely together they could not raise their arms enough to use their swords. Instead, they were being shoved helplessly into more Roman shields and stabbed repeatedly by thousands of protruding short swords.

Ben thought he had seen the worst, when the trumpets sounded again, and the Romans, still in wedge formations, started moving forward down the defile, using their shields to push the charging Celts backward while stabbing them with their short swords and trampling their fallen bodies under scores of hobnailed sandals.

As piles of fallen Celts began to rise along the five-hundred-meter front, the Roman ranks and files maintained their cohesiveness in tight formations closely linked together, rolling over row after row of fallen Celts, chopping and stabbing and trampling, to create new rows then climbing over them to create the next piles, until the remaining Celts began to falter.

The Trinovantes were the first to break, turning and trying to run back through the oncoming masses, at the same time many of them were being overtaken from behind by Romans pursuing them.

When Ben saw that, he turned to find Fiona.

He knew his faith would be tested on this day; and believed that his God, his Jesus, and their Holy Spirit would be with him. He needed their power, and the strength of spirit, to meet the impossible challenge.

"*Thank you, Lord!*" he shouted when he spied Boudica's chariot returning with Fiona safely onboard.

When the chariot came to a halt, she jumped out and ran toward him. The sight of her inspired him. By God's grace, she had returned to be with him.

"We've got to get your mother and sister out of the way of that killing machine!" he yelled as she dashed into his arms.

"Lead the way!" she shouted, as they hastily mounted and galloped back to the place where Boudica, Rand, and the rest of the royal entourage stood in shock, watching the rout.

"Mother!" Fiona yelled. "We must flee before you're trapped. The Roman cavalry is sweeping around our flanks with chariots and cavalry!"

Boudica, Rand, and Isolda jumped into Boudica's chariot. At her command, Rand yanked the two pullers around and started them running, heading down the hill, toward the killing field.

"The only place I'll go is *into* the Romans!" Boudica shouted.

"*We've got to stop them!*" Ben yelled as his mount leaped forward, and Fiona followed at a gallop.

Both reached the valley floor and were beginning to gain on Boudica's chariot when they saw Rand, impaled by a flying javelin and falling from the chariot when it careened from side to side.

Boudica stepped forward to grab the reins, desperately trying to turn the frightened pullers, as Isolda jumped from the chariot, rolled through the grass, and ran back toward Rand. Boudica was struggling to turn the chariot around, when three Romans on horseback rushed Rand and Isolda and trampled them to death, as they joined in a farewell embrace.

When Ben reached the chariot, he reached out and yanked the reins from Boudica's hands, then attempted to steer the chariot out of the melee as his horse kept up with the galloping pullers. But both the horses were wild-eyed and out of control. They turned sharply away from Ben, and the chariot tipped. As it started to roll over, Boudica jumped to avoid being crushed.

Ben dashed toward her as she hit the ground and tumbled. Fiona joined Ben, as Boudica recovered and stood up, and together they hoisted and held her between their horses while they galloped out of the defile, toward the top of the nearest ridge. When they were out of the fray, they stopped. Boudica climbed up behind Fiona and wrapped her arms around her daughter's waist. As they continued their escape at a gallop, Ben saw a Roman chariot following in hot pursuit. "*Go on!* They're after our queen!" he shouted while reining around to face the oncoming threat.

As he galloped toward the chariot, Ben spied a javelin standing vertically and embedded in the chest of a fallen Celt. At full gallop, he grabbed the javelin, flipped it around, and hurled it at the driver. The flying spear impaled the Roman through his chest. Out of control, the horses bolted. The chariot rolled over and was dragged upside down, pinning the remaining occupants underneath. Ben could hear both of them screaming when he turned to follow Fiona and Boudica up the ridge-line.

When the trio reached the top, they gathered and looked back, beholding a massacre. The Romans had shattered the Celts' charge and reached the line of wagons. The women and children were trapped between legionnaires and the barrier their wagons and livestock created. As the Romans pushed the crowd into the confines of the barrier, the grass inside the inverted horseshoe turned red.

Subsequent waves of Romans gathered together and continued to roll down the defile, cross the river and the road, to dispatch the dying and roll them for plunder. Their revenge was ongoing, and it *would not* stop.

Fiona turned her horse toward the northeast, and Ben followed until they entered a secluded grove of trees.

Without words, Ben, Boudica, and Fiona dismounted. Exhausted and in shock, disregarding potential danger from Roman pursuit, the three collapsed together on a bed of soft grasses.

Chapter 38

Ben awoke from a dream. He looked around. Fiona was an arm's length away next to her mother. Both were still sleeping. Ben's eyes began to water. Tears spilled down his cheeks. The sight of the two, so close in peaceful slumber, was more than his emotions could contain.

When he retained his composure, Ben fully embraced the reality outside the boundaries of the space he occupied in the circle of sunbeams pouring over mother and daughter, warming their bodies and melting his heart. He realized they could be lying in the defile and wondered where their souls might have gone. *If they had died in the defile and I had not, what would I do?*, he thought. *Would I ever be with them again, as we are now? Would I ever be able to find them again?*

"I *must not* forget this blessed warning," he uttered. "I must protect and cherish them no matter the cost."

He jumped to his feet, found his horse, and began riding slowly around them, forming concentric circles, expanding with each pass.

Having found no signs of Roman pursuit in close proximity, he returned to the center where he found Boudica and Fiona still asleep. He paused to look once more, then turned toward the pathway they had taken in their retreat and followed the it back to the defile.

When he was close enough to hear the sounds of men and horses, Ben dismounted and crawled to a vantage point overlooking the battlefield. At least fifty thousand dead, he estimated, and many still dying in hundreds of wind-rows with bodies stacked one upon another. The Romans were scouring the field like jackals, following blood trails, tracking down those wounded who had survived, to stop them as they crawled away in terror and finish their lives slowly with heinous tortures, laughing, as they continued to spread their merciless barbarism.

Ben could not bear the horror and the sorrow. Isolda and Rand were out there, somewhere. The thought brought a shattering vision. He winced, then shuddered uncontrollably as he thought about Boudica and Kale and the utter despair they must be experiencing, as the reality of those tragic deaths penetrated their souls.

Outraged and reeling in a rush of toxic emotions, Ben turned, crawled back to his horse, and galloped back to his charges. As he approached the place where he left them, he saw Boudica and Fiona, still safe, asleep in the grass. He thanked God as he dismounted and hurriedly awakened them.

Obviously still recovering from the effects of their trauma yet responding quickly, both mounted Fiona's horse with Boudica seated behind and holding tightly on to Fiona, who was firmly in the saddle, holding the reins, and following Ben as he spurred his mount eastward, seething with anger and burdened by remorse.

At sunset, the now-familiar landscape darkened. They continued to move, navigating by starlight, in silence, except for the muffled sounds of hoofbeats on soft ground.

Early the next morning, Ben began to recognize distinct landmarks. When the sun stood directly overhead, he could see the Iceni in distant fields harvesting and loading wagons in their haste to finish and flee with all they could carry.

"God bless you, Kale!" Ben exclaimed, surprised at the sound of his own voice.

Fiona heard him. "We're *home*, Mother," she announced.

Ben stopped when he heard Fiona's voice, relieved to hear the sound after so much silence. When the two reached him, he looked over them carefully and asked, "How are you ladies faring?"

"Like two riding dead, on one living animal," Fiona answered.

Ben understood and headed straight for the great house. As they passed, onlookers stood silently, exchanging knowing glances, then returning to their work. When the three reached the entrance, Ben and Fiona helped Boudica dismount and enter her throne room.

"Help me to my bed and let me be," she demanded.

They complied, laid her down, and covered her gently.

"Mother, do you want some broth?" Fiona asked.

"Just water. I need water," Boudica replied.

A guard came forward with a chalice. Boudica drank deeply. When finished, she motioned, "Come here…both of you…sit on my bed."

Both obeyed and took seats near her, one on either side. She gazed at them then focused on Ben.

"I know you're worried about me. But you've made the right choice. I wanted you…I grew in love…wanting you as *my* husband. Now…you'll be my *son*."

"Thank God," Ben responded with a sigh of relief.

"The thought of you and Fiona…together…brings me joy. It's *your* time," Boudica added.

"Thank you, my queen. I love you," Ben replied.

Boudica smiled and paused to draw breath. She was fading.

"I'm losing my strength. Go, Ben. Bring Salan to me."

Ben departed immediately. He saw the Druid standing alone in the center of the village, sullen as always, observing the activity around him, apparently in shock.

When Salan spied Ben, he appeared to be startled but unable to escape.

"Salan!" Ben shouted. "Come quickly. Queen Boudica has sent me to find you."

The Druid responded slowly. As they walked toward the great house, Ben said, "I thought you might run from me."

"I know you hate me," Salan replied. "I thought you might kill me, but there was nothing I could do."

"I *despise you*, Salan…but I serve Boudica now. She's gravely distressed and injured during a fall from her chariot," Ben remarked as they entered and approached Boudica's bed.

Fiona rose and came to Ben, ignoring the Druid, looking down in silence.

"I'm frightened," she whispered to Ben. "My mother is acting strangely. I've *never* seen her like this."

"Does she really want to be alone with *him?*"

"Yes. She told me to leave when she saw him."

The two went outside and stood silently. Ben noticed that Boudica's brooch was pinned to Fiona's cloak. He was about to inquire, when Salan reappeared.

"Your mother is very ill, Fiona. I've given her a remedy to ease her suffering. She wants to see you," he added, then turned quickly, about to walk away.

"*Stand fast*, Salan," Ben demanded.

The Druid recoiled. "*I'll do as I please!*" he screamed.

"No, you won't," Ben calmly replied, then grabbed his robe with both hands, and hurled the Druid to the ground.

As Fiona ran back to the great house, Ben tightened his hold on Salan. When he saw Kale coming out of his dwelling on the run and calling to three others who were repairing a chariot, Ben threw Salan to the ground and kneeled on his chest.

"*You'll regret this!*" Salan screamed. "I'll call upon powers that will destroy you! You're the one who's poisoned Boudica. You have filled her mind with your evil. You and others who anger our gods are guilty of blasphemy. You don't serve our purpose. You're a heretic, and you must be *eliminated!*"

"I fear none of your magic, Salan. Tie him up tightly and wait here, Kale. I'm going to help Boudica."

"We've got him," said Kale as Ben dashed toward the entrance of the great house.

When he entered, Ben saw Fiona kneeling by her mother's bed. She turned toward him as he approached. Her face was contorted in a fearful grimace.

Boudica was still, staring at him. "Listen carefully, my children," she whispered. "I'm feeling the same thing my husband described the night he died. Salan had been with him…They argued. The Druid said my husband was useless…He no longer wanted to kill. Prasutagus fell ill soon after. I've tested Salan. I have internal injuries from my fall from the chariot. I told him that…Now I know. He's given me the same poison he gave Prasutagus…N*ow I know*. I have the same distress as my husband…the night he died. At last. I finally know the truth."

Ben jumped up. "He's poisoned you. So that's his magic? I'm going to kill him."

"No, no," Boudica croaked, as she tried to raise her head. Her face was white, strained by distress. "Kneel, Ben. I've something to say. I'm fading, but my head is clear now. I love you both. I want you to follow in Ben's way, Fiona. It's best. I wish Ben and his Jesus had come to us sooner. I've made a grave mistake. I thought we should let the Romans gather in the defile. It would be good. All of them were together, at last. Given the great numbers we gathered for our assault…we could easily destroy them…once and for all. Instead, we're beaten. The Romans will prevail."

"Mother, you must rest," Fiona said. Her expression was somber, showing the stress of extreme helplessness as Boudica continued.

"When we went south to the first settlement we destroyed, I saw the proof of their power, what they built, how they lived. It's better. I know that. As you go forward with that knowledge to a better place where you can live in the way of Jesus, without being persecuted, and also enjoy some of the comforts the Romans have. It might produce some good. Think about it. Escape this hell. It will burn here, for a while. Go north…to the Picts…help them to understand. Think about the green island…across the narrow sea…to the west of *their* land."

Her voice was waning.

"Mother, we can barely hear you. You *must* rest," urged Fiona.

"No, my dear…I must travel on…to meet your father…again. I'm very tired. Please find a place for me to rest, Ben. Help me to go there…along the right path…My heart was broken when I came here today…Salan's medicine…and my injuries…are taking me away."

"I understand, Queen Boudica," Ben replied. "Are you truly sorry for the sins you've committed in this life?"

"I am," Boudica replied faintly.

"Then I now baptize you with this water from your chalice. And I do so in the name of the Father, the Son, and their Holy Spirit."

"Thank you," she whispered.

As a smile brightened Boudica's countenance, Ben traced the sign of the cross on her forehead using his moistened thumb, just like John had done to him.

"Now we'll pray in the way Jesus Christ taught his apostles," Ben continued.

"Our Father in heaven, hallowed be your name, your kingdom come, your will be done, here as it is in heaven. Give us today our daily bread, and *forgive* us our debts, as we *forgive* our debtors, and do *not* subject us to the final test, but deliver us from evil. Amen."

When the prayer was ended, and they were still together, hand in hand, Boudica whispered, "I must pray again."

"Of course, dearest Mother," Fiona hastened to confirm.

"Our Father in heaven," said Boudica, her voice strained with breaths taken rapidly. "Please welcome my daughter, Isolda…along with Rand…who gave his life for love of her…and accept my husband Prasutagus…who was killed by a Druid…because he no longer wished to kill others…He was truly sorry for his killings…and other evils… but died before he knew of *you*…and…please forgive the Druid Salan for his great sins against us…"

No longer a whisper. Boudica's eyes were closed. Her breathing had ceased.

Fiona leaned forward. "Mother. I hope you can hear me. I'm *with child*. We love you, and you'll *not* be forgotten."

Boudica's lips tightened, forming an unmistakable smile. It remained as she continued to rest in peace not disturbed. Her eyelashes were fluttering like the wings of a beautiful butterfly. When they stopped and were still, Fiona began to weep. Ben released Boudica's lifeless hands. The mighty hands that gripped a terrible sword could do no more. Boudica's soul had departed. Ben could feel it. Her spirit had risen with the power to free her soul, to soar to new heights with freedom and liberty forever.

The Iceni queen, the woman who might have been his wife, had given her life for others. He was certain her selfless sacrifices would be noticed. She had served and suffered enough. Her dying declaration was a request for mercy for those she loved and those most in need. Now she was gone. She would sin no more. The little girl who reluctantly became a heroic queen would feel pain no more. Her many wounds would be healed, her innocence restored. She would be renewed and remain forever rejoicing, in the spectacular beauty of her heavenly home.

Ben continued to meditate, praying until his thoughts turned to Fiona. He embraced the new mother and the new life within her. He would take them to safety. They would travel the path of faith, hope, and charity, sharing their love and good fortune all along *the way*.

When Ben and Fiona finally emerged from the great house, Kale met them with a large group of somber Iceni gathered around a pair of stout horses hitched to an elegantly refurbished chariot decorated with spring flowers carefully picked and arranged in a host of colorful bouquets.

"We know," said Kale, "and we mourn."

"Bless you, Kale," Ben responded. "Please bring Salan to us."

Kale seemed surprised by Ben's request, but hastened to help others drag the Druid forward bound with hemp and cowering along the way.

Ben stepped forward facing Salan with a menacing scowl.

"I was going to cut your head off, Salan, but Boudica intervened on your behalf as she was dying. *She forgave you.* Now you must understand that forgiveness is the final form of the thing we refer to as *love*. Cutting heads off, torturing, and poisoning people is no way to convert others to your way. Some day you and those like you will realize there's a better way. With that in mind, we've decided you'll remain a prisoner of the Iceni until you find *that way*. During that time, my friend Kale will be happy to do whatever it takes to help you change your mind and your attitude regarding the truly faithful neighbors who will surround you, for the rest of your time, in a life Boudica allowed you to continue, while you were ending hers."

The Druid priest was silent, head bowed.

Ben turned to Kale. "Queen Boudica was a hero who sacrificed everything for her people. She did her best and has gone to a new place in faith. You know it well, Kale. I pray you will spread the *good news* as you go forward with Boudica's seconds and the others who've managed to survive thus far."

"I will," Kale responded.

"Fiona and I will place her mother in the chariot, pack some essentials and some food, and leave going north," Ben continued. "We'll find a place that is suitable and bid her farewell with a funeral pyre fit for a queen. As you prepare to leave, look up from time to time. You might see Boudica in her chariot, renewed in spirit and carried upward to the source of God's everlasting spring and the living water that will refresh and sustain her immortal soul forever."

"We will do that. And God speed to you as well," Kale responded. "We'll return to our work now and be in the wilderness later today while keeping you and our dear Fiona close to our hearts and trusting you will do the same for our Rand and his life's love, Isolda."

"We shall, dear friend," Ben replied. "Until we meet again."

They embraced for the last time as the chariot came forward and Ben led Fiona, still sobbing with the sounds of a broken heart, as they passed through the entrance to the great room where her mother's earthly remains waited patiently in peaceful repose.

By sundown, Ben and Fiona had completed their ritual farewell to Boudica. They had watched the roaring fire engulf the chariot with Boudica wrapped inside and followed the smoke as a gentle breeze carried it through the treetops to vanish in the firmament.

At sunset, they mounted and continued northward toward the land of the Picts, riding in silence, both mourning deeply but finding solace in their faith and the strength it provided.

Chapter 39

The dawning of a new day was on the horizon. Ben and Fiona were riding north together, in love and knowing they would meet Boudica again, in the faraway kingdom she hoped to reach from her deathbed. She had turned to her Savior with a powerful declaration of regrets and forgiveness, revealing that her mind and her heart had embraced the knowledge and the reality of a Master of the Universe; and her soul was ready. It was never too late to embrace his redeeming love.

She emerged with the conviction of a rational mind, understanding Jesus and his mission; all he said, and all he did with the logic of a promise that revealed the ultimate truth.

The hope for a passage to the eternal life, dreamed about by millions, had been placed in the minds of human beings at the dawn of their earthly beginnings, not by accident, but by design, and would not exist without a cause, a reason, and a purpose with meaning, in a spiritual life that transcended *all else* in the brief voyage of life on Earth.

Ben knew that, when he stood with Fiona, watching the flames of Boudica's funeral pyre, with smoke rising above the lofty tree-tops. Boudica would dwell in a state of renewal, peace, and happiness with the Creator of all that is known and truly divine. She would encounter her loved ones in a new life with conscious awareness of the beauty and perfection men aspired to in art, but was *only* realized in the glory of God's creation—magnified by his presence—in the unimaginable spectacle of his heavenly realm.

Thus the mourning Ben experienced seemed to pass as he and Fiona continued their journey, riding side by side, discussing what Ben had been thinking, along with Fiona's encouraging responses.

When they crossed the border of the Roman province of Britannia, and entered the province of Caledonia, Ben spotted Romans in the distance. He knew the Roman Emperor Hadrian had ordered walls to be build walls to mark and control the farthest extents of Rome's empire, so he and Fiona reined into a forested area, found shelter, and stopped to observe. It appeared that the Romans were clearing trees and preparing to build a wall along a border that stretched east and west, as far as could be seen, between the land they had already conquered, and the land of the scottish-Picts.

When the moon had disappeared in the west, Ben went forward to find a safe pathway between Roman guard posts and camps. When he returned, they decided to wait until early morning, expecting from past experience that most of the Romans would be asleep by then.

While they waited both were reclined, gazing at the heavenly myriad of bright, shining stars.

The view caused Ben to ask, "What are you thinking, Fiona?"

"I'm thinking about my mother, Isolda and Rand," Fiona replied, "and wondering what they're doing…how far they will travel…and what form they must be in…to complete such a long journey."

"We are so much alike," Ben responded. "I'm thinking the same and also wondering if poor Rachael has completed her passing to the promised land, is safe with our trinity, and reveling in *true love* with thanksgiving."

"What have you found?"

"Exactly what Jesus promised," Ben replied immediately.

"Oh, Ben," she whispered, "please tell me more."

"I believe they have assumed glorified bodies just like John saw after Jesus's resurrection, and are traveling safely, like he did on the day of his ascension with the enormous power of God's Holy Spirit…flowing through him, with the same amazing energy, divine and capable of making, begetting, and doing all that we know and have experienced in this lifetime, like the universe we *see and feel* as we speak. It's real! And my people have been here five thousand years…longer than the Greeks, who once ruled the world. Our God sent Jesus to *my* people, not the Greeks, or any others. I have benefited mightily from that. I believe no thing…no one…but a Being of true Divinity could or would do what he did. Our loved ones are safe in his hands. *He's the Messiah.* We should know him, love him, and return his great love by serving him wisely and sharing the good news Jesus brought for people who simply *ask* for his help."

"Amen," Fiona whispered.

*****

When they were well beyond the Roman frontier Ben and Fiona encountered some Celts from the Votadini tribe. Like the Iceni, the Votadini had immigrated from other Celtic regions in reaction to pressure from Germanic tribes and Roman invaders.

Ben and Fiona received a warm reception from the Votadini and stayed with them long enough to become familiar with the area and fluent in their language. Ben related the experiences of the Iceni in their revolt and schooled the Votadini in raids, ambushes, and Roman tactics. The Votadini were not a warlike tribe, so in light of *her* tragic experience, Fiona urged them to consider cooperating with the Romans. She also encouraged them to talk with Ben further about the power of his faith and the love she and her mother experienced in their relationships with him following his harrowing journey, and arrival in their homeland.

Ben was happy to accommodate. While doing so, he learned that tribes to the north of the Votadini were forming a confederation to consider their response to recent Roman explorations. He asked his new friends to provide escorts and introduce him and Fiona during an upcoming meeting of the confederation, in the village of Graupius. The arrangements were made, and the meeting was informative. The two remained in Graupius with new friends who lived near the village, exchanged information with the leaders of the confederation, and helped them prepare for potential contacts with representatives of the ever-expanding Roman Empire.

As time passed, they discussed their interest in Erieu, the emerald-green island Boudica compared to the stone in the brooch she entrusted to Fiona on the day of her heroic, yet tragic death. In recognition of the couple's help and friendship, the leaders of the confederation provided escorts to West Caledonia, where they were directed to a harbor village along the narrow sea they would cross in order to reach the eastern shore of the island of Erieu.

They reached the village safely with the help of an escort who had lived there, then established new contacts and exchanged marriage vows, in the ancient Hebrew rite, on the day Fiona celebrated her eighteenth birthday.

Several months later they celebrated Ben's thirtieth birthday while awaiting the birth of their daughter.

And when little Boudicea was old enough to travel, friends in a Cruithin tribe ferried the new family to a harbor village in Erieu. The Cruithins had relatives there, some of whom had passed back and forth between both lands across the Erieu Sea and were familiar with the area around Armagh.

They hastened to arrange contacts for safe passage and resettlement; and the little family soon discovered that Armagh was all the Cruithins had described. The village soon became their idyllic refuge. And the home they had prayed for.

Chapter 40

On a beautiful spring morning the little family was happily settled in Armagh and they decided to hike to a meadow on the crest of a nearby hill.

While little Boudicea played in the emerald-green grass, Ben and Fiona sat nearby, watching her, and gazing across the ancient, spiritually inspiring beauty, of the land.

They were content, holding hands in their reverie, when Fiona turned to Ben and asked, "Why did you choose me rather than my mother?"

Ben thought for a moment, then replied, "On that night, with Kale and Boudica…when I first saw you, and you looked at me while your mother was introducing us, I felt something I had never felt before."

"What was it? What did you feel? What did you think about me?" Fiona asked, with an expression revealing sincere curiosity.

"I was exhausted that night, hungry, in need of sleep and disheveled. When I looked up and saw your form and realized your presence, I felt a surge of energy. I stiffened, without thinking. It was a reaction like you get when there's a storm and lightning strikes nearby and the thunderclap makes you jump. Vanity struck me. I raised a hand to my hair, realizing it was a mess, and I was also dirty, in tattered clothes. I wilted under your gaze, *not* wanting you to see me as I was, but at a better time…at my best. As you continued to stare at me, I felt the animal in me aroused and drawn to you like I wanted to touch you but had to pull back, aware of others. I forgot everything but your movements. And when your mother introduced you as *the bold one*, I was in a daze, until she called my name and brought me out of an embarrassing trance."

"Oh, Ben," Fiona chuckled.

"And to be perfectly honest with some risk, I thought of the harlots in the bazaars in my homeland and their power of seduction and deceit."

"And you thought I was like them?"

"Yes. And it worried me for some time, given my relationship with your mother…my debt to her…my fear of her, and my respect and admiration for her courage. I was also feeling tension, especially when I was *near you*, some fear of your power, and the fear of *your* seductive appeal."

"So *you did* think of *my* appeal in *that way?*" Fiona snapped back.

"Yes, and for your free-spirited attitude about everything, including your lack of clothing, which *did not* help… to say the least."

"Oh," Fiona responded coyly.

"But I soon discovered much of what you did was because of your age. That part of you was young and wicked, from my point of view. But there was a peculiar innocence that touched me deeply, along with the thought that you *might* be fond of me."

"I *did* want you to know. I was also attracted to you in spite of the crazy urgings that boggled my mind and caused inappropriate behavior, when I was near you…especially when my mother was present. I cannot account for it all. But you must've known I was moved by you in a curious way."

"I did as time passed, and your candor revealed words and actions that slowly caused me to realize you were not competing with your mother. You weren't envious, jealous, or a harlot by nature."

"Benjamin!" she exclaimed. "Are you trying to cause serious trouble *you will* soon regret?"

"Are you implying there might be another vicious attack on me, like what happened on that day, when you attacked me in the forest?" Ben quipped.

"Perhaps," she responded demurely.

"Before you seriously consider *that* again, you must understand that you truly won my mind and my heart, with the honesty you demonstrated that day, when you surprised me in the forest. And the values you later revealed in your actions, along with our discussions on a religion that's all about *cardinal values*, were also compelling. And the unselfish concern you displayed, soon gave me the notion that you were *not* using me to satisfy your ego, but instead, that you *truly did* care about me...to the point where you would risk your own life to follow me in desperation, fearing you might lose me, on that day you came after me, and so skillfully tracked, and attacked me, then gave up yourself, body and soul. It was the culmination of what I regarded as self-sacrificing, true love. *There is nothing in this life more holy.* I adored you for your rare qualities at that point, and when I realized how truly genuine and beautiful your soul was, I was astounded that someone like you would be so open, so loving, and so willing to have me as your mate.

It was astonishing, unbelievable. It was *amazing,* another of God's great miracles. I felt so blessed...honored...and in love with you. In the days that followed, I missed you terribly. I began to think that anything I might do would *not* matter...unless *you* were by my side."

Fiona was weeping. She embraced him and said, "I wish *every* woman could hear those words from such a good and faithful husband as you, Ben."

"Your wish warms my heart, Fiona. It's all I need. And as our time together passes, faith and redemption might prevail. More and more people might respond with good hope and charity to create the opportunity for a much better way of life for everyone...men women and children... just like our beautiful daughter."

Fiona smiled, deep in thought, as she continued to watch Boudicea reveling in freedom, while picking spring meadow flowers.

"Do you remember how you discovered this new life we've chosen to live, Ben?" she inquired thoughtfully.

"I think it all began when I realized I had *an idea.*"

"And what was it?"

"It seemed rather curious at the time, since I was living in a culture bounded by the law of God. It was the notion that I truly needed to behave in a certain way. It was a paradox. I couldn't get rid of it. As I matured, I realized I had difficulty living in *that way.* It bothered me. I felt as if I was one of those *hypocrites* I couldn't respect. It troubled me. I found the root of the word in the Greek language. It's what the Greeks called the people in the plays I told you about. They were 'actors,' *pretending* to be someone they were not. I was like one of those actors. It bothered me. When I was in the temple, I was acting, putting on a play to impress those around me. When I walked out of the temple, I was a *hypocrite*."

"So what did you do about this thing that was troubling conscience?" Fiona responded.

"I plunged into my studies, asked many questions, and mightily embraced my people's history and religion. I also discovered some remarkable *ideas* developed by the Greeks who conquered our land, before the Romans came, and discovered a pattern. My people had written a comprehensive history revealed in their ancient scriptures. It met all of the requirements necessary to be called 'a history,' just like the Roman 'histories' did...*and* it included a set of values learned over the ages. I studied that history, and I was perplexed by the things it revealed. I began to doubt, and was further confused as I continued with the writings of the Greeks. I came to believe that our scriptures were an *amazing* story of what my people had experienced over thousands of years, as their religion developed in the hands of men. But for me, the more I studied and memorized those scriptures, the more contradictions I would find. They could not be resolved by my teachers. They were impatient and annoyed. So I quit asking questions. I used some of the Greek ideas regarding my soul, my mind, my intellect, my ability to observe and use logic, with reasoning and common sense, to find answers to my most troubling dilemma's."

"I already know a great deal about what you discovered in your search for truth," Fiona remarked, "and it's clear that your encounter with the followers of Jesus had much to do with that seeking."

"Yes! 'Seek and you shall find.' But before we talk about that turning point, I must mention something that I might not have mentioned before," Ben interjected.

"What is that?" Fiona inquired, obviously interested and ready to hear Ben's revelation.

"I know we're made in the image and likeness of God. And I believe his '*likeness*' is the key word. To me, 'likeness' means he gave us a soul, a spirit, and *a mind* that constitutes the essence of our being, as humans. It means we have been given some things that *God also has*. And they were given to enable us to communicate with him in a trinity that includes Jesus and the Holy Spirit. We have a conscious awareness of it and ourselves, and an intellect, a conscience, and the capability of abstract thought, including the ability to reason and make choices. The Greeks cast their gods to resemble perfect human beings, but Jesus came directly from God as an incarnate human being who looked much like us and spoke the same language, in order to avoid frightening people and to facilitate precise, meaningful communication of the values he emphasized. He demonstrated true love, suffered, and facilitated communication by using *the words of God*, our Father. And I must emphasize that most of the people he met were people of goodwill. The trouble usually came from their 'leaders' who often steered them wrong for selfish purposes, like gaining power with wealth and material comforts, and sinning egregiously along the way. Those leaders were eventually called kings and queens, titles that indicated the highest forms of human life. Because of the attributes in their human nature—some good, some bad—they were allowed to govern, to control the interaction of their 'subjects'…the people who formed the societies inherent in their cultures, and their realms, called kingdoms. My people had kings like David and Solomon, his son, and the laws they followed came from the history of our religion in what became the kingdoms of Judea and Israel… then later, was simply referred to as Israel. Their values and their principles came from their religion Judaism, just as your Druidism did for your people. You are the child of royalty, just as I am, in a way. I am in the line of David, but I am a child of God, one of his many children. But God is the highest form of spiritual beings, and as such, is regarded as the King of his realm. God's Kingdom spans Earth and extends into the Cosmos, and beyond, in eternity, as revealed by our inspired scriptures and the direct Word of God we received from Jesus. Our kings sinned, so did yours, but God is without sin, and Jesus, who was begotten by and from him, was the same, and he proved it! These things are important."

"I know that, Ben, and I appreciate the love and caring you demonstrate each time you remind me about the things in our lives that *truly matter most*."

"Thank you, my love. You were right about John, Barnabas, John Mark, and the others who gathered around me and did the same for *me* as I've tried to do for you, and Isolda, and your mother and others in her kingdom. My meeting with John and the others, in the garden, was a great blessing and *much more* than a coincidence. I was naive about the safety of my body and soul until John whisked me away some nights later. But during my time with him and the others, I was at peace and had time to think more. I soon realized that my most desperate prayers for help had been answered. I was *hopeful*. I was confident. *I learned about Jesus.* I began to *know* and *trust* him. The more I knew, and the more I did what he wanted me to do, the more I settled down, shed my angst, and quit worrying so much. There was a stability in my life, with continuity that assured me that one way or another, my soul would survive this world, and I would pass on wholesome…to a life that was glorious. I wanted to explore it immediately! Then I saw *you.* And before long, I knew. God had also blessed me with a love that would go on forever. It was his gift, to compensate for all of the hardship our human nature had created in the beginning. It was the *one thing* that made this life so grand, to share the love of God with you and extend that love to Our Father, our child, and others in our daily lives. It has made me truly happy! It was the answer. *The most important and meaningful thing we could do.* And when we live in that way, we know it every day, because we feel the joy, the bliss, and the reassurance, in every part of our physical and spiritual being."

"And you began to put your many thoughts together with what they revealed about *their time* with Jesus and Peter and Paul," Fiona added.

"Yes. And there was *love.* After my wife's horrible death, the Roman atrocities, and so on, I was in dark despair. Those men made me realize that the perfection I had tried to achieve in Judaism was impossible for me to attain in this life. The Law of Moses had been expanded by men to the point where it was much like Roman law in some ways. And Jesus had said, 'Render unto Caesar what is Caesar's and render unto God what is God's'… and in my mind that translated into two basic laws that mattered. The law of God's nature, as modified for man, and the law of God, exclusively *for* man. It occurred to me that I must follow *both*, as best I could. It appeared that the laws Jesus articulated for man were clearly superior and most important, but much harder to follow daily, given corruptions in our culture's politics and its practical lessons regarding how to succeed in this life. It seemed to me, that when God placed the first creatures like us on this earth, *those in his likeness*, everything was perfect until mankind used God's gift of free will to search for more knowledge than God deemed appropriate for their well-being. They were warned, but refused to be obedient, and turned their backs on their Creator, and soon found they must suffer the consequences. They covered their nakedness, ashamed, knowing it would *now* lead to lust, upsetting their God… and chose to get satisfaction from material fantasies and, in effect, acted as if they were gods themselves. Too often they chose to pursue things that were *not* good, causing themselves great agony, rather than ecstasy, in their futile attempts to fill the void that once had been filled with the best, and *the only* true path to happiness and satisfaction. They thereby created a 'hell' of sorts on earth. The story of my people is full of examples of people who did this and others who resisted it. When Jesus came, he set the record straight by showing the former the errors of their ways and focusing most of his praise and attention on those who avoided temptation."

"So you found the basis of our faith, our hope, and our love, and you passed it on to others who would listen. And you have given me a life full of joy and fulfillment, in spite of all that has happened around us because of those who *chose* the other way and rose to positions of great power that has destroyed millions of innocents, such as we were, when we were children under authority."

"Yes, my love. We learn everything we know from *men* of authority, and if the 'authorities' could be more like Jesus, imagine how grand it would be."

"And even now, we can choose to live, love, hope, and pray that Boudicea and her children and their children in all generations will continue down the path we have taken and find more wisdom as they go on," added Fiona, "then reassure themselves of the reality and goodness that will come from men like you, who admire and respect those who first gathered around Jesus and shared his good news."

"Amen," Ben affirmed. "And as they go forward, be as Boudicea is on this day...*a child of the everlasting spring.*"

"Amen," said Fiona, watching her daughter run barefoot through the green grass of Ireland, enchanted by the beauty of fresh flowers blooming along her way.

"And there's *another thing* that might help," Ben added.

"What's that?" asked Fiona.

"It's something we've discovered about your people, and my people as well."

"What is that?"

"Many of them are losing the *reality battle* in the way they form their ideas and ideals. And in order to answer your question fully, I must tell you about a dream I've had, about a place surrounded by vast oceans on both sides. The people speak one language. They have common laws that apply to all based on the values received from Jesus. Their laws reflect those values. No one is allowed to live by other laws. There's a common name for their land. And they share it. It's their identity and their homeland, expansive and fertile. There's clear water in abundance. The people have read much of what we have in the bag John gave me, as well as the Hebrew Scriptures and some of the Greek writings that speak of politics, democracy, and how republics function in layered governments, without tyrants and Druids."

"It sounds grand. Could it be true? Could it last?"

"God only knows to what extent dreams such as mine could produce *ideas*…and how many of those ideas would be useless, void of rational, reasonable, common sense, and understanding of human nature as it *actually* exists in reality. We are sinners! We choose to commit acts that do not meet God's standards for goodness and well-being. All ideas born in ages past without an accurate perception regarding our nature…without a good grasp of the reality…have failed miserably throughout history."

"And why did they fail?"

"Because the ideas were born blind. They *cannot* visualize the truth about mankind, much less accept it in the 'politics' the Greeks, particularly Aristotle, wrote about. It was called *'polis'* in their language, meaning affairs of the cities, and *politikos,* relating to citizens, then *politcus,* in Latin, by the Romans. It basically described activities, actions, and policies that are used to gain and hold power in a government, to influence governance of a country or other areas with *the people's* opinions about the best way to manage the process. It is based on the *opinions* of human beings and therefore impossible to proceed successfully without *realizing the truth about human nature.* People must see…and fully understand that in order to develop and sustain a system of government that is capable of curbing the disease of mankind's self-conceit and corruption, a social ideology *cannot claim* it will provide happiness, satisfaction and harmony *without* fundamental moral and ethical principles based on the cardinal values…the virtues of prudence, temperance, justice, fortitude, and faith hope and charity. Those values have been proven over eons. They are God-given and *absolutely essential* in any human endeavor that seeks satisfaction and lasting peace with *any hope* of finding a result that's *not* simply a fleeting pipe dream…an idea that goes up in smoke and produces *nothing* of lasting value, holy enough to survive the rigorous test of time."

"I hear what you say. And if that dream of yours comes true for *anyone*, it should be worthy of belief, cherished by those who can appreciate its rarity and consequent value for this world replete in false prophets, who bring recurring nightmares with rotten results, like *our* Druids."

"Or the Romans who took Greek ideas and turned them into vast wastelands where virtue once ruled but was eventually replaced by chambers of madmen and perverts who sought to be gods," added Ben.

"Amen," said Fiona, nodding her head in agreement.

"Yes, indeed, my love. And there's one more thing. Do you remember the thrust of what I said about the Greeks, when your mother still lived with us?"

"I do," Fiona replied. "You spoke of democracy, republics, and city-states and the great thinkers like Plato and Aristotle and others of their time and ilk who had ideas about ways to spread power so *more people*…not just one or two…can participate and decide what is best for *all*."

"Yes. I was thinking about that. It makes sense. Someday…some way, it *could* be possible to have what we've talked about today, in the right place, and in harmony with God's will for his children to be as close as they can to a heaven on this earth, and have a chance to go forward joyfully with the comfort of knowing they've achieved their full potential to shine in the eyes of their Creator... and realize it fully, then rejoice, and be thankful for all of God's blessings!"

"Yes, Ben, it *could be* very good. We can certainly try. I have a *very* strong feeling there are many people like us, in places we might not know, who think as we do. And as time passes and Christianity spreads there will be more, and life will improve. But it will require some very special circumstances. I imagine there won't be enough of us for a while, and it might take a long time to find the right place. And what we believe to be true and beautiful in our lifetime might not make sense to some. So we must keep that faith. Your dream might not come true in our lifetime, but I think it will someday. In the meantime, we have what it takes to be happy *here*, then go on to the place where things *are as they should be*, in the presence of our almighty and merciful God," Fiona concluded.

"Amen," Ben replied while rising with Fiona to crown Boudicea's radiant red-locks with a garland of spring flowers, still fresh, and sweet smelling; kissed by their maker, with his soft morning dew.

Epilogue

In AD 432, Pope Celestine of Rome commissioned a young priest he called "Father Patrick" and sent him to Ireland. When Father Patrick arrived in Armagh, he was greeted by a statuesque woman with red hair and radiant blue-green eyes, who was wearing a gold-encrusted emerald brooch. She introduced herself as "Lady Fiona" and welcomed him with a kiss and a gift wrapped in weathered goatskin.

Father Patrick was astounded as he carefully unwrapped the bundle including a number of yellowed pages rolled into scrolls. The writings were in Greek and identical to those he had seen in Rome accepted after rigorous study as inspired by the Holy Spirit, unassailable proof of the writers' authenticity as witnesses to Jesus Christ and his revelations. The writings were therefore included in the Canon of the Catholic Bible that Patrick brought with him to Ireland after receiving it as a parting gift from Celestine the Thirty-Ninth *"Pappa"* of the Roman Catholic Church.

When Patrick was ready, Lady Fiona led him to a meadow at the top of a nearby hill where, for three hundred years, the Irish members of the Armagh Catholic congregation had gathered to celebrate Holy Mass using the contents of the goatskin bag as the format for their liturgy. Patrick celebrated the Mass for all present, and Fiona smiled throughout his homily especially when he discussed the Ten Commandments and helped the congregation to remember each of those commandments by using the shape of the Cross he described as "The Tree of Everlasting Life." Patrick said the horizontal member of the cross carried four references to God: You shall have no other gods before me, you shall not make idols, you should not take the name of the Lord, your God, in vain, and you shall remember the Sabbath day and keep it holy. He went on to say that the vertical member referred to Man: Honor your father and your mother, you shall not murder, not commit adultery, not steal, not bear false witness against your neighbor, and not covet your neighbor's wife nor his treasure.

As the Mass continued, he blessed all present and administered Holy Communion in the New Covenant. When he broke the bread of spiritual life, in remembrance of Jesus at the Last Supper, Patrick asked the recipients to follow his lead and repeat the words attributed to a Roman centurion when he told Jesus, "Lord, I'm not worthy that thou should enter under my roof. But only say the words, and thy servant shall be healed." After Mass, Patrick baptized all the children and told their parents that the Roman Emperor Constantine, in response to one of God's miracles, had embraced the Church. As a result, the Eastern (Greek) Orthodox Rite and the Roman (Latin) Rite would together make the Catholic Church truly universal spread across the known world from centers in Byzantium and Rome by peaceful evangelists, *not* by the sword.

The group then walked to the nearby cemetery where Patrick blessed the graves of the faithfully departed, and Lady Fiona proudly showed him a large stone engraved with a Celtic Cross and the faded names of Benjamin and Fiona, her great-grandparents six generations removed. They had gone to the Lord on the same day, in the springtime of AD 100. Their descendants and others in the village observed a tradition of remembering the season as Ben and Fiona's "everlasting spring." When on her deathbed, Fiona tenderly entrusted an emerald brooch to their daughter Boudicea, the great-granddaughter of the Iceni queen Boudica. Like the goatskin bag Benjamin had brought from the Holy Land, it was protected and preserved by scores of loving hands and would continue to be passed from generation to generation as a priceless icon and heirloom recalling epic events, heroic love, and undying faith in God and his purpose for those who would follow throughout the ages.

Patrick was duly impressed; and before his departure to Skellig Michael, and other locations he was considering for monasteries in his former homeland, he happily shared a feast with the members of the congregation, and announced that their village would be an ideal place to plan and build his principal church on the island as well.

Father Patrick also took some time to update his first Irish Catholic parish on the progress of their Roman Catholic Church. He confirmed the fall of Jerusalem and its destruction by the Romans in AD 70 and said it had caused the Israelites to scatter throughout the world. Those who succeeded John and the others became bishops throughout the Middle East, Asia, Africa, and Europe. The heart of the Western Church was in Rome where Peter and Paul had been martyred, and the apostolic succession was progressing well under the new Church patriarchs and bishops of Rome. The bishop at the time of Emperor Constantine's victory in the Battle of the Milvian Bridge had confirmed that Constantine did give credit to Christ for his victory and, therefore, proclaimed the toleration of Christianity throughout his empire, in the Edict of Milan. In AD 312, Constantine convened and presided over the First Council of Nicaea. It was the first Ecumenical Council in church history. Soon after, Damasus became the first bishop of Rome to be *officially* referred to as "*Pappas.*"

Beginning in 324, Constantine reorganized the Roman Empire into the Greek East and the Latin West. He changed the name of the former Arab city of Byzantium to Constantinople, made it the new capital of the Eastern Roman Empire, and legalized Christianity there, just as he had in the west.

In AD 331, Constantine commissioned Eusebius Pamphylia, also known as "Jerome" to create the official Christian Bible. Jerome was one of the prominent church fathers who assembled at Nicaea and a historian considered expert by his peers. He took the eighteen books and numerous letters that were included in the new church history he had assembled in AD 325, added them to the Hebrew Bible's Greek translation known as the *Septuagint Bible*, translated *all* into Latin and produced fifty copies of The Christian Bible containing both the Old and New Testaments. In AD 365, the Roman Catholic Church officially canonized and included nine additional Old Testament books.

In AD 379, under Constantine's successor Theodosius, Christianity became the Eastern Empire's official state religion. It was characterized by Greek Orthodoxy in recognition of the Greek culture that had prevailed in the region since late antiquity. The apostolic fathers—Clement of

Rome, Ignatius of Antioch, Polycarp of Smyrna, and Papias of Hierapolis—were also succeeded by others distinguished by their writings in either Latin or Greek.

During his conclusion, Patrick added one caution for all: The Roman Empire was declining, others would fill the void, some good, and some portending trouble. Patrick also emphasized that Ostrogoths, Arabs, Persians, and the tyranny of newly emerging monarchies would no doubt be among the latter. He then described human nature as "fickle," tending toward sins of many kinds, and urged the congregation to "stay close to Jesus" for everlasting happiness, and always and forever, in spite of worldly difficulties, "*trust in God!*"

At the conclusion of his summary, Patrick answered a wide variety of questions, lingered as long as he could, blessed and thanked the members of his new parish for their warm reception, and departed with a small retinue to continue his evangelic odyssey throughout the Emerald Isle.

The Catholic Bible, "the Book" Patrick referred to was copied at monasteries in Ireland and throughout the world to be shared for generations in many languages "to spread the good news." That, along with an infusion of Greco-Roman classical ideas, became the foundation for development of Western civilization, its laws, and its legacy beyond the Reformation. The work begun by John, John Mark, and the others who lived during Ben and Boudica's time was carried on faithfully by hundreds of dedicated evangelists. The Catholic Church expanded east and west, north and south rapidly covering vast distances, to the far reaches of the known world to became truly universal, as the *only* Christian Church in the world throughout a chaotic and critical era that lasted for fifteen hundred years. During that period, the Church made vast contributions to the creation of Western civilization. Any church, monastery, university, library, hospital, school, cultural art patronage, welfare institution, or scientific advance established for the benefit of humanity in the west, during that era, was a direct result of its influence.

After the time of Father Patrick and Lady Fiona, there were invasions, plagues, and famine of great magnitude that touched Armagh and Western world in its entirety. Viking, Norman, Angle, Saxon, Jute, Germanics, Persians, Jihadists, and the evolving European monarchies' conquests, took land and killed millions in secular conquests that often, used religion as a necessary tool to achieve goals that were hardly noble, mocking the Church Jesus founded, his apostles, the early Church fathers, the patriarchs, their disciples, millions of faithful believers, and countless others who followed to complete the task, under the most difficult of conditions.

Those who brought sacrificial love defied time and distance to draw millions more, who would also serve with profound humility at the risk of their own lives, then *be forgotten* in a history that gave utmost attention to monarchs, elite families, self-perpetuating dynasties, and even popes, who often neglected their obligations to those who served them; and thereby spread misery among millions who suffered under conditions wrought with everlasting poverty, lacking opportunity to acquire resources needed for meaningful, human life—with liberty and happiness— that was intended from the beginning, when God created Heaven and Earth from a formless, dark wasteland.

And out of it all would come a lovely red-haired Irish girl named Fiona who would fasten a tarnished gold-encrusted emerald brooch to her undergarment and hoist a carpet bag containing her meager belongings to join thousands of others who waited in long lines to board ships in Ireland's ports, hoping to survive and find a better way of life at the end of a perilous passage to the New World of the Americas.

About the Author

Francis "Frank" Audrain is an American author, who has led an extraordinary life. He is a direct descendent of North American patriarchs who immigrated from Britain and Normandy to the English colonies of Virginia and Pennsylvania. They fought in the French and Indian War, the Revolutionary War, and the War of 1812, then created a heritage of descendants who have fought in every American war since—ending with Frank's twenty years of service as an infantry officer in the Cold War.

When he retired, the Soviet Border Wall in Berlin was falling. Frank remarked that for him, the Cold War had turned out to be a very "hot war"—and he hoped and prayed that America's victory would be realized as a unique opportunity for peace on earth.

Before the ink on his retirement order was dry, he was offered the opportunity to serve as a corporate officer in a rapidly growing financial institution. Frank rose rapidly until he retired again, to become a professional author, writing short stories for magazines.

When he was advised by editors to write a trilogy suggested by one of his literary offerings, Frank began to write in earnest. The *Everlasting Spring: Beyond Olympus* emerged as a "think piece" for busy Americans to contemplate lessons in real history with action and adventure, romance, high drama, and faith and spirituality, in three epic sagas about true love and eternal values.

Frank and the love of his life have moved many times and now live in a lake home in Eden Prairie, Minnesota. They recently celebrated their 50th Wedding Anniversary with children; and Frank is still hard at work finishing the sequels of his trilogy: Volume II, *Colton and Blue Star, in the New World of the Americas*; and Volume III, *Aaron and Alana, in Post-Modern America*.

DOG LOVER

BOW WOW LABS

CPSIA information can be obtained
at www.ICGtesting.com
Printed in the USA
LVHW011545160222
711257LV00010B/74

9 781644 624555